THE DISTANCE BETWEEN US

Acclaim for *The Distance Between Us*

"Helena finds herself at the center of a murder case as strange as the Cape has ever seen, one involving stolen art, secret lovers, and some grade-A impersonating. . . Burch summons Provincetown's eclectic, art-and-barnacles ethos with an eye for detail and plenty of campy humor. . . the plot becomes secondary to the peculiar spell Burch weaves with Helena and her milieu."

-Kirkus Reviews

"A remarkable story of love, loss, and the enduring power of friendship. Burch draws his characters deftly, and the mystery he embeds at the center of the story is tantalizing and satisfying. A gem of a book!"

-Jeannette de Beauvoir
Author, The Sydney Riley Mysteries

Acclaim for *The HomePort Journals*

"Burch's exquisite descriptions of Provincetown bring the Cape to life, and the more he reveals about the delightfully crotchety Dorrie and Lola and the effervescent, tragic Helena, the more captivating they become."

-Kirkus Reviews

"Evocative, funny, and heartfelt, *The HomePort Journals* will be to Provincetown what *Tales of the City* is to San Francisco."

-William J. Mann,
Author, Tinseltown

"This is a literary work of exceptional merit. It is epic in nature, yet intensely intimate in execution, gorgeously rendered in exquisite detail, and told with heart-felt honesty. It bears a message of hope and love, compassion and tolerance, of simple joys and overcoming the roadblocks life sometimes thrusts in your path....

-GGR-Review

Acclaim for *A Book of Revelations*

"Each story draws readers into continuums of isolation and connection, introspection and expression, confusion and lucidity as its characters stumble and soar toward finding and claiming their own voices. . . *A Book of Revelations* delivers the voyeuristic aspects of social media sans FOMO (fear of missing out) thanks to Burch's stellar ability to place a reader inside the characters he's created. His short stories have an epic feel because of his exquisite use of language and penchant for deftly wielding details. The eavesdropping sensation they induce is mesmerizing, and the stream of unexpected revelations are, too."

-Yvonne Lieblein,
US Review of Books

"From the usual to the unusual, the rendering of the bubbling lives of these people will entice you from start to finish, for there is not a weak story among them."

-Carol Anderson,
Underground Book Review

"Burch weaves a collection of crackerjack plot twists in which unlikely heroes seize the day."

-Kirkus Reviews

"A. C. Burch is a quintessential observer, but without the distance that might leave the writing cold. Instead, Burch takes on voices – that of old women, young men, sex-crazed and sex-craven. We are touched by these players at the margins, artfully rendered by chapter illustrations that suit in their whimsy and wry lines. This unforgettable cast invites us to meet them "my life on my terms" (203). Think of it as less a threat than one of the several dinner invitations extended throughout the book. Black-tie, or black gown – or both! – 8pm; be there or be square!"

-Mari,
Midwest Book Review

THE DISTANCE BETWEEN US

A. C. Burch

The Distance Between Us

Published by HomePort Press
PO Box 1508
Provincetown, MA 02657
www.HomePortPress.com
ISBN 978-1-7340533-9-5
eISBN 979-8-9868654-0-9

Cover Design by James Iacobelli
Cover Painting by Pamela Parsons
Maps by Madeline Sorel

Also by A. C. Burch

The HomePort Journals

A Book of Revelations

To Ed
"My strength and stay"

"Man is least himself when he talks in his own person. Give him a mask, and he will tell you the truth."

—Oscar Wilde

"We're all born naked and the rest is drag."

—Rupaul Andre Charles
(a.k.a. RuPaul)

The Outer Cape
N
Race Pt. Light
Airport
6
Provincetown
East Harbor
High Head
Highland Links
Cape Cod Light
Herring Cove Beach
Long Pt. Light
Provincetown Harbor
N. Truro
Wood End Light
ATLANTIC OCEAN
Ballston Beach
Pamet Harbor
Mavis's House
Truro
Fisher Beach
Hideout
Cape Cod Bay
6
Wellfleet
Whydah Galley
S. Wellfleet
Wellfleet Harbor
The Outer Cape
Plymouth
Cape Cod
Martha's Vineyard
Nantucket
Nauset Light
N. Eastham
Eastham

HomePort Estate
Staunton's Lookout
Mavis's Studio
Bradford Street
Commercial Street
Studios
HomePort Mansion
Cottages
Dorrie's House
STAUNTON MUSEUM
The Moors
Pilgrims' Park

The HomePort Family

Helena Handbasket — Chatelaine, HomePort Estate
Butch — Helena's husband
Shirley-Mae — Helena's maternal grandmother
Dolores Delgado — Housekeeper, resident gorgon
Cole Hanson — Artist, curator Staunton Museum
Marc Nugent — Writer, Cole's husband
Frida — Cole and Marc's beloved Golden Retriever
Afton Walker — Head of security, Staunton Museum
Aaron Walker — Afton's twin brother
Quincy Stilwell — Attorney for the Staunton Trust
Charlotte Grubb — Financial genius and family mainstay
Brad — Charlotte's husband
Lola Staunton* — Former chatelaine, HomePort Estate
Dorrie Machado Staunton* — Lola's half-sister
Annie Machado* — Dorrie's mother
Captain Staunton* — Lola and Dorrie's father
Laetitia Staunton* — "The Captain's" mother, art collector

"Townies"

Mavis Chandry — World-renowned artist, curmudgeon
Office Chase — Provincetown Police
Lisa Kline — Detective, Provincetown Police
Clotilde Perkins — Nonagenarian, last of her line
Louie Silva — Chief, Provincetown Police (on leave)
Wally Trieste — Security technician

*Deceased

"Washashores"

Henry Boorstin — Architect manqué
Sergeant Brandt — Acting chief, Provincetown Police
Elise Stewart-Campion — Board member, Staunton Trust
Gwen Stewart-Campion — Elise's wife, board member
Melody Carpenter — Artist, busker
Frederica "Freddy" Chalmers — Reporter
Bernard "Betty" Crocker — Entertainer, bon vivant
George Miller — Security guard
Paul Schroeder — Documentary filmmaker
Celia-Jane "C.J." Strongue — Aspiring socialite
Cheswick Wilks — Socialite, crashing bore
Dr. Clarence Woodman — Would-be developer

Others

Dan Andrade — Cape and Islands District Attorney
Harold Blithe — Unemployed
Ricotta Gnocchi — Drag Queen
Lance Kensington — Entrepreneur, former model
Deidre Hamilton — Art collector
Detective Amy Morgan — State Police (on assignment)
Congressman Jack Mullins — Massachusetts 9th District
Stanley Strongue — "Scrap Metal King of Hunts Point"
Commander Raúl Vega — U.S. Coast Guard
Charles — Airplane mechanic
Kevin — A child
Lois — A baker

A Shocking Development

Aspiring socialite Celia-Jane Strongue was not prone to hyperbole or self-pity. Nor was she a fool. When she determined her recent move to Cape Cod was "a train wreck," she did so fully aware of the part she played in the debacle.

Her Wagnerian build and extraordinary tenacity gave most people the impression of a force of nature, which was both unfortunate and misleading. Celia-Jane was not so much intentionally bombastic as ill at ease around others. Far too eager for approval, she overcompensated, consistently missing social cues and assailing personal boundaries—often with disastrous results. She simply couldn't help herself.

The few who knew her beyond passing acquaintance attributed her maladroit ways to forty-three years of marriage to Stanley Strongue, the self-made "Scrap Metal King of Hunts Point." Celia-Jane knew better. She was painfully aware how her insecurities had denied her the life she desired. To her way of thinking, Stan had merely exploited her anxieties, using sarcasm and abasement to keep her under his thumb.

The day her husband died, Celia-Jane renamed herself "C.J.," setting the stage for a transformation meant to right many wrongs. Stan's frugality would make possible the one thing she'd longed for—a chance to escape the Bronx. Other than a dispiriting honeymoon in Wildwood, New Jersey, her life had been confined to the neighborhood she grew up in. She'd married the boy next door and attended the same church where she was baptized.

C.J. read voraciously to compensate for her cloistered existence. She'd often dreamed of leaving Stan and his scrapyard to live in a classic seaside village with grand old houses, white picket fences, and sympathetic, down-to-earth neighbors. County fairs, outdoor markets, parades, and church socials also featured in her re-imagined existence, which fell on a scale of rusticity somewhere between Miss Marple's St. Mary Mead and Jessica Fletcher's Cabot Cove.

When fortune smiled at last, C.J. chose Wellfleet, a picturesque town on Cape Cod with nearby theater, fine dining, and live entertainment—more than enough diversion for an elderly woman whose idea of bliss was a night in bed with Edith Wharton.

Primed with her new nickname, a host of self-improvement manuals, and the exquisite luxury of a past left behind, C.J. set out to create her new life. She joined potluck groups, attended charity events, and volunteered for everything from the OysterFest to handing out programs at Preservation Hall, a former Catholic church repurposed as an arts venue.

C.J. soon realized the only people she encountered were also recent transplants, who were equally confounded. Where were the kindly rural neighbors with their homespun ways?

For generations, individuals whose families had lived on the Outer Cape called themselves "townies." Decades before, most had rebelled against the inflated egos and unrealistic demands of an ever-increasing wave of "washashores"—a longstanding term for those born elsewhere. The townies worked hard and kept a low profile. They might raise a collective eyebrow at a specious social media post or pass an incisive comment on some new brand of entitled tomfoolery, but that was the extent of their interest in the newcomers.

It was as if two different towns claimed the same physical space while their respective inhabitants never acknowledged each other. As a result, C.J.'s bucolic New England fantasy never left its white picket starting gate.

Second Thoughts

As the Town Car descended the glacial moraine known as High Head, passed East Harbor, and entered Provincetown, C.J. wondered, yet again, where she'd gone wrong.

I wish Stan had let me learn to drive. It would have made it easier to meet people, but I'm too old and afraid to learn now.

At last, the car arrived at the fabled HomePort Estate, with its artists' colony, lush gardens filled with native plants, acres of woodland, and magnificent mansion set high atop a dune.

After giving her driver a generous tip—she was seldom, if ever, unappreciative—C.J. thought of her puppy, a Bichon Frisé she'd named Moppet. His innate joy would have made all the difference where she was headed.

Moppet would have loved a walk through these lovely grounds instead of being cooped up in a kennel. I feel so guilty. But as I told him, he's not welcome—which says a lot, if you ask me.

Striding past the newly erected Staunton Museum and stopping at a cluster of small cottages to get her bearings, C.J. stared up at the HomePort Mansion, whose Victorian ebullience dominated the nearer of two large dunes. The mansion's Italianate tower was tall enough to offer stunning views of the Atlantic and all of Cape Cod Bay. Provincetown was peppered with widows' walks, turrets, and cupolas, from which Yankee merchants had once watched for their returning vessels, but there was no better vantage point than HomePort.

Like many who viewed the place through a distant lens (in her case, the *New York Times*), C.J. had dismissed P'town as a summer playground, ill-suited for the new life she sought. This misinformed decision was perhaps her most unfortunate mistake of all.

***

Two weeks earlier, when an oil spill in Blackfish Creek had fouled a large sute of mallards, C.J. had met someone she really liked. Her fellow duck-cleaner had been surprisingly gentle with the traumatized birds—and even more so with C.J., whose frustrations had overflowed with a vehemence that surprised her.

The first person to show the slightest interest in me since I moved to the Cape. She understood how much I want to be seen for myself—not as somebody else defines me. What was her name again? Heloise? Helen? No. That's not right. It was Helena. Yes. That's it. Like Helena Rubinstein, she said. A bit odd and a flashy dresser, but hard-working and so kind. She told me she lived at HomePort and gave me her number. She was too old to be a student. She must work here. I should have arranged to see her to apologize for bending her ear. We could have had lunch.

Reaching a cluster of studios, C.J. studied the terse directions she'd received the week before. After a brief search, she found the specified path. Pitch pines, stooped and scraggy, grew near a walkway that climbed a lesser dune. The trail zigzagged across fine white sand held in check by dune grass and pressure-treated timbers.

Winded by what she soon dubbed the world's longest staircase, C.J. failed to notice the glass-fronted contemporary home at the highest point on the property. In contrast to the Victorian manse, this cedar-clad home was built to savor its surroundings. Together, the buildings, old and new, stood watch over the artists' colony, the first landing place of the Pilgrims, and the small town built on nothing but sand.

Art Isn't Easy

At last, C.J. reached her destination, a large, shingled studio partially nestled under one of the oldest beech trees on the Outer Cape. After catching her breath, she knocked twice. No one answered.

Dismayed, she tried a second time. "Yoo-hoo! I'm here!"

Again, no answer.

Releasing pent-up frustration, C.J. screeched "Coo-ee" in a tone better suited to hog-calling or grand opera. This unladylike outburst got a response—from a wedge of Canada geese whose incessant honks echoed across the estate like mocking laughter.

C.J. took a deep breath, pushed open the door, and entered the expansive workspace. Large canvases in varying stages of completion covered every wall, their figures gaunt and other-worldly. Gold leaf and brilliant colors ranging from violet to bright ochre caused the images to glow like ancient stained glass as light streamed through four skylights, flooding the space with dazzling hues.

Several unfinished abstracts of wind-sculpted dunes and towering ocean waves captured the wildness of the Outer Cape. Another work, near completion, depicted rotund, naked women capering around a flickering fire. Shadows and smoke masked some revelers, while dancing flames fully illuminated others. The effect was both joyous and erotic. C.J. quickly averted her gaze.

The portrait of a nude boy contemplating his pubescent body rested on an easel in the center of the room. His lithe form stood out against a desolate background of smoldering ash. His gaze morose and discontent, the boy was oblivious to the vivid phoenix rising from the ruins behind him. By far the most exquisite of all, the painting was a study in contrast: The boy's pale complexion and sandy hair were masterfully rendered against the haunting backdrop, which eloquently conveyed his loneliness and isolation. The bird's unfolding wings blazed with color, their vibrant, multi-hued feathers depicted in meticulous detail. The work was mesmerizing—or would have been to most people.

"I hope she hasn't set *that* one aside for me!" C.J. clutched her sunhat as if it were trying to escape. "It's simply *too* Provincetown. I doubt anyone in Wellfleet will bid on a nude to begin with—and certainly not in public. I need something far less controversial, like a nice lighthouse or fishing boat. There's got to be one around here somewhere."

"She" was the world-renowned artist and local curmudgeon, Mavis Chandry, whose work sold for some of the highest prices ever paid to a living female artist. Mavis had postponed this studio visit four times. Now it seemed C.J. had been stood up. Exhausted and near tears, she feared she'd made another misstep. There had been so many since she'd launched her fundraiser just five months before.

Build It and They Will Come

Though she was primed and ready for meaningful connections in her new hometown, C.J.'s efforts to ingratiate herself failed dismally. People were civil but pointedly declined her invitations. She was invisible unless a group was raising money for some cause or another. Then, she was bossed about by committee chairs who went back to acting as if she didn't exist when they no longer required her services.

C.J. vowed to turn things around. At last, she came up with a solution: she would give the town a gift—a monument immortalizing a local figure, which would favorably impress the townies and leave a lasting legacy.

After a life in her husband's shadow, she'd be recognized and appreciated for her generosity. It would be easy enough to arrange. She'd prime the pump with a significant donation, then host an auction of Outer Cape art—a *tour de force* guaranteed to draw a large crowd and raise more funds, which she'd supplement with state and local grants. After that, she'd find a sculptor and buy a plot of land.

For the first time in her adult life, C.J. would do something meaningful. Plus, she'd have the joy of spending Stan's money, which would have made him turn over in his grave if she hadn't had him cremated and scattered around his scrapyard in the Bronx. A high-volume, high-yield scrapyard, to be sure, but a scrapyard, nevertheless.

A potential bidding war on high-priced art would ensure great publicity, drawing sizable crowds and big money. C.J. had stalked Mavis Chandry for weeks, confident she could secure a small painting for the auction's featured attraction. Getting artists out here in the boondocks to donate their work couldn't be that difficult, could it?

An encounter on Fisher Beach near Mavis's Truro home had been the first indication C.J. might have underestimated the challenge. Her attempt to buttonhole the reclusive artist had backfired spectacularly when Mavis, brandishing a large piece of driftwood, had chased her off the beach.

A video of C.J.'s humiliation had gone viral, which may have prompted some residual guilt on Mavis's part. When C.J. confronted her in the frozen foods section of the Stop and Shop, the artist had agreed to discuss a donation in exchange for a solemn promise to be left in peace forever. C.J. had accepted Mavis's terms with alacrity and was to see the unfinished work during today's meeting.

Where was Mavis?

C.J.'s brow dripped with perspiration from the long climb. Her outfit—beige khaki shorts with a matching blouse replete with a kerchief, suspenders, and epaulets—was soaked. As she slumped into a low-slung bentwood rocker, her support hose ripped at each knee, exposing pale, white knobs of flesh. She barely heard the delicate chair as it creaked and groaned.

Fanning herself with her tattered sun hat, C.J. tried to dissipate the pungent odor of oil paint and turpentine.

I don't see why Mavis can't be on time. She's such a diva. And I've never understood all the fuss about her work. Of course, I'd never say that in public. The two hundred thousand or more a small Mavis Chandry would command at auction, say nothing of the publicity it would bring, would turn everything around.

Then C.J.'s dream—a statue of Goody Hallett in Wellfleet Center—would become a reality.

Down With the Ship

The bay side of the Outer Cape consists of marshes, tidal islands, and steep cliffs populated by expensive summer homes with views across the water to the Upper Cape. On the Atlantic side, the nearest landmass is Portugal, over three thousand miles away. The enormous sand dunes and long, isolated beaches of the National Seashore overlook a so-called "ocean graveyard," where treacherous shoals run parallel to the shore.

More than a thousand shipwrecks have been documented off the coast of Truro and Wellfleet alone. The most famous is the *Whydah*

Gally, a former slave ship carrying pirate treasure from 53 other vessels when it foundered in April 1717.

Legend has it that before Sam Bellamy became an infamous pirate and plundered the Caribbean, he and a Wellfleet girl fell in love. Her wealthy parents opposed the match, so he left to make his fortune and win their favor. Black Sam, as he came to be known, was returning to wed Maria "Goody" Hallett when a gale forced the *Whydah* onto treacherous shoals off Wellfleet. Out of the 146-member crew, only 2 survived. Black Sam did not.

Pious villagers drove Goody Hallett into the wilderness when her pregnancy could no longer be concealed. Legend has it she either witnessed the wreck or cursed the *Whydah* from atop a dune, though there is consensus she grew more eccentric and feral once her lover's vessel foundered.

Some locals insisted whenever there was a storm at sea, her ghost stalked the dunes near where the ship went down. Others, that she haunted a spot called the Devil's Pasture or Lucifer Land. This sort of ambiguity is a hallmark of Outer Cape legends, where speculation runs rampant and truth can be an afterthought—if not totally irrelevant.

If only C.J. had known. Brimming with excitement, she'd commissioned an elaborate PowerPoint presentation and gathered the necessary signatures for the town meeting to consider her proposal. It was a flawless plan. The town would benefit from a beautiful monument that preserved a piece of its history, and C.J. would be welcomed into the fold to live as she'd always wanted. What could go wrong?

The question had many answers. Though C.J. remained blissfully unaware of the growing opposition, which spread through the townie network like wildfire, all hell broke loose at the meeting. She had barely finished her presentation when a voter shouted Black Sam had left Goody pregnant to plunder the Caribbean. Another chimed in that the monument would officially sanction unwed motherhood.

C.J. responded with the first thought that came to mind. "It's not the first time a girl has gotten herself in the family way—look at Hester Prynne."

The unfortunate comparison to Nathaniel Hawthorne's tragic heroine evoked raucous laughter. Anyone in Wellfleet who'd read *The Scarlet Letter* and knew the legend of Goody Hallett was aware the two women weren't cut from the same cloth.

C.J.'s hundred-thousand-dollar request was denied by a near-unanimous show of hands. The next day, when a well-intentioned neighbor shared a rumor that Goody had killed her child the night it was born, C.J. kept her thoughts to herself. A week later, an elderly oysterman, ill-disposed toward women, newcomers, and technology, cornered her in the market. He informed her Goody's nickname had been "The Witch of Wellfleet" until the use of PowerPoint—a known tool of the devil—had captured C.J. the title.

His diatribe proved too much to bear. C.J. wrote a letter to the editor explaining her position and calling out the oysterman's misogyny. When her missive failed to appear in print, she wrote a second letter protesting the suppression of the first. This was published—alongside a lengthy editorial on libel laws and "the Wellfleet way," which, to C.J.'s eye, seemed based more on provincial inclination than either legal precedent or objective reporting.

From that point on, she'd dug in her heels. If the good people of Wellfleet chose not to support her, she'd raise the money on her own. They'd come to their senses when they saw the finished product.

The monument often appeared to C.J. in cinematic clarity: the young woman atop a dune, hand to brow, her skirts billowing in the storm as she searched the raging sea for her pirate lover, whose ship was foundering just offshore.

Them There Eyes

"I'd better just hunker down and wait," C.J. muttered, pacing the expansive studio. "I won't make this climb again if I can avoid it. The other times, Mavis called to cancel, so she ought to be here soon enough."

An electric teapot, a basket of exotic teas, and a small human skull rested on a nearby table. Polished to a porcelain sheen, the skull's sole trace of color came from the amber mounted in its eye sockets, which blazed with reflected sunlight. Unearthed at an Aztec archeological site, the chalice was allegedly used in sacrificial rites. Well in keeping with her take-no-prisoners reputation, Mavis used it as a mug.

C.J. searched the studio for a more suitable alternative.

She can't begrudge me a little self-initiative after climbing the Matterhorn to get here. I'm dying for a cup of tea.

Finding nothing, C.J. weighed the demands of her growing thirst against the indignity of drinking from such a gruesome vessel. Thirst won. She selected a packet of organic gunpowder tea, filled the teapot from a paint-smeared tap, and plugged the pot into an outlet beside the sink.

Nothing happened.

She noticed a second outlet near the bathroom door.

Again, nothing. What the hell?

C.J. spied a third outlet beneath the table.

There's an electric clock plugged into this one, and its second hand is moving. This will certainly do the trick.

As the skull's malevolent eyes stared back at her, C.J. was overcome with dread. The clock's second hand made two complete rotations while she indulged in a rare moment of indecision.

"Fiddlesticks," she declared at last. "I'm sure Mavis only uses you for the shock value."

Bending low with a protracted groan, she plugged the kettle in for the third—and last—time. Electricity surged up her right arm, searing her skin. The smell of burning flesh permeated the room as her muscles spasmed and her fingers involuntarily contracted around the cord.

Sensing her fate, C.J.'s last thought was of her beloved Moppet.

I hope they find him a loving home—

Electrons tore through every part of her body, taxing, then stopping her heart. Her final contractions ripped the teapot from its socket, spilling its contents and shorting the electricity.

C.J. slumped to the floor, arms splayed, legs locked, mouth agape, her lifeless eyes staring upward in astonishment as the skull maintained its silent vigil.

Time for a Change

The next morning, Harold Blithe rose early from his ornate four-poster in the master bedroom of the HomePort Mansion. He refused to dwell on how poorly he'd slept or how vast and empty the bed had felt. Instead, he showered, then shaved his face, chest, and nether regions with extra care before brushing his teeth, blow-drying his hair, and donning a wig cap.

Harold continued his morning ritual in the lavish dressing room adjoining the master suite. This pale purple room was filled with tall wardrobes crammed with evening gowns and accessories. Staring at his nakedness in an enormous gilt mirror, he pondered a paradox that had stymied him for as long as he could remember: Were this reflection another man's body, he'd be attracted if not aroused. Yet, when he studied his image, all he saw was the dire need for a makeover.

"When it comes to panty lines, where there's a penis, there's a problem," Harold said as he stepped into a white cotton gaff. With a rapid motion of his right hand, he pushed the troublesome bits between his legs while snugging the gaff into place with his left.

The entire process took just a few seconds. Harold studied his reflection again, made a minor tweak, then sat down at an ornate dressing table to do his makeup. That meticulous effort complete, he donned a padded white bra and a black pageboy wig.

Then, as he did at the start of every new day, Harold smiled into the mirror and said, "Good morning, Helena. Welcome back, darling. What shall we wear today?"

We Are Family

All traces of Harold safely tucked away, Helena Handbasket, tastefully attired in a purple business suit with matching purse, waited outside a nearby bedroom for the sound of gentle snoring.

Once confident her grandmother had made it through another night, Helena tiptoed to a window near the kitchen stairs. As she did most mornings, she surveyed the cottages and studios scattered over the twenty acres of the HomePort Estate. Despite the early hour, many artists in residence were already hard at work. The notion of so much creative energy in one spot always made Helena smile. She was, after all, in charge of the place.

Looking over at the former servants' wing, Helena recalled the days when it was a grotesque ell known as "The Bates Motel." It was now faculty housing, perfectly integrated with the mansion's architecture, its elegant suites furnished with modern amenities.

If those temperamental painters and writers only knew what the place was like when I lived there, there'd be fewer faculty meetings. The guy next door turning tricks, the wind rattling the windows. . . It seems like another life.

Even with the renovation, some still found fault. In a recent meeting, an illustrious faculty member had declared the lack of an ice maker to be "an inhibitor to [his] creative output."

Glancing to her left, Helena watched Dolores Delgado, faithful family retainer, park her vintage Edsel near the kitchen door. Dolores was the only person allowed to park near the mansion. Even Helena used the staff lot off the service road to avoid disturbing the artists at work. Immaculately dressed as always, her towering beehive hairdo reminiscent of a Beefeater's helmet, Dolores was the guardian of HomePort's traditions—and its resident gorgon.

Helena blew a kiss her way.

Dolores treats this place like a royal abode. Imagine Buckingham Palace guarded by a hundred elderly women wearing black uniforms and beehives, like something out of an old Monty Python skit. God bless her. She's an anachronism—and still scares me half to death—but I don't know what I'd do without her.

Dolores had tended the reclusive heiress, Lola Staunton, with regard bordering on fealty until her death at ninety-six. Two years later, when Dorrie, Lola's half-sister, passed away, Dolores transferred her devotion to Helena, the estate's current chatelaine.

Not a day passed when Helena didn't think of the Staunton sisters, whom she helped reconcile after decades of estrangement. In their final years, they'd created a family of their own from a diverse group of young people—gay and straight—who were devoted to both women. In appreciation, Lola and Dorrie had left significant portions of their vast fortune to their chosen family, who remained close to this day.

Rituals established during the reign of Lola's grandmother, Laetitia—breakfast trays, afternoon tea in the parlor, and dinner in the formal dining room—continued even once the grounds were filled with faculty and students. These outmoded practices were often a challenge, but memories of Lola and Dorrie outweighed the inconvenience.

Besides, no one dared tell Dolores to change her ways.

Gandma

When she'd shown up unannounced at HomePort's front door a year after Dorrie's death, Helena's beloved "Gandma" had cut short an effusive welcome. "Don't use that name for me anymore," she'd insisted. "The moment someone knows you're a granny, they watch what they say. If I'm gonna live in this two-bit town, I'll want all the dirt—all the time. Call me Shirley-Mae or Shirley from now on."

A former Hollywood bit-player with brief appearances as a "bombshell" on *Dragnet* and *Perry Mason*, Shirley-Mae became a local celebrity soon after her arrival. She loved going out to all the revues, gay, straight, or anything in between. With her towering hairdo, seventies earrings, garish makeup, signature beaded purse, and vintage-twenties flask filled with Beefeater Gin, Shirley revved up a crowd better than any warm-up act. The more risqué the performance, the louder her catcalls and hilarious commentary. Every drag performer in town hoped she'd be in the front row on opening night.

In July, annoyed neighbors had summoned the police to *The Naked Hunks Review*. Shirley's voice had carried through a rickety sliding door to a nearby condo, whose owners insisted she'd single-handedly violated the town's noise ordinance.

Her response quickly became town lore: "Boys, I was married to the same man for thirty-two years. I never knew the Good Lord could make anything close to the paraphernalia I'm seein' up on this here stage tonight. Why take a harmless pleasure away from an old broad—especially one with one foot in the grave and the other on a banana peel? Karma can be a bitch, and so can I! Get offa your high horses and don't take life so serious."

The cast carried Shirley on stage for the grand finale. Two weeks later, she'd been made Grand Marshal of the Carnival Parade.

It didn't surprise Helena that Shirley had become the town's grandmother. She'd been a fierce and loving protector from the moment Helena's mother had walked out.

Artistic Temperament

The recently completed Staunton Museum was the new home of the Laetitia Staunton collection, an extensive array of Impressionist and Provincetown art. Collected by Lola and Dorrie's grandmother over decades of travel, the works had remained out of the public eye for nearly a hundred years. When informed of the collection's value, the Staunton sisters added a detailed bequest to their wills to provide for its permanent care. Helena, executive director of the Staunton Trust, had followed their instructions to the letter with help from her dear friends, Marc Nugent and Cole Hanson.

Studying their contemporary home high atop its dune, Helena contemplated how much the two men had matured in their three years together. They'd each arrived at HomePort as refugees: Marc had fled an abusive relationship. Cole, a talented artist, had been paralyzed by self-doubt and turned his back on a promising career. They'd eventually recognized their love for each other, married, and built a new life together.

Finding strength and stability in their union, Marc had become a published author. Cole began to paint again and became the museum's curator. Helena considered the two men the colony's greatest success story—as well as the brothers she'd never had.

***

Glancing at the clock, Helena decided to check the museum before the eight-a.m. walkthrough with Mavis Chandry.

Who knows what fresh hell awaits me. Mavis will probably turn everything inside out just for the sheer fun of it. I'll text Cole to meet me ahead of time, so we're prepared. Better to anticipate her inevitable tantrum than be caught unaware.

When Mavis joined the faculty, Helena and Cole—intrigued and intimidated by the temperamental artist whose largest paintings sold for millions—had performed everything expected of them and more. In time, the old woman had lowered her guard. Gradually, a wary friendship evolved. Even so, Helena had been speechless when Mavis broached the idea of donating 63 never-before-seen works to the museum for its gala opening.

At the sight of her stunned expression, Mavis had burst into laughter for the first time Helena could recall. "You've got a good head on your shoulders," the artist said in her husky contralto, "even if your hair's a different color and length every day, and your cup size changes four times from noon to midnight, you care about doing things right—the way I do. I like that.

"I won't be around forever. These works are intensely personal, and I need to know they'll be cared for. P'town's been good to me.

You've been good to me. If you don't mess up my show, maybe—just maybe—I'll be good to you."

When it had been announced that Mavis would display the large cache of paintings as the museum's first major exhibit, interview requests had overwhelmed museum staff. Helena came up with the idea of a press walkthrough the morning of the private view, where those who had helped build or contributed to the museum would be the first to see the finished product.

Paul Schroeder, a documentary filmmaker who lived in town, asked to film the event. If Mavis agreed to an interview with him, PBS would air his documentary. Despite intense media scrutiny, her intention to donate the paintings remained a closely held secret. The bequest was to be signed after the press briefing and announced that night.

Clean Up Your Act

Leaving the mansion by the front door, Helena stopped to stare out over the moors, a stretch of sand and reeds between the stone breakwater at the end of the harbor and a portion of Long Point. The view from a nearby bench was her favorite on the estate. She often sat there to pay her respects to Lola and Dorrie, who were buried close by. Today was no exception.

Helena studied the narrow stretch of sand beyond the moors, then gazed across Cape Cod Bay to the hills of Plymouth and Kingston. The sea was calm, the cloudless sky a rich blue. A few of the boats still moored in the harbor had not yet aligned with the change of tide. The haphazard pattern occurred only at slack water and slowly yielded to symmetry as the tidal flow strengthened.

As she often did, Helena thought of the town's history, especially the community once situated on Long Point.

An entire village out on that tiny spit of land. Even a schoolhouse. Not a single structure remains. They floated them all back here. What pragmatism—and insistence on continuity. Back then, P'town was so isolated the ocean was a highway. In some ways, folks were more comfortable at sea than on land. No wonder Provincetown whalers traversed the globe. Have we captured that unique, seafaring spirit in the museum's design and exhibits? I guess we'll find out tonight.

An enormous black yacht set out from the long dock at Fisherman's Wharf. Helena watched the vessel pass through the harbor, then accelerate with surprising speed.

That's Scamp, the monstrosity docked near my boat. Good riddance!

Helena followed the yacht's progress until it was out of sight, then gazed down at the museum tinged with gold light from the morning sun. Cole's suggestion to use unpolished granite blocks for the exterior walls had been a masterstroke, recalling ballast used on whaling ships. Its simple lines and organic composition also allowed the HomePort Mansion to hold sway over the site as it had for so long.

It had been a wise, though extremely expensive, decision to build a satellite parking lot near the town center to protect the estate's fragile ecology. Cole had designed unobtrusive studios and housing in ways that belied the number of people in residence. The service road, the guard shed, and Dorrie's former home, where the head of security lived, were surrounded by native vegetation. As a result, the outer grounds of the HomePort Estate appeared as timeless as they had been the day Helena arrived.

The museum's interior could not have presented a more dramatic contrast. While everything on the outside blended with its surroundings, the high-ceilinged galleries, with their crisp angles and ample wall space, could accommodate art of almost any scale. The soaring rooms with their glass ceilings drew the eye upwards to clouds borne by ocean breezes. The view was like looking up from the deck of a sailing ship.

This morning's walkthrough was the first opportunity to view Mavis's show in the light of day. The museum's north roof, constructed of hurricane-proof glass, was designed to maximize Provincetown's famous light. The glass had been Helena's idea, and so far, the results had been impressive. Mavis's dazzling assortment of landscapes, seascapes, and iconic portraits would be the ultimate test.

As Helena descended the winding path, a text from her husband arrived.

(Butch) *Break a leg tonight and don't forget to send pictures.*

As she often did, Helena stared down at the memorial stones of Pilgrims' Park and thought of those commemorated there. She couldn't imagine what it would be like to lose the man she missed so much it hurt.

(Helena) *You're always with me in spirit.*

She prayed Butch still felt the same way, then descended the short flight of stairs to the museum entrance, where she met Cole Hanson. Tall and breathtakingly handsome, with a firm jaw and a mane of black hair, he was immaculately dressed in flat-front chinos and a blue polo shirt that accentuated his athletic physique. He and Helena hugged, then waited for Afton Walker, the museum's head of security.

Afton was a mountain of a man, almost seven feet tall, with bulging muscles, a close-cropped beard, and perceptive brown eyes. He wore a smart uniform of white slacks, a white shirt, and a blue blazer with the museum's signature compass rose embroidered on its lapel. As he arrived, he burst into a wide grin. It was obvious he adored Helena, though, as he'd once put it, "At first, she'd took a bit of getting used to."

"Everything OK?" Cole asked Afton as he keyed in the security code and unlocked the steel-reinforced gate at the front entrance.

"Quiet night here. Not so much downtown, though. Sergeant Brandt called around one-thirty to tell me Aaron was rip-roaring drunk outside the Squealing Pig. He picked me up so I could drive the damn fool home, then gave me a ride back here. Poor Aaron has had a tough time since Aurelia ran off with that gal from Northampton. He's got no other family here but me. Everyone else is back home in Jamaica."

"How is he?" Helena asked, genuinely concerned for Afton's twin.

"Near dead to the world when I left him. He'd never have made it nine miles to Truro without hurting himself or somebody else."

"Awfully kind of Sergeant Brandt to look out for him—and you," Helena said. "And somewhat out of keeping with his reputation. Perhaps I've been too rough on him, though there have been several rumors—"

"That you've helped circulate," Cole said, grinning at Afton, who confidently awaited Helena's retort, his eyes alight.

"Well, I'm not one to spread rumors," she said, splaying her palms in a supplicating gesture, "but what else can you do with them?"

Quite the Exhibition

As Afton and Cole exchanged knowing glances, Helena entered her security code. The main door clicked open, and they stepped into the museum's two-story atrium. Sunlight poured through the glass ceiling, illuminating the multi-hued marble floor whose embedded compass rose was based on that from a map belonging to the first Captain Staunton.

The atrium was set up with forty high-top tables, a lavish buffet area, and a bar. Sail-shaped fabric hung from the thin metal rafters as if a fleet of ships were about to depart, one of many touches contrasting the past and the present. Galleries of differing sizes fanned out from the atrium on the major points of the compass. The content of these rooms alternated between permanent and revolving exhibits.

Helena headed to the main gallery. As she'd hoped, its indirect north light made Mavis's work glow with divine radiance. It also highlighted the obscene graffiti spray-painted on every canvas: A kneeling monk, meant to be in prayer, faced an enormous, erect phallus, his devotions a monstrous caricature. A beautiful female nude wore hastily drawn tassels on her breasts. A priest sported a sombrero and carried what appeared to be a surfboard. The adjacent piece, a tranquil seascape, displayed a swimmer followed by an ominous black fin. At the entrance to the exhibit, Mavis's artist statement, in raised silver lettering on a Plexiglas panel, was defaced with the words, "Can't paint for. . ." A spray-painted pile of excrement completed the critique.

The graffiti had been applied in haste, spattering walls and the floor with a fine, black spray. Faint lines trailed from painting to painting. The contrast between the iconic figures and their mutilations was grotesque and revolting.

Helena's shriek summoned the others, who, at first, stood in silence, their mouths agape. Then, Cole ran to the Plexiglass panel, and Afton sprinted to the Mansion Suite, where HomePort's formal parlor and study had been relocated. Everything from both rooms, right down to the draperies, light fixtures, and furniture, was as it had been in the family home.

The entire Laetitia Staunton Collection of Impressionist and Provincetown Art, conservatively appraised at four hundred million dollars, hung undisturbed in the reconstructed parlor and study. The discovery of those forgotten Corots, Monets, Corbets, Hartleys, Lazells, and a multitude of others—some considered lost forever—had taken the art world by storm.

Relieved those works were not damaged, Afton checked the Historical Society exhibit and the galleries dedicated to Provincetown's maritime past. Those artifacts, as well as the extensive photographic collection of wharves and whaling ships, were also untouched. Completing the circle with quick checks of the remaining galleries and the small theater, he reported back to Helena, who was still standing where he'd left her.

"Looks like the masterpieces are OK, as well as the rest of the galleries," Afton said, breathing hard. "These are the only paintings with graffiti. We've got to be sure nothing was stolen, though. I'll call in all the other guards and have them take inventory. If we each take a room, it won't take long."

"My God," Helena said, finally finding her voice. "Who would do this? And why?"

"And how the hell did they get in?" Afton asked. He was striding around the room, unable to contain his outrage and bafflement. "I was on the estate grounds all night save when I took my brother home. And the guard on duty monitored the security system while I was away."

"We may be OK," Cole said, holding up a black-coated index finger. "It looks like they used spray chalk, so we should be able to clean it with water. I'll call the house and have Marc bring all the buckets, towels, and sponges he can find. Afton, when you contact the guards, please ask them to keep this to themselves. After that, please locate as many ladders as possible."

As Cole stabbed at his phone, a stentorian voice yelled, "What in the name of God?"

Mavis Chandry stood at the entrance to the main gallery, hands on her ample hips, her face red with rage. Mavis was just over five feet tall, what Helena lovingly described as a "four-square gal"—compact and broad in the beam—with blue eyes and close-cropped white hair. She wore black slacks and a white Oxford shirt that sported the museum's compass rose logo on her right lapel.

"You bitch," Mavis screamed, pointing at Helena, "I trusted you to keep my paintings safe. I was about to sign them over to you, for Christ's sake. What sort of perverted joke is this?"

Helena raced to her side. "Mavis, darling, we just discovered this travesty a minute ago. We don't know who's behind it, but we can get everything cleaned up before anyone else sees."

"It's chalk, Mavis," Cole said, completing his call. "It's used to mark lines on turf for sporting events. And it's water-soluble. Marc is bringing everything we'll need to wash off the graffiti. The paintings will be cleaned up in time for the press viewing."

"There won't be any goddamn viewing," Mavis said, "I trusted you fools with my best work. Now you've allowed this to happen. I'll have everything out of here within the hour. Don't you think I won't."

Helena took the artist's arm and propelled her forcefully to a terrace overlooking the moors, whose span of tall reeds offered a tranquil contrast to the chaos in the main gallery. "Mavis, I'm devastated and can't imagine who would want to do this. I'll take photos, then we'll clean this mess up. When we're done, I'll call the police. After that, you and I will talk things through.

"We've got the *New York Times*, *Art in America*, and *Vanity Fair* here for the walkthrough, say nothing of our interviews for Paul's documentary. You shouldn't lose such a marvelous opportunity because of some deranged, hateful person. We can't back down. If we do, the bastard wins. We can fix this in time. I know we can."

"I suppose you're right about the publicity," Mavis said, with less of an edge to her voice, "but I'm not signing the bequest."

"I understand. Let's figure out who did this and why," Helena said, her voice gentle and encouraging. "Then you can make a final decision. If you choose to take the paintings back, I won't fight you. Fair enough?"

Mavis's eyes were rife with distrust. "I suppose so."

"Excellent. I'll photograph the damage. Then we'll clean things up. And while we're doing that, Afton will review the security footage.

"C'mon, let's get back in there. We need your guidance so we don't damage anything."

All Hands on Deck

Cole's husband, Marc, arrived with several buckets and sponges. He was wearing jogging shorts, a purple T-shirt, and leather sandals. His blond hair was awry, and he hadn't shaved. When he saw the damaged paintings, he halted in his tracks, speechless.

Some distance behind him were Dolores Delgado and Shirley-Mae, who was wearing a lime green pantsuit and stuffing the gooey remains of a chocolate croissant into her mouth. Dolores's famous beehive had every strand in place, and as usual, her black uniform was spotless.

"I was with the gals when Cole called," Marc said. "They insisted on coming along to help. We have enough supplies for everyone."

Cole smiled at his husband, delighted by the rapid response and extra help. "Marc, please fill a bucket from the sink in the janitor's closet. I'll do a test where the chalk is sprayed on the floor. If that goes OK, we can get to work."

The sound of running water soon echoed through the room.

Shirley-Mae spied the defaced art as soon as she entered the main gallery. "Cheese and crackers! I ain't seen nothin' this perverted since they tore down the Dew Drop Inn in Mount Venus, Nevada, in 'sixty-six."

Watching Mavis turn purple, Cole worried that Shirley's outrageous remarks might undermine Helena's peacemaking efforts. Much to his relief, the artist took a deep breath and remained silent. As tempting as it might be to watch these two forces of nature square off, this was neither the time nor place.

"Here you go," Marc said, handing a damp sponge to Cole, who began wiping the marks off the floor.

"Perfect. Not a trace left. We're in business," Cole said. "I'll keep going here while you fill the other buckets, then I'll test a small bit of canvas to be extra sure."

"The photos are just about finished," Helena said. "Marc, turn off the vibration sensors for Cole, would you please? As soon as Afton brings the ladders, we'll start with the tallest paintings and work our way down. I'll wait to call the police. They'd want to keep the graffiti as evidence. We can't allow that with the press walkthrough in just three hours."

Cole looked up from his work. "Tell them we had to remove the chalk before it bonded with the glaze."

Mavis clenched her fists. "Send them to me if they give you any lip, the goddamn fools."

Helena smiled to herself.

That's more like it. There's hope for us yet.

Restoration

Cole and Marc tackled the high spots where the spray had diffused while the others worked where the chalk was most concentrated. Mavis raced from painting to painting, wringing her hands as if fearing for a child in peril. Which, Helena thought, was just about what the works were to her.

"Careful with that spot, Cole," Mavis yelled. "Just dab it. Don't scrub. Watch out for the gold leaf. The glaze doesn't harden completely to avoid crackling. Too much pressure could loosen the gold or even tear the canvas."

"You got it, Mavis," Cole said, gently dabbing the spot. "Looks stable so far, but keep your eye out for tricky areas like that one. OK? Don't hesitate to tell me what to do."

Dolores tackled the artist's statement, scrubbing vigorously until every trace of chalk disappeared. The group, seeing her rapid progress, took heart.

Helena focused on the portrait of the mother and child, which seemed to have suffered the worst onslaught. A series of black slashes had obliterated the mother's face, while priapic grotesques reminiscent of Hieronymus Bosch marred the painting's background, a distant landscape in the style of Renaissance Masters. Only the child remained untouched. Mavis often returned to this painting as Helena worked, pointing out minuscule traces of chalk that might be overlooked. Her tone was more subdued around this work—almost reverent.

"That's it, Helena. Good. You got that tough spot. Now that bit over there. See it? Just above the child's left foot. Yes. Yes. You got it. That's perfect."

Helena painstakingly removed the graffiti with a small sponge, much as a restorer would eradicate the grime of centuries. When that work was complete, Mavis moved on, looking over the cleaners' shoulders and pointing out places they'd missed. When Cole finished cleaning a delicate seascape, she wiped away a tear.

Shirley-Mae was scrubbing the walls and floor with surprising speed as Dolores emptied buckets of dirty water and refilled them for her. The friends continued until no trace of the damage remained. After a lengthy inspection, Mavis confirmed the paintings were back to their original state. Eyes moist, she managed a choked thank you before retreating to the terrace. Watching from a discreet distance, Helena sensed, for the first time, the potent anxiety beneath the artist's bravado.

The Long Arm of The Law

After one last survey of the art, Helena called Sergeant Brandt. Despite numerous complaints from residents, Brandt, though new to the force, had recently become acting chief of police. He was filling in for Louie Silva, who left on a leave of absence two weeks earlier.

Helena kept her opinion of Brandt to herself.

From all I've heard, he's a hothead, a misogynist, and a homophobe. If Chief Louie were around, any of the things Brandt's done would get him fired on the spot. If word gets out about the vandalism, our reputation will never recover. And Brandt will undoubtedly want to show off for the press. Whatever he's up to, I wish Chief Louie was here instead. But I'm not going to say that to Brandt. That's for sure. Time to channel Madame Director and toe the not-so-straight but oh, so narrow.

Afton returned from the security office just as the friends stowed the last of their buckets and sponges. Seeing his downcast expression, Helena summoned the group to the atrium.

When they'd assembled at the compass rose, she said, "OK, Afton. Quick, before the police show up. What have you got for us?"

His reply was tentative and anxious. "Helena, I've scanned ten hours of last night's video on fast frame. I didn't see a damn soul inside the building until we arrived this morning. I saw one odd thing: it's like the security cameras rewound themselves. There's no way everything that happened last night was recorded."

"So you suspect someone tampered with the video feed," Marc said as Cole nodded in agreement.

"I think so. Somebody had to get in to make the mess, but the feed doesn't show anyone entering the building."

"How could they do that without being detected?" Helena asked.

"The cameras are wireless, so someone could have replaced their signal with images from another source. But to do that, they'd have to break the network encryption for starters."

"What's encryption?" Shirley asked.

Seated at one of the high-top tables, she'd just pulled her silver flask from her purse.

"It's a way of jumbling the wireless transmission so that hackers can't see what it contains," Afton said, raising his eyebrows slightly as Shirley took a long swig then smacked her lips.

"If they broke the encryption, then what could they do?"

"They could substitute earlier images from the feed to make it look like no one was in the museum when they actually were."

"The bastards," Shirley said, slamming her fist on the tabletop. "If I get ahold of them, I'll encrypt them all right."

"You saw no one except the police last night?" Cole asked Afton, who seemed impressed by Shirley's reaction, though he clearly felt he'd let everyone down.

"Nobody but Brandt and George Miller, the guard on duty. George stayed in the guardhouse watching the monitors as an additional precaution while I tended to Aaron. So, by rights, the cameras should have recorded anyone on the premises while I was gone—except they didn't."

Just the Facts, Ma'am

The sound of an approaching siren grew louder, then stopped as a police car careened into the drive. A short, bald man with a thick neck and broad shoulders burst from the vehicle and strode toward the museum door. He wore a blue police officer's uniform with a prominent badge. A Glock 22 hung from his belt, along with handcuffs and a collapsible baton.

Helena ran to meet him, ignoring his scowl as she drew near. Cole followed close behind. He knew Sergeant Brandt's reputation and wasn't about to let Helena face him alone. Sensing a confrontation, Shirley, her jaw set, tagged along.

"Sergeant Brandt, thanks for coming so quickly," Helena said.

The officer recoiled at the sound of her voice. "What's going on here?"

"We've had a horrible act of vandalism inside the museum."

"Who are you?" the sergeant demanded, ignoring Helena and focusing on Cole. "What can you tell me about this?"

"I'm the museum curator," Cole said warily, "but Helena is the exec—"

"I don't have all day. Tell me what I need to know. Nothing more. Every minute you stand there babbling is a minute lost."

Helena thought better of making a reply, signaling Cole that he should take the lead. She shot a glance at Shirley-Mae that telegraphed, *Don't you dare say a word.* Her grandmother scowled but remained silent.

Mavis joined the group as Cole walked the sergeant through the main gallery. "Every single work in this room was defaced with some sort of spray-on chalk. We needed to remove it quickly before it bonded with the glaze Mavis uses. Here are some photos of the damage."

Brandt scrolled the images on Helena's phone. Twice, he raised his eyebrows and seemed about to smirk. "Quite the mess," he said at last. "How'd they get in?"

"That's the big question," Cole replied. "Everything was secure when we got here. The gates and doors were locked, and all the alarms were activated."

"So tell me," Brandt asked. "Aren't the pricey pictures from the big house down here now?"

"Yes. The paintings, the original rooms, and furnishings are all in the Mansion Suite."

"If I'm understanding correctly, those paintings are worth a hell of a lot more than the ones that got messed up. Am I right?"

"Yes, you are," Mavis said, barely masking her contempt. "The three major works in that collection would be worth more than all of mine combined."

"So why not steal those paintings, then?"

"Sergeant, I'm not sure anyone could steal either those or Mavis's," Cole said.

"What do you mean?"

"The entire museum is wired with sensors inside the walls. If any piece of art moves even a sixteenth of an inch, they activate and immediately shut down the galleries. Metal grates drop in less than three seconds to lock any suspects inside."

Brandt surveyed the room. "OK. Let's assume no one could take anything. What's so special about these paintings that someone would want to mess them up?"

A thin woman in a white blouse and blue jeans drew near. Her blonde hair was tied back in a ponytail, and she wore no makeup. Her long fingernails were painted bright red, and her vibrant face, wrinkled from years of sun, was inquisitive and good-natured. Helena discreetly signaled her to remain silent.

"Mavis's works are the only items that aren't museum property other than family artifacts on loan to the Historical Society exhibit," Cole said, his voice much quieter than before.

"Meaning?" Brandt said, staring intently at Cole.

"Meaning the goal might be to get her paintings removed from the museum by demonstrating they weren't properly protected."

Then Brandt noticed the woman, who was writing things down in a small blue notebook.

"Freddie! How many goddamn times do I have to tell you to stop following me? And don't pull any of that freedom of the press nonsense on me again. I've got a right to do my job in peace—first amendment or no first amendment."

"Who's that?" Shirley whispered to Helena, who, realizing her proximity was annoying Brandt, had escorted her grandmother back to the high-top table.

"Frederica Chalmers. Everyone calls her Freddie. She's a reporter for the local paper, and a damn good one at that. She must have been monitoring a police scanner and chased after the story. I'm going to talk to her once Brandt leaves. She's a bit of a horse trader but has always been fair. She might be willing to keep this out of the papers—at least until we figure out who did it."

The sergeant said, loud enough for everyone to hear, "Things were fine when I was here around one this morning. I double-checked the monitors in the guard shack before I took Afton downtown."

Freddie caught Helena's gaze, then rolled her eyes.

By the Light of the Silvery Moon

"Take me to the master security console," Brandt ordered, looking for an instant like a caricature of Mussolini. "Not the one in the guard-house. The one in the command center."

Afton led him up a spiral stair to the security office on the museum's second floor. Helena signaled Freddie to wait, then joined Brandt, Cole, and Afton in the office.

Brandt, appearing tiny in contrast to the head of security's height, seemed eager to compensate. "OK, explain the configuration of the entire system."

Afton covered the positioning and range of the cameras. Then he mentioned the encrypted wireless signal.

"Yeah, yeah. He already explained all that," Brandt said, folding his arms on his chest and staring at the array of monitors.

Afton looked at Helena as if to ask, *What the hell is wrong with this clown?* When she shook her head, he shrugged and continued his explanation.

Brandt, oblivious to the exchange, spoke at last. "So everything's covered by the cameras? Floor to ceiling, indoor and out?"

"Yes, sir. Everything. The cameras on the girders give a three-sixty-degree view."

"Did any of the feeds show anything unusual?"

"Yes, sir," Afton said with equanimity. "It was a full moon last night. The rooms on the north side should get brighter as the moon passes its meridian and its light shines through the glass roof."

"So what?"

"For a while, they do, but then things go dark, then get lighter again. That's during the section where the timestamp repeats itself. This happens for both the internal and external feeds."

"And did you see anyone on the outside cameras before this morning?"

"No, sir. Except for you and George Miller, who was in the guard shed when you and I left."

"Show me the segment you're talking about."

Afton pressed the play button. An image of the main gallery flickered on the monitor. The cameras repeatedly panned the room, showing the paintings in their original state. As the moon began to set, the interior got brighter. Video of the exterior displayed the empty entranceway and parking lot. The timestamp reached 2:45. Then it was 1:10 again, and the galleries were dim. Afton explained the video repeated that way for three iterations.

"You're right," the sergeant said. "Someone intercepted the wireless feed with a loop from earlier footage."

"But how did they get in? I can't find any trace of forced entry."

"Good question. Have you got the access logs?"

"Not here. The security company has them. I've asked them to send the log file for the last twenty-four hours."

"Nice work. Better than I'd have expected from the lot of you," Brandt said.

Again, Afton caught Helena's eye. Again, she signaled for patience. Cole watched the exchange with a puzzled expression but said nothing.

While less than impressed with Brandt, Helena, too, kept her thoughts to herself.

Why is Brandt so damned confrontational? It's probably just a week or two before Chief Louie gets back. What's the point in getting folks all riled up while he's away? It's bound to backfire in the long run. Oh well, I'm going to remain optimistic even if I have to hurt somebody.

The sergeant's radio squawked, "Three-car collision on Route Six and Conwell. Injuries reported."

Brandt said, "I gotta go. Email all the pictures to the police station. Don't make me come back for them."

Then he raced to his car and drove off, siren blaring.

On the Beat

Returning to the group in the atrium, Helena said, "In case you haven't already introduced yourselves, this is Freddie Chalmers from the *Provincetown Free Press.* You've probably read her insightful articles. I need a couple of minutes alone with her."

Helena said little as she escorted the reporter to the theater beyond the Mansion Suite. When they were behind closed doors, Freddie said, "OK, now. What the hell is going on here?"

Helena took in the stillness of the small room with its leather viewing seats and dim lighting. The tranquil spot seemed a million miles away from the turmoil outside the door.

"I've got no choice but to trust you, Freddie. You've always been decent to me, so I'm going to appeal to your sense of fair play. Something horrible happened today, and if word gets out, all my work, as well as Lola and Dorrie's last wishes, might be for nothing."

Freddie took Helena's hand in hers and motioned that they should sit. "I loved those two old broads. You know I did. After all Lola did for me during my divorce, I'd walk over hot coals for her. What's happened? Off the record. . ."

Helena quickly explained the break-in and defaced paintings.

Freddie paused, then said, "I'm not sure you have much to worry about, Helena. I've been following Brandt closely, and there's something not quite right with him. Before I say more, I want to ask you a few questions—again, off the record—to see if my theory holds water.

"First, when you reported the break-in, did you call the main police number?"

"Yes."

"But you must have wanted to speak with Brandt, right?"

"Yes, but I didn't have his direct number."

Freddie smiled. "Tell me what he said when they put him through."

"Well, the strangest thing happened. He picked up the main number. Come to think of it, it was almost as if he was expecting my call."

"OK." Freddie looked smug. "And then?"

Her reaction puzzled Helena, who paused before responding, "I hardly got two sentences out, and he said, 'I'll be right there.'"

"That fits right in with my theory."

"And what's that?" Helena asked, leaning close. "Are you suggesting he *was* waiting for my call?"

"Yes, and that he doesn't want word of this break-in to get out. I suspect he won't log it officially. You should get back to your crew. I'll explain more later. But for now, if you play ball, let me ask you questions, and keep me informed of developments, I won't publish until you say so."

"Deal," Helena said, shaking hands with the reporter. "I owe you big time. You're part of the team from now on. Let's go back and hear what Afton has to say. But I want to know what you find out, too."

"You got it, I promise," Freddie said with a grin and a fist pump. "Let's get to work."

Time After Time

When Helena and Freddie returned, everyone moved to the lounge, where three solid glass walls overlooked Pilgrims' Park, the breakwater, and Long Point. An old-fashioned ice cream parlor had been installed at the back of the room. Marc stepped behind the counter, poured cups of coffee, and offered them around as Helena addressed the group.

"Folks, you can say anything you need to in front of Freddie. Everything will be off the record for now. She may be able to help us, so don't hold back.

"Afton, could someone have tricked you into leaving last night?"

"Not sure, Helena. Maybe." He continued to pace the room as he spoke. "But Aaron was so drunk he'd have hurt himself, or somebody else, had he tried to drive. And, besides, the only person I dealt with was Brandt. Except, of course, George Miller, who was on duty."

"And you're confident neither of them went inside?"

"The police have an access code for emergencies. But theirs wasn't the one used, Helena."

"What do you mean? You already know whose access code was used?"

"Yes, ma'am. A copy of the log is kept on the backup computer here."

"I thought so," Cole said. "Why didn't you tell Brandt?"

Afton looked uncomfortable. "Because it was Helena's."

"What?"

"Helena's code opened the main door at half-past one this morning."

Mavis Chandry's jaw dropped. It was a few seconds before she stopped staring accusingly at Helena and composed herself enough to growl, "What the hell?"

Her inference stunned Helena. "Mavis don't go there. Why would I deface your paintings when the museum stands to gain so much from a successful show, say nothing of your donation?"

"Because you're stark, raving mad," Mavis said, pronouncing each word slowly and stressing the last. "I should have known. I tried to make exceptions. To each his own and all that bullshit. But the bottom line is you're certifiable."

Belatedly, Cole stepped between them. "Now, just a minute, Mavis."

"Listen to me," Helena said, clasping the elderly artist's hand and not allowing her to remove it. "Stop and consider who has the most to lose. I do. If word gets out that the Staunton Museum can't protect its collection, everything we've worked so hard for will be ruined. I'm the executive director, and the museum is my responsibility. This isn't an attack against *you*, Mavis. It's an attack against *me*. In fact, I'd stake my life on it."

"Do you have any idea who would do something like this, Helena? And why?" Freddie asked, taking out her notepad and pen.

"I don't. It makes no sense whatsoever. Clearly, this wasn't theft—it was pure vandalism, and I can't for the life of me figure out why. How long do you think we have before word gets out?"

"There was nothing on the scanner after your call to Brandt. He passed me, going like a bat out of hell. Since I hadn't heard anything from dispatch, I followed him here. My gut is damn near convinced he won't log an official police response. If he does, it will become public record, and I'll be able to tell you. But I bet you good money he won't.

"And I'll keep all this quiet—in exchange for an exclusive at the private view tonight. I've already got my press pass, but I'd love to report your thoughts about the opening firsthand. Yours too, Mavis, if you'd be willing?"

"Sure, why not," Mavis growled. "But if one single word gets out before we're ready, you'll wish you'd never crossed me."

"I'd expect nothing less," Freddie said, grinning. "I just want first dibs on the story when you are."

"Oh, Freddie," Helena said, "you've got all that and a bag of chips."

Concern clouded Shirley-Mae's worn features. "That don't take away from the fact that someone may be out to get you, Helena. What you gonna do about it, dahlin'? How are we gonna find the sons-a-bitches if we can't even see who they are?"

Helena spoke soothingly. "I'll leave a message for Sergeant Brandt saying we found a backup of the security logs and that my code was used to gain entry."

Shirley-Mae frowned. "You sure, honey? That fellow don't seem to cotton to you all that much."

Helena laughed. "Speaking of cotton, I've already got a long row to hoe to prove my innocence to Mavis, so I'm not getting tangled up in lies before I even begin. Darlings, everything I've said is the truth, and that's the way it's going to stay."

Mavis nodded her approval.

Round one, Helena, Cole said to himself.

Set Me Free

Returning to the HomePort Mansion to dress for the luncheon, Helena raced up the grand staircase to her bedroom. She'd never once imagined she and her husband would move into the main house and sleep in the master suite that had been locked for over seventy years. For that matter, Helena had never imagined having a husband until the moment Butch proposed.

Their marriage, two years earlier, had begun well. An avid sportsman most at home on the open ocean, Butch had told Helena the night of their wedding, "You're a man who needs to do gal stuff, and I'm a man who needs to do guy stuff. We've got all the bases covered between us, and I like that. A lot. Let's never let marriage confine us."

They'd tried to remain faithful to that pledge, but Helena's forty-million-dollar inheritance from the Staunton sisters had transformed her from a quirky P'town character to a local celebrity. Soon, everyone wanted a piece of her, and the couple's marital tensions escalated. Things had come to a head on a rare evening when there wasn't a fundraiser, cocktail party, or some other command performance.

Helena recalled how Butch looked that night during dinner. Normally unflappable, his handsome face was flushed, his eyes brooding. He'd worried her for the first time since they'd met.

Butch waited until Dolores had cleared dessert to drop his bombshell. "I've got a chance to deliver a sailing yacht from Marseilles to Aruba," he'd said, looking like a man ready for a fight. "I'll have to leave tomorrow. It's short notice, I know. But when you think about it, the timing is perfect. All my work for the museum is done. And I've got to get a break from the social bullshit, or I'm gonna lose it. This trip is the answer to a prayer. I need it, Helena, and trust me, you'll be better off with me out of the way."

Helena struggled to contain her astonishment before asking, "Can't it wait until after the opening when things settle down, Butch?"

"No. There's a group of yachts gathering for an around-the-world trip. The new owner wants an expert to help him acclimate on the way to Aruba, and the guy he was working with broke his leg. They set out in three days, so I've got to get him an answer now. This is something I want for a change, Helena. Given all I've had to put up with, I've earned the right."

After a tension-filled moment of silence, Butch adopted a less hostile tone, "I know you're run ragged and don't need this, but let me ask you something. Have you ever considered how all the social bullshit has affected me?"

When Helena, confused and intimidated, didn't answer, he'd slammed his fist on the table. The sound, echoing around the ornate dining room, conjured painful memories. The dentist had replaced her broken teeth. The bruises on her face and pain in her ribs had taken months to disappear, but they had, at last. Unbeknownst to her, a gripping fear had burrowed deep inside, only to resurface at the sound of her husband's fist striking polished mahogany.

Never again. Not anyone. Ever. Not even Butch. I should have told him the whole story before we were married. Instead, I played things down, afraid I'd seem like a victim and drive him away. If I tell him now, it will look like manipulation. I've got no choice but to sit this one out.

Butch paced the room, too worked up to notice. "I can't stand all these new folks, moving here at the same damn time, foisting themselves and their privilege on us. Why do they think they can buy their way into a community where you always had to earn people's respect? They're gobbling up all the property, forcing good people to move away, and then complaining because they can't get the things they can in 'the city.' I've lived here for sixteen years, but now—all of a sudden—the town is losing its history and its people to a bunch of spoiled jerks who will never measure up to those they're forcing out."

Butch's voice took on a cynicism Helena had never heard before. "You're sitting on one of the most valuable rediscovered troves of artwork since Pompeii, and then there's the Cinderella tale of your inheritance. City folks dine out on stories like that—who knows who and who said what. You've become a sideshow, Helena, even if you can't see it. This isn't one of your performances. This is our life—our marriage and our town—they're co-opting. And I've had more than enough."

Helena struggled to remain calm as Butch strode back and forth in the elegant dining room, his height incongruous amid the China cabinets and Victorian bric-à-brac. It wasn't easy. One sweep of his long, muscled arm could kill her.

She wasn't the only one worried. Dolores cracked open the kitchen door, clutching the handle of a cast-iron frying pan with both hands. Helena shook her head, and the door closed without a sound.

Don't argue, even though you know he's missing the point. Most of these folks love P'town as much as we do. Butch hears what the guys down at the wharf are saying and feels loyalty to them—as he should. Their work is dwindling, and it's hard to find a place to live. But if he remembered what some of these recent arrivals have been through, I know he'd see both sides. The biggest threat to this town is the people buying up properties and flipping them—and those in town who enable it. Their greed is fracturing our community, not the newcomers. That's an important distinction, and Butch knows that when he's not riled up.

Don't get so freaked out because he's upset. He's not that bastard that beat you. He's not. He's Butch—a good man, but not equipped for the strain he's under right now. Don't overreact. Don't push back. Just love him while you still can.

Butch took a seat beside her and reached for her hand. "Helena, trust me, I can't stand even one more day. I've done my bit for the past two years, played the dutiful husband, stifled my boredom, and kept my mouth shut. I know myself. I'm going to be thirty in a few months. It's time to get my life back on track. If I don't, I'm gonna end up killing my spirit. Or worse, somebody else."

Helena's breath came in shallow gasps as everything she'd ever wanted hung in the balance. Butch was her rock. The man who grounded her and made life bearable. She no longer knew where she ended and he began. How could he leave her at a time like this?

Butch's eyes had grown soft and pleading, with a hint of mortification, as if he'd realized how close to the edge he'd come.

"You'll be fine without me," he said, his voice almost a caress. "The hard work is done. You, the gang, and the board can handle the last lap. I've got to get out of here, set my sails, stare up at the stars, and get my act together. It won't make a damn's worth of difference if I'm not here for the opening. You'll be too busy to notice, and no one else cares. So let's keep things honest like we always do. Right? No bullshit, ever. Remember? Let me go, Helena. Let me go before it's too late."

Helena's thoughts came so fast she could barely keep track of them.

Why didn't I see this before now? Have I been that self-absorbed? And what does he mean by 'let me go?' Does he think I'd tell him what he can or can't do—or is this his way of saying he's leaving me?

Then, though she knew she was losing her strongest ally, Helena took a deep breath and said, "By all means, go, Butch. But before you do, answer me one thing. Is this the end for us?"

He'd looked as if he hadn't understood the question, then left without another word.

She hadn't mustered the courage to ask a second time.

Just One Thing

The ache that surfaced in Helena's chest whenever Butch was away served as a compelling reminder of their robust physical connection.

She'd never expected to be loved for her feminine side, never mind the capricious man-child hidden underneath an ever-changing array of costumes and personas. Before they'd met, Helena had never imagined the intense joy and desire that had become a constant from the moment he'd sought her out.

She recalled something he'd said early on after one particularly intimate and powerful moment.

"I don't give a damn about outside appearances. If we were two sea slugs at the bottom of the Atlantic, I'd still have to get next to you. Being with you just makes sense for me."

Helena smiled wistfully.

But we fell in love in a time and place that no longer exists. He was a fisherman. I was a housekeeper/companion. He was out on his beloved ocean often enough to stay balanced, and I had more freedom cleaning the mansion than I do now as its mistress. Then the money came, and everything changed.

Helena selected a thin gold necklace with a matching bracelet as a finishing touch for her elegant, knee-length luncheon dress. Faithful as always to her personal goddess, she recited Coco Chanel's mantra, "Before you leave the house, look in the mirror and take one thing off."

Helena returned the bracelet to her jewelry box. Fortified by this time-honored ritual, she returned to the museum for the press walkthrough and luncheon.

It's always easier to face adversity in drag.

Calm Before the Storm

The morning's events were a triumph. The weather cooperated to present the new building in the best possible light, and Mavis was almost effusive—at least when reporters were around. Other than to her chosen family, who watched intently from the sidelines, and Mavis, whose eyes seldom left her, Helena appeared poised and in her element.

Mellowed by a significant amount of wine at lunch, Mavis attempted a rapprochement as the last of the reporters returned to their accommodations. "I'll be honest with you, Helena. I might have gone off the deep end a bit. At first, all I could see was the damage to my work. I see now nothing has changed as far as your commitment is concerned."

Helena clasped the old woman's arm. "I'm so relieved. Your paintings have such spiritual simplicity and grace. Defacing them shows hatred for all that is beautiful. I'll sort this out. I promise. And I don't want you to sign them over to the museum until I do."

"I'm tempted to believe you," Mavis said, her features softening. "What say we go up to the studio later? I painted a little something to thank you for all your hard work. After all you did to rescue my artwork today, it means even more to me that you have a piece of your own."

Helena tried to mask her astonishment. "Thank you, darling. I'll have some free time around two. Would that work? I can be ready in two shakes of a tart's tail."

Letting Off Some Steam

Cole Hanson called Frida, his beloved golden retriever, to the back door of his house atop the dune. He'd named it Staunton's Lookout after an observation tower on that spot that predated the HomePort Mansion. Though having designed the house, living in it still seemed like a dream. A home of his own, a husband, and a family of decent people who accepted and believed in him; four short years ago, he'd never have thought any of it possible. Now this house—his house—had become a locus for his chosen family.

Cole surveyed the calm blue ocean. There was just enough time for a much-needed swim. He and Frida ran down the sloping dune to Commercial Street, then crossed the moors, the moist sand giving way beneath their feet.

Within a few hours, the entire stretch of sand and reeds would be covered by water. The constantly changing ocean was a source of joy and inspiration for Cole, who had made sure it could be seen from every room of his new home.

They reached a secluded stretch of outer beach just as the first breeze of the day rippled across the bay. Cole scanned for seals, which might attract sharks. Seeing none, he shed his jogging shorts and charged into the ocean, swimming near shore as a precaution. Frida ran along the water's edge, ready to sound a warning. She'd sensed and accepted the change in their routine when an increase in Great White sightings forced him to abandon his sunrise swims.

The water's refreshing chill lowered his anxiety, as it always did.

Better to think of tonight as just another event than the critics passing judgment on your efforts. Go with the flow. Don't freak out. An opening like this will only happen once in your lifetime, and you can either dread it or revel in it. Helena's going it alone without Butch; you need to do all you can to support her. Besides, Marc will be right there with you. Be grateful for that, along with everything else.

Frida and his daily swim were the only remaining links to the years of isolation and loneliness before Cole met his husband. The loyal Golden Retriever made room for Marc in her pack, but her bond with

Cole was more profound than ever. Her wise and soulful eyes followed his every move, her simple devotion making his world complete.

Life was good.

There Is Nothing Like a Dame

As he swam, Cole recalled Helena's most amazing prank of the season. He, Marc, and Frida were bringing *Valkyrie*, their forty-five-foot Oyster yawl, from the boatyard for the summer when they spotted a fifty-foot Hinkley ketch with bright purple sails coming toward them. Every time Marc changed his course, the magnificent vessel did likewise until it pulled alongside at the last possible moment. Whoever had been at the wheel ducked out of sight, and Helena appeared in a striped sailor suit with a cap and trailing ribbons.

"Ahoy, sailors," she'd shrieked into a vintage brass megaphone as Marc and Cole stood gaping. "I thought I'd surprise you. I've had such fun racing *Valkyrie*, I got a boat of my own. Butch has been showing me the ropes on the way over. I've just figured out port and starboard. Port has four letters, and left has four letters. That's how you keep track of which is which. And, darlings, I have the most perfect name. . ."

At that, Butch had come out of hiding. Seeing the incredulity on their faces, he'd shrugged as if to say, *You know how it is.* Then he'd taken the helm, and *Dame Edna* had surged toward Provincetown, leaving Marc and Cole speechless in her wake.

From that day on, Helena had thrown herself into sailing, taking daily lessons from a local pro. She'd even had special falsies made that doubled as a life vest—or, as she called them, "life breasts." When asked why, she'd explained, "I don't have the heart to create the perfect racing ensemble and then cover it up with a life jacket, even if it is called a 'Mae West.'"

***

Cole swam to shore, toweled off, put on his shorts, and ran back to HomePort with Frida leading the way. He'd have just enough time to wash off the salt in the outdoor shower and change before the caterers arrived.

"Pray for me," he said to Frida as they climbed the path to Staunton's Lookout. "If Mavis gets through this evening without a tantrum, maybe things can get back to normal—whatever that means, given we've got a break-in, an insane policeman, and a pissed-off featured artist. Then again, when has 'normal' ever applied around this madhouse?"

Into the Woods

At two-ten, Helena and Mavis met at the base of the winding path C.J. Strongue had followed the day before.

"Your studio is certainly out in Siberia, darling," Helena said, as she and Mavis walked arm-in-arm up the stairs, tensions diminishing. "I can arrange for someplace closer if the hike ever becomes too much."

Mavis leaned on her slightly but seemed to have little difficulty with the climb. "Nah. You built it where I asked you. If I slow down too much, I'll use the service road. I love the beech tree, and I need the exercise. Besides, working way up here, depending on my mood, I can step in and out of the fray. I may seem ready for a fight twenty-four hours a day, but I need downtime to get in the right frame of mind to paint."

Mavis stopped suddenly.

"What is it?" Helena asked, fearful the climb was becoming too much.

"I just remembered I was supposed to meet someone up here yesterday. After the Art Center board meeting, I got to talking over cocktails and forgot. I'll call her and reschedule when I get home."

They walked in companionable silence until reaching the clearing near Mavis's studio. The building's south side was dappled by what light made it through the leaves of the magnificent beech tree. The spot was quiet, save for the distant sound of songbirds.

"I closed that door when I left. I know I did," Mavis said, as Helena, sensing her anxiety, sprinted the remaining distance to the building.

In the hours since C.J.'s death, the water from the teapot had seeped into the wooden floor, but little else had changed. The tall fence surrounding the colony had kept the coyotes out. Other than a small swarm of flies feasting on some of its exposed flesh, C.J.'s body remained untouched.

Helena grasped the doorframe and tried to take everything in: the electrical cord in the victim's hand, the teapot on the floor, and the skull, which still rested on the table above the body. C.J.'s contorted legs convinced Helena this was not a peaceful death.

It's the lady from the Audubon rescue. C.J. Strongue. The one who was having such a tough time in Wellfleet. I'd recognize those big purple glasses anywhere. Was she the one Mavis was supposed to meet? If so, why? Or does this have something to do with the museum break-in last night?

Given the skull's malefic glare, and its position above C.J.'s body, she might have been an Aztec sacrifice. The gaunt figures on the canvases scattered about the room looked like ghostly witnesses, while Mavis's empty easel resembled a blood-spattered instrument of torture. Amid all this, C.J.'s straw sunhat looked glaringly out of place. Staring at it, Helena fought back her tears.

She was supposed to get in touch with me and never did. She couldn't have come all the way up here looking for me, could she? The poor soul. So mistreated, frustrated, and unappreciated. I wish I'd said more about a part-time job with the Trust. Our young artists would have given her a sense of belonging. Instead, she died alone, out here in the dunes.

Determined to spare Mavis, Helena walked to where she was standing and took several deep breaths before speaking. "Something dreadful has happened. It's not your artwork. That's fine. Someone's been hurt. I've got to make some calls. Please wait for me on that bench over there. Trust me, you don't want to see what I've just seen."

Mavis paused, then found the bench and slumped onto it, her face pale, her hands trembling as if she already knew.

Helena called Afton Walker, who answered on the second ring. "We've found a body in Mavis's studio. Please call the police, then get over to the service road to let them through the gate. Make sure they silence their sirens. On your way, please call Marc and have him arrange to hold the press reception somewhere else. I want the reporters away from the estate. Once Marc has made that call, I need him to find Cole and come to Mavis's studio. And remember, the press can't get wind of this."

Dead to Rights

For the second time that day, sirens screamed down Bradford Street. Suddenly, all was quiet. Afton had prevailed. Seated outside the studio, Mavis and Helena awaited the inevitable grilling from Sergeant Brandt.

Helena was unable to block the memory of C.J.'s body.

What the hell is going on? Was her death an accident? If not, why would C.J. be the intended victim? She was a harmless, lost soul—if a trifle naïve and single-minded. Who'd do this to her? And why?

Mavis withdrew her hand when Helena reached for it. "I'm sorry, Helena. I'm not big on being comforted. Especially when somebody has it in for me. I'd rather spend the time figuring out how to fight back."

Helena knew enough to remain silent.

***

When Sergeant Brandt, the rescue squad, and most of the town's police force arrived, Helena led them to Mavis's studio.

"You again," Brandt said to Helena after looking at the corpse. "Who is she?"

"C.J. Strongue. From Wellfleet," Helena said.

Mavis walked over to where they were standing and hastily surveyed the body. She began to speak, then stopped.

"You two go back to the bench and wait," Brandt said. "I'll want statements later."

The sergeant and his second in command, Officer Chase, a short, harried-looking man, strode into the studio and bent over the body.

"OK. Let's see what we've got here," Brandt said. "Looks to me like electrocution. The medical examiner will be here soon. She can confirm it, but I'm fairly certain."

"How'd you know that so fast?" Chase asked.

"The burns on her wrists where the jewelry touched her skin." Brandt pointed at the scorch marks underneath one of C.J.'s many bracelets. "Get the men searching for anything that might identify the killer. Have someone tell the rescue squad they can go. We'll be sending the body with the medical examiner."

Helena watched as the police began to search the grounds.

Poor C.J. lying out here for who knows how long with that horrible look on her face. All she wanted was a chance for a new life. Now, she'll never have it. I'll find out who did this to you, C.J.. I swear I will.

"Take pictures of the entire area," Brandt told one officer, "Then the body—from every angle—and be sure to get the teapot up close from both sides."

Addressing two other officers, he said, "Judging by the considerable number of maggots, the victim's been dead from seven to twenty hours or more. It takes that long for them to hatch. Survey the area and look for discarded items—anything suspicious. And try to isolate the victim's footprints from those of the two who found the body."

Once the photographs were complete, Brandt donned a pair of nitrile gloves and picked up the kettle. "Look," he said, showing Officer Chase, "someone shaved off the insulation on the underside of the wire, right where you'd plug it in. Then, they painted the copper white to match the rubber coating. See the traces of paint that didn't get scorched? No doubt about it. This was no accident."

Leaving his officers to their work, Sergeant Brandt summoned Helena and Mavis to a grassy spot some distance from the studio. "Early days yet. But I'm seeing evidence of foul play. What do you two have to tell me?"

"It was supposed to be me," Mavis said, glaring at Helena.

"Why do you say that, ma'am?" Brandt asked, his dark eyes scanning her face.

"Because this is my studio," Mavis answered, her voice rising in pitch and volume as she pointed at Helena. "She had it built especially for me. Way out here. Away from everything and everyone."

Helena paled. "Mavis. What are you saying?"

Brandt pointed at Helena. "Save your theatrics for the stage. Wait for me over by the cruiser." Turning to Mavis, he said, "And you? Who are you?"

"Mavis Chandry."

Brandt didn't seem to recognize her from earlier in the day. "Tell me what you know about the victim. Why was she in your studio?"

"C.J. Strongue," Mavis said, her husky voice subdued, "was one of those old battleaxes who never give up until they get their way. She hadn't lived on the Cape long. In Wellfleet, I believe. Hounded me to death—uh, excuse that poor choice of words—to donate a painting for some godforsaken charity. As if I don't get thirty requests a week for just that."

"And that's why she was in your studio?" Brandt asked.

"She shouldn't have been inside, but yes. I was supposed to meet her here yesterday at three, but it slipped my mind until now."

"What were you meeting about?"

"She was a strange old bird. Couldn't understand why I didn't want to give her a painting I could sell for a couple hundred thousand dollars. I hoped to convince her to look elsewhere."

"Is there anything out of order in the studio? Anything missing?"

"I'm sorry, Sergeant. I really can't remember right now. And I can't look at her body again. I just can't. Can I get back to you on that? Once things are cleared away?"

"I'd appreciate knowing now, ma'am," Brandt said, his tone less harsh but hardly empathetic.

"OK. I'll go," Mavis said, her voice unsteady, her eyes dull.

***

Marc and Cole ran to the police barrier near where Helena was standing. Cole was still in his shorts and hadn't had time to dry his hair. He looked incongruous next to his husband, who was immaculately dressed in tan chinos and a white shirt.

"I got Afton's call." Marc reached over to hug her. "Someone actually was killed?"

She pointed to the studio where Mavis was peering through the open door, pinching her nose. Two police officers were flagging footprints, while another three were methodically moving about inside the building, unaffected by the stench of death. When Mavis stepped back, C.J.'s body became visible. Marc and Cole gasped at the sight.

"Are you OK?" Cole asked.

"Fine," Helena said. "Just a nasty shock. But not as nasty as the one poor C.J. got, by the look of things."

Overhearing, Sergeant Brandt waved the two men through the police barrier, where a solitary officer stood watch. "Not as nasty as the one someone would get if they still used the electric chair in this state. We have to wait to let the medical examiner do her job, but it seems a clear-cut case of deliberate electrocution. The question is why."

Pointing to Marc and Cole, he said, "You two, you're familiar with this place, right? Take a look and tell me if you see anything out of order.

"And you, artist lady. Anything missing?"

Mavis hesitated a moment before shaking her head. Only Helena noticed her discomfort before she walked back to the bench.

"One thing, Sergeant," Marc said after a brief survey. "The clock says three-ten. It must have shorted out because the time is two-forty."

"Chase. Check the fuse box," the sergeant bellowed, seeming irritated someone had noticed a point he'd overlooked. "The rest of you, step outside the crime scene and wait for me by the cruiser. I'll have more questions."

Helena, Marc, and Cole did as they were told. Mavis hesitated, then followed a few steps behind.

***

From inside a utility closet at the far end of the room, Officer Chase called out, "Sergeant. You gotta see this."

"What is it?"

"All the breakers in the fuse box are off except the one the kettle's plugged into. It's as if someone was trying to lead the victim to that outlet."

Brandt inspected the fuse box. "Get a picture. Then shut the power off at the main. Why didn't the active breaker trip when the wire shorted?"

"I'm not an electrician, but that breaker looks different from the others," Chase said slowly. "And see how it's melted around the edges? That shouldn't happen. It should have tripped, but the wires burned through instead. I say we get someone to pull it and see what's up."

"Call the Bureau of Criminal Investigations," Brandt said. "Tell them I want a complete evaluation of the electrical system. Then take notes while I get preliminary statements from the two wack jobs who found her."

***

Brandt crossed the short stretch of grass to where Mavis was sitting. Helena was standing just a few feet away, staring into the woods.

The sergeant spoke assertively. "I've got some questions to jumpstart my investigation. I'll take official statements from you individually later. First, where were you yesterday at three-ten?"

Mavis answered quickly. "I was at the trustees meeting at the Art Center from noon to sometime around two-thirty."

"Weren't you supposed to meet the victim here at three?"

"Well, yes. But as I said, the appointment slipped my mind."

"Where'd you go then?"

"I'd had wine after the meeting. I went home to take a nap."

"Can anyone vouch for you?"

"Yes. My cleaner was finishing up when I got to the house."

Brandt turned to Helena with visible distaste. "And you?"

"I was working in the museum."

"Do either of you know any next of kin? A husband?" Brandt asked.

"She was a widow," Helena said somberly, "with no living family members."

"So you knew her, too?"

"I only met her once."

"Did she mention anyone in particular? Any friends?"

"No," Helena said. "She didn't seem to have any. She'd had a tough life and was having difficulty adjusting to living on the Outer Cape."

"Do you know why?"

Helena chose her words with care. "As I said, we only had one conversation, but my impression was she'd had a difficult marriage and may have expected too much from the move to Wellfleet."

Sergeant Brandt changed the subject. "Can anyone vouch for you being at the museum yesterday afternoon?"

"I was with Marc, Cole, Afton Walker, and other museum staff, preparing to hang all of Mavis's work."

Brandt summoned the two men. "You three were together yesterday?"

"Yes. We started working just after noon," Marc said, "then had a quick dinner in the lounge while waiting for Mavis's paintings to arrive. Helena wasn't out of our sight all afternoon and evening."

"Why hang the show so late?"

Marc signaled Cole, who stepped forward to answer. "The delivery truck got in an accident en route from the secure storage facility. Repairs took two days, so the art didn't arrive until yesterday evening around seven."

"I can vouch for that part, at least," Mavis said. "Cole told me about the delay, and we rescheduled my walkthrough to this morning."

Brandt scowled at Helena. "It may seem you're in the clear—whatever you are. But I'm not buying it."

"Hey!" Cole yelled."Don't treat her that way!"

As Marc grabbed his husband's arm, Brandt laughed. "OK. Mr. Politically Correct. If you're so bothered by my interrogation, we'll continue this interview at the station. You, artist lady, are free to go while I deal with this one. But I'll want a statement from you first thing in the morning."

"Marc. Call Quincy and have him meet me there," Helena said before addressing the sergeant. "Despite your ignorant behavior and misguided suspicions, I'm eager to cooperate in any way I can, but I'll have nothing more to say until my lawyer is with me. Lead the way."

The medical examiner arrived and set her bag beside the body. When she swatted away the flies covering C.J.'s flesh, they swarmed out the door, causing everyone to look.

"The poor old bat finally got her moment of fame," Mavis muttered, then slipped into the woods.

Counselor Stilwell

Quincy Stilwell, lawyer for the Staunton Trust, was on the seventh hole at Highland Links when his phone rang. He was a tall, thin, distinguished man with a slight stoop, white hair, and a walrus mustache. At seventy-eight, he kept himself fit by getting in at least a round of golf every day the weather permitted, regardless of the season.

"Marc, what is it?" Quincy asked.

"It's Helena. Sergeant Brandt has taken her in for questioning."

"Slow down. Tell me what's happened. Just the highlights."

"C.J. Strongue was found dead in Mavis Chandry's studio."

"Oh, my. The woman Mavis chased? I met her once. Definitely an acquired taste, but what's that got to do with Helena?"

"Brandt is implying Helena set a booby-trap to kill Mavis, and C.J. died instead. It was a veiled threat, but I think he means it."

"How was C.J. killed?"

"Brandt said electrocution. He practically accused Helena of tampering with a circuit breaker."

"Nonsense. I'll drive over to the police station and sort this out. It's a shame Louie Silva isn't around. Brandt's one pheasant short of a full brace. He wouldn't know a murderer from a Sister of Mercy. I'll have Helena back home within the hour."

A Good Man

Quincy marched into Brandt's office without knocking. The sergeant, seated behind his desk, reddened, then glared at the dapper attorney. "Look, Stilwell, this is just routine questioning. No need to get your shorts in a knot."

Quincy turned to Helena, who sat to Brandt's left. "Have you said anything?"

"Only how I met C.J. once, that she was a widow who recently moved here, and that I'm happy to cooperate."

"OK, Brandt," Quincy said, sitting next to Helena, his voice calm but assertive. "Here's the deal: Five minutes with my client so I can get up to speed, and we'll go on the record. One word of your usual bigoted nonsense, and we're out the door. Understand? And get a female officer to witness the interview."

"But that's not—"

"Those are our terms," Quincy warned. "Take 'em or leave 'em. Don't blow the deal with the first words out of your mouth."

Brandt stomped out of his office, slamming the door behind him.

"OK, Helena. Talk to me. What's going on?" Quincy asked, his tone encouraging and affectionate.

Helena thanked him for his prompt arrival, then described what she'd discovered at the studio along with Mavis's and Brandt's accusations.

Asked what C.J. was doing at the estate, Helena replied, "She needed something to lift her spirits, and I'd thought seriously about hiring her, if only part-time, to work at the trust. When I discovered her body, my first thought was that she'd come looking for me. Later, it became clear C.J. was there to see Mavis. Why Brandt would think I'd want to kill either of them is beyond me."

Quincy patted Helena's hand. "Sheer nonsense. And don't worry about Mavis. She'll get over it. Our problem is that Brandt won't. What else can you tell me?"

Helena took a deep breath. "There was an incident at the museum yesterday. It isn't widely known, but someone broke in and used water-soluble chalk to deface Mavis's paintings."

Quincy looked stunned. "That doesn't make much sense."

Helena agreed. "I'm only speculating, but the intent might have been to spook Mavis into removing the paintings—or not donating them. It's the only scenario that makes sense to me."

"So, you're saying someone wanted to harm the museum's reputation but not the art?"

"I suspect they were out to discredit the museum's security and, most likely, me."

As Quincy wrote in his notebook, Helena studied him.

From the moment I met this man, he's been a force for justice. I'll never forget how kind he was to me after the attack. No judgments. Always there, going the extra mile. In a way, he's like someone out of Jane Austen—dignified, but slightly comical, and that rarest of all things: a good man.

"Has Mavis signed the bequest I drew up?" Quincy asked.

"No. She planned to sign it during Paul Schroeder's interview tonight but changed her mind after her work was damaged. I don't blame her. She has to be certain the paintings will be safe."

"OK. We'll talk more about that on the way back to HomePort. Let's get the troglodyte in here so we can get you out of here."

Quincy opened the door to Sergeant Brandt and a very pregnant woman waiting in the hall.

The attorney was delighted to see her. "Well, hello there, Detective Kline. Glad you could join us. I thought you were on maternity leave."

Brandt's scowl deepened, but Lisa did not try to hide her regard. "Just in to tie up some loose ends on that opiate sting. A new detective will be here next week to cover for me. She's associated with the DA's office, and I hear she's a real pro. How are you, Quincy?"

"Fine, Lisa. Simply fine, save for needless interruptions to my golf game," he replied, looking pointedly at Brandt. "Let's get this over with, so I can get back to it. Are you arresting my client, Brandt?"

"Not at this time. But I am limiting her travel to no more than thirty miles from town."

"You can request that, but no one has to obey you. You'd know that if you were up on Massachusetts law. Is Helena a suspect?"

"Let's say a person of interest."

"Cut the Inspector Morse routine and put your cards on the table."

Brandt regrouped. "All indications are that an attempt on Mavis Chandry's life resulted in the death of C.J. Strongue."

"I agree, but why do you suspect my client?"

"Your *client* stood to benefit if Ms. Chandry died."

"How do you figure that one?" Quincy asked, silencing Helena with a curt glance. "C.J. Strongue was in Mavis Chandry's studio—not that I'm inferring Mavis had anything to do with this."

Brandt sneered before catching himself. "I plan to talk with Ms. Chandry in the morning. For now, all I'll say is that art goes up in price when the artist dies."

Quincy turned to Helena. "Do you own any of Mavis's work?"

"I'm not sure. We went to the studio to get a painting she planned to give me. That's when we found C.J., so she never did. I don't even know what it looks like."

"So let me see if I understand." Quincy winked at Lisa, who was watching intently. "You think Helena, who inherited forty million dollars, tried to kill Mavis to increase the value of a single painting she hadn't been given?"

Lisa turned to hide a smile as Quincy's eyes twinkled. He loved an audience no matter what the topic.

Brandt was apoplectic. "No. Of course not. Chandry's paintings in the museum would be worth over one hundred million if she died."

"You're quite up on the art world, Sergeant. A hidden passion we haven't heard about? But I beg to inform you your theory won't hold water. Mavis hasn't signed the bequest."

"If she were dead, someone could pay a crooked notary to authenticate a forged signature. It doesn't take a genius to figure that sort of stuff out, Quincy. What say we stop speculating and hear what your client has to say."

The attorney nodded. "I want the interview recorded and reserve the right to halt it at any time. I also request we keep all news of the death to ourselves until there's a better idea of what really happened. There are people from all over attending the museum opening tonight and a boatload of press in town. If I were you, I wouldn't want them mobbing my office when I don't have any answers to give. I can't imagine you would, either. Are you on board with that?"

Brandt paused, then said, "Fine. You've got until tomorrow afternoon."

"Good," Quincy said. "And thank you for being so considerate. I appreciate it. OK, Helena, tell the sergeant everything you just told me. Leave nothing out."

***

Sergeant Brandt completed the interview and grudgingly allowed Helena to leave. When she and Quincy were in the privacy of his vintage Avanti, he said, "Helena, there's more to all this than you realize. I need your permission to share what you've told me with another attorney. Please trust me and don't ask who. Do you agree?"

"Sure, Quincy. I'd trust you with my life."

"Thanks. I know you've got a big night. Can you spare me some time first thing tomorrow morning?"

"Of course. Where and when?"

"Let's meet at Highland Links for a round of golf. Say six a.m.?"

"Darling, I've never played golf in my life."

"Good. I prefer winning. I'll have clubs for you. Just wear something sporty and, for once, understated. Muted colors and sensible shoes are a must. Leave the rest to me."

It was five o'clock by the time they arrived at HomePort. Quincy kissed Helena on the cheek. "Don't worry. Focus on your preparations, and let me deal with the rest. The show must go on. I'll see you in two hours at the private view."

Battle Dress

Helena attempted to fend off the grim realities of the day by taking meticulous care with her makeup and wardrobe. Billy C., a recent graduate of HomePort's fashion program, had tailored her blue satin evening gown. The strapless creation with its silver-edged décolletage was specifically designed to showcase the famous Staunton diamonds. Helena had been eager to wear it until the evening's gala had become more ordeal than celebration.

I can't cancel the private view. Everything has to go on as planned to keep C.J.'s death from dominating the coverage. Butch isn't here, and the gang can only do so much. This is up to you, Helena. Your public awaits what might be the most important performance of your life.

Then she recalled what Billy had said at the last fitting, *"Gurrrl. . . Hanging this big a rock on your neck with that low a cut and not hauling out the falsies takes real balls! You're gonna get a ton of people trying to figure out how you made it work. It's like shining a searchlight under the Boatslip deck at two in the morning—you just know every queen in town will dine out on what they thought they saw."*

Helena, spirits lifted, grinned at herself in the mirror and, in her best Ethel Merman impersonation, began to sing, "There's No Business Like Show Business."

The Family Jewels

The trove known as the Staunton diamonds included a silver tiara studded with fifty white stones and a large sapphire at its center, two diamond teardrop earrings, and the famous necklace with its pear-shaped, forty-four-carat solitaire on a chased-silver chain. Dolores carried them from the safe with reverence befitting a coronation, then laid them out on a large piece of red satin.

"I still remember the first time I saw them," she said, closing the empty cases. "Miss Lola was hosting a party to raise money for the families of the *Patricia Marie*—the fishing boat that went down with seven crew on board. It was October of 'seventy-six, and the jewels hadn't been seen in fifty years. She'd always refused to wear them."

Dolores grew wistful, as she always did when reflecting on HomePort's illustrious past.

"This time, I told her, 'Miss Lola, your grandmother wore them, and whatever you may think of her, so did your mother. People appreciate continuity, especially at a time like this. So I say, show them the rocks, fill them to the gills with booze, then sit back and watch the money jump from their wallets. I've heard that's just what Miss Laetitia used to do.' I think bringing up her grandmother did the trick."

Dolores centered the tiara on Helena's head, then stepped back to admire her handiwork. Helena did a turn, showing off the elegant gown.

"Miss Helena, you look lovely. I've never seen you more beautiful. You do Miss Lola—and all the Stauntons—proud."

With that, Dolores withdrew, leaving Helena to contemplate herself in the mirror until a text message interrupted her reverie.

(Butch) *Have a ball tonight. Will arrive Majorca tomorrow mid-day.*

(Helena) *Enjoy yourself, darling. I'm jealous.*

She stared at the screen, gathered her thoughts, then walked carefully down the staircase for one last pre-performance ritual.

Come Into My Parlor

Helena crossed the darkened hall to what was once the mansion's formal parlor. With the room's contents installed in the museum, this space and Captain Staunton's former study would host student exhibits. Helena remained ambivalent about the move, though knowing the days of splendid isolation she'd enjoyed with Lola and Dorrie were already a thing of the past.

Cole oversaw the redesign of both spaces, rebuilding everything to exacting detail, hoping to temper the loss for Helena, who thought he hadn't noticed her ambivalence. He, too, had struggled between protecting the originals and keeping things as they had always been. In time, he'd grown certain the furnishings and décor were too old and fragile to remain where they were.

Helena was still not entirely convinced.

Rooms have personalities and unique characteristics. I'd never say this to Cole, but the replacements lack the patina of use and the comforting gloss of a century's application of bee's wax. Newly lathed wood and crisp new fabric can never replicate the indescribable feeling of a hundred years of daily airings, say nothing of all the conversations and memorable moments they've absorbed. The replacements look like they've just had a facelift—taut, tentative, and unsettled. And I guess that's the way they'll remain for the next few decades, at least.

Alone, dressed in her couture gown and bedecked with the Staunton jewels, Helena poured a shot of whisky and sat in the replica of Lola's swan chair, which was nowhere near as comfortable as the original.

Seeing herself in the large mirror over the fireplace, Helena teared up.

I won't give in. I won't. Too many people are counting on me. I can do this without Butch. I can—and I shall.

Portraits of Two Ladies

Cole's portraits of Lola and Dorrie were the only contents that remained after the move. Helena had insisted. In her darkest moments, she'd found her way to this room—as she had when the sisters were alive—to share her hopes, fears, and, most recently, the protracted unfolding of their last request.

Helena raised her glass to the portraits. "I hope you'll find everything to your liking at the opening tonight, darlings. If all goes well, this should be the beginning of the end for those interminable parties and insufferable dinners."

The two paintings highlighted similarities in age and alacrity while capturing the unique and lovable quirkiness of the two women. They were both seated in swan chairs, having "tea." Somehow, Cole's artistry made it as if they were in the room.

Dorrie's portrait played on her forthright nature. Her eyes shined with mirth as if she were assessing the impact of a caustic remark. Lola seemed about to respond, and Dorrie, leaning forward in her chair with a teacup in her hand, looked as though she was ready to make her next move. As they often did in life, the two sisters seemed to be playing to an audience.

Helena felt the tingle in the back of her neck she often got when in the parlor.

I miss the old days when I could be anyone I wanted, and neither Lola nor Dorrie ever said a damn word. I'd try to get a rise out of them by wearing a crazy costume, but they both played along as if it were my uniform. Things have changed so much now they're gone. This lady of the manor role isn't what I thought it would be. People depend on me, and now, with all that's happened, I'm in over my head. I used to become someone else just to get through my day. Now, my drag is responsibility, leadership, and problem-solving. I'm not a corporate hack. I'm a goddamn person underneath all of this—at least, I used to be.

These days, people expect glamor and wit as if I'm their own personal entertainment—and to hell with a donation unless I deliver. I love challenging roles, but I see where Butch is coming from. This fundraising Barbie routine is scraping my last nerve. I'm tired. Damn tired, and I. . .

Helena forced herself to stop. "But enough negativity, ladies," she said, practicing the upbeat tone she'd need for several hours to come. "It's showtime. I'll pull myself together now. I always do after our little chats."

Just then, Cole arrived to escort her to the private view. As they walked to the museum, arm in arm, he said, "Helena, we've got another problem."

Room for a View

Word had gotten out about the documentary being filmed at the private view. A noisy group of people without invitations had assembled, insisting they were VIPs. The doors would open to the general public in two hours, but this crowd refused to wait. Afton and his staff had cordoned off a path so those with invitations could enter the building, but the vocal group had confronted the guards and was hassling the invited guests.

"On the brighter side," Cole said as they reached the museum's rear entrance, "No one seems to know about C.J.'s death. So I guess everything's relative."

"Thank God," Helena said. "That won't last long, though. Even if Brandt tries to hush it up overnight, word will get out. I just need to survive this party, then I won't care."

"Well, here goes nothing," Cole said, kissing Helena's hand. "Smile, sweetie. We're on."

Entering the museum through a side door, Helena and Cole were greeted by a round of applause from the museum's board of directors. Then, Elise and Gwen Stewart-Campion brought them each a glass of champagne. Elise's blue eyes sparkled, and her approving smile was radiant. She was dressed in a black silk tuxedo with wide lapels. Her short gray hair was swept back from her forehead.

"We hosted the reporters at the house for cocktails as Marc requested," she whispered to Helena. "We used the trolleys from the downtown parking lot to get them out there. They loved the trip through Truro's back roads. Every one of them believed us when we said you were double-checking the exhibits. No one gave your absence a second thought."

"You've done it, Helena," Gwen exclaimed.

She, too, wore a tuxedo, its dark blue complimenting her wife's ensemble. A tall and elegant former model, Gwen's hair was exquisitely coiled into a spiral, with tight braids cascading over both shoulders. She wore no jewelry other than her wedding band. Gwen was the more subdued of the couple, and Helena had never seen her so excited.

"After this morning's tour, they're calling the show a 'triumph,'" Gwen said, "And Cole, several critics told me the curation couldn't have been better if it were at the Metropolitan Museum."

Cole shut his eyes to stem his tears of relief as Helena pulled him close and whispered, "This is your night, darling. Enjoy every last friggin' bit of it."

Onion Rings

Gwen escorted Helena away from the crowd for a private word. "You've got quite the night ahead of you, honey. There's a host of reporters outside the Mansion Suite, all lined up for their exclusive interviews. Cole must have already told you there are a bunch of 'onion rings' out front, thinking they can crash the private view. I don't know what about the term invitation-only those damn fools can't understand. Afton and his crew have done an amazing job. He's added extra security in case there's a ruckus. Just flag him down if you need backup when these clowns are let in. I think some of them will be coming for you."

Helena had recently coined the phrase onion rings as a secret code between board members to identify those unlikely to support the museum's fundraising efforts. The term harkened back to Mary Heaton Vorse's book, *Time and the Town.* In it, the author and local treasure described Provincetown as "*. . .like an onion. . .There is here layer on layer, whorl on whorl. Three civilizations have met here and formed a unique strain. The old New Englanders, the Portuguese, and the summer folk have made a town individual in the world.*"

The social ascendancy coveted by the onion rings was new to Provincetown. Longstanding residents often donated whatever they could without fanfare, satisfied to give something back to the place they loved. They also served meals at the soup kitchen and sponsored kids at camp, their largesse known to few, if any. Butch had been right: free food and unfettered social access were proving too tempting to ignore for those who defined their social status by the fame of their connections.

Elise motioned to a nearby staffer who positioned the board members for a group photo. Then, Helena offered a pep talk to those about to enter the fray.

"Fundraising is a lot like doing drag, folks. Fake it until you make it. Pretend you have everything under control, focus on the person talking to you, let them ramble on, act like you're having fun, make sure they've got plenty to drink, and then take their money. Now let's get to it."

Turning to Cole, she said, "I feel like Fagan sending out the pickpockets. God, I want all this over and done with. Lead the way, darling. We who are about to die salute you."

***

The private view was meant to acknowledge supporters of the museum project, especially those often overlooked. As a result, servers, bartenders, and contractors were sipping champagne with local business owners and philanthropists. The group was enjoying themselves immensely, perhaps a bit more because of the indignation of those waiting outside.

To many in the room, the moment was long overdue. Work often meant two or three jobs. For contractors, the extraordinary number of renovations required nights and weekends. With little time to decompress, a party like this was just what everyone needed. Despite their diverse talents and incomes, the guests' love for P'town united them just as Lola and Dorrie knew it would.

On the Record

The Mansion Suite was the backdrop of choice for the hordes of reporters and television anchors covering the event. When it was time for her interview with the filmmaker, Paul Schroeder, a makeup artist approached Helena, cosmetics at the ready.

She held up both hands. "Not on your life, honey. I do my own makeup. No exceptions. Not even for Public Broadcasting."

"Have it your way," the man huffed, flouncing off.

Laughing, Paul beckoned Helena into the space containing HomePort's original parlor. He was an attractive man of fifty, well-known for his sartorial flair. His ample mustache was impeccably trimmed, and his bald pate glistened in the bright light. He wore a vintage tuxedo jacket with a white shirt, hand-knotted black bowtie, tapered black slacks, and purple boat shoes.

"Hi, Helena. I've had a fabulous time interviewing the folks here tonight," Paul said. "The one downer is that Mavis has changed her mind. She didn't rule out doing a segment some other time, but I'd be lying if I said I'm not disappointed."

Helena clasped Paul's hand. "She's had a long day. I'm sure she wants to be her best for you, darling. I'll be happy to schedule staff to stay after closing hours so you can have all the time you want when she's ready."

Paul seemed mollified. "It will take a couple of weeks to edit tonight's footage and tighten things up. If I treat her interview as the last segment, we can stay on schedule. By the way, I got your note about Freddie."

Paul pointed to where the reporter stood outside the entrance to the Mansion Suite. Her hair was up in a French twist, and she was wearing a red, sleeveless evening gown ablaze with sequins. Realizing they were watching, she raised her large glass of Scotch in a salute.

"Perfect," Helena chuckled as she blew a kiss. "I owe you one, Paul, but rest assured, she'll add an extra dimension to the discussion. You'll see."

"Before we get started," Paul said, "I have a couple of off-camera questions. We've got your cameos in the prior footage, but they're labeled with your name and title. This will be the first time we hear you in a live conversation. How do you want to present yourself?"

Helena was baffled. "As likable?" she ventured at last.

Paul colored slightly. "I'm sorry. I wasn't clear. What pronouns do you prefer? His/Him? She/Her? They/Them? And do you describe yourself as a drag queen, gender non-binary, gay, transgender, or transvestite? It's important to me to get things right."

"So considerate of you, Paul. My pronouns are She/Her. I've been using them forever, and that's what works best for me. As for the rest, I used to call myself a cross-dresser, but these days I bill myself as a full-time female impersonator—twenty-four-seven, 'living the dream.'"

Paul's interest was piqued. "What do you see as the difference between a drag queen and a female impersonator? And may I also ask—just for my edification—exactly what does 'living the dream' mean to you?"

"Never hold back your questions on camera or off, Paul. In my mind, there's a subtle distinction between drag and impersonation. A female impersonator has the leeway to be as outrageous as the wildest drag queen—but also subdued when they want to be. Since I dress as a woman pretty much all the time, that description works best for me in real life and on stage.

"As for 'living the dream,' it's a term Ellie, the legendary Provincetown showgirl, taught me. It means living my 'T'—my truth—as I define it. Being the best person I can be and not kowtowing to society's expectations or demands."

"I hear you, Helena," Paul said with a grin. "That's the reason I moved here, so I get it. Well, it looks like they're ready for us. This is going to be a great conversation. Just follow my lead."

Helena removed a compact from her slim evening clutch, did a quick scan, then powdered her nose. She sat in Lola's swan chair, and Paul sat in Dorrie's as a large crowd gathered to watch.

When the countdown was complete, Paul said, "And now a conversation with Helena Handbasket, Executive Director of the Staunton Trust and the driving force behind the amazing Staunton Museum, which opens tonight. We've tracked the construction of this building from the beginning. Now we're going to have a wide-ranging conversation with the person who made it all happen."

Paul struggled to suppress a smile. "There's no better way to start this interview, Helena, than with an observation: 'Goodness, what beautiful diamonds.'"

In her best Mae West impersonation, Helena patted her tiara and intoned, "Goodness had nothing to do with it, dearie."

Delighted, Paul directed the cameraman to zoom in on the jewels. "Let's get a good look. Am I right in understanding that these spectacular stones were part of your inheritance? All throughout our filming, I've wanted to ask you about what they call your 'dust rags to riches' story. Is it true you started as the housekeeper in the fabulous mansion where you now live?"

Helena took a deep breath. Her Cinderella story came with the territory. It was "the hook," as she thought of it—the human-interest angle that got people to pay attention to more important things.

"Lola Staunton, the heir to a vast whaling fortune, took me in after a homophobic attacker put me in the hospital," Helena said in a matter-of-fact tone. "When I recovered, she hired me as her housekeeper, and we became dear friends. The diamonds have been in the Staunton family for over one hundred forty years. Though both sisters were kind enough to mention me in their wills, I'm merely the jewels' current caretaker. The family has been the town's benefactor since the days of whaling ships, and their two-hundred-million-dollar Staunton trust is intended to perpetuate that legacy."

Helena explained how the jewels belonged to the trust, as did the HomePort Estate and the museum.

Paul moved on to his next question. "Could you spend a few moments talking about the discovery that turned the art world on its ear?"

"You must mean the Laetitia Staunton collection," Helena said, her eyes twinkling. "I'd be delighted."

Helena shared that Lola Staunton was a recluse, so only a handful of people saw her grandmother's art collection for nearly eighty years.

"As dumb as it makes me look," Helena said with a sheepish grin. I used to dust the paintings every week without a second thought."

"You're kidding!" Paul exclaimed. "That story's actually true?"

"Scout's honor," Helena said, holding up her right hand. "I kept my head down and my feather duster in high gear. And if that makes me a philistine, I guess the stiletto fits."

"And they say the collection rivals those in major cities," Paul said with reverence as the camera zoomed in on several of the more significant works.

"So I've heard," Helena replied. "It's a good thing I didn't know that when I was dusting them. I'd have been an absolute wreck. I'm sure glad I didn't use Pledge on them. I can't tell you what a relief it is that they're safe here in the museum. I hope your viewers will visit and support our efforts to endow their permanent home."

"I'm sure they will," Paul replied. "Now, for something a bit off the topic of art. I'm fortunate to have another guest, Frederica Chalmers, a reporter from the *Provincetown Free Press.* Freddie, c'mon over and join us if you would, please?"

Stunned, Freddie checked her makeup, then broke into an enormous smile as the camera followed her movement across the room.

Helena enjoyed her confident entrance.

This is going to be good. She'll be revved up and help me make my points. Nothing like jazzing things up a bit to get the best effort.

Freddie sat in a chair beside Paul, ready for whatever came next. He wasted no time.

"The Staunton Trust has funded a group to deal with gentrification and climate change. Freddie, could you describe those challenges and how they affect Provincetown in particular? Perhaps start with some history, given where we are tonight."

The reporter described a small town surrounded by ocean on three sides, isolated, self-sufficient, and dependent on the sea for its livelihood. Provincetown whalers made large profits for their owners; for a brief period, the town was one of the wealthiest in the Commonwealth of Massachusetts. In later years, P'town had a large and prosperous fishing industry dominated by Portuguese families whose ancestors once manned those whaling ships.

"But things have changed since then, haven't they, Freddie?" Paul asked. "Can you describe the reasons for—and magnitude of—the change?"

"Sure," she said, looking directly into the camera. "Few vessels set sail from Provincetown anymore. As the fleet dwindled, tourism offered an alternative that worked well for a while. These days, the town's tourist economy is more than two hundred million dollars a year, rents have gone through the roof, and property values have skyrocketed. As a result, the town has changed dramatically."

"What's causing the increases? And what do these changes mean, Helena?" Paul asked.

In clear, concise tones, she explained how Provincetown's beauty, diversity, ferry service, and airport made it so desirable to second-home owners. Many built or bought after visiting for years, while others relocated when remote work became an option. As a result, rents and property prices had escalated to the point it was now difficult for the average person to work and live in the town year-round.

"I'm one of those people," Freddie added. "My beat is Wellfleet, Truro, and Provincetown. I rented in P'town for fifteen years. Now, the only place I can afford to live is at least a half-hour away. It's hard to be the first on the scene when something happens here. And that's the least of the problem. Some of what's being lost can never be regained."

Paul turned to Helena. "I sense you have more to add."

"You're right. There's a genuine paradox. The very things that make the town appealing to newcomers are at risk of disappearing because of them. And many of these things are irreplaceable."

Helena took a moment to solidify her thoughts. "Here's an example: Not that long ago, in the U.S. and elsewhere, gay people were beaten in the streets, persecuted by governments, and demonized in the press. Throughout those troublesome times, the Portuguese community in Provincetown made us feel welcome in a way few others did. A strong partnership developed that placed a high value on personal dignity and mutual respect."

Paul leaned forward in his chair. "Are you saying this recent influx threatens that?"

"It could, if not handled properly. The descendants of those who welcomed gay people may well be forced out. Many others—gay and straight—who have called this town home for years face the same fate. Both outcomes, in my view, are unconscionable."

Paul, sounding sympathetic, asked Freddie, "But shouldn't a person be able to buy a property if someone wants to sell?"

Freddie smiled as if the question were a gift. "Of course. But there's an enormous distinction between *wanting* to sell and *having* to sell. If you can no longer find a job where you live, you have to either rent your home to pay the mortgage or sell it and move where you can get work. This is a free country, and those who own property can do what they like with it within the bounds of the law. That's their right. But it's our right to push back as best we can with all the legal tools at our disposal. There's never a condition of stasis; everything's in flux, always has been, always will be. And that's the very thing that makes this town vital and unique."

Members of the audience were nodding in agreement as Helena weighed in. "I want to be clear. Neither of us is placing blame. There's a lot we all need to understand about the town's fragility and resiliency. It's a question of finding commonality and balance, not pitting one side against the other—or choosing the past over the present."

Helena looked up to see Gwen and Elise blowing kisses. Elise raised her fist in the air and mouthed, *You go, girl!* Cole, standing beside her, telegraphed, *Don't stop now.*

Paul sensed the tension in the audience and directed the cameraman to scan the crowd, buying time to formulate his next question. "What can you do, though? Isn't gentrification inevitable in highly desirable communities such as this?"

Freddie pointed to Helena as if to say, *this one's yours.* Helena adjusted the diamond necklace, taking comfort in its timeless solidity. "Wealth without community can smother whatever it encounters. Think of some places you know—we all know them—where there's a disproportionate amount of money. The owners are seldom around off-season, and the towns have become brands. Furniture collections and even cookies are named after them, and their zip and IATA codes are printed on T-shirts. Where's the community in that?"

"So true," Paul said, "but how does a town built on two square miles of sand counter such a trend?"

Helena's necklace and tiara sparkled with fire that seemed to channel her passion. "You might say we're a town with little land but a vast populace scattered around the globe. As one of our most famous residents, Norman Mailer, once said about us, 'This is a town worth fighting for.' And that's what those who live here—and those who don't but love the place—are doing. We're fighting to protect the town's history, maintain its socio-economic balance, and adapt to climate change as much as we can."

The camera zoomed in on Freddie, who gestured for Helena to continue.

"This is why we created the Artisans' Fund—to retrain displaced workers and preserve skills that could vanish forever in a generation. The way we see it, if you can afford to pay millions to buy and convert a guesthouse into a private home that sits vacant ten months of the year, you can afford to support training for those whose jobs your purchase eliminated. If you paid a fortune for a waterfront residence that may well be washed out to sea within a decade, you might consider joining us to fight climate change—if only to protect your investment."

"That makes sense," Paul said, "but solutions to these problems have eluded large cities. What do you have here that they don't, Freddie?"

The reporter's eyes sparkled. "The Atlantic serves up violent storms that shape the very land we live on. Mother Nature sees to it you appreciate your community and forces you to understand how important it is to protect it.

"We also have other advantages: passion, creativity, diversity, talent, and a powerful love of place. Some folks may still need a wake-up call, but many good people are already hard at work finding solutions. And, with enough support, I'm certain we shall prevail."

"I am, too," Paul said, visibly impressed by Freddie's response. "And now, we have something special to share. Throughout the filming of this documentary, we've set aside images we felt reflected the town's unique beauty and extraordinary residents. Here they are together for the very first time."

A montage of the town played across the far wall of the atrium: striking sunsets, stately buildings, whales breaching off Herring Cove, the ubiquitous drag performers and street musicians, and the crowds on Commercial Street. An assortment of races, ages, gender identities, and sexual preferences graced the screen. As the images morphed from one to another, a near-religious silence enveloped the room.

Helena surveyed the beaming faces in the audience.

You were right, Norman Mailer. It's a town well worth fighting for. I wish Butch understood that.

When the film clip ended, Paul said, "You've undertaken quite the project, Helena. And Freddie, the public is well served by your vigilance and insight. I wish you both—and the town I'm proud to call home—every success."

The assembled crowd broke into spontaneous applause once the cameras were shut off. Many in the audience were crying.

"It's been a genuine pleasure working with the two of you," Paul said, shaking Helena's hand. "This opportunity has been everything I could hope for and more. And adding Freddie here was a stroke of genius. Even if it was last minute."

Freddie answered first. "Talk about a surprise. But you made it so easy, Paul—your questions were right on point, and I appreciate the opportunity. Getting the word out is essential, and there are limits to what I can do at the paper."

"Freddie, darling, you were magnificent," Helena said. "I've got to circulate, but will you be around for a bit? I'd like a chat once I've done my rounds."

"You bet," Freddie said, then turned to a large crowd eager to congratulate her.

As Helena rose, Paul grabbed her elbow, drew her close, and whispered, "I'm one of those people you described. I've been coming to this town since college and finally achieved my dream of living here three years ago. It touches my heart to see a community pull together like this—especially given the divisions we've seen across the nation. My husband and I will be sending you a check for the Artisans' Fund as an expression of our appreciation. Call me if there's any other way we can help. Don't hesitate. We'll do whatever it takes. For starters, I'll make sure everything we discussed tonight makes the cut."

Helena, relieved and emotionally exhausted, was momentarily speechless—a rare thing indeed.

Behind the Velvet Rope

As Helena left the Mansion Suite, she cast a quick glance at the line of so-called onion rings beyond the locked doors. It seemed as though every one of them was glowering at her. She'd never shed the memory of how invisible she'd been when she lived in a single room, worked three jobs, and performed as a busker, singing on Commercial Street to make ends meet. Many people avoided her then as if she were dirty or diseased. Helena, exhausted and missing Butch more than ever, found it hard not to resent some of those same people waiting in line. Their entitled behavior—and the way they'd treated Afton and his team—made her reaction harder to contain.

You shouldn't hold a grudge. But just for once, it feels damn good to see them on the outside looking in—though I'm beginning to understand how Marie Antoinette felt when the mob was at the gates of Versailles.

As was often the case, Cole read her thoughts. Standing beside her in a fitted tuxedo that accentuated his muscular frame, he whispered, "I just don't get why they're all pissed off. The invitation was to a private view for those who contributed to the museum. The rest can damn well wait two hours and pay their twenty bucks to get in.

"Watch out for Cheswick Wilks, the tall guy with the big gut and half-glasses. I think he's the ringleader. He started in on me when I arrived. Why has it become so important to see and be seen in this town? It's just a small fishing village, not L.A., for God's sake."

"I don't think it's the size of the town, darling," Helena said, mimicking Bette Davis. "It's the size of their egos. They can't stomach the notion of being shut out of a private event that has drawn national attention. They want to be able to say they were there—every last tremendously special one of them.

"When Lola and Dorrie planned the private view, they never could have imagined such gauche behavior."

Kissing Cole's cheek, she murmured, "'Once more unto the breach, dear friends, once more.'"

Continuity

Nearly two hours had passed when a short, elderly woman with white hair piled high atop her head drew near.

Helena's mood improved at the sight of her. "Clotilde, darling, I'm thrilled you could grace us with your elegant presence. How are you?"

It was difficult for Helena to speak to the woman without crouching since she'd have been talking to nothing but a tangled mass of hair.

"Doing OK for an old warhorse," Clotilde Perkins replied with a winsome smile. "Glad to see you hauled out the rocks. Lola would be delighted. They threw away the mold when they made her and Captain Staunton. Did you know he bailed out my father's hardware business during the Great Depression?"

"No, I've never heard that," Helena said, filled with admiration for the stylishly dressed woman who admitted to ninety but was closer to a hundred years old.

"Captain Staunton lent my father the money without interest. When Father went to pay him back, the captain said, 'I don't know what you're talking about, Harry. That's your daughter's college fund.' And that's how I ended up at Radcliffe."

"That sounds like the captain," Helena said with pride. "I'm glad we put those rumors about him to rest a few years ago."

"My father never believed a word," Clotilde said vehemently. "He always said they'd been there for us—and so many others—when we faced a crisis. I suppose there's no better time to tell you it's my turn to give something back."

"What do you mean, Clotilde? You've been more than generous with your time and donations of family items."

"Now, Helena, hear me out. I won't take no for an answer. Without the captain's money, we'd have lost the store and our home. My family has lived in that house since it was built out on Long Point in eighteen twenty. It was one of the last to be floated back to town, and I'm proud to say we've kept it in its original condition.

"When my Robbie died in Vietnam, that was the end of the Perkins line. I'm donating the house and its contents to the Staunton Trust. It's my way of giving something back to the town *and* the Stauntons."

"The Stauntons are gone, dear," Helena said, suspecting Clotilde may have lost the thread of her thoughts.

Another link to a more caring, gentler past. Another person who intuitively knew what it meant to be part of a community. They had to depend on each other back then for survival—and something marvelous happened because of it. Can we ever find our way back to that kind of existence?

Clotilde raised herself to her full four feet eleven. "Like hell they are. You're as much of a Staunton as any of them, if not more. I'm settling the debt with their heir. That's you, dearie, just in case you're wondering. I've had Quincy set the transfer in motion, and that's that."

Helena brushed away a tear, not only for the sentiment but also for the notion that her dear friend was anticipating the end of her days.

"I'm touched and honored, darling. But I hope you won't mind me saying I pray it will be some time before the curtain comes down on your last act."

"It's neither here nor there to me," Clotilde said emphatically. "I've done my living. Now that I've settled my affairs, I live in the moment. For now, life is good. When it isn't, I'll know it's time to move on.

"Nice chatting with you, Helena." The old woman held up her empty glass, her eyes brimming with affection. "I'll be damned if I know where my bourbon gets to. Time to head to the bar for a refill before the unwashed masses descend. Anyhow, Your Majesty, you've got a crowd waiting for an audience; say nothing of angry peasants at the gate. Better you than me, dearie, that's all I can say. Better you than me."

As Clotilde hobbled away, Cole, who had heard the entire exchange, said, "I knew we'd start something with the Artisans' Fund. Now there's another project to keep the crew engaged. Can you imagine what that place will be like when it's fully restored? And we can probably house five people when it's done."

"Yes," Helena said pensively. "Another project."

Cole whispered, "Things won't feel so overwhelming after tonight. I promise. We just have to get through the next few hours. After that, everything will be OK."

"Well, the doors open in ten minutes," Helena said. "The onion rings can get their shot at me then, I guess. Before that madness begins, though, there's one last person I want to talk to."

Networking

Helena strode over to a handsome young man standing alone in a corner. He was six feet tall with a dark beard. Dressed in a navy-blue suit, he wore dark-framed glasses and was constantly checking his cell phone.

Helena studied him before speaking. "Wally, darling. Let's get out of the crowd for a moment. I need a word."

Wally Trieste tensed, then followed Helena up the stairs to her large office overlooking the atrium. The room was subtly decorated in shades of light blue, with several paintings and bronze sculptures bathed in soft light. An elegant oak desk with two armchairs across from it took up the center space. Through a glass wall, they could see the crowd milling below and the line of angry people still waiting to get in.

"OK," Helena said once they were seated, "I'm not making any accusations, but I've got some questions for you."

"Sure, Helena. Ask away." The young man said, staring at the floor.

Helena snapped her fingers. "Wally, look at me. Someone has my museum access code, and our network has been compromised."

"Shit!" Wally struggled to hold her intense gaze. "I didn't set up the encryption, but you know I installed the access system."

Helena gave a terse nod. "How could someone get my password?"

Wally stared down at the floor again. "I'm not one hundred percent sure, but I've got my suspicions."

"What? You knew and said nothing?"

Wally colored. "No. Not about your password. I'd tell you in an instant if I knew. It's just that weird things have happened to some of my other customers."

Helena held his troubled gaze. "What sort of weird things?"

"Their codes have been used to gain unauthorized entry, and stuff's been stolen. I've got to figure out how the thieves got the codes. Helena, I'd never—"

"I know that, Wally. Give me a minute to digest all this."

They watched silently as security guards formed a human cordon, and Afton unlocked the front door. The guards stared straight ahead as those entering pushed and shoved their way into the building. When the onion rings reached the atrium, they greeted each other with air kisses and vociferous complaints. The noise was deafening.

Wally looked down into the throng and grew pale. "I can't talk now, Helena. Not here. It's too dangerous. I'll get in touch real soon. I promise."

Then he bolted from the room.

Noblesse Oblige

Helena scanned the crowd to see who had spooked Wally. The new arrivals were already gorging at the buffet (the sauteed lumps of foie gras, oysters, clams on the half shell, and platters of jumbo shrimp, despite their valiant numbers, didn't stand a chance). Other newcomers were flagging down waitstaff for drinks. Many were sizing each other up with taut, calculating smiles as if weighing the best social conquest. No one seemed to be looking up at Helena's office.

She descended into the fray and was immediately accosted by the very person Cole had warned her about.

Big Bird

Cheswick Wilks' shiny, worn tuxedo emphasized his odd shape—spindly legs, ample gut, and long, narrow neck. Half-moon-shaped glasses magnified his beady eyes, which looked like two cigarette burns against his pasty skin. The lenses perched on an elongated nose, which narrowed to a point above a pencil-thin mustache. As was her wont, Helena searched for a visual tag to aid her memory. She dubbed the man "Big Bird" for his odd, gangly appearance.

"*Heh-layn-a,* my dear," the man squawked in a pretentious tone aligning perfectly with his new moniker, "at last, we meet. Why is it our paths have never crossed before now? Have you been avoiding me? I've tried several times to reach you about a board seat and an invitation to the *vernissage*. Apparently, your etiquette training was sub par—I've not received a reply. Surely this is no way to treat one of your potential patrons?"

Helena took a deep breath.

It's never a good sign when someone throws around arcane art terms within minutes of meeting you—especially if they're in French. His snobbery rivals Lady Catherine de Bourgh's. They probably knew each other. Time to channel my inner Joan Crawford.

Helena spoke slowly. "Since *you* introduced the topic of etiquette, might I suggest it's simply good manners to pronounce your hostess's name properly? My name is Hel-*eh*-na—as in Bonham Carter, not He-*layn*-ah, which sounds like a 'thirties telephone operator with a faulty connection. Furthermore, at the Staunton Museum, we prefer the term 'private view' as in 'invitation-only.' While meaning nearly the same thing, *vernissage* has snobbish connotations some of our artists find off-putting."

Helena seized the advantage while Wilks was still at a loss for words. "Tickets to our private view were so in demand they conjured up a legion of friends I never knew I had. I've lived in this town for years, yet to hear some people speak tonight, you'd think I arrived yesterday on a clamshell—like Botticelli's Venus."

Wilks laughed disdainfully. "Bette Midler's already done that routine. Surely you can come up with a more original metaphor."

Helena took her time crafting a reply.

Look at him. So entitled, so self-assured, and about as interesting as a used Q-Tip. If I weren't in this satin gown, I'd toss him in the reflecting pool. Time for a little Bette Davis, if only to make my escape.

"I said *on* a clamshell, not *in* one. To an entertainer such as myself, that's the difference between first class and steerage.

"Getting back to your complaints: Support for the museum—with either a donation or time—was the Staunton sisters' criterion for entry to tonight's private view. Not mine. You did neither, so you had to wait for general admission. That was *your* decision. Again, not mine. I'm not surprised our paths have never crossed. Given the tenor of this conversation, that might just be a good thing. As for your second point, all board memberships must be offered in strict compliance with criteria set by the Staunton sisters."

Wilks took another long sip of his drink. His eyes had narrowed to small, black bullets. "An unfortunate and unnecessary impediment. I've owned my home on Commercial Street for over thirty years—longer than you've lived here, I suspect. I'm an important member of this community with world-class connections and a trove of Provincetown history at my disposal. I should have been featured in Paul Schroeder's documentary, but he refused to give me the time of day. You and your staff need some pointers as to who matters in this town. And if I may be so bold, you could also have used my help with the design of this place."

"May I ask you something, Mr. Wilks?"

As Helena said this, she stared with such intensity he traded his indignation for an anxious grin.

"But of course."

"How long have you lived here? Not summered. Actually lived here?"

"I moved here full time two years ago when—well, it doesn't matter why I moved here."

Helena let the detail slide. "Did the thought ever occur to you that your experience might differ from those whose families have been here for generations? Or that they might be entitled to additional recognition because of their longstanding commitment to the community?"

"Why, yes. I'm sure there's a distinct difference. You can hardly compare living in Manhattan to living in this backwater."

As Helen turned to leave, Wilks quickly adopted a hearty tone. "No use crying over spilt milk, though. What's done is done. Let's start again, my dear. I'm Cheswick Wilks. I own the Stull House. You may have heard of David Conwell Stull. He was known as the 'Ambergris King.'"

"No, I'm devastated to say I haven't," Helena said, accepting his tacit offer of a truce. "Was that a prototype for Burger King?"

Wilks twittered, smirked, then shook his head, looking like a giant canary. "No, my dear. Ambergris is a waxy substance from the digestive tract of sperm whales used as a fixative in perfume. It's still quite valuable today. Stull did a tremendous amount of business with the Staunton Fleet. I have more information on him and Captain Staunton in my extensive library. You must come and see it sometime."

Helena waved to a passing couple.

Lord love a duck. If I can't get rid of this clown in less than a minute, I'm going to end up making Attila the Hun look like Mr. Rogers.

"That would be lovely," she said, mentally filing his invitation in her "cold day in Hell" file. "It sounds fascinating. Perhaps we can discuss it some snowy night in front of the fire. I'm sorry I can't talk more just now, but as you can see, several others are waiting to castigate me for crimes against 'Society.'

"Enjoy your *visite de l'art* and be sure to try the *Clams à la Marinière.* They're superb. Oh, and fear not; we always serve them *on* the half shell."

***

The sound of popping champagne corks and the smell of savory hors d'oeuvres filled the atrium. The space worked well as a social venue, and Helena surveyed the festive scene with pride.

Keep enough champagne flowing and food circulating, and we'll pry their wallets open without them even noticing.

She flagged down a server, who filled her champagne flute to the brim. Then Helena smiled encouragingly at the next person in line, leaving Wilks to seek other victims. There were plenty to choose from: the heir to a liquor fortune, an aging pornstar, a retired airline executive, a former child actor, now a "lifestyle coach and promoter," and, as Helena thought of them, a "slither" of real estate agents—all talking at once in self-important tones.

She barely listened as one self-anointed critic after another informed her of the merits and flaws of the exhibition.

Gay men. One purchase from Pottery Barn, and presto, they're a designer! I love you guys, but tone it down now and then, will ya? I should trot out Big Bird to show them what happens when one gets too hung up on esthetics.

Fluff Follows Function

Local architect, Henry Boorstin, cornered Cole near the buffet table. Boorstin was a short man with an enormous nose and a pockmarked face who had a way of waving his index finger in the same rhythm as his words. Little snippets of his monologue wafted Helena's way during the brief intervals when someone in her circle wasn't offering their opinion.

"I don't think you made the right decision moving the furnishings and decor from the house," Boorstin said, pointing to the Mansion Suite. "People don't care about those sorts of things anymore. They want function, not fluff. And I'm not sure I'd have done a stone exterior for the museum if I'd been given the chance. This town has classic bones, like Chatham and Nantucket, even if, thank God, our buildings are only now emerging from under a century of funk. I'd have done something more in keeping with Cape Cod traditions—white clapboard or shingle style, which is widely established and easily recognized. I'm telling you now, this building will be an anachronism within five years. . ."

Helena caught Cole's eye. Making a pistol out of her thumb and forefinger, she pointed it at Boorstin and pretended to pull the trigger. With a sigh, Cole turned back to the architect, who hadn't stopped talking long enough to notice.

The Battle Royal

While scoring yet another refill from a passing server, Helena felt a sharp poke in the ribs. She turned to see local bon vivant Bernard Crocker glaring at her. Known as "Betty" and resplendent in an off-the-shoulder, chartreuse gown with train, he was a pale, willowy man in his mid-fifties with flowing white hair and taut features.

"Darling," Helena drawled in an intentionally insincere tone as she leaned in to kiss his pale cheek, "How kind of you to take time away from your sailing lessons to attend my little soirée."

For an instant, Betty's eyes gleamed with affection and mischief. For him, throwing shade was more than a pastime; it was a vocation.

Betty drew himself up as though preparing for a duel. "Helena, dearest, I'd have thought you'd be outside sacrificing some poor, unsuspecting houseboy to Neptune. It will take divine intervention by the god of the sea for you to beat me on Sunday. I've only let you win so far because it makes things more exciting for the little people."

Betty's arch reply drew the attention of several onlookers, who moved closer to eavesdrop.

Winking at Helena, he lowered his voice. "Nice job on the boobs. Most queens who try to go without falsies mess up the shading and end up looking like the front end of an old Buick. By the way, have you seen the coverage in the local rags? Looks like we'll have quite a crowd for the race. Life is always better with an audience, n'est ce pas? We've got one now. Let's make the most of it."

No sailing race had gotten more attention that season than the battle between Helena's *Dame Edna* and Betty's *Tough Cookie*. Their alleged feud was intended to draw attention to the weekly races at the Provincetown Yacht Club, a venerable, if small, organization founded in 1867. The series was tied six-six. The final race was the following Saturday, and excitement was riding high. Even the Provincetown II had been pressed into service to accommodate additional spectators once Helena and Betty had agreed to race in drag to benefit the Artisans' Fund.

Turning her back to the other guests, Helena beamed at her sparring partner. She genuinely admired Betty, a free spirit who lived life on his terms. They'd been close since Helena "worked the streets," as she called it, performing for chump change in front of Town Hall. Back then, Betty had been a headliner for a drag review, and once he'd heard Helena sing, he'd offered her a part in his show, launching her professional career.

Betty leaned close and whispered, "I know you've got a roomful of social climbers who all want a piece of you, and we don't want people thinking we're getting along, so I'll say congratulations on your superb interview, well done, and goodnight, bitch."

Helena recoiled dramatically, raising both hands to her cheeks as if something rude had been said.

Betty winked, then sashayed away as Helena felt someone grab her arm.

The Tin Man

"Clarence Woodman," the man holding her elbow said in a portentous tone. "*Doctor* Clarence Woodman." Seeing Helena's puzzled look, he added, "We haven't met."

The doctor was bald and of moderate height, with neither beard nor mustache, which gave him the appearance of a peeled potato. His beady eyes scanned the room, never resting on any person or thing for too long. Their gaze was stony, acquisitive, and unnerving.

"It's a pleasure to rectify the situation," Helena said, switching to autopilot. "So kind of you to support the museum."

"It's nothing, trust me. I'm new to town, and I figured this was a great way to meet people."

"I'm not so sure about that," Helena said, her eyes twinkling. "One doesn't necessarily meet like-minded people at these sorts of things."

The man seemed taken aback as if his twenty-dollar entrance fee had been ill spent, though he rebounded quickly. "Wherever I go, I make it my point to meet the movers and shakers. The others I couldn't care less about. I don't have time for chitchat."

"That's an interesting notion for a party, Mr., ah?"

"Woodman, *Doctor* Clarence Woodman."

Helena fought the urge for a moment, then gave in.

As in the Tin Woodman. Yet another onion ring, no doubt.

"Forgive me, Doctor Woodman," Helena said, "but what sort of movers and shakers do you expect to find in a little fishing village at the tip of Cape Cod?"

"You may still think that's what this place is," the doctor said, leaning close until the potent odor of Scotch forced Helena to take a step back. "If so, you're one of the last. P'town is on the map. Money from around the globe—big money—is coming here in droves. People who matter. And it's so much easier to get to them here than it is in the city."

"Get to them? Might I ask what you mean by that?" Helena inquired, wondering how Lola would have dealt with the statement.

Of course, in her day, no one bothered the actors, writers, and performers who lived or vacationed here. Now, people like the Tin Man are creating a cult of celebrity where the famous once went to escape it. Go figure.

Doctor Woodman smirked. "I'm a developer, and when you build things, it helps to know people who can pave your way."

"Where *do* you come from?"

Helena waited for his answer, which he whispered when the expectant silence could no longer be sustained.

"Newark, New Jersey."

"You're a developer in Newark?"

"Nah. I'm a doctor in Newark. You could say development is a recent development for me." The doctor chuckled at his own joke while Helena remained silent. "I'm doing my first real project here. I'll ditch the medical racket once the place sells out. Then I'll take on bigger projects."

Helena took a deep breath. "What place might that be?"

"Oh, it's early days. I can't go public with the specifics. But I tell you what, if things go the way I'm hoping, I'll let you in on the ground floor."

"How thoughtful of you," Helena said, trying to temper the irony in her voice. "So considerate. I have so many questions for you, such as how you decide which people matter, what criteria you used to determine P'town is up-and-coming, and several others I'm just dying to discuss. Unfortunately, I have to keep circulating. It's been a pleasure meeting you, Mr. Tin, ehr, *Doctor* Woodman."

Helena walked away as fast as her stilettos allowed, their red soles reflecting on the polished floor. When certain he was no longer watching, she fanned herself with a program and downed her fourth glass of champagne.

Vissi d'Arte

The clink of crystal, the waitstaff's rapid circuits through the crowd, and frequent bursts of laughter reassured Helena the umbrage of those kept outside had diminished enough that everyone was enjoying themselves. No doubt there'd be repercussions and recriminations tomorrow, but she would focus on those then.

Helena was delighted to see Mavis escort the critic from *Art in America* around the room, stopping to talk about each work as a large crowd watched in respectful silence. When the tour was done, Helena saw the mask drop from the artist's face.

She's still worried about something. Is it the break-in, C.J., or both?

Suddenly pensive, Helena returned to the Mansion Suite, where Afton had replaced the red velvet cordon that kept the public at a distance. She gazed into the formal parlor and saw Lola and Dorrie sitting in their chairs, smiling at her. Uncertain whether what she saw was real or the product of too much champagne, Helena raised her glass in a tentative toast. The sisters each blew a kiss, then vanished. As Helena stared at the now-empty room, complex emotions—relief, loneliness, anxiety, and bewilderment—overwhelmed her.

Sensing her granddaughter's confusion, Shirley drew close and whispered, "You did it. You brought it home for them. Did you see how proud they were of you? So am I."

Helena was about to ask exactly what her grandmother had seen when Shirley said, "When you get up there in years, there's not as much distance between the here and now and the hereafter."

Then she swept away to corner a handsome waiter for a refill and, with any luck, his phone number.

Melody

With minutes left before her second speech of the evening, Helena studied the work she'd focused so much care upon that morning. Mavis's seven-foot portrait of the woman in white holding a baby with a misshapen leg dominated the room. The mother's smile was both loving and protective as the child nursed at her bare breast. Tranquility and acceptance radiated from the canvas, though concern for the baby's future was visible in the mother's eyes.

"That's my favorite, too," Helena said, standing beside a young woman entranced by the work. "You have good taste."

"If only I could paint like that," the woman replied, smiling at Helena. "I'd give anything to capture a fifth of the emotional range in that portrait."

Helena studied her. "Don't I know you from somewhere?"

The woman appeared to be in her early twenties. Her red hair was short with bangs that complemented her penetrating blue eyes. Her pale skin was smooth, with the slightest trace of freckles around her nose. She wore a long, black cotton dress and sandals that, despite their extreme simplicity, were more than suitable for the occasion. Helena suspected she was a student at the Arts Center.

"You've probably seen me performing on Commercial Street," the girl said in a voice devoid of its earlier enthusiasm.

"But of course. You're that marvelous musician with the autoharp. My music teacher played it as if she were strumming a washboard. You make it sound so angelic, I've finally put those horrid memories to rest. You've saved me thousands in therapy."

"Wow. Thank you." The woman's radiant smile returned even brighter. "I'm a painter. I perform to pay the rent since my paintings never sell. I didn't think anyone ever noticed my music. They certainly don't open their wallets."

"It's a tough life out there on Commercial Street. What's your name?"

"Melody. Melody Carpenter."

"How perfect. Well, Melody, when I used to busk, I'd have to stop myself from tripping people. They'd spend twenty dollars on some cheap T-shirt or forty for a doormat with a ransom note from a cat but never drop so much as a quarter in the hat to encourage talent."

"You were a busker?" Melody looked stunned.

"Busker, server, bookseller, short-order cook, bartender, chambermaid, dog-walker, window washer—you name it. I did anything and everything to keep my little room on Bradford Street until I became the housekeeper at HomePort. Like everyone who loves this town, I figured out a way to stay."

"Where on Bradford?" Melody asked.

"That old guest house where performers rent rooms. Or at least, they used to. You must know the place."

"Buskerville Hall?"

"Is that what they call it these days? What a fabulous name—right out of Conan Doyle. I wish I'd thought of it. It's the dilapidated house at the crest of the hill, right?

Melody surveyed Helena's elegant figure as if looking for some residual trace of her earlier days. "That's the place. I can't believe you lived there."

"I certainly did," Helena said. "We lived on the edge and had nothing. In a way, though, we had all we needed and more. Those were wonderful times."

Helena's voice trailed off as she gazed up at the painting.

Melody seemed eager to continue the conversation. "It hasn't changed all that much from the sound of it. We can still take a chance on our dreams—if only for a summer."

Helena clapped her hands. "That's the best description I've ever heard—a place to take a chance on your dreams. Why don't you come and see me next week, and we can talk more? And bring your portfolio.

I'd love to see your work." Helena pointed to a line of people queued up behind them. "Unfortunately, right now, I must deal with these onion rings."

"Don't you have caterers for that?" Melody asked.

"Did I say that out loud?" Helena gasped, clutching her necklace in mock astonishment. "I should be more careful. That's my admittedly petty name for the phonies. It's the same game here as it is on Commercial Street, trying to separate people from their money. You just have to wear fancier clothes and do a better job of keeping your thoughts to yourself."

Melody laughed and turned to view the next painting: a tall man in an embroidered robe presiding over a religious ritual, all traces of the sombrero he'd been wearing just hours before successfully eradicated.

Marc, who had been waiting to speak to Helena, offered a tray of hors d'oeuvres and, raising an eyebrow, said, "Onion rings?"

"*Time and the Town*, darling. *Time and the Town*." Helena made a circle with her index finger. "Look it up when you get a chance. It's a book. You're an author. The two of you should get along famously."

"OK, whatever. Cole sent me to tell you it's time for your remarks."

"Let me dispose of this last committee of culture vultures, and I'll be right there."

Keystone Kop

Nearly three hours later, Helena and Freddie escaped to the little theater, where Helena was confident no one would overhear them.

Freddie pulled her notepad and ballpoint from her evening clutch. "Thanks again for the guest appearance on the documentary. If you wanted to get me to play ball, you couldn't have chosen a better way."

Helena shrugged. "It's a question of decency, Freddie, and when I tell you what you need to know, I don't think you'll require a bribe to keep it secret until tomorrow."

Helena spoke of finding C.J.'s body, the interview with Sergeant Brandt, and his agreement to keep the murder quiet for twenty-four hours.

"Tell me, why is he suddenly being so cooperative?"

Freddie thumbed through her notepad. "Thanks for being so up-front. I'll reciprocate. Three weeks ago, my editor asked me to investigate complaints about Sergeant Brandt, including homophobia, harassment, and unlawful arrest. I decided to do a profile on him, thinking I could massage his ego and get him to go on the record. He jumped at the chance.

"I asked the usual basics: Where he came from. Prior job. All that sort of stuff. Of course, I fact-checked what he told me, and that's where things went off the rails. The secretary at the police department where Brandt allegedly worked had never heard of him. There was no record of him at the college where he claimed to have gotten his Criminal Justice degree."

"You're kidding! Is he actually a police officer?" Helena asked, lowering her voice and leaning close.

"That's an open question. What happened next is even more bizarre. Of course, I went to see Chief Louie. He showed me Brandt's application and the notes about his references. They all seemed legit. When I told the chief what I'd found out, he did the oddest thing."

"What?"

"He asked me to ride with him in his car."

"Not his cruiser?"

"Nope. That old Volvo he loves so much. We went out to Pamet Harbor and looked out over the bay. For a while, he made small talk. Then he thanked me for bringing things to his attention, asked me to hold off on the story, and said he'd be going away. When I quizzed him, he told me to trust him and keep a close eye on Brandt. Two days later, I was stunned to learn he'd made Brandt acting chief. I couldn't believe it. Other, more qualified officers knew the town much better. It made no sense why the chief would leave a lunatic in charge."

"Wow. You don't think Louie is in cahoots with Brandt?"

Freddie shook her head. "More likely, he's gone undercover. One of our reporters saw him coming out of the DA's office. But why leave Brandt in charge?"

Helena took a moment to reflect. "Earlier today, you told me Brandt wouldn't report the museum break-in. Why do you think that?"

"There have been several robberies he hasn't made public, both in private homes *and* galleries. I'm not sure why. Maybe he's trying to hog all the glory if he solves the crimes. But there's something fishy about the way he's behaving. I'm sure he won't report the vandalism of Mavis's artwork. At least not right away."

"And is that why he agreed to hold off on publicizing C.J.'s murder? He's going to have to say something eventually, right? The medical examiner, rescue squad, and other officers witnessed the scene. He can't keep it quiet for much longer."

Freddie pulled up a text message. "According to my editor, there's already gossip at the paper—and vague innuendos on the community Facebook page. To be frank, Helena, I haven't the faintest idea why Brandt agreed to keep silent with so many people involved. Keep me posted, and I'll do the same for you."

A Motley Crew

Bedtime was when Helena missed her husband, Butch, the most. She loved how they would relive the day's high points before falling asleep. On this most special of nights, she was alone with her thoughts.

Cheswick Wilks. Big Bird, with his snobbish ways, half-glasses, and pointed nose. So sure of himself, lecturing one and all about his taste and social standing. Speaking of lectures, you'd think Henry Boorstin would have figured out by now that no one has the slightest interest in his architectural opinions. Pointing his finger all the time certainly brings out the "boor" in Boorstin. The more he does it, the more idiotic he seems. And now, there's another self-important male dinosaur joining the herd. Doctor Woodman—the Tinman—with his round face and tiresome notions about "movers and shakers."

Just my luck. I throw a gala and am visited by the three assholes of the apocalypse. It's amazing how much bullshit can be served up at one gathering. There was a time Butch and I would have laughed about it. Given his mood when he left, I should temper what I say about tonight. Better to skip C.J.'s murder and the graffiti altogether.

Helena texted pictures and commentary to her husband.

(Helena) *It went well. Mavis made all the right moves and was gracious in her remarks. We raised an additional one hundred thousand dollars. The museum is off to a brilliant start.*

As Helena hit send, she thought, *At least to the outside world. And I never thought I'd say this—even to myself—but taking on the Staunton Museum may have been the biggest mistake of my life.*

The Summit

The next morning, Helena reached Highland Links just minutes after Quincy Stilwell. The parking lot was empty except for the two of them.

"Morning, Helena. Great bash last night," Quincy said, his usual effervescent self. "A bit of a crush with all those onion rings barging in, but the party will be talked about for decades. You did one hell of a job as hostess."

While thanking him for the compliment, Helena pondered how, at his age, Quincy could function with just five hours of sleep. He'd been one of the last guests to leave.

Fore!

The course was a lovely expanse of dark green in the early morning light. Traces of fog drifted in from the ocean, whose waves could be heard in the distance—an ostinato not unlike a heartbeat. Birdsong emanated from the woods, and as the sun rose, gulls flew out to sea in formation. Helena suddenly understood why Quincy was so insistent on spending his limited free time at this beautiful spot. He beckoned her to sit beside him, and they set off for the first tee.

The morning dew was heavy. Helena's Balenciaga sneakers were soaked by the third hole. When not focused on his expert shots, Quincy patiently offered pointers as she struggled to make sense of the bizarre outing.

He's up to something. There's no reason to play golf this early, not after being up until all hours. Why the subterfuge?

The two friends played through the first five holes without encountering another party. Then, on the sixth, as Quincy planned his putt, Helena surveyed the Atlantic from high atop a steep cliff. Waves rolled over shallow sandbars, crested for an instant, then subsided in deeper water only to foam again when they reached the shore. The beach, smoothed by a recent high tide, seemed to stretch into infinity in either direction. As Helena savored the tranquil beauty, Quincy tossed her ball into the woods.

When she objected, he whispered, "Let's pretend we're looking for it. There's a clearing to the left. Start over there."

When they reached the spot, Helena was surprised to see a tall, familiar-looking, blond man in jeans and a green polo shirt sitting on a log.

What's the District Attorney doing here?

"Morning, Quincy," the man said, rising. "And this must be your client. Morning, ma'am."

"You're Dan Andrade," Helena said, looking to Quincy for an explanation.

Dan seemed pleased to be recognized. "Right in one. Quincy told me what happened. It seemed best we meet somewhere out of the way to avoid notice. He and I are members, so Highland Links was the obvious choice."

"Meet about what?" Helena asked.

Before Dan could answer, a short, muscular man with a broad chest and tattooed arms stepped into view from behind a stand of blueberry bushes. His brown hair was cut short in military style, and he wore black jeans and a matching T-shirt.

"Louie," Helena yelled, throwing her arms around him.

Chief Louie Silva, looking embarrassed, said, "Try to keep things low-key, Helena. I know it can be difficult, but I'm undercover."

Quincy savored the chief's embarrassment before saying, "OK, gentlemen, and lady, let's get down to business. Let me say right off, Helena, I know you're going to have difficulty with this conversation. We have a lot of questions for you, but we can't say much about why we're asking. Please trust us and keep that natural curiosity of yours in check."

"Well, Quincy," Helena said, "you picked the right moment. I was up until two drinking champagne, and what is it now? Seven in the morning? I don't think I'd be curious if you told me you were taking up drag."

Quincy chuckled, then said, "Dan, would you begin?"

The DA cleared his throat. "Helena, it's unorthodox for me to meet with you like this. I must ask you to hold everything I'm about to say in confidence."

Dan explained there had been a series of art thefts across the Outer Cape over the last three months. The MO was always the same: high-priced art stolen from private homes and galleries with no visible sign of a break-in. Most houses were robbed earlier in the season before the homeowners arrived. Then, in July, the action shifted to the galleries. The thefts had been kept out of most news outlets, though it wouldn't be long before the public learned of them.

"The thieves appear to be getting bolder as the season ends. Two galleries in Provincetown were hit just last week," Dan said.

"And now the Staunton Museum," Helena said, "except those paintings, which may be the most valuable of all, were vandalized."

Dan nodded. "The goal in that case may have been to stop the museum's acquisition. But I need your help to prove it."

"I'm happy to do whatever I can. What do you need?" Helena asked.

She was already confident Dan was on her side. Quincy would never lead her astray.

Dan returned to his seat on the log. "I think we've got the security hack figured out. Tell me what protects the works inside the museum. The stuff no one ever talks about."

Helena described the vibration sensors and the metal grillwork that sealed off the galleries if they were engaged.

"But the spray chalk didn't activate the sensors, right?" Chief Louie asked, opening a thermos of coffee.

Helena refused a cup. "No, it didn't. I suspect it was light enough to circumvent them."

"A crucial point. Someone would have to know that. What happens if the power goes out?"

Helena explained that, given the risk of hurricanes, the electrical and security systems were solar-sourced. All electrical and video cables were embedded in steel conduits, so they couldn't be cut. There were solar panels on the southern roof and massive batteries in a secure room accessed by a special key. Protecting the power source was an integral part of the museum's security.

"So the likelihood of paintings being stolen is next to nil?" Dan asked.

Helena liked his intelligence and dogged determination. "I don't want to jinx things by saying so. We hired the security firm that handles the Getty to map out the system and had consultants from the Louvre approve their design. Given the aggressive lockdown mode, we were told there was no need for guards inside the building at night. Even so, at least two are on the grounds at all times."

Dan gave Quincy a thumbs-up before saying, "They knew they couldn't remove the art without getting caught."

Chief Louie grinned. "Let's assume the accident with the delivery truck was a failed hijacking. If so, it follows that the museum break-in was an attempt to get Mavis to remove the paintings, allowing them to be stolen once outside the museum."

"But what *about* Mavis?" Helena asked, surprised to realize that, despite the early hour, she was energized by the discussion. "Where does

C.J.'s murder fit in? Why didn't they just steal everything Mavis had in the studio instead of trying to kill her? She swears she was the intended victim."

The solemn look on Quincy's face confirmed Helena's worst fear. "Mavis has allowed me to reveal certain information under the condition you keep it to yourselves. If she were to die, the paintings would increase dramatically in value and revert to her estate. And they'd have to be stored somewhere until probate was complete.

"As for the art in her studio, her paintings go through a final glazing process right after she signs them. The signed works are photographed and cataloged immediately, then she ships them to her dealer as soon as the glaze sets. She'd even cataloged the one she was planning to give you. Is it still in the studio, Helena?"

"I don't know. But it should be easy enough to find out."

"Ask Mavis to check," Dan said. "I haven't heard they found any signed works."

Quincy volunteered, then said, "Let's assume the spray chalk was a fallback strategy after the failed attempt on Mavis's life. That plan almost succeeded."

"It makes sense," Helena said, "and explains why the graffiti was water-soluble. But why is Brandt so eager to pin C.J.'s murder on me?"

Dan pulled a handkerchief from his pocket and wiped his brow. "I'd asked Louie to go undercover to investigate certain issues with Sergeant Brandt. He was made acting chief at my insistence, even though he'd only been on the force for three months. I thought the more high-profile he was, the easier we could monitor him, but his obsession with you makes little sense. We need to figure out whatever game he is playing in case it points us to the killer, which is another reason I wanted to talk to you.

"I have to ask you to prepare for some unpleasantness, Helena. Brandt has informed me he is treating you as the prime suspect in C.J.'s death. I'll let him have his search warrants but try to block any arrest. I need Louie watching Brandt in case he gives something away. Please play along with us and be treated as a suspect?"

"I'm OK with that," Helena replied, "though I can't say I'm looking forward to the experience."

Chief Louie spoke next. "I have several questions about C.J. Strongue."

Helena offered the slightest trace of a smile. "Of course, Louie. You know I'll do anything I can to help."

"Thanks, Helena. For starters, what can you tell me about C.J.?"

Helena felt sadness overtake her. "I only met her once. At an Audubon rescue. She was a classic washashore, new to Wellfleet, and disillusioned by her reception. We see it all the time in P'town, too—people who expect to finally live the life they always wanted, only to hit some hurdles. Some folks move to the Outer Cape because they've vacationed here and found our way of life compelling. Others insist they know better and will whip things into shape—though that seldom goes well. C.J. had a foot in each boat."

When Dan looked puzzled, Quincy seemed eager to weigh in. "The washashores usually fit into one of three groups: The first is made up of those who are drawn here by the beauty and our small-town ways. These folks are patient and seldom have unrealistic expectations. Gradually, they become part of the community, supporting local causes and participating in town government.

"Then, you have the second group: those who may appreciate the natural beauty but want to adjust the town to their liking. These folks are often corporate types who consider the locals backward and unwilling to change. They quickly make a name for themselves and are avoided whenever possible.

"Lastly, there are those who think a change of scene will change their lives. Everything is about them. Of course, they bring along all the baggage they'd hoped to leave behind.

"The first group eventually fits in. In time, the other two groups usually make the necessary adjustments."

"And just what are those adjustments?" Dan asked. "I've often heard life on the Outer Cape is significantly different from that in Onset, where I live."

Quincy nodded. "The 'experts' often get frustrated after a few failures and the inevitable pushback. Their dissatisfaction mounts until they buy a second home elsewhere, which works well for all concerned. Then, the experts are away for the winter, which the locals like because that's when the town meeting makes all the important decisions. By the time these folks return for the summer, everyone's busy working, and these corporate types are lost in the crowd."

"And the last group? The ones who want everything to be about them?"

"They remain isolated in a circle of similar people, entertaining each other with mindless prattle while trying to convince themselves—and their social media followers—that they're living their dream."

"Or," Helena said, unable to resist, "they move to Daytona Beach."

"Back to the topic at hand," Chief Louie said, fighting to suppress a smile. "Why was C.J. in Mavis's studio?"

Helena sighed. "As I understand it, she thought if she donated a statue to the town of Wellfleet, she'd be accepted by the locals. C.J. was going to have an art auction to raise money for a monument to Goody Hallett, and she was after Mavis to donate a work."

"Goody Hallett!" Quincy exclaimed. "That must have gone over like a lead balloon."

"Exactly," Helena said. "From what I heard through the grapevine, C.J. botched her town meeting presentation, then wrote an incendiary letter to the *Free Press*."

"I saw that video where Mavis chased her off the beach," Chief Louie said. "There must have been bad blood between them after that."

Helena shrugged. "Mavis said something about a meeting with C.J. the day of the murder, so I assume they patched things up."

"How likely was that donation, though?" Quincy asked. "Even a small Mavis Chandry can go for hundreds of thousands."

"You'd have to ask Mavis, I'm afraid," Helena said, staring down at the ground. "She seems to think I tried to kill her. I'm not likely to get much out of her."

"I'd heard that," Chief Louie said. "Unfortunately, we can't comment on an ongoing investigation."

"Even if it's being handled by a lunatic sergeant," Quincy said, sounding frustrated for the first time. "Helena. Listen to me. You need to be careful."

"I get that, but I've got a few questions. If you can't answer, you can't answer, but I want some things out in the open."

"Ok," Dan Andrade said with some hesitation. "But remember, if we can't, it's not because we aren't concerned about you."

"I get that, too," Helena said. "Here goes: George Miller was in the guard shed when Afton took his brother home. Even if the thieves hacked the network, shouldn't he have seen someone entering the museum? Or is he in on it with Brandt?"

Chief Louie hesitated. "I want to be clear; I'm *not* suggesting Sergeant Brandt is involved with the thefts. I *can* say there aren't clear lines of sight between the museum entrance and the guard shed. I should have written it up as a finding when I did my security walkthrough, but the rest of the system was so impressive I thought it wouldn't matter. So it is possible George might not have seen anything. You've got to hand it to these crooks. Whoever they are, they're sophisticated."

"You're telling me we relied so heavily on technology we overlooked the obvious." The chief nodded, and Helena pursed her lips. "But my security code was used to gain access. What do you know about that?"

"Not much," Chief Louie said.

Quincy signaled for silence when the sounds of a passing foursome reached the clearing. As they waited for the group to move on, the soothing rhythm of the waves offered a pleasant antidote for Helena's frustration. Once the party was out of earshot, she shared what Wally Trieste had told her.

When neither the chief nor the DA had any questions, Quincy cleared his throat, which was always a sign an oration was to begin. "I'm going to offer a theory—just a theory, mind you: The thieves wanted those paintings out of the museum and back on the road. When Mavis escaped the electrocution attempt, one alternative was getting her to tear up the bequest. Using your access code almost accomplished that, Helena. It also set you up to take the fall."

Helena stamped her foot, causing her sneakers to squeeze out a small puddle of water. "Damn these shoes. Remind me never to wear high-fashion footwear on a damp golf course! Have you spoken to Wally? He's been fantastic—and dedicated."

"I can't answer that, Helena. I'm terribly sorry," Dan replied.

Helena shrugged. "That's OK, but I suppose I can still tell *you* something: When I spoke with Wally in my office last night, he grew agitated when he saw someone—I don't know who—downstairs in the crowd. I'll never believe he'd share security codes unless forced to do so."

Quincy spoke up. "I saw him race out the side door. I agree he looked stricken."

Helena frowned, her right foot toying with a fallen leaf. "He's a good kid and shouldn't be left to deal with this alone. OK, guys. Tell me everything you need me to do. And don't waste time sugarcoating it. I can damn well take care of myself."

Two Sides of the Coin

Quincy Stilwell and Mavis Chandry met outside Sergeant Brandt's office at ten that morning.

When he saw Quincy, the sergeant tensed. "No way, counselor. You can't be here when your other client is my prime suspect. I'm going to have to ask you to leave."

The attorney removed a paper from his briefcase. "I have here an informed consent document signed by both Helena and Mavis. They specifically state no objection to my representation of them both at this stage, and I agree to represent only one of them if charges are made against both. We can go to court, or you can let me advise my client. Which will it be?"

Brandt heaved a deep sigh and said, "OK. Let's get going. Ms. Chandry, why was C.J. Strongue in your studio the day she died?"

Quincy nodded, and Mavis answered, "She wanted a donation for some fundraiser. I decided to show her a work in progress, hoping she'd change her mind."

"Why would you do that?" Brandt asked.

"My paintings do rather well. Buying them at auction and reselling them undermines the value of my work. I decided the best way out was to offer her a painting she wouldn't take."

"How do you know she wouldn't take it?"

Brandt peered across his desk as Mavis shifted uncomfortably in her chair. "Well, it was just a hunch. But she seemed such an old maid, I figured she'd find the subject embarrassing."

"What was the subject?"

"Nothing all that exotic. Just a bunch of naked lesbians dancing around a fire as part of a witchcraft ritual."

Brandt grinned. "Oh yeah, I saw that one in the studio. Great detail. Very realistic."

"I'm glad you liked it, Sergeant," Mavis said through clenched teeth.

Brandt smirked, then continued his line of questioning. "So you forgot about the meeting with the victim?"

"Yes, as I said yesterday. It totally slipped my mind."

"You'd had an altercation with her previously, right?"

"You might call it that," Mavis said, taking a deep breath. "She'd been stalking me. I got sick of it."

"So why did you subsequently agree to give her a painting? Was she blackmailing you?"

"No. Nothing like that. C.J. Strongue was one of those strong-willed women who keep coming at you. I've seen it a few times before—someone who never gives up until you give them what they want, even if it's just to make them go away."

Mavis spoke in short, staccato bursts. "I felt bad when the video of me chasing her went up on the Internet. Then I read in the paper how she'd made a fool of herself at the Wellfleet town meeting. I thought if I gave her a way out by offering a painting I knew she wouldn't take, she might cut her losses and move on. You haven't been here long, Sergeant, but once you've got a reputation, the Outer Cape can be a very lonely place. Take it from me."

Brandt made a note, then said, "Why do you think that Helena person tried to kill you?"

Quincy shook his head. "We won't answer that question, Brandt. Mavis's position is that she was overwrought by the discovery of the body and spoke inappropriately. She has no wish to go on record as making an accusation of any kind."

"How did I know that was going to be your game?" Brandt said with a scowl. "You might as well go. I've got other ways of getting what I want."

Standards Must be Maintained

Helena returned to HomePort from the golf course both troubled and intrigued. After showering and changing her clothes, she walked down to the museum, greeted patrons on the terrace, then strode purposefully up the stairs to her office.

No point in giving in to despair. Quincy, Louie, and Dan have my back. I need to focus on getting this place running smoothly so I can figure out how to patch things up with Butch. What I wouldn't give for a spa day and a chance to think things through. No way that's gonna happen, though. Maybe I can give myself a pedicure tonight instead. Ah, the life of the idle rich.

Over thirty bouquets filled the room, including an elaborate one from Butch. Dozens of congratulatory cards had been hand-delivered. Newspapers covered Helena's desk. Freddie's article in the *Free Press* filled most of the front page with a glowing review of Mavis's show and an insightful summary of the conversation with Paul Schroeder. At the bottom of the pile was a long manila envelope. When Helena opened it, she found a white sheet of paper with a single sentence in cutout letters that read, "*You're next bitch.*"

"Proper punctuation is *so* important," she said before taking a marker, inserting a comma, and placing the threat in her desk drawer.

***

At eleven-thirty, Cole tapped on her office door. "Sergeant Brandt would like a word. Do you want me to call Quincy?"

Helena looked up from her work. "Tell Brandt I'm on the phone. Make him wait five minutes, then let him in. I'll call Quincy."

The attorney answered on the first ring.

"Helena here. Just as you predicted, Brandt is in Cole's office, wanting to see me. Can you get to the museum quickly?"

"I'm back at the office, so it will take less than ten minutes. Stall as long as you can, and keep this line open so I can listen in."

At the appointed time, Cole escorted the sergeant to a seat by Helena's desk. Brandt seemed to have traded his swagger for a smoldering rage. His jaw was set, and he kept his right hand near his holster.

The sergeant wasted no time once Cole left. "No doubt you already know there was a dummy circuit breaker. That old lady got hit with a hundred-twenty volts that just kept coming. Nothing could have saved her."

It was idiotic of Brandt to share such an important detail, but Helena wasn't surprised.

"How would I know that, Sergeant?"

"Because you built that studio especially for Mavis Chandry. I'm sure we can find who you paid to turn that outlet into a direct feed. The kettle's frayed cord would have tripped the GFCI outlets, but the dummy breaker allowed the power to flow until the spilled water shorted the entire system."

Brandt's eyes probed Helena's, searching for some sign of weakness or fear. She stared back, composed, with the slightest hint of a smile.

Brandt looked away first, then spoke more forcefully. "I hate saying so, but it was pretty smart to set the trap in a way you didn't have to be there. I'm on to you, though. Your alibi is toast."

Helena chuckled. "Sergeant, that is the stupidest thing I've ever heard. Why would I go to such lengths to kill someone who was donating a fortune in art to the museum?"

"I'm saving motive for your preliminary hearing. I've already contacted the DA and merely came to remind you not to leave town. I didn't like the way Quincy handled our meeting yesterday. If I say you don't leave town, you don't leave town."

"It's a lovely day, is it not?" Helena flashed her most radiant smile while glancing pointedly at her phone. "May I offer you something? A cup of coffee or tea?"

A brain transplant?

"You've got to be kidding." Brandt spat the words out.

Helena sat back in her chair. "Why are you really here, Sergeant? I find it intriguing and hardly a convincing demonstration of superior intellect that you're sharing information so readily. Aren't you concerned about a procedural misstep?"

Brandt's eyes grew wide. "Are you threatening me?"

Helena laughed out loud. "I'm doing nothing of the kind, just saying you are way out of line having this conversation with me in the first place. No professional law enforcement officer would say such things to a suspect. Where did you get your badge? The Dollar Store?"

Brandt started to rise, then thought better of it. Helena realized she was taking a risk by antagonizing him but found she was enjoying herself too much to stop.

Just what the doctor ordered, a dumb straight man for me to piss off. Some gals do yoga to work off stress. Give me an idiot like Brandt to sharpen my claws on any day. I'm feeling better already.

"All I'm saying is that I thought a legitimate murder investigation might involve a few more resources than a lone cowboy cop."

Brandt's mouth curved into a grotesque sneer as he struggled to keep his cool. The effect was like watching a poor imitation of Dirty Harry. Then, finally noticing Helena's cell phone where she'd prominently displayed it, Brandt calmed himself with visible effort.

"Detective Kline is on maternity leave. Her replacement starts in a few days. I'm perfectly capable of conducting an investigation until then."

Again, Helena looked pointedly at her phone. "Without a police chief or a detective in a town you moved to three months ago? Forgive me, but it seems a trifle cavalier."

Brandt turned purple. "Listen, you freak. You may think you're so smart, but where I come from, we don't put up with perverts like you. It's just a matter of time before I'll find enough evidence to lock you up, and that will be the end of your hifalutin', crazy ass. You heard it here first."

"Why take the trouble to warn me, Sergeant?" Helena was as calm as if she were talking to an old and trusted friend. "Surely a more seasoned professional would use tactics other than threats and intimidation?"

Brandt looked as though he might explode. "I'm telling you one last time, you're underestimating who you're dealing with. You may think you're above it all, but you'll be singing a different tune within the next twenty-four hours. That's a goddamn promise."

A stentorian voice, filling the room, interrupted Brandt's diatribe. "Mass General Laws, Part Four, Title One, Chapter Two Six Eight, Section Thirteen-B: 'Witness intimidation, shall be punishable by imprisonment in the state prison for not more than ten years.' You have ten seconds to get your sorry ass out of that chair, Brandt, and three minutes to leave the grounds."

The sergeant pivoted to see Quincy standing in the doorway, with Cole right behind him, arms crossed.

"You haven't got a thing on me!"

"Really?" Quincy said with a taut smile as he held up his phone. "Would you like me to play back what I've recorded?"

Brandt pushed past the two men and strode toward the exit. Helena followed.

"So long, darling, do come back to enjoy the exhibits when you're in a better mood," she yelled down the stairs as he stormed past a group of gawking visitors.

Returning to her friends, she said, "That was fun. Nothing like starting your first day at work by upsetting an officer of the law."

Quincy took Brandt's seat. "Look, Helena. Dan Andrade's willing to drag his feet on Brandt's arrest warrant, but he can't quash it without showing our hand. You won this round but be under no illusions; you're not out of the woods yet."

Helena's tone changed immediately. "You don't have to remind me, Quincy. This is reminder enough."

Reaching into her desk drawer, she removed the manila envelope, opened it, and handed him the threatening note.

Quincy put on his glasses to inspect it. "They put a comma in with a marker? Why didn't they just cut one out like the other letters?"

Helena laughed. "I did that, darling. If I'm to have my life threatened, I insist the threat be grammatically correct. As dear Lola used to say, 'Standards must be maintained at all times.'"

Quincy and Cole shook their heads. Helena caught their worried exchange and abandoned her bravado.

"I hear you. I really do."

Quincy looked into her eyes as he spoke, "I'm going to take this to Dan Andrade. It's only marginally a threat in legal terms because 'next' is vaguely defined. Still, there might be forensic evidence on the paper.

"I need to repeat this, Helena, to be certain you understand. It would be greatly appreciated if you were a little less reckless."

Helena lowered her gaze. "I hear you. I've had Afton add extra patrols of the grounds, and we're installing more security cameras." Then, unable to resist, she became the performer once again. "Whatever your retainer is, Quincy, darling, it's nowhere near enough," she said, using her Bette Davis voice.

"I can fix that," Quincy said, stroking his mustache to mask an involuntary grin. "But we've got a few other fish to fry first."

***

Two days passed in disquieting silence. The last event of opening week was a new donors' benefit for the Artisans' Fund at Elise and Gwen's Truro home. Two of the museum's earliest supporters, their expansive property was set high atop a cliff overlooking Fisher Beach. To the left, the dim lights of nearby houses reflected in the still water, while across the bay, the red beacons of three cell towers pierced the darkness, pale in comparison to the starlit sky above. To the right, Provincetown was a radiant necklace, the illuminated Pilgrim Monument its lavalliere, the night sky a black velvet backdrop.

Elise and Gwen had gone to considerable lengths to make their forty guests comfortable. Nearly fifteen thousand dollars was raised in the inevitable appeal.

Get the Guests

Helena was baffled to see Cheswick Wilks, Doctor Woodman, and Henry Boorstin in the crowd. None of them had been invited.

Wilks soon cornered Gwen and Elise, peering over his half-glasses and holding forth about his illustrious family. Doctor Woodman, round-faced and a bit too hearty, moved from group to group, eager for entrée. Once again, Henry Boorstin sought out Cole. Within a minute, the architect's index finger was accentuating whatever points he tried to make. None of the men acknowledged the other, and Boorstin left a room whenever Wilks or Woodman entered it. Watching them throughout the evening, Helena grew concerned.

All three attended the museum opening. Now, they're crashing this new donors' event. Wilks is trying to bully his way in. No doubt Woodman is in search of his "movers and shakers." But why the hell is Boorstin here? Is he trolling for clients? And I use the term "troll" advisedly.

After reviewing their paltry donations with Marc, Helena avoided the three men for as long as possible. They were gatecrashers who should not be encouraged. Helena remained uncharacteristically averse to Wilks, who had focused much of his time on one of the HomePort fellows. There was something predatory in the way Wilks hung on the student's every word, peering over his half-glasses with a hungry look.

***

As the evening wound down, Helena watched Mavis's departure with anxiety. Afton had informed her earlier that she had refused all offers of protection.

Seeing Wilks still had the young man in his clutches, Helena reluctantly decided a rescue was in order.

If I took a strong dislike to every older gay man that falls all over a young guy, I'd never get another donation. No, it's not that. There's something unsettling about Big Bird—a cold streak just below that simpering façade, visible only when he doesn't think anyone's looking. Well, no point prolonging the inevitable.

The Witching Hour

"Cheswick, darling, how nice to see you again." Helena summoned her most sincere tone while grabbing his hands to fend off a kiss. "Gwen just told me of your generous contribution. How can I ever adequately express my appreciation?"

Wilks puffed his chest and turned his attention away from the young man, who raced to the bar where a large drink—and a sympathetic bartender—awaited him.

"That's why I've been so eager to get to know you, Helena, dear," Wilks croaked. "My family, the Wilks of New York City—related to the Astors, don't you know, and Hetty Green, the 'Witch of Wall Street,' who was my great-great-aunt—have a long history of supporting worthy causes. Well, not so much Aunt Hetty, but her daughter, cousin Sylvia, did a hell of a lot of good with Hetty's millions when she finally inherited them. And Art is my passion—it's in my blood."

Unlike their last meeting, Wilks seemed to be making a significant effort. "I told that delectable young man I'd put in a kind word for him about a job at the museum. Surely you and I know each other well enough now that I can? He has excellent taste and a tremendous interest in antiquities. In fact, I've invited him to come and visit my collection. It's *so* important to support today's youth."

Helena struggled to keep a smile on her face.

No doubt he considers you an antiquity. I suppose, in the grand tradition of collectors such as yourself, you offered to show him your etchings. Of everything I hate most about begging for money, it's 'the witching hour' when the onion rings come out of the woodwork and circle like birds of prey. That's what's best about performing for an audience. The lights come up when the show's over, and everybody leaves. If the entire crowd tonight were like this guy, I'd have to set the house on fire to make my exit.

As Helena contemplated a retreat to the bar, a server delivered a Martini.

"Melody! Darling! I didn't realize you were here tonight." Relieved to see her, Helena ignored Wilks' hostile stare. "And how thoughtful of you to know what I needed just when I needed it most!"

"The bartender's been sending care packages to folks in the trenches," Melody whispered. "I've been in the kitchen most of the night. It sucks, but it pays."

"Oh, I hear you there. I did everything and its aunt when I was in your shoes. Everything legal, that is. Mr. Wilks, have you met Melody Carpenter? She's an extremely talented young musician and artist."

"I don't believe I have."

Wilks' glacial tone was at odds with the warmth he'd lavished on Helena just moments before. It was clear to her he saw no reason to waste time on someone so young, unimportant, and female.

So much for supporting today's youth.

Melody cleared her throat. "I'm sorry to interrupt you, Helena, but a young man came to the kitchen door asking for you."

"What did he say?"

"He needs to speak with you in private on the stairs to the beach. I thought you could take your drink and go out through the living room."

Wilks drained his glass. "Quelle drama and intrigue. A secret admirer, eh, Helena? Well, the party is breaking up, so I guess it's time for me to be on my way. I'll leave you to your gentleman caller then, my dear, and be in touch to arrange your visit."

Helena forced a taut smile. "Yes, of course. I'll look forward to it. Just call my assistant at the museum, and we'll set up a date."

When Hell freezes over.

Ill Met by Moonlight

As Wilks said a lengthy farewell to his hosts, Helena passed through the French doors to the ample terrace beyond. The waning moon cast a golden trail over the calm ocean, a vast pool of darkness with the slightest trace of a ripple where small waves hit two large rocks exposed by the outgoing tide.

There was still a small crowd of guests gathered on the terrace. As Henry Boorstin held forth on architectural trends of the 1840s, those near him looked as if rigor mortis had set in.

Using her cell phone to light her way, Helena took a swig of her Martini, then gingerly tottered down the steep stairs to a platform at the center of the span. Reaching it, she saw a man's shadow at its farthest corner. His back was to her as he scrolled images on his phone.

A chill overtook her.

Why does he want to see me all the way down here? Why couldn't we meet in the house or even the driveway? I don't like the feel of this.

As she drew close, the man heard the sound of her heels on the stairs and turned to face her.

"Wally! What is it that can't wait until morning?"

"I heard you'd be here tonight. My house is just up Fisher Road, so I came to tell you what's been going on."

His hands were shaking, his voice barely a whisper. Helena moved close to hear better.

"Do you know how the thieves got the access codes?"

"Yes. Somebody hacked the list on my phone. At least twice."

Helena's gaze followed the stairway back up to the terrace. She could hear the clatter of utensils being loaded into the catering van and the occasional bits of conversation between the staff.

My gut tells me we're in danger. We better make this quick.

Helena turned her attention back to Wally, whose voice had grown even softer. "I keep a spreadsheet on my phone with the access codes I assign after an alarm installation. Many business owners are dead in the water if they forget theirs, so giving it to them saves a ton of time."

"And somebody got hold of the list?" Helena asked, working hard to mask her incredulity.

Oh, Wally! How like you to try to be helpful and create a disaster instead.

"Yes. It took a bit of doing, but I had a trace waiting when the hackers returned. The IP address is in Eastern Russia."

"Russian hackers? Why would they bother with an alarm company in Provincetown?"

Wally nodded. "I know. It doesn't make a hell of a lot of sense. But my customers have had high-end works stolen—the kind the Russian Mob might use to launder money."

Helena softened her tone. "OK. That explains a lot. I'm glad to know you aren't involved in the thefts."

"Helena, I'd never. . ."

Despite the shadows that surrounded them, Helena could sense his mortification. "I know, Wally. But I must ask, who made you so nervous at the private view?"

Wally stammered, "I can't get into that. You've gotta trust me, Helena. You don't want to know who, or you'll be a target—like me."

Helena placed her hand firmly on his shoulder. "Look, Wally, I've not questioned your poor judgment, but I'm accused of murder and could be in jail by this time tomorrow. You've got to tell me all you know and then get some legal advice. Right away."

"Oh God, Helena. I'm so sorry. I thought it was just me he'd gotten his hooks into."

"Who? Who's gotten their hooks into you?"

A quizzical look crossed Wally's face, then he slumped onto her chest, blood oozing from his mouth. Helena dropped her drink. The glass shattered, spreading its shards as she lowered him to a nearby bench.

What do I do? If I start up the stairs, I could head right into more gunfire. But I don't have the medical skill to tend a wound like this.

Helena peered up at the house. There was no sign of anyone on the terrace.

He's not dying on my watch if I can help it.

Helena leaped over the broken glass, then kicked off her heels and ran up the stairs.

Halfway to the house, she met Melody running in her direction. "Helena, I heard a strange noise near the kitchen door. Did you hear it?"

"Wally Trieste has been shot and is bleeding from the mouth. We have to get help right away."

"I'll call an ambulance," Melody said without hesitation. "See to him until you hear me coming back, then make a run for it. I'll take over until the paramedics get here. Don't forget your shoes."

"But I'm a witness."

Melody grabbed Helena by the shoulders and shook her. "Look, Brandt is going to try to pin this on you. I just read the web article about the murder at HomePort. Freddie Chalmers quoted him as saying his prime suspect stood to benefit from Mavis Chandry's death."

"He said that? No sane officer would say something like that on the record."

"My point exactly," Melody said. "No sane officer. . . I've seen this guy at work. Now, go."

***

Helena returned to Wally, used her phone for light, tore the sleeves from her dress, and stanched the flow from his chest wound. Then, she sacrificed part of her skirt to secure the bandage.

Thank God I took the first aid intro when I worked at that camp in the Adirondacks. The bullet just missed his heart. I was standing so close to him, it's a miracle I wasn't hit. Were they after him—or me?

Helena heard Melody talking loudly to Gwen and Elise. "I heard this muffled pop. I went down to investigate and found a man who'd been shot. I'll go back to him. You guys call an ambulance and handle the guests. No one should leave."

Taking her cue, Helena grabbed her heels, crept down the stairs to the beach, and disappeared into the darkness. Rifling her handbag, she retrieved her phone and texted Cole and Marc

(Helena) *Danger. Leave now. Go right home.*

Don't stop no matter what you see or hear.

Don't answer this. I'll be in touch.

She shut off the phone and waited for the distinctive sound of Marc's Porsche. Then she set out along the base of the cliff toward the Fisher Beach parking lot. In the distance, she heard Gwen and Elise's agitated voices trying to calm the remaining guests.

On the Beach

The cliffs rose to more than eighty feet in some spots. Staying close to their base to avoid being seen, Helena stumbled over driftwood more than once as sand shifted beneath her bare feet. Illuminating her hands with her cell phone, she saw they were covered in blood.

She ran to the water's edge at a spot where the beach narrowed, bending low to avoid detection. There were few sounds but the occasional lapping of a wave against the shoreline as she tried to wash her hands and clothing. Under normal circumstances, the beautiful spot would have been enchanting. Instead, Helena caught herself cursing the moonlight.

The irony wasn't lost on her.

Ten minutes ago, I was at a cocktail party fending off onion rings. Now, here I am, wandering the beach in the torn remains of a dress, carrying my high heels like some shipwrecked broad from a B movie. There may even be a shooter out there somewhere. There simply has to be a better way for a gal to have a night out in this two-bit town.

Helena returned to the relative safety of the cliff. When she got within sight of the path to the parking lot, she spied a dark shape moving toward her. As she pressed against the base of the cliff, sharp blades of beach grass scratched her back and sleeveless arms. The shadow moved closer, and Helena dropped to the ground. The mysterious shape turned toward the water before stopping. Helena remained stretched out on the sand, face down.

After several minutes, the solitary figure rambled on. Helena rose to a crouch and scuttled along the beach like a wild animal. At last, she reached the path where Mavis Chandry chased C. J.. Creeping across its shifting sands, she heard the departing ambulance in the far distance.

At last, Helena reached Fisher Road. After a brief walk, she approached an old Cape nestled in a grove of oaks. The two-story house was painted white and had a pitched roof. A sizable, one-story ell protruded from the back of the building. There was a large, shingled studio with a wall of glass in a hollow behind the house. Beside it was an ancient oak tree.

Seeing a dim glow from the ell, Helena pounded on the back door. It opened a crack, and Mavis Chandry peered out into the darkness, a vintage shotgun in her hands.

When she saw Helena, she took a step back, "You! I just saw you at Elise and Gwen's. What do you have to tell me at this time of night? You look a fright! What on earth is wrong?"

Helena, covered in sand and blood, took a moment to calm herself. "After you left, someone shot Wally Trieste. I don't know if he was the intended target—or I was. The police will know I was there, and Brandt has as much as accused me of killing C.J.. You've got to let me in. I've nowhere else to go."

Mavis, looking squat and immovable, took time to answer. When she did, her effusive response was the last thing Helena expected.

"Get the hell in here, you." Mavis's rugged face was bright with excitement. "Glad you came to me. What's your poison? Bourbon or Gin? We've got a long night ahead of us. And a lot of ground to cover."

Sanctuary

Mavis's home was a classic Cape Cod saltbox, with wood-paneled walls and a narrow staircase that made a sharp turn to the left before ascending to the second floor. A fire glowed brightly in a fireplace equipped with its original cast-iron cauldron, sending flickering light across the room. The firelight partially illuminated wide plank floors and wainscoting while leaving the upper part of the room in shadow. Time seemed irrelevant inside this snug refuge that had housed countless generations for nearly three hundred years.

Mavis waited while Helena cleaned up and changed into the pair of jeans and pullover she'd provided. Then, pointing her to a wingback chair and handing her a large tumbler of Scotch, Mavis said, "OK. Pull yourself together and tell me everything that happened. Don't leave anything out."

Helena recounted the events of the evening, including how Melody came to her aid and insisted she leave the scene. "I'm sure Brandt will be looking for me once it's light, if not before."

Mavis downed half her drink in a single gulp. "Brandt's a fool. Technically, this is a Truro investigation, though the two forces often work together. Doesn't matter. You're already the prime suspect based on the interview with him that Freddie posted on the *Free Press* website. He's going to go after you for her death and this shooting. The thieves used your code for the museum break-in, and Wally installed the alarm system. Brandt will make hay out of all that."

Helena heaved a sigh. "Which means I've got to get back to Provincetown. Cole and Marc will back me up if I ask them to and say we went home together. I can tell Brandt I dropped my glass earlier in the evening if he finds fingerprints on it."

"You shouldn't use your phone," Mavis said. "Brandt might get the records. Which of the guys do you want me to contact?"

Helena set down her Scotch. "Damn. I just remembered. I texted Cole and Marc and told them to leave right away. Brandt will find that message if he subpoenas my phone records. He's probably put in a request already."

Mavis didn't hesitate. "Then it might make sense for you to stay here for a while. I doubt the police will think of looking for you at my house, given the battles we've had in front of them."

Helena thought for a moment. "I've got an idea. Call Charlotte Grubb. You met her at the museum opening—the stock market wizard with the handsome husband. She was Lola Staunton's financial adviser."

Mavis grinned. "I remember her. Quite the powerhouse. Not bad to look at, either."

"She's an amazing organizer. She'll figure out what to do and communicate with everyone else. Brandt doesn't know her, so it's unlikely he'll monitor her calls."

Helena dictated the number to Mavis, who promptly dialed it on her rotary phone. When Charlotte answered, Mavis said, "We need you folks to figure a way to get Helena from Truro back to Provincetown early tomorrow morning without being seen. Got it?"

Charlotte must have understood, for Mavis said, "Good. Perfect. Call me at this number when you've figured out the details. And let me know how I can help. Yes. Yes, I do. Of course, I would. Goodnight."

Mavis set down her phone and picked up her drink. "Well, Helena. You're right. She's smart as a whip and putting her mind to it. Nothing will happen until tomorrow morning at the earliest."

Helena shifted in her chair. "I can't begin to thank you. Not sure if I'm ready to sleep yet, if you don't mind. I really appreciate—"

Mavis held up both hands. "Don't go all weepy on me. I hate that shit. Nobody does anything like that to any friend of mine and gets away with it. I never should have doubted you, but from now on, trust me, we're on the same team."

Rising from her chair, Helena studied the artist, who, in the flickering firelight, seemed so solid, righteous, and determined. She kissed Mavis on the cheek and was pleased to see a thin smile cross her lips.

As Helena warmed herself next to the fire, they talked intermittently about topics of little consequence, intentionally avoiding the events of the evening and the day before. The cozy old house kept the world's ugliness at bay as Helena's pounding heart slowed and her thoughts regained their equilibrium.

When she yawned contentedly, Mavis was quick to notice. "Nothin' like a good bit of shut-eye before a big day. The guest room is upstairs, second door on the left. There's a flannel nightgown under the pillow. Not too glamorous, I'm afraid, but I didn't know you'd be dropping in unannounced. I'll guard the fort while you get your beauty rest. I suspect you're gonna need it."

The Great Race

Mavis shook Helena awake at four in the morning. "Hurry up. Your friends have figured out how to get you out of here with no one the wiser. We don't have too much time before daylight. Here's what we're gonna do. . ."

Within minutes, Helena was walking Fisher Road toward the beach. Once there, she turned right and sauntered to a seawall at the mouth of Pamet Harbor. Clad in one of Mavis's old sweatshirts and a pair of jeans held up with a piece of rope, she looked like a local eccentric out to watch the sunrise. Helena clambered over the stone revetment to a hidden patch of sand facing the harbor. Several minutes later, a small motorboat appeared with Mavis at the wheel. She expertly beached it a few feet from where Helena stood.

"Tide's ebbing, so there'll be no difficulty getting out."

"Out where?" Helena asked.

"Lie down so no one sees you. I'll tell you once we clear the harbor."

Helena climbed on board. Mavis backed off the beach, steered through the narrow channel, then opened up the engine to full throttle. Helena, still stretched out on the boat's floor, could feel the bump of the waves and see the spray behind her. Looking straight up, she saw nothing but darkness.

In minutes, they were a half-mile offshore, and Mavis yelled, "You can sit up now."

"Where are you taking me?" Helena asked, barely making herself heard over the engine's roar.

"We're going to check my lobster pots over by Long Point," Mavis said, laughing, her white hair blowing in the breeze. "At least that's the official story. Ah! There she is. Right on time."

By the Dawn's Early Light

Helena spied the navigation lights of a boat leaving Fisherman's Wharf. The shape was too long for a trawler, and the illuminated masthead indicated a sailing vessel. As first light struck the water, Helena saw the vessel was towing a blue powerboat.

"*Dame Edna*!" Helena yelled as the sunrise illuminated the polished black hull of her beloved yacht. "Brilliant! I can hide out on her until the race starts!"

She teared up as if seeing a long-lost friend.

"Charlotte knew you'd never forfeit the race," Mavis said. "So she and the boys decided to hide you on board. If no one saw us leaving the harbor, you should be OK for a few more hours. But only a few."

In ten minutes, they'd reached Long Point and were alongside *Dame Edna*. When Helena climbed aboard, Cole, Charlotte, and her husband, Brad, clustered around her. Marc remained at the helm, guiding the vessel through a maze of buoys marking the lobster traps below. Mavis gunned the engine, and Helena blew her a kiss, which was acknowledged with a terse nod. Then the artist raced to a cluster of nearby buoys marked by a cerulean band.

Turning to Helena, Marc said, "I figured we'd head out past Race Point. The fewer who see us, the better."

Helena gave two thumbs up.

"We'll stay offshore until just before the starting gun," Cole said. "Brandt will assume you're still holed up in Truro somewhere. That should buy us the time we need for the race. Then we'll get you out of town."

"For now, let's get you below," Charlotte insisted, decisive as always. "Then you can tell us what the hell happened last night, and we can plan our next moves."

Once in the salon, Helena allowed herself to relax in the familiarity of one of her favorite spots.

Cole stepped behind her to rub her tense shoulders. "Have to say I'd never thought I'd see you with a rope belt as an accessory, Helena. The last person to attempt it was Ellie Mae Clampett on *The Beverly Hillbillies*."

Helena laughed, relieved to be back on *Dame Edna*. The salon, with its teak walls and brightly covered seating, displayed two of Cole's paintings. A brass oil lamp hung from gimbals on the port wall. Across from her, a built-in bookcase held many of her favorite books. The space, lit by portholes and three partially open hatches, felt contained, safe, and exquisitely comforting. More and more, it seemed, *Dame Edna* was what HomePort had been until recently—the place where she could be herself. And right now, there was no better place in the world to be.

Charlotte may have been Lola's financial adviser, but her role in this group of friends fell somewhere between governess and moral compass. Appropriately dressed in white boat shoes, white slacks, and a blue blouse, Charlotte seemed even more self-possessed than usual.

Helena spoke directly to her. "I don't know if it was an actual setup, but I was this close to finding out who Wally Trieste was afraid of."

She described Wally's misguided effort to help his customers, how he was shot and toppled onto her, and how Melody and Mavis helped her escape.

Helena ended by asking, "What have you heard about his condition?"

"Shirley-Mae's monitoring the scanner back at the house," Cole replied. "The details were sketchy. She heard they were taking someone to Cape Cod Hospital, but there was nothing more before we came out here."

"Brandt will have controlled all information once he got involved. I've no doubt of that," Helena said. "Now, listen up, boys and girls; we've got a lot of work to do before the race. First, I've got a few calls to make. Charlotte, will you lend me your phone? I shouldn't use mine. After that, I want to talk to Marc, Cole, and Brad about some adjustments to our racing strategy."

***

Two hours later, Charlotte and Brad cast off from *Dame Edna* in the small, blue motorboat. Brad was transfixed as he watched the yacht recede into the distance. Helena was putting Marc and Cole through their paces in preparation for the race. The Dame was heeling to port in the breeze, which had strengthened to eighteen knots. A pod of dolphins frolicked off her bow. Some rode ahead of the bow wave, using displaced water to propel themselves. Others breached near the wake that foamed on each side.

The vessel was on a broad reach, her purple sails filled, sunlight reflecting a rich gold off her varnished brightwork. As she heeled, her white waterline offset the darkness of her hull. A flag bearing the compass rose flew from the top of her main mast and from the mizzen, a large gay flag, vivid and celebratory. An enormous American flag fluttered from her stern. *Dame Edna* was a sleek and elegant empress of the sea, breathtakingly beautiful in the morning light.

Brad roused himself from his reverie. "I could stare at her all day, but there'll be plenty of time to see her in action once we get the racing marks in place. I don't want the committee to think we're not doing our job. Especially today."

"I don't know whether I should be jealous," Charlotte said, putting her arm around him. "I think Helena's right when she said *Dame Edna* is your 'other woman.'"

Brad hugged his wife, then looked at his phone. The coordinates had just arrived from the race committee. He steered toward Truro to set out the marks—yellow, inflatable tetrahedrons that could be seen for miles.

The Last Leg

Five minutes before the starting gun, *Dame Edna* rounded Long Point. Helena was at the wheel in a white sailor's top with navy-blue piping and black leggings. A large blue bow spanned her enormous breasts, and she sported a jaunty sailor's cap.

Onboard *Tough Cookie*, Betty wore an old-fashioned polka-dot bathing dress replete with pantaloons and an enormous sun hat with a length of polka-dot ribbon flowing from behind.

Betty's yacht, a sixty-foot Hanse sloop, was a sleek racing machine. Its white hull glistened in the light while its tan deck accentuated the yacht's low profile. Portholes just above the waterline looked like cannon mounts on an old frigate—gaping black maws that could strike a lethal blow. Betty had softened the boat's military appearance by trailing large pieces of polka-dot fabric from the aft stays. The result was slightly off-kilter—much as if festive streamers trailed a fighter jet.

The crowd was enjoying the sight as *Tough Cookie* tacked back and forth behind the starting line. The *Provincetown II*, a large flotilla of smaller craft, and two whale-watch boats had assembled to view what had been billed as the "nautical drag race of the century." When *Dame Edna* came into view, loud cheers were augmented by the raucous sound of boat horns.

The first mark was halfway between Long Point and Wellfleet, while the second was near the mouth of the Pamet River. The third was in deep water off North Truro, and the finish line was back at Long Point. The winds were brisk from the south, running at twenty-four knots, which worked to both yachts' advantage.

In an expert display of seamanship, *Dame Edna* crossed the starting line just as the starting gun fired. *Tough Cookie* compensated for a slower crossing and drew close to the Dame halfway to the second mark. Helena maintained a decent lead and rounded that mark with ease, coming about and setting her sails with surprising ability. *Tough Cookie*, with a more seasoned sailor at the helm, made an impressive tack, which allowed her to draw closer to the Dame. Approaching the North Truro mark, *Tough Cookie* was just off *Dame Edna's* stern and gaining. The Committee Boat followed nearby while the other vessels watched from a respectful distance.

Provincetown was in clear sight as the yachts approached the third mark. Cole saw several flashing red lights on MacMillan Pier, as well as the rotating blue lights of the Harbormaster's Boat, which was just clearing the mooring field. He tapped Helena's shoulder and pointed. She nodded but said nothing, hands gripping the helm, eyes scanning the horizon.

In minutes, the two yachts were in close proximity, heeling to port in the strong breeze. As Helena approached the third mark, *Tough Cookie* overtook her to windward, stealing *Dame Edna's* wind. The Dame slowed and quickly righted herself only fifty feet from the mark.

Helena yielded the helm to Cole and raced to the bow. Standing on the pulpit, she tore open her blouse, exposing enormous false breasts, and shrieked, "Buoy Room!"

As fast as it had crowded *Dame Edna*, the *Tough Cookie* headed into the wind, coming to a complete stop. With the strong breeze no longer blocked, the Dame heeled hard to port. Helena was suspended in mid-air for an instant, then landed in the water with a tremendous splash.

Marc yelled, "Man overboard," as Cole, at the helm, hit the MOB button to flag their exact location. Then *Dame Edna* headed into the wind alongside *Tough Cookie*.

The spectator boats raced to the spot. One of Betty's crew quickly donned a wetsuit, snorkel, and fins, then dove into the water. Three scuba divers from a nearby charter dropped a diver below flag and followed him.

There was no sign of Helena other than her life breasts, the blouse with its scarf still attached, and her sailor's cap. When the snorkeler reached them, he dove beneath the surface as arriving vessels formed a protective circle around the search area, their engines idling.

A tense silence reigned as scores of anxious people scanned the waves. The Harbormaster's Boat approached, and Sergeant Brandt's authoritarian tones blared over a loudspeaker. "Prepare for boarding."

"Approach with caution. We've got a man overboard," Cole yelled as Marc used the electric winches to furl the sails.

"All other vessels, stand clear," was the only response as the Harbormaster's Boat drew alongside.

Brandt hesitated before making the jump to *Dame Edna.* His right foot landed outside the coaming. Marc grabbed him by both arms and pulled him into the cockpit. The sergeant looked flustered and green. As two others boarded, his arrogance quickly returned.

"Where is he?" Brant demanded.

"That's what I'm trying to tell you," Marc said, struggling to control his irritation. "*She* fell overboard."

"It's a goddamn trick," the sergeant sputtered, turning to Officer Chase and a trim woman Marc had never seen before. "You two. Search this entire boat. Now."

The woman had dark black hair and a muscular build. She wore jeans, boat shoes, and a brown sweatshirt. Unlike the two men, the mysterious woman seemed comfortable on board.

Officer Chase raced to *Dame Edna's* bow, where he stood clutching the forward stay, seeming unsure what to do next. The woman surveyed the cockpit, then went below, asking Cole to accompany her. Cole yielded the helm to Marc and followed.

Brad, who had been part of the spectator fleet, idled his blue motorboat near the third mark. He, Charlotte, and the others on board peered into the water, only to be driven off by another command from Brandt.

"All unauthorized vessels leave the area at once or face arrest."

The Committee Boat drew alongside.

The sergeant waved them off until the woman, who had just climbed up the companionway, said, "The race officials are on that boat. I'd suggest letting them stay. They'll have been observing everything up close."

Brandt said nothing as a Coast Guard Fast Response Boat, lights flashing, joined the cluster of vessels just above the mark. Two divers with wetsuits, masks, and oxygen tanks tipped into the ocean before the FRB was fully stopped.

"The Coast Guard will conduct the search from this point on," a bullhorn blared. "All other vessels, get your people out of the water."

The snorkeler swam to *Tough Cookie* and climbed the boarding ladder. A diver who surfaced was informed his team should return to their vessel.

Jumping onto the Harbormaster's Boat, Brandt took to the microphone again. "Crews of the two sailboats and the guy in the blue powerboat report to officers stationed at Fisherman's Wharf."

Most vessels remained at the site, but Brad steered his blue powerboat westward, pulling up to the dinghy dock at Captain Jack's Wharf. He stayed for only a moment to offload Charlotte and their two guests, then returned to Fisherman's Wharf just as *Dame Edna* arrived.

Rule Eighteen

A police officer escorted Brad and both crews to the captains' lounge. The marina's outdoor space had several Adirondack chairs, a fire pit, and a view over MacMillan Pier. The sailors conversed among themselves while waiting for Sergeant Brandt and his officers. Their tone was subdued, with none of the usual post-race camaraderie.

Clutching a sheaf of papers, Sergeant Brandt stepped up to a makeshift podium and addressed the group. "The Coast Guard has just informed me they've curtailed the search until tomorrow due to high winds, strong currents, and poor visibility. That's their public position—but I believe they share my opinion there will be nothing to find.

The individual who jumped overboard is a person of interest in a murder investigation and a related shooting. Said individual may have avoided us for now, but I can assure you that's only temporary. There's something you all need to understand. Once the DA files charges, the individual that calls himself—"

"*Herself,*" Cole said, staring at Brandt.

"Whatever, yet again," Brandt snarled, not taking his eyes off Cole. "Once charges are filed, this *person* becomes a fugitive in a murder investigation. Those of you taking part in this so-called race could be material witnesses. And any of you who helped this *person* escape will be considered accomplices. Is that understood?"

The men exchanged incredulous glances.

"I want to start with the crew of the, ah. . ." The woman who boarded *Dame Edna* whispered something to Brandt, then he continued, "the *Tough Cookie*. Please stand over here."

He pointed to a spot just past the fire pit.

"I can't believe she's gone," Marc said, clutching Cole's hand as they watched Betty and his crew saunter past.

"Me neither," his husband replied, wiping away a tear as Brandt stared at their entwined fingers.

Just then, Quincy Stilwell entered the enclosure, and the sergeant yelled, "Quincy, get lost. This doesn't concern you."

"It most certainly does, Brandt. Mr. Crocker is a client entitled to my presence during an interview, as are Messrs. Hanson and Nugent."

When Betty, still in the antique bathing costume, blew his lawyer a kiss, Brandt threw his papers in the air. "Damn it, Quincy. Have you got this entire town sewed up?"

"My business is not at issue, Brandt. I'm here should my clients need my advice. Please proceed with your interview or let them leave."

"So let me see if I understand." Brandt turned back to the crew of the *Tough Cookie*. "You were alongside the other boat."

"Upwind from the other vessel," Betty said imperiously, looking dignified despite the veiled sunhat and pantaloons.

Brandt heaved a sigh. "Upwind from the other vessel. And then you pulled away. Why was that?"

"Rule eighteen. The windward vessel must yield."

"Windward? What?" Brandt reddened. "Just tell me why you backed off before the jump."

"Helena didn't jump, Sergeant. She fell overboard when my yacht no longer stole her wind."

"Stole her what?"

Betty frowned. "Sergeant, let me use that whiteboard in the office over there to explain, or we'll be here forever. I've got a massage at five-thirty I simply can't miss."

Brandt rubbed his brow, then nodded. Two officers pulled a portable whiteboard into the enclosure. Betty drew the mark and the two yachts' relative positions, then drew an arrow to show the wind direction.

"I was above *Dame Edna* and blocking most of her wind as she approached the third mark. When Helena ran to the bow and yelled, 'buoy room,' she was under her rights according to rule eighteen. That meant she was signaling a risk of collision with the mark unless my boat changed course. I headed upwind to slow my momentum. When I did so, *Dame Edna* got the full brunt of the breeze and heeled to thirty-five degrees."

Brandt looked so befuddled it was hard for the sailors in the room not to laugh. "Heeled?"

"She tipped to port as the wind I'd been blocking hit her sails."

"She who? What port?"

"*Dame Edna.* When the wind hit after I turned away, the yacht tipped to the left. The rapid movement appears to have tossed Helena overboard."

"So you're trying to tell me the individual in question didn't jump?"

"Sergeant, if I may have a word?" Quincy asked.

"You're going to anyway, so what is it this time?"

"I've sailed for over sixty years, so I know what he's trying to say. I urge you to consider the forces in play: The boats were competing in close quarters in a strong breeze. They were about to round a mark when Betty's yacht crowded *Dame Edna* to the extent that she couldn't get past the mark without hitting it. He was also blocking *Dame Edna*'s wind, which meant she wasn't tipping. When Betty pulled up to allow enough room, the wind was no longer blocked and hit *Dame Edna* full force. She tipped way over, and the momentum tossed Helena off the deck.

"No one could plan for something like this. There were two different crews, two different boats, and the Race Committee was nearby. Jack Mullins called me, which is why I'm here. He saw it all from the Committee Boat and said it was an unfortunate accident, nothing more."

Brandt reddened. "Jack Mullins? *Congressman* Jack Mullins?"

"Yes," Quincy said. "He was a guest of Dan Andrade's on the Committee Boat. They're both avid sailors and have a long history of racing all around the Cape. I can ask him to explain things to you, Brandt, but he's already told me everything went according to the rules."

"Nobody told me the DA witnessed anything. Where is he?"

"I'm not sure now, Sir," Officer Chase said. "You didn't ask me to sequester the Committee Boat."

Brandt slammed his fist on the podium, took a deep breath, and started again.

"But *she*," Brandt said, beckoning Cole and Marc to where he stood, "had a lifejacket on, right?"

"After a fashion. It was a vest of her own design," Cole said, making no effort to hide his hostility. "It seems to have come undone when she hit the water."

"So when she went overboard, what did you do?"

"I headed into the wind," Cole said.

"What?"

"I stopped the boat so we could look for Helena."

"And you?" Brandt pointed at Betty.

"I stayed where I was. It's standard procedure for a MOB situation." Betty delivered each initial slowly, as if talking to a child.

"MOB?"

"Man overboard."

"And I suited up and went in," said the crew member who had snorkeled to the mark. Again Brandt looked puzzled, so the man tried to clarify. "I'm a certified diver. If she were unconscious and couldn't make it to the surface, I could have helped her, but it's over eighty feet deep with a strong current out there. I couldn't see to the bottom. I only found traces of her—the vest, the hat, and the blouse floating on the surface. When the Coast Guard ordered everyone to leave the water, I went back to my boat."

"How did you happen to have scuba gear on board?" Brandt asked, his eyes narrowing.

"Most large boats carry dive equipment in case they get entangled in fishing gear or need emergency maintenance below the waterline."

"And you?" Brandt said, summoning Brad. "You were in the blue powerboat, right?"

"Yes." Brad's handsome features gave nothing away.

"You came awfully close to the scene. Why?"

"Helena's one of my dearest friends. I was watching the race, saw her fall overboard, and came over hoping to find her."

"What did you see in the water?"

"Her life vest, her hat, and her blouse. Nothing more."

Brandt's withering glare swept the room. "Thanks for nothing. All of you. I'll tell you right now, if I find any of you are lying to me, there'll be hell to pay. Don't leave town and call me at once if you see or hear anything from this Helena person."

He strode from the enclosure with Officer Chase close behind.

"Gentlemen, after that childish display of unprofessionalism, I think a drink is called for," Quincy said, summoning a server. "I'm sure Helena would have appreciated your efforts on her behalf."

When the drinks were served, Quincy said, "A toast. To Helena."

"To Helena!" the group responded, then a heavy silence overtook them.

Drag Net

Brandt doubled the police presence on Commercial Street and stationed surveillance outside HomePort. As word of Helena's disappearance made its way around town, two factions soon emerged: a small group who mourned Helena's death and a significant majority who were confident she was in hiding.

"She's a master of disguise," one queen told another outside the Post Office. "For all we know, she could be standing in line inside."

His friend grinned. "Or even behind the counter. I'm not giving up on Helena yet."

***

A day passed. Then two. Mavis Chandry refused to see visitors or accept phone calls. When she spied Marc and Cole outside her studio, she insisted they leave, claiming she was hard at work. Dolores went about her duties in somber silence, while Shirley-Mae never left HomePort. Concerned Brandt might have bugged their homes and phones, the friends' important conversations took place as they walked the estate's extensive grounds.

"Never underestimate Helena," Shirley said one night when the group had gathered for dinner at Charlotte's house. "If she went into hiding, you can be sure it's for a damn good reason. I always had one."

Her observation was met with uncharacteristic silence.

Road Show

By Wednesday afternoon, Melody had heard that Helena was missing, presumed dead.

She's probably in Europe by now. Why would someone with her money hang around? Just as I was getting to know and like her. It's too damn bad.

Let Me Entertain You

Melody strummed her autoharp listlessly and stared out onto the street as people passed in front of the venerable town hall with its varnished oak doors and soaring clock tower. Tourist trolleys departed on schedule, their drivers reciting their scripts while trying to mask their boredom. The smell of fried food wafted from restaurants on the far side of Commercial Street.

Melody had no appetite for any of it. The passing crowd seemed endless, but no one stopped to listen. She was about to give up for the day when a gangly young woman wearing a plain black sweater with a white collar and a knee-length black skirt sauntered over to where she sat. The woman had dark eyebrows, a pale, white face, and long black braids that fell over her shoulders. Melody's first impression was of a taller version of Wednesday from *The Addams Family.*

"How's business?" Wednesday asked.

"It sucks," Melody replied. "Nobody's bothering to listen, but I can't say I blame them. I'm not that into it today."

"What's wrong, hon? You look like you lost your best friend."

"Not quite, but close enough."

Wednesday offered a tight smile. "Maybe you should play some livelier music to cheer yourself up."

Melody stared at her empty tip hat. "It won't make any difference. These people are zombies."

Wednesday's smile grew wider. "Wanna bet?"

"Sure. How much?"

"Half the take—if you let me sing with you."

"Do you have a performer's license? I'll lose mine if you don't."

"Yes, I do."

"Let me see it."

"Here."

Wednesday pulled a laminated card from her hip pocket. Melody looked at the license, then at Wednesday, whose warm smile was comically at odds with her grim costume.

"Your name is Harold?"

"My parents wanted a boy."

Melody shrugged. "Whatever. I'm not pulling them in today. Might as well give it a try. What do you want to sing?"

"'Let Me Entertain You' from 'Gypsy.' It's straightforward: G major, A minor, D seven."

"I can play anything by ear."

Wednesday turned to face Commercial Street. "Fabulous. Let 'er rip."

"I don't have a mic other than the one for the autoharp."

"That won't be a problem. You'll see."

The crowd had swelled to more than forty people before the first chorus was complete. By the time the song ended, that number had doubled. Cheers, sustained applause, and cries for an encore stopped passing traffic. The tip hat came back three-quarters full.

"Wow! You're good," Melody said, not quite believing what had just transpired.

Wednesday stared down at her black shoes. "A bit rusty, I'm afraid."

"If that's rusty, I can't imagine what top form looks like."

Wednesday patted Melody's arm. "We make an excellent team. Stick around and find out."

"Deal. My time is up, though. I should start packing."

Just then, Dolores Delgado, in a black trench coat that covered her uniform, made her way through the audience, strode toward the two performers, and dropped several bills into the hat. Wednesday surreptitiously turned off the mic as Dolores blended back onto the crowded street as quickly as she'd appeared.

Melody retrieved the bundle of bills and counted it at once. "Oh my God! That woman left over six thousand dollars!"

"How kind of her," Wednesday said. "She must really like Styne and Sondheim."

Melody grabbed Wednesday's arm. "OK. What's going on here? Are you laundering money or something?"

"Whatever gave you that idea?"

"This never happens. That woman's not a tourist. She's an old Portuguese lady with baggy nylons—not somebody off a yacht or something."

"Darling, keep your voice down! We shouldn't draw attention to ourselves with this kind of money around. Let's go somewhere quiet where we can talk."

Melody stared for a moment. "Helena. . . Tell me what's going on. Right now!"

"Shush! Let's go over to Bradford Street, get up on the roof deck, and divvy up the take. I promise I'll explain the whole damn mess."

Behind the Facade

Melody's questions began in earnest once they reached Buskerville Hall. Helena played down her escape from Truro, which was easy since

Melody was much more interested in the alleged boating accident. She repeatedly asked for more details than Helena wanted to provide.

At last, she gave in. "It's not as much of a mystery as you might think, darling. Before Butch and I got married, he insisted I take scuba lessons. I'd always loved to swim, and he wanted me to go diving with him on our honeymoon. We keep gear on *Dame Edna* for emergencies or to dive a wreck, so everything was already on board.

"Charlotte and Brad always lay out the course for the races. When he set the third mark, Brad tied my tank, flippers, and mask ten feet down on the mooring line. I had a wetsuit under my outfit. When I jumped overboard, it was simple enough to make my way down the rope, put on the mask, jam the regulator into my mouth, and pull on the oxygen tank. The fins were a little trickier. I almost lost one, but I got it on, eventually.

Melody was wide-eyed. "How did you get to shore?"

"I called in a favor from Hank at Outermost Divers and arranged to masquerade as one of his crew. Sergeant Brandt had no way of knowing how many divers were underwater, so I surfaced and went ashore with them when he ordered them out of the water."

Melody was insatiable. "But what about the Coast Guard? I heard their divers responded. Didn't they see you?"

Helena shook her head. "Darling, I trust you; otherwise, I wouldn't have told you this much, but I'm afraid I can't talk about that part. At least, not yet."

"OK, Helena. I know you love being a woman of mystery. I don't know if I could have done what you did."

"With the right training, you would have. Don't underestimate yourself. Though I have to say, I've had better gigs than hanging from a rope thirty feet underwater, hoping someone would signal that I could surface. Even the time the DAR booked me by mistake was better than that."

Hoping to change the subject, Helena surveyed the harbor. On the horizon, vivid colors were growing in intensity as sunset approached. To the east, windows reflected what the locals called "Truro Fire."

"I've always loved the view from here."

Melody was not to be put off. "Tell me something."

"Yes?"

"I can't figure out why—with all your money—you didn't just get away while you could. Instead, you're cracking jokes and acting as if you don't have a care in the world. How can you do that?"

"My dear," Helena said in the tone of a grand dowager who sounded just like Lola, "Whatever can you mean?"

"I'm serious, Helena. From what I see, you're in a colossal mess, yet you're acting like your biggest problem is a broken nail."

"Broken nails can be devastating. I remember once—"

"Helena!"

"Oh. All right. All right. It's like this, darling: For as long as I can remember, I've felt safer being anyone other than me. I got really good at it. I always thought clothes were more like armor than anything else. I've never told anyone this, but when I do drag, the person I really am, Harold Blithe, ceases to exist. Not only do I assume the style and mannerisms of the character I'm impersonating, I adopt the personality as well—the thoughts, the reactions, and, sometimes, even the memories. It's as if I write a book inside my head then step into its pages."

Melody looked puzzled, so Helena gave an example. "Take the museum gala the other night. I had multiple interviews and tons of schmoozing to do, even though I'd found a body, and that idiot, Brandt, had practically accused me of murder. I convinced myself the dress and diamonds were a shield, reflecting negativity back on whoever might project it onto me. For the night, I was an invincible artistic diva. And I became the glamorous, successful museum director I needed to be. Does that make more sense?

Melody still seemed perplexed. "To an extent. Are you saying the gorgeous professional woman I met that night was not you?"

Helena wiped her hand across her brow. "Darling, I'm always someone else—it's my superpower."

"Is that what you're doing now?"

"There's some of that, though not a lot because I trust you. I do use snide remarks to keep myself up to snuff, though. Humor and camp help me cope better than anything else."

"So you're saying you compartmentalize your problems."

"Melody, my dear," Helena said, adopting the matronly tone once more, "when I become someone else, I'm not compartmentalizing. I get so into the role the person I really am disappears. That's the whole point. Otherwise, I'd be stuck with myself and paralyzed with fear of what people might think of me. I could never have done those interviews as myself."

Melody's tone grew gentle. "But why, Helena? Everyone loves you. Don't you see that?"

"Not everyone, darling. Besides, Helena may be me, but she's not the *real* me. I could tell you stories about Harold's mother and her boyfriend—what he did to Harold and what she let him get away with—that would curl your hair.

"Let's move on to a more pleasant topic. I haven't revealed this much since I had a wardrobe malfunction during the Esther Williams Festival at Herring Cove. I was playing Little Edie Beale at the Country Club and dove off the boat in a cloche number only to end up as naked as the day I was born—"

"Helena!"

"OK. OK. Thanks for your concern, darling, but I've already said much more than I should. Let's talk about this place for a bit. I used to do my best thinking up here, staring out over Long Point, just watching the waves."

Melody sighed. "It's a shame those days are coming to an end. I'm going to miss this."

Helena sat upright. "What are you saying? Are you planning to leave town? You simply can't!"

"No. The owner has put the house up for sale, and the potential buyer is a developer who wants to turn it into condos."

"Oh, no. Not another wonderful old place sacrificed to greed and ignorance."

Melody nodded. "With Airbnb, investors make a lot more money than running a guest house or doing yearly rentals. Before long, there won't be a place someone like me can afford to rent."

Helena rapped her fist on a nearby table. "That makes me sick. People don't realize it's the mix of humanity that makes this town unique, say nothing of keeping it running. Who's the developer?"

"The clown next door. Doctor Woodman."

"The Tinman?"

"Huh?" Melody said, her face registering confusion.

Helena put her hand to her brow. "Oh dear, you've caught me at it again. You know how I make up names for people I don't like? That's my name for him. He seems to think I'm the key to improving his dreary social life. Is he an actual doctor?"

"Yeah. A proctologist. He flies his plane up from New Jersey on weekends. We call him 'the Flying Asshole.'"

Helena laughed. "I should be more careful. I'm taking flying lessons, and I shudder to think what my name might be."

Melody grinned. "You should see his architect. The guy made me sick, wandering about, measuring for a pool and jacuzzi, talking about making room for high-end appliances and walk-in wine cellars. He said each unit could go for two million dollars. And he kept wagging his finger and laughing like a mad scientist from some horror film."

Helena held her hands to her face like a silent film actress. "Oh no, not Henry Boorstin! He's nuts."

Melody shrugged. "I don't know his name, just that he was weird, short, and stooped, with a buzz cut and an enormous nose. He looks like a garden gnome."

Helena laughed. "That's Boorstin, all right. He's responsible for more damage to this town than anyone else in its history. Everything he designs is the same: uninspired and suburban. I've always called his style 'early Pepperidge Farm.'"

Helena began to pace. "What a travesty! As Empress Livia allegedly said, 'That child should have been exposed at birth.' Boorstin always finds a way to get around the rules. Of course, people have the right to buy a property and make it the way they want. But people should also have the opportunity to remain in a town they love, and Boorstin is partially responsible for driving them out. It's all money, money, and more money with him. I wish something could be done to save this old place. It allowed me to stay on in Provincetown when I had next to nothing."

Melody lowered her voice. "We've started a resistance group."

Helena took a long, satisfying sip of her Martini, her left pinky extended. "That sounds promising. May I join? What's the plan?"

Melody giggled. "We've been trying to upset the Flying Asshole with little things that might make him move."

Helena drew close. "Little things like what?"

"Well, he spends hours a day strolling his garden and goes wild if a dog even sets foot in the yard. We've been sneaking over at night to dump leaves on the lawn. We've also got a catapult, and whenever a dog takes a dump nearby, we shoot that over the fence. It's working. Yesterday, the doctor was out in the yard all by himself, screaming bloody murder."

Helena peered down at the house next door. "I can see that elaborate floral bed from here. It looks like something the Third Reich would have commissioned. There's not a dead leaf or a color out of alignment. Does he whip the gardener if he finds a weed?"

Melody laughed. "A few weeks ago, before the garden was laid out, and the plants were still in pots, we snuck over and spelled out 'free anal exams' in Shasta Daisies. He always flies over his house before he lands his plane, so we knew he'd see it from above. He went batshit and spent twenty minutes yelling over the fence even though no one was in sight."

"What on earth do you expect to achieve by tormenting him like that?"

"We want him to know he can't just walk all over us. We have year-round leases and need time to find other apartments. Worst case, he won't push us out before the season's over. And best case, maybe he'll give up on buying this place. . ."

Helena grew pensive. "Perhaps we should fight back on a larger scale. Have you got a cell phone? I shouldn't use mine."

Melody offered hers. "The only place it has reception is up here, though."

"Thanks, darling. Would you be kind enough to go downstairs and get me a few more olives? I've got a business call to make. It's a private matter."

Once Melody was out of earshot, Helena dialed. "Charlotte. Yes. I'm fine, darling, but I have little time to chat. I need you to get on something right away."

A Waiting Game

That evening, back at the HomePort Estate, Helena's chosen family assembled under a pergola near Marc and Cole's house where they could talk without fear of being overheard.

"Did she get the money?" Charlotte asked Dolores, who was knitting a sweater.

"Yes. Miss Helena was where she said she'd be. The girl she was with took the cash from the hat right away."

"Who's the girl?" Cole asked, reaching for another canapé.

"Melody. The busker who plays the autoharp," Charlotte said. "She covered for Helena when Wally Trieste was shot."

"Oh, yeah. She seems nice," Cole said. "I remember seeing her with Helena at the private view."

Shirley-Mae shifted in her chair, then took a sip from her glass. "I'm tired of sitting on my butt and doing nothing. We all know Helena wouldn't hurt a fly."

Marc weighed in after pouring himself another glass of wine. "Helena was insistent when we talked on *Dame Edna.* She has a plan she expects us to follow, and we're to wait for our instructions. I'm in favor of any steps that keep her safe. I know you are, too."

"But not letting Butch know," Shirley said, "that just don't seem right. He's her husband, for crying out loud."

Cole knew better than to argue. "Once the yacht is past Gibraltar, Butch will have to use a satellite phone, so we'll just have to wait until he checks in with us. But Helena was adamant he's not to be involved."

"Has anyone other than Dolores seen or talked to Helena today?" Marc asked.

"I have," said Charlotte. "She called me on someone else's phone this afternoon. But I'm forbidden to discuss our conversation. Client privilege, I'm afraid."

Working the Street

When she learned Melody had a busking slot from seven to nine the following evening, Helena asked to join her. The sooner Wednesday was known as a regular, the less likely Sergeant Brandt would be to question her presence—and the more sleuthing she could do.

With Helena's adroit interpretation of show tunes and Melody's inspired accompaniment, it wasn't long before a sizable crowd gathered on the sidewalk in front of the library. The former church, with a glorious harbor view, housed one of the best libraries in the country. Helena and Melody played next to the iconic sculpture "Tourists" by Chaim Gross. The statue of the short, round man and his buxom wife never failed to bring a smile to long-suffering townsfolk.

Just minutes before the performance was to end, Helena noticed a blue flashing light on Commercial Street. She tensed but continued to sing. The cruiser stopped across from the library. Sergeant Brandt and another officer got out.

Brandt was the first to address the two performers. "OK, folks. Move along now. Showtime's over."

When Melody protested she had a permit and ten minutes left in her time slot, Brandt replied, "Sorry, but we have the right to ask you to move under extenuating circumstances."

"Seems like there have been an awful lot of them lately," Melody sputtered.

Helena silenced her with a touch to the elbow, then whispered, "Let's play along and see what happens."

As Melody packed, Brandt returned to the cruiser and drove down Commercial Street, leaving a young, part-time officer behind.

"Oh, I can tell you what's going to happen," Melody whispered. "Whoever has the next slot will be told to go somewhere else, and a rogue busker will take their place."

Helena placed the microphone in its bag, then led the way across the street. True to Melody's prediction, the remaining officer sent the scheduled performer away. Soon after, a young man with a guitar sauntered to the library steps. He seemed indifferent to his surroundings as he set up his mic stand and started to play. His guitar was woefully out of tune, his voice nasal and often flat.

Helena put her hands to her ears. "He's horrible. How can he break into the schedule like that?"

Melody was quick to answer. "It's been this way for a couple of months now. He must have some special deal with Brandt because the guy is so consistently bad no one stays to listen. In fact, he clears the street."

Helena handed the day's take to Melody. "Fascinating. Head home as if there's nothing unusual. I'll stay and watch what happens next."

Melody frowned. "I can save you the trouble. He stands there, sounding like crap. After a while, he packs up and leaves. There's nothing we can do."

"Why not?"

"Because it will just make things worse. One guy already complained to the police. Brandt delivered a message not to interfere real quick after that."

"It makes little sense. Why would Brandt care about buskers?"

Melody shrugged. "Because he's nuts?"

"Oh, he's egotistical, misogynistic, homophobic, arrogant, and abrasive as hell, darling, but he's not nuts. Trust me. There's a reason he's doing this, and I need to find out what it is.

"I'll see you back at the house."

Standing Watch

Twenty minutes into the interloper's lackluster performance, a white van parked in a nearby lot. By then, Commercial Street was almost empty, and Helena had taken up a position in an alley across from the Harris Gallery.

The sun was just setting as a man exited the van carrying a roll of brown paper. He sauntered to the gallery door, fumbled with the lock, entered, and punched in an entry code. The gallery was in a basement, and little daylight penetrated through the few windows facing the street. Helena saw the faint glow of a small penlight as the man roamed inside.

A cruiser appeared on Commercial Street. In the middle of his lame performance, the busker switched to a discordant version of "Wichita Lineman," and the light went out. Once the cruiser was out of sight, the singer began an atrocious rendition of "You Picked a Fine Time to Leave Me Lucille," and the faint light returned.

Ten minutes later, the man exited the gallery, punched a code into the alarm system, and placed two wrapped parcels in the van. As he drove off, the singer stopped mid-song, packed up, and shuffled away.

Helena waited until the coast was clear, then started back to Buskerville Hall, planning to call Chief Louie when she arrived.

Trouble in Paradise

At Buskerville Hall, Helena found Melody in a shouting match with Doctor Woodman. They were nose to nose across a chain-link fence. Every spotlight in his yard was illuminated.

"If I catch any of you doing anything on my property, I'm calling the police," the doctor yelled.

"What's going on here?" Helena asked, striding to Melody's side, all thoughts of calling the chief forgotten.

Doctor Woodman stepped back from the fence. "Who are you?"

"Candice Lagasse."

"Well, Candi-girl, you'd better not be part of the high jinks around here."

"What high jinks?

"Someone violated my flowers. Again."

Helena surveyed the immaculately landscaped property.

Violated? What an intriguing choice of words. Can one violate a violet? Oh God, this undercover stuff is getting to me.

Melody stepped away from the fence, her fists clenched. "I didn't do it. Why are you accusing me?"

"Because you're one of those disgusting people crowded into that stupid old house. All I can say is you won't be there much longer."

Helena waved her hand. "Excuse me, Mr., er, what is your name?"

"Woodman. *Doctor* Clarence Woodman."

"Well, Doctor Woodman, do you have any evidence to support your claims? How, exactly, would you define 'violated?'"

"Come over here, and I'll show you." Woodman pointed to a gate at the far end of his property.

Helena stepped onto a manicured lawn with well-trimmed hedges and what appeared to be a giant bull's eye on a lush green canvas.

The doctor's round face was red, his eyes bulging. "See. See what they did? It's not the first time."

Helena scanned the display. "I'm not sure I see what's wrong."

"Right there. In the center. See it?"

Helena took a closer look. In the middle of the elaborate planting, a pink, plastic flamingo straddled a patch of black petunias, making a mockery of the forced symmetry. It was a masterstroke, which Helena appreciated at once.

She chuckled despite herself. "Oh, I'm sorry. I thought that was part of your design. Plastic flamingos have been making quite a comeback."

Woodman stamped his foot. "You're just as bad as the rest of them. Get the hell off my property and take the goddamn bird with you."

The doctor reached into the circle but couldn't extricate the offending lawn ornament. He turned to Melody, who was still watching over the fence. "How did you put it there? I can't get it out without crushing the blooms."

"Doctor Woodman, for the last time, I didn't do this."

Helena intervened before the war of words could escalate into a scuffle. "Is that a garden shed?"

"Yes."

"May I look inside? I've got an idea."

Doctor Woodman escorted her to the shed, where she retrieved a pole saw. Returning to the garden, she extended the saw, looped its rope over the flamingo's neck, and lifted the offending yard ornament from the flowerbed with ease.

The doctor's tone changed in an instant. "Thank you so much, Candi. I'd have hated to destroy this beautiful design by tromping through it. I appreciate your resourcefulness."

Helena smiled. "No problem. Just be careful who you accuse in the future."

"There won't be a problem in the future. I'm buying the place next door."

"It must be lovely to be so sure of yourself—and the future," Helena said, passing through the gate before he could respond.

***

Greeting Helena on the roof deck, Melody sputtered, "Such an asshole. He does nothing for the community, just takes up a space on summer weekends that someone else could live in all year long."

"He did donate to the Staunton Museum," Helena said.

"Yes, but I'll bet you that was only to buy entrée to other rich people. You can't tell me he appreciates art. Anyone who did wouldn't spend money to create a giant bullseye in the middle of their lawn."

Helena laughed. "Point taken. Trust me when I say I struggle with folks like him. A lot."

"For sure. Well, the hell with him. Look at how the moonlight reflects on the water. There's no place like P'town. I want to enjoy it while I still can," Melody said, tearing up. "By the way, you still haven't explained that business with the Coast Guard. . ."

Helena sighed and put her hand to her head. "Darling, give it a break, please? Things are happening so fast and furious lately I can't keep track of who I'm supposed to be. Which reminds me, I've got a call to make."

The Game's Afoot

Early the following morning, Quincy Stilwell fired a straight shot that landed just feet from the sixth hole. Someone picked up the ball and scuttled into the same clearing where he'd met Dan Andrade. Quincy raced his cart to the spot and strode into the woods, where he found Helena sitting on the log, holding the ball in her right hand.

Quincy was not amused. "Helena, you ruined a damn good shot!"

"I'm so sorry, darling, but there was simply no other way. I've been waiting since before sunrise so no one would see me."

Dan Andrade, Chief Louie, and the young woman who had accompanied Sergeant Brandt on *Dame Edna* stepped out from behind the stand of blueberry bushes.

Quincy's jaw dropped. "Dan! Louie! What are you doing here?"

"Sorry for the subterfuge," the chief replied, "but I didn't have a secure way to invite you to this meeting. You're such a creature of habit; I knew you'd be playing golf early."

Quincy looked baffled. "Meeting? What meeting?"

The chief asked the group to sit. "Helena called me last night and asked that we meet. But before we get started, please let me introduce Detective Amy Morgan. She's filling in for Lisa Kline, who's on maternity leave. Given all Helena's uncovered, I thought Amy should hear things firsthand.

"For the record, we're logging this meeting as Amy interviewing Helena as a witness to Wally Trieste's shooting. You are here in your capacity as Helena's attorney, Quincy. That should keep everything aboveboard."

Amy nodded to the group, hugging herself to fend off the morning chill.

Quincy looked questioningly at Dan, who said, "It's OK. Amy is one of ours. I made sure she was with Brandt during the race. I'll explain in a moment."

The attorney then pointed at Helena and addressed the group in his courtroom voice, "To start things off, perhaps this one here might care to explain how she rose from the dead and where she's been hiding since the blessed event?"

"I'm sorry for the deception, Quincy," Helena replied. "I'll explain. But first, can anyone tell me how Wally is?"

"He's stable," Chief Louie said, "but still in a coma. They think he'll recover, but he obviously can't tell us anything yet."

"Thank God," Helena said, wiping away a tear. "After he was shot, I had little time to think. So at first, I hid at Mavis's."

Quincy stared at her. "Mavis's? I thought she hated your guts."

"The vandalism upset her, but she came round just in the nick of time to help me get out of Truro."

"Mavis is Mavis Chandry, the world-famous artist whose work was defaced," Dan told Amy.

"Famous, indeed," said Amy. "She's a household name."

"We think she was the intended victim in the electrocution that killed the woman from Wellfleet."

"Got it."

"Mavis smuggled me out to *Dame Edna*—that's my boat," Helena said, turning to Amy to avoid another dose of Quincy's wrath. "I'd agreed to a race to raise money for the Artisans' Fund, so it made sense to hide on board so I could still participate. I jumped overboard when I saw Sergeant Brandt was on his way."

"Why didn't you just cancel?" Quincy asked. "I ended up in the middle of that mess without a clue. It wasn't until Marc told me the following day that I learned you weren't dead."

"Quincy, you're a dear friend, and I do apologize. I wanted to protect your reputation by keeping you in the dark. The event had been weeks in the making, and the Artisan's Fund would have lost thousands had I failed to race. Once Mavis had smuggled me on board *Dame Edna*, I decided jumping overboard might be the best way to avoid arrest. That would mean we could schedule a rematch instead of having a default."

"Well, I suppose," Quincy grumbled, "but you know I hate surprises."

"That's why we're here, darling," Helena said. "When I called Chief Louie, he suggested we meet and get everyone on the same page. To continue, once I was aboard *Dame Edna*, I got in touch with Betty Crocker."

Amy raised her eyebrows.

"Betty Crocker is Bernard Crocker's nickname," Dan Andrade said. "No doubt you recall his polka-dot racing outfit. There'd been an ongoing competition meant to culminate in the race we're discussing. Helena, please continue."

"I got a hold of Betty using a friend's phone. He and I worked out how I could escape Brandt. We knew he would figure out I was aboard *Dame Edna* if the race went on as planned. My friend, Brad, tied scuba gear to the anchor line of the third mark. When Betty made my boat tip, I pretended to fall overboard, shed my life breasts and top, put on the mask, fins, and tank, and hung on to the line about thirty feet down."

"Life breasts?" Amy asked, her head tilted to one side.

"A special set of fake boobs that double as a flotation device."

"Oh, OK," Amy said, still sounding puzzled. "That water's cold, though. How did you avoid hypothermia?"

"I incorporated a wetsuit into my sailor's drag. From a distance, it looked like a leotard with leggings."

"It was something to see," Dan said. "Helena toppled off that deck, and we could see nothing in the water but a giant set of boobs, a blouse, and her sailor's cap. If I hadn't known what to expect, I'd have sworn she'd drowned."

"You knew about all this beforehand, Dan?" Quincy asked, his voice tinged with annoyance.

Dan winced. "I think there are some other things I'd better explain."

"I'd certainly say so."

Dan winked at Amy. "When Helena escaped to *Dame Edna*, her friend Charlotte filled Louie in on the plan, and I came down to Provincetown to keep an eye on things. We couldn't warn you, Quincy. I'm not sure who is doing it yet, but my tech folks tell me several in Helena's circle appear to have unauthorized taps on their phones. Once we figure out who's hacking the cellular network, heads will roll. But for now, you should assume your phones and financial transactions are being monitored."

After a pause meant to drive the point home, Dan continued. "When Louie told me Helena's plan for the race, I called in a favor and got invited on board the Committee Boat. As Charlotte requested, I also contacted Congressman Mullins for help with the Coast Guard. It will please you to know I'm still in the dark on certain other points."

Quincy appeared mollified, so Dan asked, "Helena, how *did* you get away from that circle of boats? There are Great Whites in those waters. Did you swim all the way to shore?"

Helena laughed. "I'm not that dumb. That many boats in a circle were likely to scare off any sharks, but I'd be a free lunch swimming more than a mile to the beach. Charlotte arranged for Outermost Divers to have a crew in the area. When Brandt ordered them from the water, they gave me a prearranged signal. I came up when they did, got into their boat, and we headed back to the wharf. We got there well ahead of Brandt."

"With him none the wiser," Louie said. "He must have thought they just happened to be on the scene. I'm impressed."

"Don't forget you guys left me to handle Brandt without so much as a clue," Quincy said. "I'm billing you for my time, Helena. And keep in mind, I hate being the last to know."

Helena rose and kissed him on the head. "I'll keep that in mind, darling. I promise I will. You're the father I never had. I'd never do a thing to upset you if I could possibly help it."

Quincy smiled lovingly and said, "The defense rests."

"And Dan," Helena said, "Please thank Congressman Mullins. The one colossal risk in my plan was if the Coast Guard noticed I didn't have the Outermost Divers' logo on my wetsuit.

"There I was, hanging from the line, when one of the Coasties looked right at me, waved, and swam off in another direction. Boy, was I relieved! I appreciate the congressman using his clout and letting them in on the ruse. I'm so glad I contributed to his campaign."

Dan seemed pleased. "Officially, the Coast Guard called it a drill. We owe Commander Vega and the congressman for that bit of subterfuge. I had a hell of a time trying to explain to Mullins that men in women's clothing racing million-dollar yachts were part of an investigation into police corruption. I think he went along with me just to see for himself."

Quincy couldn't contain his amusement. "I'd have paid damn good money to watch you pull that one off, Dan. It must have been the legal argument of your career!"

The group shared a much-needed laugh when Dan nodded in sheepish agreement.

"So what happened after that, Helena?" Quincy asked.

"Betty has a small cottage near Ballston Beach. I laid low there for a couple of days. Then, I connected with my housekeeper, Dolores, to get some cash, which has come in handy for an upcoming event I'm headlining. Melody Carpenter, a lovely young girl who's a busker on Commercial Street, let me stay at her place on Bradford Street."

"And this turns out to be a lucky break," Dan Andrade said with obvious delight. "Tell them what you discovered."

Helena described the break-in at the Harris Gallery the night before.

Quincy was incredulous. "You're singing on the street? After everyone thinks you're dead?"

"No better place to hide than in plain sight, darling," Helena said.

Amy nodded her approval.

"What do you know about this woman you're staying with? Can you trust her?" Quincy said, his voice suddenly solemn.

"With my life. She saved my bacon when Wally was shot. Melody is smart, talented, and committed. Don't worry about her, Quincy. She's true blue.

"Now, back to the robberies. They've got a fake busker who alerts the thieves when the police are nearby. He literally changes his tune. And when the burglars leave, he abandons his post. Brandt clears the way for him by kicking out whoever rightfully has the time slot."

"You spoke with Wally Trieste more than once. Do you think he's in on the thefts?" Amy asked.

"Absolutely not. Wally is a pawn in all this. He was about to confide in me when he got shot."

"That was at the party in Truro, right?"

"Yes."

"Any idea who the shooter might be?"

"It was the end of the evening," Helena said. "A few diehards were lingering, including the architect, Henry Boorstin, and Doctor Woodman, who flies up from New Jersey on weekends. Most everyone else, including Cheswick Wilks and Mavis Chandry, had left. Except for the hosts, of course. Marc and Cole remained as well."

"Could the shooter have been waiting outside?"

"Yes. That's possible," Chief Louie replied. "It's an extensive property, high on a cliff with access from the beach or a dirt lane behind the house. Plenty of hiding places."

"Did anything strange happen at the party itself, Helena?"

"It was the usual production," she replied. "Expensive food and cocktails, endless schmoozing, and the big appeal for contributions once everybody had a few drinks under their belt. If I had to describe those in attendance, I'd say that eighty percent of them were well-known locals, and maybe twenty percent were onion rings."

"Onion rings?" Dan and Amy asked at the same time.

"It's our nickname for aggressive social climbers who don't contribute."

"Oh, OK," Amy said, still looking baffled.

"When you're dealing with Provincetown people, Amy," Quincy said with a wink, "you can spend your entire life trying to figure out all the hidden layers and meanings."

Amy smiled, then asked, "Helena, do you think the shooter was a guest?"

"I'm not sure. It's the best theory, but it could have been anyone."

"Any signs that Wally's being out of commission has affected the robbers?"

"No," Dan replied. "They went right ahead with another break-in."

"They already had the information they needed," Helena said, then described the hack of Wally's phone from the Russian IP address.

Louie seemed pleased. "So the likelihood is that the Harris Gallery was also a customer of Wally's."

Amy said, "Thanks, Helena. You've helped me with the big picture. I read your interview with Sergeant Brandt, but do you have any other insights about the murder victim?"

Helena paused to gather her thoughts. "C.J. was trying to make a new life for herself since her husband's death, but it wasn't going well. She was well-intentioned, lonely, disheartened, and had alienated a lot of people. I know she had a puppy she was crazy about. But that's about all I can tell you."

Amy wrote a few notes, then said, "You do know your description of C.J. varies significantly from Mavis's."

"I'm sure it does. I don't think Mavis was prepared for how indefatigable C.J. could be. Mavis expects people to skitter away when she shouts, not come back for more. Those two would never have gotten along. Oil and water."

Chief Louie said, "Thank you, Helena. Since you're being so forthcoming, I'm comfortable admitting it's proving harder to get Brandt to show his hand than I thought it would be. I figured my departure and Amy's presence would do the trick, but so far, it hasn't."

"There may well be a better way," Helena said, looking off into the distance. "Amy, if I may ask, do detectives ever wear a uniform?"

"Huh? Well, no. Seldom, if ever. I'm usually dressed like this, or in more high-profile situations, a suit. I have a badge holder I can wear on my belt or around my neck in situations like crime scenes and so forth. Why?"

"I've been hoping to fulfill my commitment to S.K.I.P.—the Soup Kitchen in Provincetown next week. It's an important event, and I'd hate to cancel on them. There may be a way I can do the show *and* smoke Brandt out at the same time. Louie, it's your call, but I've got a plan."

On the Case

At nine-thirty that morning, Sergeant Brandt and Officer Chase arrived at the Harris Gallery. Detective Amy Morgan was already hard at work.

"No signs of forcible entry," Amy said, pointing to the front door. "Isn't that the same MO as the others?"

Brandt answered, "Yup. We have little more than that to go on with this one."

"Why do you say that?" Amy pulled a small tape measure from her bag. "It's clear from this footprint that one perp wore a size twelve shoe and was approximately five feet, two inches tall."

Brandt strode to her side. "Who do you think you are? Sherlock Holmes?"

"No, Sergeant Brandt, I'm a trained detective, and I say we have four obvious things in our favor: One, the muddy footprints that appear to be size twelve. Two, the distance between the prints is twenty-six inches, which indicates a height of just over five feet. Three, their shape indicates the perp is most likely male."

"And what's the fourth?" Brandt said, significantly less at ease.

"That I'm the detective in charge of this case."

Turning to the sales assistant, she asked, "Works by Franz Kline and Hans Hoffman were taken. Do you have a *catalogue raisonné* for them?"

The salesperson handed her a thick volume. Brandt stepped over to study it. "What is that, and why do you need it? She showed us photographs of the missing paintings."

"It's a complete catalog of an artist's works. These aren't the first works by these artists to be stolen. I'm trying to see if there's a pattern. Ah, here are the Hoffmans. His Provincetown period. Now, let's look at the Klines. Yes. These too."

"And what does that tell you?"

"That the thief or thieves are working to order. Someone, somewhere, is craving Provincetown art."

The Show Must Go On

The posters appeared overnight, stapled to telephone poles and taped to shop windows. There were few businesses on Commercial Street without at least one poster prominently displayed. Several had five or more.

A picture of Helena made up as Norma Desmond sported a caption in bold letters:

"IT'S NOT A COMEBACK; IT'S A RETURN"

This Saturday, the annual S.K.I.P. fundraiser

Gay Men's Chorus,

Ricotta Gnocchi,

and special guest artist,

HELENA HANDBASKET

singing the American Songbook

8 p.m. Town Hall
$30 suggested donation

Officer Chase brought a copy to Sergeant Brandt, who took one look at the poster and tore it in half.

"What's all this?" Amy asked.

"I knew that bitch wasn't dead! She's messing with me again. This time she won't get away with it."

"Just what are you saying, Brandt? Dan Andrade told us there wasn't enough evidence to secure a felony arrest warrant. You're not planning to take liberties with the law, are you?"

"Well, no," Brandt said, avoiding Amy's probing gaze. "I've got a good gut for these things. I know she, or whoever it is under all that shit, killed that old woman and shot that Trieste guy."

Amy snapped her fingers in front of his face. "Sergeant, look at me. As I said earlier, I'm the detective on this case, and, per the DA, you must always coordinate with me. Now, tell me what you intend to do."

"Well, if she's going to show herself in public, we should at least keep a tail on her."

"That's within bounds, for sure. So, what's the plan?"

"I say we haul her in for questioning after the show. Let her think she's getting away with things, then nab her when the crowd's gone."

"On what grounds?"

"That drowning scam, for one. We could charge her with wasting official time. The harbormaster, the police, the Coast Guard. . . Her disappearing act cost time and resources, after all."

Amy looked directly at him. "You have a good point, though I'd urge caution. Folks in this town *adore* Helena. Say nothing of the fact that she's extremely well-connected. Whatever you do will have to be discreet. If you try to haul her in with a crowd watching, you'll have a riot on your hands."

"Oh, I've got that all figured out. Discretion is my middle name."

"I'd never have guessed."

Broadway Baby

Alone in her dressing room, Helena felt more than the usual pre-performance jitters. The minimal police presence outside the dress rehearsal had been a welcome, though puzzling, surprise.

Amy warned me Brandt was setting a trap after the show, but I thought he might double-cross her and try to stop me from performing altogether.

There was a knock at the door. Helena remained still until she heard Shirley's gravelly voice.

"It's me, doll. Let me in. We gotta rehearse that last bit one more time."

After decades of TV reruns, Shirley-Mae was making her onstage debut.

***

By seven-thirty, there wasn't an empty seat in the spacious auditorium. When the curtain opened for Helena's first number, the standing ovation was instantaneous and heartfelt. Bowing low to the crowd, arms outstretched, she reveled in the affection flowing over the footlights. The accolades ceased only when she gestured for silence a third time.

Using her best Norma Desmond imitation, Helena waited a beat, then said, "Reports of my death were greatly exaggerated. I promise you I'll never desert you again."

There was another standing ovation.

Signaling again for silence, Helena pulled a snorkel and face mask from her ample cleavage and, with the chorus backing her up, sang the first words of "The Morning After." The crowd went wild, and she had to signal the band to stop playing. Then she raised her long skirt to reveal she was wearing swim fins. Sergeant Brandt, watching from the sound booth on the balcony, banged his head against the wall until the sound engineer made him stop.

The magic of live performance soon cast its spell. Helena's comic timing had audience members clutching their sides in laughter. The dancers from *Naked Hunks Review* drew bawdy whistles, and their version of "Macho Man" inspired dancing in the aisles. In fine voice, the chorus performed a medley of show tunes that alternated between romance and comedy. Throughout the performance, spouses and boyfriends beamed with pride.

Helena joined the chorus for a special number. Before starting it, she said, "We dedicate this next song to the 'chorus wives' whose support makes it possible for these men to do what they love. I'd like them to stand so we can give them a hand."

The proud partners stood to deafening applause.

Again, Helena signaled for silence. "This is the first of my shows my guy missed since we met. Please give an enormous hand for my fabulous husband, Butch."

As the camera moved in for a closeup, Helena said, "Butch honey, I don't know what I'd ever do without you. This one's for you."

Then Helena segued into her much-loved Streisand imitation of "My Man," flawlessly executing the challenging song. By the time she finished, there wasn't a dry eye in the hall save Sergeant Brandt's.

***

The second half of the evening peaked with a moving rendition of "I Am What I Am" by Helena, Ricotta Gnocchi, and the chorus. The audience sang along—their voices loud and proud.

The performance ended with the duet, "Sisters," sung by Helena and Ricotta, both in nuns' habits, which morphed into a rendition of "Climb Ev'ry Mountain," complete with ropes, carabiners, and ice axes. The chorus provided a stirring background while the two performers upstaged each other. Just before the song ended, Ricotta knocked Helena to the floor and stood like a prize fighter with her foot on her stomach, which did not stop Helena from hitting—and holding—the famous high note.

The crowd screamed for more, stamping their feet and demanding an encore. Eventually, the curtain opened to reveal the chorus facing the audience in a large half-circle. In front of them was a solitary microphone bathed in dim light. Helena entered, flawlessly done up as Judy Garland, wearing a black turban and a long black gown with a rhinestone belt that glistened in the spotlight.

The room fell silent. Taking a deep breath, Helena nodded to the chorus, who hummed an extended introduction to "The Man That Got Away." The tempo was slow and sultry, with rich male voices adding a pensive note to what had been, until then, a madcap evening. In an instant, the audience was still. Many of the older men smiled at each other, recalling younger days.

The band joined in when Helena began to sing. At the start of the second verse, one of the hunks from the review burst on stage, clad in nothing but a pair of torn undershorts. His muscles bulging, he glanced behind him, his features contorted in panic. Moments later, Shirley-Mae entered stage right in a tattered version of Helena's costume, her white hair flowing from beneath a dented turban. She was deftly twirling a lasso while pursuing the virile young man.

The audience erupted in catcalls, which only inspired Shirley to greater heights of inanity. She capered around the stage doing rope tricks, sometimes drawing close only to have the youth escape her clutches. Her facial contortions and frantic gestures evoked raucous laughter. Many in the chorus struggled to maintain their focus.

Amid the pandemonium, Helena sang with total concentration, the genuine tears in her eyes mirroring the pain in her voice. Her rich tones rose above the fray, filling the hall with exquisite sounds that soared over the mayhem. To those paying close attention, this performance was one of her best. Many in the audience watched in awe, confident they were witnessing a historic moment. Marc and Cole stared into each other's eyes, fully aware she was singing about Butch.

Helena remained focused on the wall above the rear balcony. Reaching the last verse, she gazed upward to the ceiling, her hands clasped in prayer, mascara streaming down her face.

As the band brought the song to a close, the chorus parted to reveal all but one of the naked hunks—in torn, leopard-skin loincloths—manacled to what looked like a dungeon wall. Then Shirley entered stage left, dragging the lassoed escapee back to his place among them.

The auditorium shook with laughter, stomping feet, and thunderous applause. The curtain calls lasted for five minutes, with the performers taking several solo bows before returning hand in hand to acknowledge the band and chorus. At last, Ricotta signaled their final bow, and the performers left the stage for good.

Only then did the applause fade away and the crowd depart.

Busted

Once the hall was empty, Sergeant Brandt marched down from the balcony, up the center aisle, and sprinted backstage to the dressing room door.

"Is she in there, Morgan?"

"Someone's in there. I arrived after the last curtain call, as we agreed. The door was already closed. You've got to hand it to Helena; she's incredibly talented."

"I'm not handing her anything but an arrest warrant if Dan Andrade ever gets off his ass and asks Judge Willis for one."

"Sergeant, remember our agreement. You are only to question her. No arrest."

"Yah, yah, I hear you. I've had enough farting around. I'm going in."

Brandt pushed open the door and barged into the room.

Shirley-Mae, clad only in a slip, let out a shriek. "Why Sergeant, I'm not decent. Then, of course, I never was. What are you doing here? The statute of limitations on that little business with the joint and Customs was up five years ago."

"Where the hell is she?" Brandt yelled, bringing Ricotta Gnocchi, still in her nun's habit, and a group of stagehands to the doorway.

"Who, dahlin?" Shirley-Mae asked, completely at ease.

"That, that drag queen that was performing out there just now."

"You've got to be more specific than that in this town, I'm afraid. And put away that popgun, all right? It might go off."

Brandt, looking like a guilty choirboy, returned his gun to its holster.

There was a glimmer of amusement in Shirley-Mae's eyes when Ricotta sidled closer to him, twirling her rosary beads.

"What's your problem?" Brandt yelled, trying to assert his authority. "This is a police action. Stop interfering, both of you, or I'll turn you in."

"Turn me into what, lover boy?" Ricotta asked, shimmying in front of him until he pushed her away.

Shirley-Mae pointed her gnarled forefinger at Brandt's chest. "Listen, Sonny. I've had more than a few run-ins with guys like you in my day. You're on thin ice. I was just changing out of my costume, and you practically broke down the door. You could have sent a note telling me you were interested, and I'd have met you in the bar. If anyone's got a problem, it's you, not me."

When Ricotta licked Brandt's badge, he slammed his fist against the wall. "I give up. This whole damn town is insane. Morgan, go outside and see if anyone saw where that lunatic went. I need a drink."

"I'll see ya at the bar in five minutes, sweetie," Shirley yelled as Brandt stormed from the auditorium. "Order me a Harvey Wallbanger to get the ball rollin'!"

Reflections in the Dark

In the dim light, the two shadows were mirror images: the same height, hair, build, and wardrobe. Each wore black slacks, a black blazer with a light-blue blouse, and black sneakers.

As Detective Amy Morgan escorted Helena down an alley to the beach, she asked, "Did he fall for it?"

"Hook, line, and sinker," Helena replied with a laugh. "I wish you could have seen the look on his face when he barged into the dressing room thinking he'd cornered me and found Shirley instead. By the time she and Ricotta were done with him, he was off to the nearest bar."

"Perfect," Amy said. "You can't imagine what it's like dealing with that fool day in, day out. He's certifiable. Technically, you're still a suspect, and we shouldn't be going rogue, but we've got to nail him somehow."

Sensing Amy's ambivalence, Helena sought a bright spot. "How did you enjoy all those curtain calls? I had more than enough time to change and position myself outside the dressing room. He never realized he wasn't talking to you. I felt like one of the The von Trapps making my getaway."

Amy burst into a grin. "To be honest, I loved it. I've always wanted to be on stage, and somehow the costume gave me the courage I lacked. Knowing Brandt was in the booth as I took your bows made my day. He was so sure of himself. Do you think we've gotten under his skin?"

Helena cackled. "In a big way. It was as easy as shooting fish in a barrel."

"So, what's the next step?"

"If I'm right, he'll overreact and shift into a massive search and destroy mode. It won't surprise me if he does one of those house-to-house numbers like Nazis in war movies."

Concern showed on Amy's face. "That bad, huh? He's not authorized to do anything like that. Is it time for Chief Louie to step in?"

Helena clasped her hand. "Not yet. Remember, darling, the goal is for Brandt to lose control, move too fast, overlook something, or mess up. And when he does, we'll be right there waiting for him."

Amy seemed satisfied. "I've got an idea where he'll go next. Dan subpoenaed Wally's cell phone and got someone to break the encryption. It took a while; Wally wasn't slipshod when it came to protecting his clients. Only two galleries are left on his list: the Ventura and the Amalfi."

"How do we know which one they'll choose? And if we see something, what do we do?"

Amy paused. "We have to be careful. I'm an officer of the law, though I'm authorized as an undercover agent, which gives me a bit more latitude. Still, we need a case that will stick. Let's video as much as possible and hold off on an arrest, so we don't scare off the ringleader."

Helena smiled. "Right as usual. Don't know what I'd do without you, darling."

"Likewise, Helena. You're the best partner I've ever had. I should get back in case Brandt comes looking for me. Is there anything you want me to report to him?"

"Yeah. Tell him someone whispered in your ear, 'Next time, I'll lead a conga line down Commercial Street.'

"Thanks for everything, darling. I owe you. Big time."

Helena hugged Amy, then vanished into the night.

On the Lam

Sergeant Brandt reacted as expected. All over town, police presence was expanded, with officers stopping anyone they thought might be Helena in disguise. With help from Amy, she stayed one step ahead of them.

***

Several days later, Helena had changed into her Wednesday Addams outfit when she saw Clarence Woodman inspecting his garden. The doctor wore a Panama hat, sleeveless T-shirt, cargo shorts, and sandals.

Helena studied him for a moment.

He looks like a spud in drag. I never have gotten over that dancing potato routine with Betty at the Crown and Anchor. It's scarred me for life, which will make it tougher to deal with the mad doctor without cracking up.

"You have an eye for color and detail, Doctor Woodman," Helena said, suppressing the memory to the extent she could.

"I appreciate all things done well, whether it's elegantly executed surgery or a perfectly trimmed hedge," Woodman said once he'd recognized her as Candice, the girl from next door.

"That's a real gift," Helena said, struggling not to groan. "I find too many people settle for second-rate."

"How would someone like you know what's second-rate?"

Woodman's tone was both suspicious and supercilious. Despite this, Helena remained cordial. "In my line of work, you see second-raters all the time."

"What *is* your line of work?" the doctor asked, striding over to the fence.

Helena was delighted by the question.

I can't tell if he's interested or just trying to get information to use against the folks in Buskerville Hall, but he wants to talk.

"I'm a performer. Even if I'm just singing on Commercial Street, I give it my all."

"That *sounds* good," he said. "But does it get you anything?"

"Of course it does. There's the satisfaction of knowing I've done my best and made people happy."

"I can agree with the former but see no point in the latter."

As the doctor turned away, Helena responded quickly. "I think of my music as a painting. Maybe it's being around so many artists, but I find many things in common between the art forms."

Doctor Woodman came back as she'd hoped he would. "Say more."

Helena struggled to suppress a smile. "There are several important components to painting great art that aren't dissimilar to giving a virtuoso performance. Your foundation must be solid, your perspective clear, and you must know how much is enough."

The doctor relaxed. "It makes a certain amount of sense when you put it that way. Have you studied painting?"

Helena nodded. "I majored in art history and restoration in college. That gave me a decent sense of what's good and what isn't."

He's in over his head in this town and needs a mentor. Someone to give him talking points so he can impress his social conquests.

Doctor Woodman mustered an insincere smile that was at once disingenuous and unnerving. "Really? I'd never have imagined someone with a degree like that would end up singing on the sidewalk. Why aren't you at a museum or university?"

"I worked in restoration at a museum, but it wasn't for me. I don't miss the politics and snobbery, but I sure miss the art."

"C'mon over, then. I've got an extensive collection," Woodman said after a moment's hesitation. "I'd be interested to know what you think of it."

The Wall of Bad Art

The doctor met her at his front door. They stepped into a large, contemporary room, all in white, with minimalist furniture and gaudy paintings covering every available bit of wall space. Helena had seen several old houses gutted in similar fashion—the downstairs reduced to a single room to accommodate large gatherings.

Henry Boorstin again. I'd bet my last set of falsies on it. He must think there's an endless market of gay boys who all want the same thing. Maybe there is, but Woodman doesn't run with that crowd. He's more like Uncle Fester than an "Instagay."

Doctor Woodman took her extensive survey as a compliment. "When I bought this house last year, I went hog wild buying paintings. Of course, the place had to be entirely rebuilt before I could hang them. It had been in the same family since eighteen fifty, and I swear they hadn't done a thing to it since then. Can you imagine people living that way?"

Helena looked around the vast living room, seeking a diversion to temper her response. "It certainly is a large space."

"You like? I wanted maximum flexibility for social events. It was all tiny rooms with these weird doors with iron latches. They'd covered that fireplace in blue Delft tiles that had to be chiseled off. I think it looks great painted black, don't you? There was wainscoting on the walls and warped pine floors. Some planks were over two feet wide, and none of them matched. And all that old horsehair plaster. Pure crap. I had everything hauled away.

"I told Henry Boorstin, he's my architect, to make the place as open-plan as possible. I refuse to live in a rabbit warren. We got shit from the town because it was one of those—what do they call them? Floating houses? But we prevailed in the end. You just threaten a lawsuit, and they back right down. They always do, according to Henry."

Helena tried to keep the sadness from her voice. "Oh yes, Floaters. Houses brought over by barge when they dismantled the little village out on Long Point. Some of those places have wonderful histories."

The doctor tensed. "I appreciate history. You might not think it, but I do. The fact is nobody in my line of work gives a tinker's damn about it. No buyer who can afford it wants a property that isn't up to date these days."

Helena tried to sound impressed despite the despair rapidly overtaking her. "I see."

Doctor Woodman seemed mollified. He flipped a series of switches that illuminated several large canvases hung around the room. To a one, they were high-priced tourist art.

"I got a great deal on some of these."

Staring at the portrait of a topless woman surrounded by a cascade of chicken feathers, Helena could only manage a faint-hearted "Wow."

Woodman seemed eager to share his triumph. "An artist who ran his own gallery was going bankrupt. The way I figure it, I got these five for thirty cents on the dollar. I've got a real nose for a bargain."

"You sure have," Helena said. "I don't think I've *ever* seen a collection quite like this. Are you still adding to it?"

I hope to hell not. What could possibly augment this mess? Clown portraits on velvet? Or a series of Panda bears on bicycles? I'll never get these images out of my head.

The doctor pointed to a parcel wrapped in brown paper at the far end of the room. "Funny you should ask. I haven't found the right frame for this one, so I haven't hung it yet. It's not my typical style, but they tell me it's worth a pretty penny. Do you want to see it?"

Once again, Helena mustered enough enthusiasm to sound convincing. "I'd love to!"

"Well, why not? Unlike the philistines next door, you seem to appreciate the finer things in life."

The doctor walked over to the package, unwrapped it, and extracted the luminous painting of the young man and the firebird.

I know this style, Helena thought, deeply moved by the troubled young man's face and the mythical creature's vitality.

"It's a Mavis Chandry," the doctor said, his eyes fixed on Helena. "The dyke who had the opening at the Staunton Museum the other night. I had to wait to get in, which I didn't like one bit, but I had to see her other work to decide on this one. I don't get all the fuss, but it's a damn good investment given the price I paid."

Helena stepped closer, confirming the painting's technique and the signature under the glaze.

This has got to be the missing painting from Mavis's studio. My painting. Could he have killed C.J. and stolen it? I doubt it. He doesn't seem the type. But then, how did he get it?

This time, it was easy for Helena to convey her excitement. "You've made quite the find, Doctor Woodman. Mavis Chandry is one of the most well-known artists in the country. This painting is the best example of her work I've ever seen. What a coup.

"I went to an auction at Sotheby's, and one of her large pieces sold for over a million dollars. Would it be indiscreet of me to ask where you found it and what you paid for it?"

The doctor seemed to inflate with pride. "I'm not allowed to reveal who sold it. But, I can say I helped someone who was down on their luck. I only paid ten thousand."

Helena didn't believe him for an instant. "Isn't that marvelous? I congratulate you. Some collectors and museums would *kill* to have a Mavis Chandry at twenty times that price."

Doctor Woodman's greedy smile convinced Helena she'd won him over. She glanced at her watch. "Oh, look at the time. I've got to pick up my mail before the post office closes. Thank you for the tour. It's been most informative. And congratulations on your purchase. You're quite the connoisseur."

The doctor's grotesque smile grew wider with each bit of flattery. "Any time. This should be back from the framers in a few days. Come back and see how it works with the others."

"I'll hold you to that," Helena said as she beat a hasty retreat.

If Hell exists, it's probably decorated like this place.

Provenance

Helena had donned a gray pageboy wig and dark aviator glasses to avoid being recognized. A patrol car was parked on Shore Road across from High Head and another at the North Truro intersection. Despite that, she drove Melody's battered Honda Civic to Fisher Road without incident.

Parking in the beach lot, Helena walked to Mavis's studio and stood outside the large north window. The artist had her back turned but sensed a presence. Covering her easel with a dark cloth, she walked to the door.

"Who's there? What do you want?"

"It's me, Helena. What did the painting you planned to give me look like?"

"I never recognize you with all your disguises. Why do you want to know about that painting?"

"I may have just seen it."

"Where?"

"At the home of this creepy guy who lives next to my current hideout. Was the painting of a nude young man and a phoenix taking flight?"

The artist's features clouded. "Yes. That's the one they stole, the bastards."

Helena took a seat on a nearby stool. "That painting had a powerful effect on me from the moment I saw it. There can be no mistake, right? It had your signature, but you've done nothing similar, have you?"

Mavis dismissed the praise with a wave of her hand, but Helena sensed a softer tone when she spoke. "No mistake whatsoever. Tales of the phoenix have always intrigued me. I'd never found the right context until I realized you changed your life through sheer strength of will. I'd even planned a companion piece."

Helena bowed her head. "I was lucky. Shirley-Mae was an excellent role model when it came to doing your own thing."

Mavis chuckled. "Still is. I thought I'd cornered the market on being a forceful old broad, but she could teach a masterclass."

"That painting is magnificent, Mavis. I appreciate the perception that went into it. I promise you here and now, I'll get it back."

Mavis's eyes were bright with admiration. "Something tells me you will. That's why I never told Brandt it was stolen. He couldn't find coffee in a Starbucks, that one. But you; that's a whole other story."

Comparing Notes

Helena returned to Fisher Beach and walked to the mouth of the Pamet River. As she climbed the seawall, she spied Freddie Chalmers standing at the far end.

"I hope I haven't kept you waiting, Freddie," Helena said to the reporter as she approached. "I appreciate you meeting me like this."

"Not a problem," Freddie replied, continuing to face the water.

From shore, she and Helena looked like two friends entranced by the sea.

"That was an intriguing article you wrote about C.J.'s death," Helena said. "Am I right that you edited out some of the worst bits from Brandt's interview?"

Freddie groaned. "It was a *trip*. He as much as said you were the murderer. I had to keep reminding him of libel laws. Now, I'm totally convinced he doesn't know his job.

"Remember that precinct where Brandt claimed to work? Their chief learned of my inquiry and called to set the record straight. He knew Brandt as a vigilante who followed police cars and had a history of aggravated assault. The chief, Logan was his name, was stunned to hear Brandt has a badge, say nothing of being in charge."

"No surprise there," Helena said. "Brandt threatened me the day after C.J. died and is far too eager to pin her murder on me."

"He is. And you should be *very* careful."

Helena grew solemn. "I will be, darling. Do you have anything more on C.J.'s death?"

"My sources confirm the circuit breaker had been tampered with. Brandt made a big point of the fact you had the studio built for Mavis—as if anyone else couldn't have sabotaged the breaker. It sounds like Dan Andrade isn't buying his theory, though. Brandt has filed paperwork to arrest you on a murder charge, and I hear he's furious Dan is taking his time reviewing it.

"Now—not that I'll use it immediately—what's the inside scoop on your disappearance the other day?"

Helena whispered, "Brandt was already breathing down my neck, then Wally Trieste was shot. I decided to go underwater. You know, it's like going underground, only wetter."

"I knew you were with Wally when he was shot," Freddie said. "I've interviewed Gwen and Elise. They were circumspect but gave enough away that I could put two and two together. You can share the details later. For now, who do you think is behind all that's going on?"

Helena felt grateful for Freddie's comfortable presence. "I'm quite sure Brandt is involved in the museum vandalism and maybe even in C.J.'s death. He's not the mastermind, though."

She told Freddie about Brandt forcing the buskers to move on and the atrocious singer who alerted the thief during the break-in.

The reporter seemed pleased. "That's well in keeping with what I'm seeing on my end. Brandt's not giving the art robberies a lot of oxygen. Officers I've talked to are furious he's so intent on finding you he won't let them investigate the thefts—or much of anything else.

"Amy Morgan seems to be the only one working on the robberies. Apparently, she and Brandt have argued about that. Dan Andrade had to get involved since she's out of his office and Chief Louie is still away. This is the part that bothers me the most. The situation has deteriorated to the point Dan had to intervene, yet Louie is still MIA."

Helena put her arm around her friend's shoulder. "Don't underestimate him, Freddie. I've known Louie Silva for years. I'm sure he took what you had to say to heart."

Freddie hugged her. "No doubt, you're right. On another note, I've been digging into C.J.'s background. There's not a lot to find. She inherited a fair amount of money from her husband, had next to no friends, and didn't have any surviving relatives.

"One thing, though: she dropped off a puppy at a kennel in Eastham the day she died. It's been there almost a month. With no heirs, the kennel owner isn't sure what to do."

Helena recalled the way C.J. doted on her pet. "I saw that pup at the Audubon rescue. He's called Moppet and is absolutely adorable. I may know someone who might give the little cutie a wonderful home."

On the Stroll

The Friday evening gallery stroll was winding down. Patrons and grazers (those who attend openings not for the art but for the food and drink) were gulping their last glasses of champagne. Anyone watching Detective Amy Morgan closely might have noticed she was tracking a deliberate course between two venerable West End galleries: the Ventura and the Amalfi, a mere two blocks apart.

Buskers performed within yards of either venue. Amy took an active interest when she spied Brandt talking to a violinist near the Ventura. She had just positioned herself across the street when someone in a trench coat, slouch hat, and thick leather boots sidled up to her.

"Helena," Amy sighed, "how in the name of Mata Hari can you manage these wardrobe changes when you're on the lam?"

"I have help. My housekeeper, Dolores, is amazing. After all, disguise is essential to good detective work."

Amy shook her head. "Not since Sherlock Holmes returned alive from Reichenbach Falls. Changing the subject, I think the Ventura is on the docket for tonight."

"I agree. Here comes the bogus busker."

The man set up his mic stand and launched into the same torturous medley.

"The Ventura closes at ten," Amy whispered, "but buskers can sing until eleven. I suspect the thieves will show around ten-thirty."

At ten-twenty-five, a white van pulled into an adjacent parking lot. Inside the gallery, the staff was cleaning and hanging a new show. At ten-forty-five, they were still at work.

"I don't like this," Helena whispered. "If they don't leave soon, someone could get hurt."

Minutes later, two men exited the van and strode to the gallery door. One fumbled with the lock, then they both entered as Amy crossed the street. Peering through the window, she saw the two young employees being held at gunpoint. Amy stepped away from the window, called for backup, and moved to a position where she could observe without being seen.

Within three minutes, a cruiser appeared on Commercial Street. Again, the bogus busker switched to "Wichita Lineman." He began screaming the lyrics when the cruiser parked next to the gallery. The two men had just tied up the staff and were removing two paintings from the wall. Not stopping to wrap them, they ran out the door.

"Halt. Police," Amy shouted, pointing her pistol at them.

The man holding the paintings froze, but the other man, unaware Officer Chase was sneaking up behind him, drew his gun and fired. The shot missed Amy, who returned fire, striking the shooter in the leg. As he collapsed on the ground, clutching his knee, Officer Chase tackled him, pulled the gun from his hand, and handcuffed him.

Helena ran to Amy, who was holding the second suspect at gunpoint.

"I'll take care of this one. Make yourself scarce. Now," Amy whispered. "Brandt will be here soon."

Just then, Sergeant Brandt arrived, leaped out of his cruiser, pointed his revolver at Helena, and shouted, "Stop, or I'll shoot."

Helena froze. When Amy turned toward Brandt, the second culprit began to run.

She lowered her gun and yelled, "Sergeant Brandt, a suspect is fleeing with valuable artwork."

Brandt waved her off. "Stand down, Morgan; this is my bag. I've been waiting for this moment for far too long."

As he brandished his weapon, Helena signaled Amy to step back. When Brandt was within ten feet of Helena, she heard a muffled noise. Without a word, the sergeant toppled to the ground.

Amy raced to him, crouched by his side, then yelled, "Chase, what happened?"

"I'm not sure. One second, he was going to handcuff her. Then I heard a popping sound, and he fell over."

Amy took Brandt's pulse and tried to stanch the bleeding as Officer Chase called for more backup and an ambulance. Then he took over for Amy as she surveyed the area around the gallery for traces of the second burglar.

Helena leaned against a nearby telephone pole for support. Amy snuck behind her and whispered, "Brandt's unconscious, but there's a pulse, and he's still breathing. I know you didn't shoot him, Helena, but he may claim you did. You've got to go somewhere safe, preferably out of town, and lie low. Let Louie know where you are, and I'll try to communicate with you through him. Go. Now. While you still can."

Helena stepped into the shadows, raced up Brewster Street, found her way to Buskerville Hall, and called Chief Louie. Getting no answer, she tried Dan Andrade, who picked up immediately.

"It's Helena. Two men broke into the Ventura Gallery and held the staff at gunpoint. Amy confronted the robbers and wounded one of them. Then Brandt showed up. The second robber started to run, then someone shot Brandt from behind. Amy doesn't think the runner pulled the trigger, but he has two paintings."

"Is Brandt badly hurt?"

"I don't know, Dan. Amy said he was still breathing. He was about to arrest me when he was shot. They must have used a silencer. I didn't hear a thing."

"Where was Amy when this happened?"

"On the sidewalk. Officer Chase had just handcuffed the robber she shot."

"Was her gun out of its holster when Brandt was shot?"

"I think so, yes."

"And, just to be certain, you said she'd shot the perp who's in custody?"

"Yes," Helena said, struggling to catch her breath.

Dan's tone grew more forceful. "OK. Listen carefully. Amy has to go on administrative leave because she's been involved in a shooting. My office does the review, but it's a matter of protocol she be taken off the case until the investigation is complete. I'll track down Louie Silva right now. He'll have to take over for Brandt. But for the short term, at least, you're on your own."

It pleased Helena that the chief would be back on the job. "Have Louie call me. I couldn't get him, and we must talk. Some other things have come up."

"What things?"

"I know where the painting stolen from Mavis's studio is, and I've got an idea who's behind the theft."

"You know who's in charge?"

"Maybe. Lots more digging to do before I can say for sure."

"Be careful. We can't watch out for you as we'd planned until Amy's back from her leave. I'll try to expedite things, but it will be a few days, at least."

"OK, Dan. I'll figure out how to cope."

"And Helena?"

"Yes?"

"This is no stage show. It's real life. With real consequences."

"That's for damn sure."

The Soccer Mom

The next day, Helena was sunning on the roof deck at Buskerville Hall. Birds were singing in nearby trees, and out in the harbor, the weekly sailboat race was underway.

Melody arrived and sat beside her. "You got home late last night. Is everything OK?"

"Two thieves hit the Ventura Gallery," Helena answered. "Amy shot one of them, then Brandt showed up. The other thief ran off, then somebody shot Brandt. He's still alive, last I heard."

Melody paled. "You're kidding. Do you know who shot him?"

"Afraid not. I've got an idea, but nowhere near enough evidence to prove it."

"What's our next move?"

"Our?" Helena raised herself from her chaise. "Who said you're in on this? I appreciate your letting me hide here, but there's a killer out there. And, if I'm caught, the police could charge you with harboring a fugitive."

"That's one way of putting it, I suppose," Melody said. "The other is that you need my help to prove your innocence. I'm not backing down, so if you think you can just ditch me, get over it."

Helena embraced her. "You've become such a dear friend. Just when I needed one most."

"Speaking of friends," Melody said, "we have to go to a meeting."

Helena looked perplexed. "I'm in hiding, remember?"

Melody laughed and said, "Trust me and go get changed. We can't be late. Your lady friend—the one with the beehive and baggy stockings who likes Sondheim—just dropped off a bunch of stuff. She said to be sure you wore one outfit and brought the rest with you. We have to be at Ryder Beach by noon."

Three garment bags, Helena's professional makeup case, and several wig boxes were on the bed in Melody's room. The bags contained an array of clothing Helena had never seen before. None were her style; all were soccer mom outfits.

"Apparently, Dolores no longer trusts my fashion sense," Helena said, stepping from the bathroom in black leggings with a gray long-sleeved sweatshirt, a long, blonde wig, and wide, gold hoop earrings. "I feel an immediate urge to buy a beige minivan!"

Melody laughed, gathered up the clothing, and led their way to her car.

A Strategic Retreat

There were no police on Route Six, which offered hope Louie Silva was back on the job. The Ryder Beach parking lot was deserted save for an enormous F150 King Ranch, more like a Humvee than a pickup, with leather seats front and back. Helena was stunned to find Marc behind the wheel.

"Marc? When did you buy a pickup truck? It's about as far from your 'gayboy' image as a card-carrying queen can get."

"Hey, Helena! What do you think of my new look? Does it work?"

"About as much as water wings on a cat, but you didn't answer my question."

Marc blushed. "I borrowed it from a friend. He's an electrician and needs room for his equipment. He also uses it to get out to Race Point when the bluefish are running."

Helena studied the massive truck. "Any particular reason you need an off-road vehicle?"

"Get in, and I'll show you. You too, Melody. I'll load the bags."

Marc revved the engine in a display of masculine bravado that at once fell flat. Exiting Ryder Beach Road, he turned onto a narrow track of sand. Reaching a driveway that wound its way up a dune, he arrived at an elegant cape-style house with views over moors to the ocean. Hidden from the road, the shingled house had a broad porch facing the water, natural plantings, and freshly painted white trim. Modern but understated, the residence was ample and welcoming but not extravagant.

"What are we doing here?" Helena asked. "Whose place is this?"

"For the next six weeks, it's yours," Marc said, enjoying her puzzled expression.

"I don't understand," Helena said as they walked to the front door. "Will someone please tell me what's going on?"

"I'll try," Butch said, opening the door, wrapping his arms around Helena, and lifting her off her feet. "Dig your new look! What time's the soccer match? Or perhaps lacrosse?" He stepped back. "Hm, no, definitely not lacrosse."

Helena stood where he'd deposited her, mouth open, struggling to catch her breath. "Butch. Oh God, Butch! You're really here. I've missed you so much!"

Shirley-Mae stepped into view. "Right where he should have been the whole damn time."

"And not a moment too soon," Cole said, striding up the path from a nearby garage.

"Why are we out in the middle of nowhere?" Helena asked as they escorted her inside.

"We need a headquarters. Someplace no one can find us," Charlotte said, descending the front stairs. "These are dangerous people, Helena. We'd already been thinking you should leave town. Brandt's shooting sealed the deal. Come see the place."

Helena entered a large, sunlit room overlooking sand dunes and blue ocean. The sea breeze cooled the house, and the musky smell of the nearby moors added an earthy touch. The home's interior décor was simple but functional, with none of the cutesy plaques, wooden seagulls, and lobster buoys often found at beach houses. This was an elegant, cultivated retreat, both comforting and tranquil.

Turning to Melody, Helena asked, "Were you in on this?"

"Nope. When your friend came to Buskerville Hall this morning, all she said was to bring you to the Ryder Beach parking lot."

"Dolores. Wait until I get hold of her. This getup is just too much. I feel like I've died and come back as Missi Pyle."

"I think you'll find you fit right in now, Miss Helena," Dolores said, stepping out from an extensive library that took up an entire wing of the house. "Your usual wardrobe was not appropriate for these surroundings, sorry to say."

"Dolores!" Helena raced to hug the bemused old woman. "I've so much to thank you for."

"Now, now, Miss. Don't worry about any of that. I'm just doing my job."

"Your job? The clothes? The money?"

"Not that different from any other day, in my book. Besides, I had plenty of help. Your grandmother's a real go-getter."

Butch was quick to agree. "It astounded me that Shirley figured out how to reach me on my satellite phone."

Shirley, watching from the kitchen, took a bow.

Helena struggled to hold back tears. "How did you get here, Butch? I thought you were in the middle of the Atlantic."

"We were near the Azores when Shirley called to say you were in trouble. I got off the boat at Santa Maria and hopped the next flight to New York. Charlotte arranged a private flight to P'town, and I arrived at nine this morning."

Cole looked sheepish. "I'd argued you'd be mad if Butch interrupted his trip. Looks like I was wrong."

"I'm so glad he did. Things took a horrible turn last night," Helena said. "And Butch, I apologize for taking you for granted. I never will again."

"Not now, hon. Not now," Butch whispered, wrapping his arms around her. "We'll talk about us. I promise. But later. Right now, let's focus on making sure you're safe.

"Charlotte filled me in on what happened at the museum and the murder of that old woman. What else can you tell me, Helena?"

She paused as her insecurities overwhelmed her.

Has Butch returned just because I'm in danger, or has he come to a decision about our future? What exactly did Shirley tell him when she called?

Suppressing those fears, Helena leaned against the kitchen counter and took a deep breath. "Someone's been stealing artwork from homes and local galleries. Last night, Amy Morgan—a detective who works with the DA—shot one of the thieves."

"The scanner said there was an officer down outside the Ventura Gallery last night. That wasn't her, I hope?" Shirley asked, taking her grandchild's hand.

"No. Sergeant Brandt was shot right in front of me. He was still alive when I beat a hasty retreat."

Charlotte pointed to a room where a large dining table overlooked the moors. "Let's sit over there. We all need to get up to speed."

"How did you pull this hideout together so fast, Charlotte?" Helena asked, surveying the isolated home with its priceless view.

"It belongs to clients of mine. I knew they were in Asia for two months, so I called and offered to rent it."

"They must know you have a house in P'town. What excuse did you use?"

Charlotte colored slightly. "I told them I was having marital difficulties. In truth, I was so worried about the twins that Brad took them back to New York, which just happens to make it appear our marriage is in trouble."

"A wise move," Butch said, looking around the large room. "I heard about Helena's escape. Thank you, Melody, for all you did to protect her when she had to go underground."

Helena clutched her husband's arm. "I still can't believe you're here."

Butch squeezed her hand. "Tell me everything from the beginning. Don't leave anything out. You never know what detail might be important."

The group listened, spellbound, as Helena recounted her conversation with Doctor Woodman, Mavis's confirmation of the phoenix painting in his possession, and the events at the Ventura Gallery the night before.

"You came damn close to getting killed," Butch said to Helena, who, this time, let that reality settle in. "If Brandt took you out, he could pin C.J.'s murder and Wally's shooting on you to protect himself."

Helena nodded, relieved her husband's strength would temper her fear.

"We need more on this Woodman character," Butch said.

Charlotte agreed to research him, wondering aloud if he were an actual developer.

"I've got a hunch where you can get the scoop on developers in town," Cole said. "Henry Boorstin, the architect, is hungry as all get out. He'd come running in a heartbeat if you told him you wanted an addition to your house."

"He's as dumb as a sack of hammers," Helena said, "and always hungry. He pestered me during construction of the HomePort Colony; even did a three-dimensional model for the cottages and studios."

"You never told me I had competition," Cole said, raising his eyebrows. "Just out of curiosity, what was his model like?"

Helena shuddered. "Clapboards, faux black shutters, fancy little moldings above the windows. The houses, the fences—all painted white. Boorstin wasn't too happy with me when I told him his design looked more like a retirement home for white supremacists. He's probably the best way to get dirt on developers *and* Doctor Woodman, though. And I want to be there when you talk to him, Charlotte."

"Now there's a surprise," Butch said, casting a furtive glance at Shirley, who sighed and shrugged.

A Voice from the Past

When everyone but Shirley left, Butch and Helena decided to explore the grounds. They followed a narrow path over a dune, through tall grass, and out onto the beach. In the distance were two small cottages built in the nineteen twenties—the sort of places where screens went up on Memorial Day, sand was swept out every morning, and there was little else to do but relax. Instinctively, Butch and Helena walked in their direction.

Butch spoke first. "I realized on the flight to Boston that I'd frightened you the night before I left. I love you more than I do myself. I'd never hurt you, but I should have remembered what Dorrie told me."

"What do you mean?" Helena asked, stopping to stare at a section of beach covered in round, polished stones. "What did she tell you?"

"Do you remember how she gave me the third degree when we first met?

Helena chuckled. "I remember your being bowled over by how much she cared for me."

Butch grew solemn. "I didn't tell you the entire conversation. We'd talked for about forty-five minutes when she said, 'I'm between a rock and a hard place, Butch. There are things you should know about Helena, but they aren't mine to tell. You're a good man and the right man for her—if you weren't, I'd throw you out on your ass in a heartbeat. Instead, I'm gonna share my personal observations. The first time I saw Helena, someone had beaten her up real bad. And I don't mean just physically. Has she told you what happened?'"

Butch stopped to gaze into Helena's eyes. "You were so nonchalant about that attack. I waited for you to say more, but you always avoided the subject. And I should have been more careful about being angry in front of you. I just never thought you'd think I could ever—"

"I don't, Butch. I know you'd never hurt me. My reaction surprised me. I didn't know what to say or do. I'll tell you everything. I promise. But can it wait until we're out of this mess? What else did Dorrie say?"

"I've never quite understood the second bit. She said, 'Something else happened to Helena as a child. I sense it more than know it, but I'm certain it was terrible. Not her mother walking out—something before that. What you need to know, Butch, is that Helena's a "runnah," just like Marc and Cole. Just like most everybody who comes to HomePort—maybe even you, for all I know.'"

He paused. "I remember thinking how righteous she seemed—and how troubled she was when she said, 'What I'm trying to say is that Helena's hiding something terrible from herself, or at least not coming to grips with its consequences. That's why all the costumes and drama. She's running hard to avoid whatever it is, and if you love her, you're going to have to keep up with her. I'm sorry, but that's all I should say. You're the best thing that could ever happen to her, Butch. Be strong. Stay true. And most of all, be yourself. Someday, it's likely all this running will become too much, and Helena will have no choice but to stop and face her demons. That's when she'll need you most of all.'"

Butch sat down on the sand. "I wasn't true to myself or you that night before I left. I was tired, angry, and frustrated by just about everything. You need to know that it wasn't more than ten minutes after the plane took off that I saw the error of my ways.

"We've got to get you out of this mess—and we will. Then, we'll sit down and figure out where we go from here. For now, I want to apologize for letting you down."

Helena sat next to him and placed her arm around his waist. "Butch, I apologize, too. There's so much I did to—"

"Not now, Helena. We need to sort out this murder first. Let's wait a bit on the rest, and we'll work things out somehow. OK?"

The Consultation

The following day, Charlotte, in a prim, black business suit, and Helena, wearing green contact lenses, the blonde wig, tight jeans, beige shoes, and a white blouse with a red jacket, waited outside Henry Boorstin's inner office.

Cape Cod novelties lined the walls and shelves: a tarnished weathervane with a codfish on top, several wooden sandpipers, and a fleet of plastic sailing ships. The general impression was that of a low-priced gift shop.

"This place is like Chatham on crack," Helena whispered to Charlotte, who struggled to contain a laugh. "Or if Martha Stewart went to

Nantucket, got juiced up, dug through everyone's trash, and had a yard sale."

The door opened. Henry Boorstin strode out, clasped Charlotte's hand, and shook it rapidly. "Ms. Grubb. How lovely to see you again. I've been hoping to be involved with the HomePort Colony ever since the Staunton Trust was established."

Charlotte introduced Helena as Kelly van Dusen and informed the architect that Kelly was the one in need of his services.

Boorstin hesitated, tried to mask his disappointment, then pointed toward his office, where two captain's chairs faced a vintage partner's desk. Enlarged photographs of various projects covered the walls. To a one, they were suburban, cookie-cutter copies of each other.

Helena shuddered and pulled her jacket around her.

"Is it not warm enough, Ms. van Dusen? I'll be happy to turn up the heat," the architect said.

Helena shivered again, then responded in a voice both breathless and seductive. "Perhaps a tad. I've just flown in from the Cote d'Azur and haven't adjusted to these temperatures."

"Right away," Boorstin said, striding to a thermostat. "We mustn't have you catching cold. How about a cup of coffee? Perhaps with a dash of cognac?"

"How kind of you," Helena purred. "That would be delightful."

Boorstin fussed with a coffee maker and, when it was ready, pulled a bottle from his desk drawer. He hummed while he served the two women as if extremely pleased with himself.

Once he'd finished, the architect returned to his side of the desk. "Now, how can I be of service?"

Helena launched into the spiel she and Charlotte had worked out: "Kelly" intended to build a house somewhere in Wellfleet or Truro. She had to have a minimum of twelve acres with lots of ocean frontage and needed architectural plans to give context to the site choice. Interior space for entertaining mattered more to her than architectural style—so long as she had the water view.

"That's a tall order, Ms. van Dusen," Boorstin said, taking a sip of his spiked coffee.

"Please call me Kelly," Helena said.

"Well, Kelly," he said with a nervous chuckle, "property like that usually stays in the same family for generations."

Helena laughed. "Money is no object, and everyone has their price. My agents have already found four properties. When I decide which one, I'll buy out the owners and tear down the existing house. I'd like you to provide a design so I can visualize my new home on the sites in question. Clarence told me you are a master at knowing what a client wants—sometimes even when they don't know themselves."

Boorstin was suddenly wary. "Clarence?"

"Doctor Woodman. He's an old college friend of my husband's. He spoke highly of you."

"Oh yes, Woodman," Boorstin said. "I've had dealings with him, but he's asked me not to discuss them."

Helena feigned indignation. "Surely that doesn't apply to me. My husband's his financial backer. Didn't Clarence tell you?"

Boorstin scowled. "Actually, no, he didn't."

"We're in on that deal with the old guest house on Bradford Street."

"You've heard about that? Clarence hasn't submitted a bid yet."

Helena said she and her husband had come to discuss funding and inspect the property.

Boorstin mustered a strained smile. "This is a different kettle of fish. It sounds as though you're the principal investors."

"We'd never say that publicly. Clarence will have a free hand with the design. He's got exquisite taste, don't you think? You did such a wonderful job rebuilding his home, by the way. Once he gave me the tour, I realized there was no one else for me but you. I love what you did with the fireplaces."

Boorstin grinned, revealing his canine teeth, as Helena discreetly studied him.

He looks like a piranha about to attack. Given the size of his nose, maybe a shark would be the better metaphor.

She suppressed the thought with difficulty. "I believe you helped him set up the gallery in his home, did you not? I own an extensive art collection and am buying more paintings for this new house. It *was* you who helped Clarence with his purchases, was it not?"

"Oh, of course," Boorstin said so fast he had to be lying. "He doesn't make a move without my input."

"Then you *are* the right person for me," Helena said, leaning forward seductively. "I desperately need your help. Clarence won't tell me how he got that exquisite Mavis Chandry, and I'm simply green with envy. She rebuffed all my attempts to buy from her directly when I was here last summer. The things she said to me cannot be repeated in polite company."

"If you're that close to Clarence, I suppose there's no harm in telling," Boorstin said. "He bought it from me."

"How fascinating! Ms. Chandry said she doesn't sell except through Sotheby's, and then only once every few years. Where did you get it?"

"From a client who was behind in paying his fees. I took it in exchange for writing off his outstanding balance and sold it to Clarence at cost."

"Who was that? And how did they get the painting?" Helena asked, trying hard to mask her excitement. "Maybe they have more?"

"I'm afraid I'm not at liberty to say," Boorstin said, his features darkening for an instant.

Helena glanced at Charlotte, who signaled they should leave. Within five minutes, the two friends were back on Conwell Street.

"I'm not certain how much that got us," Charlotte said once they were alone in the car.

"Not all the way. But a lot further than where we were," Helena replied.

"Care to explain?"

"Boorstin knows who had the painting. That person most likely got it from Mavis's studio. We also know they are, or were, a client. But what's our next move?"

Charlotte explained that a computer search of recent building permits would show Boorstin's projects and their scale.

"You're amazing. Have I ever told you that?" Helena said.

"Not often enough," Charlotte replied as they wended their way along Shore Road.

From Bad to Worse

Back at the hideout, Helena summoned Marc and Cole to discuss their next move. While waiting, she saw a young fawn grazing by the moor's edge as its mother watched from the nearby woods. It was a different world in this isolated spot.

When the two men arrived, she had them sit at the dining room table.

"We've gotten the word out that Shirley-Mae has gone back West," Marc said. "Dolores returned to HomePort with a story that will reach the entire gossip network by sundown. Shirley will be safe enough here."

"Just try telling her that, darling," Helena said, patting him on the back. "She'll have a loaded shotgun pointed at the front door the moment I leave. Let's get down to work."

Helena described the meeting with Boorstin and shared her suspicion that the stolen painting was payment for a bill. She finished by asking Marc to search for the building permits.

"Do you have any idea how many projects that guy does?" Marc sputtered. "He's cornered the market. All the gay guys who don't know which end is up—outside the bedroom, that is—use Boorstin. Most of them have lived in apartments or condos and are sitting ducks for a con artist like him. You want me to search through all that crap?"

"Yes, Marc. I do." Helena said. "I know it will be torture for someone as esthetically sensitive as you, but I need you to take one for the team."

Cole laughed and said, "C'mon, Marc. I'll help you. It won't take that long."

Helena's burner phone rang shortly after they left. Turning to her husband, she said, "It's Louie Silva. I've got to take this."

She spoke little during the call. When she hung up, her face was ashen.

"Brandt's dead. Somebody poisoned his IV drip when the guard outside his hospital room left his post. They think it may have caused a heart attack, but it's too early to be certain."

It was a good minute before Butch spoke. "I hate to state the obvious. This is bad, Helena. You may have had fun playing detective and escape artist, but we've got two deaths now and who knows how many thugs on our tail. International criminals may be involved. We should get out of town for a while. Go somewhere on *Dame Edna*. Bermuda, Barbados, or even Europe. I'm sure we could sneak her out of the marina at night and provision her en route."

"I appreciate that you'd do that for me, Butch." Helena placed her head on his shoulder. "My friends are being threatened because of me. Innocent people like Melody are involved because they sheltered me. A sweet guy like Wally Trieste is hovering between life and death because he tried to tell me the truth. There's so much more than our privileged existence at stake now. I can't run away just because I can afford to."

"Never thought you would," Butch said. "Just thought I should ask if only to be certain you fully grasped the situation."

"I do, but think of it this way; I have a unique set of skills at my disposal. Not everything I do is as crazy as it might seem—sometimes, there's a method to my madness. We all make different contributions in this family. Mine is the ability to go places without being recognized. If we're to get out of this mess, I should be undercover finding things out, not running away."

"I'm with you, Helena, as long as you understand the risks. What's our next move?"

"I need you to help me flesh out a plan. Let's walk the trails and put one together."

***

Hours later, Butch, Helena, and Shirley-Mae gathered in the large kitchen. Butch was leaning over the sink, and Helena was dying his hair after having cut it short.

"I've never seen you without your beard," Helena chuckled as she did a final rinse. "You look like a chipmunk."

"Cut the commentary and just dry my hair."

"Reminds me of Samson and Delilah," Shirley said, her eyes bright, the corners of her mouth twitching. "His power was in his hair. With that trim and shave, you look like you just came out of a PTA meeting. What a comedown."

"Look, I agreed to help, not to be a punching bag," Butch said, smiling all the while. "Does my hair *have* to be this blond?"

"Yes, but don't worry. With the stubble on your by tomorrow, you'll look hot," Helena said, "Or as hot as one can get with chipmunk cheeks."

Shirley-Mae spat out part of her drink, then covered her mouth.

Reconnaissance

The next day, Butch parked a Kelly-green Land Rover across from the HomePort Estate. Gazing wistfully up at the mansion, Helena yearned for her chats with the Staunton sisters and her favorite view over the harbor.

Butch clasped her hand. "You'll be home soon enough. Right now, it's all about ensuring our friends and family are safe."

He nuzzled her neck with his scruffy face. To anyone looking on, they were typical tourists from one of the wealthier, up-Cape towns, oblivious to everyone around them.

"It's the two guys in the Ford Explorer at the far end," Butch said, nodding toward the parking spaces encircling Pilgrims' Park. "They have that look I remember from Iraq—not focused in any specific direction, always scanning. Let's get over to Charlotte's and see who's watching her."

The short drive to Telegraph Hill was uneventful until they reached the bottom of the street, where two men sat inside an identical Explorer displaying the same rigidity and lack of affect. As Butch and Helena drove up the hill, the manicured lawns and substantial houses seemed packed together compared to the isolated expanse of the Truro hideout.

They found Charlotte staring out her living room window. "Are they still down there?" she asked once her friends were inside.

"Yes, and there's a matching set outside HomePort," Butch answered.

Charlotte sighed. "I'm not convinced they're all that competent since it's easy enough to lose them. Still, they give me the creeps when they follow me."

"Don't worry," Butch said. "If we need to meet from now on, Afton will provide a way to get you and the guys to Truro without being followed."

"Got it. What's up?" Charlotte asked Helena, who sat on a leather sofa in front of the fireplace.

"I should feel bad that Brandt is dead, and I do, but I'm hoping that with him out of the picture, we can find who killed C.J. and shot Wally."

Charlotte studied her closely. "Are you sure you're OK? You were in the middle of Wally's shooting—and Brandt's, for that matter."

"OK, now that Butch is back," Helena replied, taking his hand.

"So am I," Charlotte said, smiling at him. "Do you still think C.J. and Brandt's death are related, Helena?"

"Yes, more than ever. And now we know Brandt was not the mastermind. The goons spying on us would have run for the hills by now if they worked for him."

"That's not the greatest leap of logic," Butch added, "But it's enough to get us started."

"I can't get used to the two of you," Charlotte said. "You look like you both stepped out of an L. L. Bean catalog."

"Please don't remind me," Helena said with mock anxiety. "If Betty Crocker ever sees me in this outfit, he'll drum me out of drag."

"Say nothing of the guys down at the wharf," Butch added. "If they get a load of me looking like this, I'll never live it down."

"How do you figure you'll trace the painting to the thief or thieves?" Charlotte asked. "And are your outfits going to help or hurt the effort?"

Butch laughed. "By figuring out who owed Boorstin approximately three hundred thousand dollars. That's what the phoenix picture is worth, according to Mavis. I don't believe for a moment that Woodman paid ten grand for it."

"Let me show you something." Charlotte herded them into her office, typed on her laptop for a few moments, then displayed the results. "I got this list of liens for non-payment from the Registry of Deeds. Boorstin filed all of them."

From the list of fifteen, four were still pending. None were for an amount close to what the painting was worth, though there were several counterclaims for improper specifications and cost overruns due to building code violations. One claim was from Doctor Woodman.

"That's the best news I've heard in quite some time," Helena said. "I swear Boorstin is to Provincetown architecture what Robert Moses was to New York City neighborhoods. I'm glad people are calling him on his crap."

"Where does this get us, though?" Butch asked.

Charlotte looked up from her screen. "It suggests significant cash flow problems that may have forced Boorstin into illegal activity."

Helena clapped her hands. "You're brilliant, Charlotte. God knows his reputation is shot already. So now the question is whether he'd deal in stolen art to save his flabby butt."

Alone Again, Naturally

Melody plucked random notes on her autoharp and stared off into space.

Helena had a heartwarming reunion with her gorgeous husband, and it's as if I ceased to exist. I felt a part of something for a fleeting moment, but I'd better accept that there's no place for me in all that love and money.

She played her gig with as much enthusiasm as she could muster, but the crowds in front of Bubala's were sparse, and the donations even more so. During her last set, Melody's temper flared when a stylish couple sauntered up to watch.

Look at her with that perfect tan, wide green eyes, and blonde hair tucked under a Gillie's Cap. And him with that sculpted chest and fancy clothes, say nothing of the designer haircut. They've got every advantage in the world, and they're staring at me as if I'm a freak.

Melody began to pack. As she put her autoharp in its case, the man tossed a hundred-dollar bill in her tip hat.

When she looked up in astonishment, he winked and said, "Follow us at a distance." Then the couple strolled down Commercial Street toward the center of town.

Melody grabbed her equipment and followed them. When they reached Town Hall, the couple turned left and sauntered to the Bas Relief, a bronze tableau commemorating the signing of the Mayflower Compact in Provincetown Harbor.

As she crossed Bradford Street, Melody noticed the couple laughing and sprinted toward them. "OK, you two. What's so funny?"

A familiar voice stopped Melody in her tracks. "How foolish we look, darling."

"Helena?"

"Not so loud."

Melody stood transfixed. "I didn't even suspect it was you."

"That doesn't surprise me one bit. I feel like a creature from outer space in this getup."

Melody struggled not to laugh out loud. "I should have known it was you, Helena. You're wearing the same wig."

"Wigs are the least of drag, sweetheart. It's makeup, shadow, and most of all, posture, right, Butch?"

"Butch?" Melody took a second look. "No way. You look like some guy from an aftershave commercial."

"Gee, thanks," Butch said, looking sheepish. "I've never gotten a compliment like that before. Good to see you again, I think."

Helena laughed. "Look, kid," she said, "I'm reluctant to ask yet another favor, but we need your help."

Melody was ecstatic to be back in the game.

"I must see your paintings as soon as possible," Helena said. "There weren't any at the house on Bradford Street. Where do you keep them?"

"I use a part of my friend's studio out at the warehouse on Route Six. Why?"

"Can we go there right now? I'll explain on the way."

The Art of Deception

Helena rummaged through stacks of canvases leaning against the wall of a large, well-lit studio. "Melody, these are remarkable. I love your use of color."

Melody remained slightly unsettled by the couple's transformation. Butch's in particular.

Does he become another person the way Helena does? It's getting hard to keep up with all these wardrobe and personality changes.

"This one," Helena mused. "This one will do very well. Will you sell it to me?"

She was holding a portrait of an exquisite young woman in a diaphanous gown, vaguely reminiscent of the blue satin she'd worn to the museum opening.

"You can have it," Melody said.

Helena shook her head. "No. I want to buy it from you. But only if you understand it could be lost or destroyed."

"You've got to say more. I'm confused."

"We're setting a trap for an art thief. If things go the way I hope, your painting will smoke them out. But there's a chance something could happen to it."

"Sure. Anything that helps you guys. That one is my favorite, though. I raced back here and painted it after the Mavis Chandry opening. I called it *Grace*."

"Great name," Helena said. "I can see Mavis's influence in the figure's treatment and the reflected light. Your own voice comes through loud and clear, though. Mavis will be impressed."

Melody caught her breath. "You *can't* show it to her. I'd just die."

"We'll settle that bit later. I'll have Charlotte cut you a check. How much do you want for it?"

"A thousand?"

Melody's hesitation revealed her discomfort.

"That sounds reasonable," Butch said. "Ten thousand it is."

"No. I said a thousand—"

"And I heard ten thousand," Butch said, grinning.

"So did I," Helena said. "Besides, we need a believable provenance for this painting to work as bait."

"Speaking of believable, I can't believe the two of you," Melody said.

"There's no reason you should, darling. We're about as real as Barbie and Ken. Oh, and if you get inquiries, you sold the picture to Kelly van Dusen for ten thousand. Be sure and reveal the name and amount."

Melody shrugged. "All right. Sure. Why not?"

"We must get going. I don't want 'Kelly' to be seen too close to you—or Buskerville Hall," Butch said.

Melody smiled. "No worries. I'm going to see if I can snag another performance slot. I feel a song coming on."

Into the Woods

After a conspicuous lunch at Ross' Grill, a Provincetown favorite overlooking Long Point, Helena and Butch parked at the fire road leading to Race Point Light. Cole's Porsche was among the few cars parked there. As Butch and Helena strolled along the path, he soon caught up with them.

"Charlotte clued me in," he said, grinning. "Do you think Melody's painting measures up?"

"Absolutely," Helena said. "She has extraordinary talent, and as luck would have it, there's one that will work perfectly."

"What's it called?"

"*Grace*," Butch said. "It's a portrait of a young woman in a beautiful gown who looks a lot like Helena. I sent a picture to your phone a minute ago."

"It shows Mavis's influence but has its own merits," Cole said after viewing the image. "Let me make sure I have the details right. You want me to do a letter on museum stationery offering fifty thousand for this work?"

"Yes," Helena said. "Use the same lofty terms you'd use if you were writing about a new acquisition. An important piece, indicative of outstanding talent, follows in Mavis Chandry's footsteps yet offers an exciting fresh style, blah, blah, blah. Play it up as though you'll go higher. Please sign and deliver it to Charlotte as fast as you can. Text me when you have, and we'll pick it up."

"You got it, Boss. By the way, love the look. Yours too, Butch; it's so. . . butch!"

The Frame

Butch found a parking space near Henry Boorstin's office and removed Melody's painting from the Land Rover. When Helena pounded on the inner office door, the architect opened it looking bothered, though his features quickly changed.

"Mrs. van Dusen, how delightful, if unexpected, to see you."

"Mr. Boorstin, this is my husband, Gregoire van Dusen."

Butch stepped forward and said, "Call me Greg."

Boorstin seemed dumbstruck by that simple gesture. His hungry eyes scanned Butch's body as Helena struggled to hide a smile.

In that outfit, Butch is every fantasy that poor queen has ever had: bucks, basket, and booty. Seems sort of cruel to stand here watching him drool over my husband, but then, I suppose if someone has to, it might as well be me.

"How can I help you good people?" Boorstin asked.

Helena admitted to a mistake. Doctor Woodman didn't know Greg was in town to view the property. Clarence would be furious if he found out, so she asked Boorstin not to say anything.

"I hope you are on board with this harmless deception?" Butch asked.

"Of course," Boorstin simpered. "I have many clients who rely on me for total discretion."

The poor fools, Helena thought, searching for something to focus on besides the ghastly models and photographs.

"Is there anything else I can do?" Boorstin said, looking quizzically at Melody's painting after yet another discreet scan of Butch's physique.

"Yes," Helena replied. "Given the need to tiptoe around Clarence, I thought you could help us with a dilemma. The strangest thing has just happened. Greg and I were at an artist's studio when some fellow from the new museum came in." Helena pointed to the painting. "I'd just bought this, and he offered me three times what I paid for it on the spot."

"Really?" Boorstin said, surveying the portrait of the woman in the sheer gown. "An impressive effort. May I ask what it cost you?"

"Chump change. But now this letter was hand-delivered to our hotel not twenty minutes ago. I couldn't think of anyone else to advise me, so we came to you."

"What does it say?"

Helena handed the letter on museum stationery to Boorstin, who read it. As he did, she studied him.

Bent over that letter, he looks like a troll out of a fairy tale. Did his profession make him this unattractive? It's an intriguing notion. I wonder if grasping after money can change the way a person looks? I better check the mirror when I get home. I can't have all these unsavory financial transactions wreaking havoc with my beauty regimen.

Boorstin handed the letter back to Helena. "It's from Cole Hanson, all right. He's number two over at the museum, and I suppose he's running the show now that his boss has gone underground."

"Who's that, and why did she go underground?" Butch asked.

"A fabulously wealthy do-gooder named Helena Handbasket. She inherited an old whaling fortune and oversaw the museum's construction. Hard to take sometimes, but with more money than God. She's on the lam for—"

"What do you think?" Helena asked, eager to avoid Boorstin's speculation. "Should we sell it or keep it?"

Butch weighed in. "The painting—it's called *Grace*, right?—has increased five times in value in a few hours. Isn't it likely to increase even more?"

Boorstin hesitated, then said, "There's a lot of interest in Provincetown art these days. It almost doesn't matter what we think. If the Staunton Museum thinks it's good, it's good. Let me ask you a question, Kelly. Did Cole Hanson buy any other paintings?"

"He bought three but said *Grace* was the most striking example of the Chandry influence. Apparently, he feels it's essential to have it because of that."

"Well," Boorstin said, showing his pointed teeth, "he'll pay more, then. They've got money to burn over there. Let him sweat for a few weeks, and I bet he'll go higher."

"Good enough for me," Helena said. "Do you have a recommendation for a good frame shop?"

"There is an excellent framer in town," Boorstin replied. "He works from his house. I'd be happy to take it to him for you."

"Oh, we couldn't put you to such trouble," Helena said, her voice coy and enticing.

"It's on my way home. I'd be delighted to help. He'll email you several shots with different frames so you can choose the one you like best. Put it over there. I'll take a photograph so he can start choosing sample frames, then I'll write a receipt for you."

"Well, if you insist," Helena said, smiling at Butch, who moved the work as instructed.

Boorstin took several photographs then wrote the receipt.

"Email sounds perfect," Helena said. "We have *tons* to do before Greg leaves. Oh, by the way, our agent has found a nice fifteen-acre parcel on the ocean side of Wellfleet. Looks like it might be the one. I'll be in touch once I've toured the location, and you can start the plans."

"And remember," Butch said, "not a word to Clarence on that other business. I need time to bring him around."

"Mum's the word," Boorstin said, wiping his brow as he escorted them out.

Country Life

When Butch and Helena returned to their Truro hideout, Shirley-Mae was waiting at the door. "It appears I'm chief cook and bottle washer around this joint. If so, there's a ton of stuff I need."

"You know, darling, I don't think anyone's given food a thought," Helena replied, winking at Butch.

Shirley-Mae caught the exchange and raised her voice. "What sort of crazy game are you playing with me now?"

"Just pulling your leg, Gandma," Helena said. "We stopped at the grocery store and the fish market. We've got your favorite: lobster."

"Lobster, huh?" Shirley said, still petulant. "Who said that was my favorite?"

Helena laughed. "You did. Don't you remember watching *Grey Gardens* with me and what Big Edie Beale said about making time for sex? How did it go? 'Who has time for that? Wouldn't you rather eat a lobster any day?' You said you felt the same way."

"Hell no," Shirley-Mae said, rising to the bait, her pique forgotten. "I never said that. Or if I did, it was because I was plumb wore out. Sex comes first with me. Always has and always will. Given I'm stuck out here in the middle of nowhere without a chance of gettin' any, I guess I'll damn well have to settle for lobster."

A Wrench in the Works

Later that afternoon, Marc watched Boorstin load Melody's painting into his BMW and then followed him from a distance. When the architect reached the West End parking lot, he parked facing the water, and Marc slipped into a nearby space.

Within seconds, Boorstin was on his phone speaking with animation. Then, he hung up and stared out his side window until a Ford Explorer parked next to him.

When Marc recognized the men he'd seen outside HomePort, he slid down in his seat to watch. One man placed the painting in the Explorer and drove away. The other tied Boorstin's arms behind his back, then appeared to force him into his car. The assailant got behind the wheel, and the BMW raced from the lot. The entire operation took less than three minutes. Marc called Chief Silva, then Charlotte.

"Our priority is making sure no one else gets killed," Chief Louie said when Mark arrived at the station. "My guys are tracking his vehicle from a safe distance."

The chief took a call. "They parked on a side road in Wellfleet. By the time the officers approached, there was no one inside the vehicle. They're searching the area."

***

Boorstin's BMW was found next to a patch of scrub pine at the bottom of a hill. As the officers examined the empty car, they heard a voice yell, "Over here! Help me!"

The architect stood atop the hill, arms still tied, his shirt untucked. The officers scrambled up to him.

"They threw my keys and phone somewhere and just left me," Boorstin said, sounding panicked.

After freeing him, two officers searched the area while the third radioed a report. They found the missing items within minutes and escorted Boorstin to the police station.

"So, is his story accurate?" the chief asked Marc and Charlotte, who had watched Boorstin's interview over a closed-circuit monitor.

Marc shrugged. "Everything lines up except for one point: he didn't receive a call. He called someone. He must have told them about the picture then—unless he made that call from his office."

"There are no office calls between the time Butch and Helena left until Boorstin was kidnapped," Chief Silva said. "While you were following him, Boorstin called a number we can't trace. I'm glad Dan Andrade finally got those wiretaps."

"And you figure whoever he called sent those two goons to get the painting?"

"Yes. The question is whether it was taken against his will."

"There are some odd angles to all this," Charlotte said. "If you wanted to steal the portrait, why drive Boorstin to Wellfleet?"

"To buy time?" Marc asked.

"Or to ensure the vehicle with the painting in it wasn't followed. A kidnapping would be the primary focus of any police response," said the chief.

"And I thought we were so smart," Marc said. "I wonder how Boorstin will describe the loss to Helena. Maybe that will tell us something."

***

The architect's email was a brief statement of the facts followed by an abject apology and hopes the van Dusens were well insured.

Helena glanced at her husband. "You're not convinced either?"

"Not at all. How would robbers know about the painting unless he told them?"

"So, what's the best response?"

"Let him stew," Butch said.

No Accounting for Taste

Melody answered a knock on her door two days later to find Helena in her Wednesday Addams outfit. "We want you to have a burner phone so we can stay in touch. I've added all our numbers."

Melody didn't try to hide her appreciation. "Great. I wanted to let you know I've sold two more paintings since I saw you. I didn't know how to get in touch."

Henry Boorstin had bought a harbor scene in Mavis's style, and a man Melody didn't recognize had purchased an earlier self-portrait.

"That's not surprising," Helena said. "Boorstin must figure he can make money like 'Kelly' did. I'd asked Cole to make an offer for *Grace* to convince Boorstin your works were skyrocketing in value."

"If only they were," Melody sighed.

"Don't think that way. I'm sure you'll show at the Staunton Museum someday."

"That doesn't mean much. You built the place. You can put whatever you want in there."

"That's not true. Cole's the artistic director. He and an acquisition committee made up of several local artists, including Mavis, make the final decisions."

"Mavis Chandry?"

"Yes."

"I'll *never* get in. She's as tough as shoe leather."

"So you might think." Helena paused. "Is the Flying Asshole next door?"

"I saw lights over there last night. Why?"

"It's a crazy hunch and probably won't amount to anything, but I'm going to pay him a little visit."

The Connoisseur

Clarence Woodman cracked open his front door to find Helena smiling at him.

"What do you want, Candi?" he asked, stepping back in surprise.

"I was hoping you could spare a moment," she said, adopting a tentative tone. "If the Mavis Chandry painting is back from the framer, might I take another look? You have such an amazing collection. I haven't been able to stop thinking about it."

The doctor made no effort to hide his pleasure. "It just came back today. C'mon in."

Helena followed him into the house. "Oh, there it is. What a magnificent work! Even more beautiful than I remember. You are *so lucky* to have it. When I was at the museum, I almost bought an original Thomas Kinkade. I'll never forget. I saw it at a yard sale but couldn't afford it."

"Kinkade is all right," the doctor said with a sniff. "I've got some from what I'm told is his school, but I never thought his originals were worth the price."

"If I ever have the dough, I want a collection just like yours," Helena said, while thinking, *Lord, forgive me.* "I could sit here for hours looking at everything." *But not without inflicting serious trauma.*

Woodman beamed. "Why, thank you. I have something new that might interest you. Wanna see?"

"I'd love to. Perhaps you'd also share your reason for buying it? I'm always fascinated to learn what distinguishes a good work of art from a not-so-good one."

The new painting was *Grace*, Melody's portrait of the young woman in the satin gown.

"What a find," Helena said, thrilled her hunch had been correct. "This is an impressive effort. Wherever did you get it?"

"A friend tipped me off this artist was going to be hot. I went to her studio, and she gave away the store. She's young and doesn't realize the value of her work. I got a great deal, don't you think?"

"Why, yes. So astute of you to recognize talent in an emerging artist. You've made a significant investment that will only appreciate in value. Where'd you get the tip?"

"I promised not to tell." Puffing with pride, the doctor added, "But I will say that I snatched this one right out from under the Staunton Museum."

Despite internal resistance, Helena offered an admiring gaze. "Well done! Bravo! I won't take any more of your time, but I so appreciate seeing your new purchase. Is it OK to check in now and again to see if you have any more finds? I've learned so much from you already."

"Of course," Woodman said, a predatory grin crossing his smug features. "You're always welcome."

Encore

Back at Buskerville Hall, Helena let loose. "Melody, you sure were right. That jerk told me he bought the painting from you when it was stolen from Boorstin. I doubt he even understands what he has. All he sees are dollar signs."

"Now, don't be too hard on him, Helena," Melody said, enjoying her friend's outrage. "There are plenty of others in town just like him, if not worse."

"I suppose you're right, darling. It's just that when I see people taking advantage like that, it makes my blood boil."

"That's sweet, Helena, but I'm not feeling all that exploited at the moment."

Helena paused her tirade. "I wonder who the other buyer was. You're sure you've never seen him before?"

"Never. He was nondescript, looked like he had money, and seemed to appreciate my work."

"That's fascinating."

Helena stared into space until Melody put on her jacket. "Hey, while you're here, want to hit the streets? You're already in your busker outfit, and I've got a slot in a half-hour at the library."

"Sounds like just what I need," Helena said, "This Kelly van Dusen drag is making me feel like Eva Braun. It would help to strut my stuff in front of an audience—if only for old time's sake."

The Bradford Street Irregulars

The next day, at the Truro hideout, Helena waited anxiously at the dining room table for her fellow sleuths to arrive. Seeing the first vehicle pull up, Shirley set out a plate of cookies.

Amy entered and sat next to Helena, who patted her on the shoulder. "Glad to see you, darling."

Dan Andrade said, "Detective Morgan is back on the case. I still have significant political concerns, Helena, which is why I asked to meet out here."

"Yes, Dan," Quincy said, hanging his coat on the back of his seat and pulling out a chair for Afton. "Even if we can safely say Helena is no longer a suspect, your political adversaries would have a field day if they knew you'd involved a group of civilians in an investigation. We're doing our damnedest to cover for you."

"I appreciate that, and I'm grateful for your support in what I know is a significant inconvenience—if not outright hardship—for some of you."

"It sure as hell is a hardship for *me*," Shirley said. "I'm stuck out in the middle of this cranberry patch with nothing but a lobster. My libido is in danger of exploding."

"Don't ask," Helena said to Amy, hand to brow. "The image will scar your psyche for decades to come."

Chief Silva spoke next. "We hire temporary police for summer traffic and special events. I can deputize these folks if you think it would help protect your position, Dan."

Only Shirley balked at being sworn in. "Last time I was a deputy, I got a badge. Still got it somewhere. No badge, no dice."

When Louie assured her there were badges for everyone who wanted them, she said, "Then what are you waiting for? Sign me up. Now, all we need is a name for our squad."

Helena didn't need but a moment. "The service road enters HomePort from Bradford Street Extension. How about 'The Bradford Street Irregulars?' Has a nice ring to it. Right out of *Sherlock Holmes.* All in favor, say aye."

The vote was unanimous.

"All this is rather unorthodox," Dan said, somewhat baffled by Shirley's comment. "Given we have two deaths, one of them an officer of the law, I believe there's a case for extenuating circumstances. Having solved that dilemma—I hope—Detective Morgan needs to hear everything of importance since the night Brandt was shot."

The Mystery Man

Chief Louie described the prisoner from the gallery shootout as more like a tech nerd than a Russian operative. Dan confirmed the man's identity was false. The court had agreed he was a flight risk, so the mystery man was still in jail.

"Has he said anything useful?" Afton asked, grabbing a chocolate chip cookie as Shirley passed them around.

"Very little. It's not quite a code of silence, but rather a bizarre combination of recalcitrance and what could be genuine ignorance."

"Define ignorance?" Afton asked.

"He doesn't seem to know who hired him. We can see from his burner phone he communicated by text with a person or persons using code names. Of course, everything's stopped since his arrest."

"And no one has come forward to represent him?" Quincy asked.

"A public defender has been assigned."

Amy jotted a note on her pad. "So you don't think he's foreign? Even though the breach of Wally's phone came from a Russian IP address?"

Dan explained internet traffic could be routed through foreign servers and that he thought the man hailed from the Florida panhandle. His English was good, though he used regional phrases such as spigot instead of faucet and commode instead of toilet. There was nothing more to work with than that.

Amy distributed a list describing seventy-six stolen paintings spanning Provincetown's artistic history.

"This is a travesty," Cole said, studying the document. "Most of the major breakthroughs in the Provincetown art scene are represented: White line prints, works from the Hoffmann and Hensche schools—there's value in the individual items, but the collection as a whole is priceless."

"I'm glad you share my thinking," Dan said. "What more can you tell us?"

Cole responded eagerly. "These aren't the most iconic works; those are in museums or well-guarded private collections. This is the next tier—those that inevitably will grow in value. Works worth tens of thousands, not hundreds of thousands like Mavis's. That said, I'm not convinced this is primarily a financial job."

Amy looked up from her notes. "Say more?"

"These stolen pieces are more like a town-wide portfolio, worth more in the aggregate than as individual works."

"I'd wondered if there was a pattern," Dan said.

Helena raised her hand. "Your theory may explain the sudden interest in Melody's paintings. Cole, is her work in the same league as the contemporary artists on Amy's list?"

"I think it will be before long. I did gild the lily a bit with that letter I wrote, but she's got what it takes to go the distance."

Helena took a sip of water. "If that's the case, it may mean the thieves are looking for long-term investments. Here's what I think we should do: One, get a profile of Melody in the local papers to draw attention to her. Two, get more bait to smoke out the thieves."

"You're right with me," Dan said. "Is anyone good at press releases? I don't want to bring my secretary into this."

"I know just the person," Helena said with a grin.

The News of the Day

That Thursday, the *Cape Cod Gazette* and the *Provincetown Free Press* had extensive features on Melody Carpenter, a "newly discovered artistic sensation." The *Free Press* also carried Freddie's interview with the chair of the Wellfleet Historical Society, which had appropriated the art donated to C.J.'s fundraiser.

"It's a tremendous windfall," said society chair, Blanche Hopkins. "Mavis Chandry's donation of a painting from her Phoenix series in C.J. Strongue's memory has me over the moon! I'd also like to single out Cole Hanson and Melody Carpenter, among many others who have contributed their newest works. The auction will be held at the Staunton Museum two weeks from today. Any artists wishing to donate should drop off their art at the museum during normal business hours."

Finishing the article, Charlotte stared out her office window at the tranquil harbor beyond, then said, "And so the trap is set."

Replay

At one the next morning, Cole was photographing artwork for the auction website. As he worked in the basement of the Staunton Museum, he heard technicians in the gallery above installing a set of hard-wired security cameras.

***

Two days after that, Afton, Cole, Marc, and Amy were watching the monitors in Afton's cottage when the hard-wired cameras picked up three shadows at the museum entrance. One masked man keyed in an access code. Once the door was opened, two others made their way through the lobby to the basement stairway while he stood watch outside. The wired feed showed both men opening a door at the far end of the cellar where the auction works were stored, while the original monitors did not.

"A spot of brilliance to assume they'd use Cole's code, Afton," Amy said. "I agree that if we hadn't changed Helena's, they'd have suspected something."

"It was a calculated guess," Afton replied. "Good thing we knew they'd hacked Wally's entire list."

The intruders selected five pictures. When one of the men held open the stairway door, his shirt sleeve slid up to reveal a tattooed snake.

"That will come in handy as identification," Amy said. "I was hesitant about this approach, but it may be working."

The newly installed external cameras followed the thieves' progress from the museum to Pilgrims' Park. The paintings were loaded into a Ford Explorer, which quickly left the area. A few minutes later, the wireless feed returned to normal.

"I doubt they're controlling the video from the car," Afton said. "They're communicating with someone who does it from a greater distance."

"Not knowing who the boss is. Getting orders remotely. These individuals are just foot soldiers," Amy said.

Cole agreed. "And we're still nowhere near knowing who's behind all this. But things could change as early as tomorrow."

"Amen to that," said Marc.

A Meeting of the Minds

Dolores had laid out a sumptuous brunch of seafood, fresh greens, and homemade bread at Staunton's Lookout. The Bradford Street Irregulars were enjoying the meal under the grape arbor, which had been scanned for listening devices. As they ate, Chief Silva explained that tracers installed on the stolen works were transmitting properly. At eight that morning, three paintings—those by Mavis, Melody, and Cole—had been moved from a house on Creek Hill Road to Henry Boorstin's home. Less than an hour later, they'd been relocated to Doctor Woodman's house. Two other tracers remained at Creek Hill Road.

"And no sign that Cheswick Wilks has any of them?" Helena asked. "I can't get him out of my head. It's probably just his weird appearance, but he bugs me."

"None," Amy replied. "The tracking devices aren't signaling anywhere near where he lives. I do suspect the house on Creek Hill Road is the hideout, though."

"Damn," Helena sputtered. "It looks as though Henry Boorstin is the one, after all. Though it makes little sense."

"From what I gather of Wilks," Melody said, "he's a harmless old queen who lives in the past and is always hitting on the young guys."

"That could be half the men in P'town," Marc observed. "Especially in winter."

"Watch yourself, buster," Shirly-Mae said, prodding his arm with her index finger. "Take it from someone who's got more mileage on her than you do. You'll appreciate a nice piece of man flesh a helluva lot more when your own has wrinkled up like a raisin."

Charlotte turned away to hide her laughter as Marc blushed.

"Thank you for that, Shirley. Illuminating perspective, as always. Now back to the subject at hand," Cole said, savoring his husband's embarrassment. "What do we do with this information?"

"We use it to anticipate their next move," the chief said, reaching for another shrimp. "Which means a bit more brainstorming."

"Sounds good," Amy said. "You guys get things started. I'll take notes. But save me some oysters."

The chief sat back in his chair. "OK. First of all, who's running the show? Someone's pulling the strings anonymously, but the thugs on the ground have to deliver the goods to him at some point."

"Or her. There could be an evil queen atop this food chain," Helena said, taking a sip of wine.

Marc reached for a lemon pastry. "Which could still be a him in this town. God knows there are plenty of evil queens."

Helena raised her glass. "Point well taken, darling. I bow to your greater wisdom and expertise. In either case, we'll search out the evil queen."

"OK, folks," Amy said. "Enough Disney. What are the most important questions we haven't answered?"

The chief said, "Mine is, why are they stealing such a wide range of art?"

"A collection of related works is rare outside a major museum," Cole said. "These thefts are as if someone stole all the known Impressionist paintings—works by multiple artists bound together by their concept of the transient effects of light and color. In our case, Provincetown is the binding concept."

Charlotte nodded her agreement. "Then that means the stolen paintings will end up at the same destination despite being stored in separate locations. Chief, what's the current count?"

"More than eighty that we know of—if you count the five taken from the museum last night."

"Assuming the other stolen works are at Creek Hill Road," Amy said, "why did these three end up with Doctor Woodman? If you count *Grace* and Mavis's original phoenix painting, which he already had, he's got five now. What do you think, Cole?"

"He has two of Mavis's; the others—mine and Melody's—are in her style. Perhaps someone wants to keep Mavis-related paintings separate."

"Let's be sure to note that," Chief Silva said. "Two other things bug me. The thieves had just about finished Wally's list. But then they took our bait, broke into the museum a second time, and stole those five paintings. Why? And, most importantly, how will we know when they've got everything they want?"

Girl Talk

That afternoon, Helena strolled Commercial Street in her Kelly van Dusen drag. She was dressed in white linen, and a pair of wide sunglasses rode atop her blonde wig. Her mind was full of potential answers to the questions raised earlier, but none were satisfactory.

As Betty Crocker approached, Helena lowered her sunglasses and peered into a shop window. When Betty passed, she whispered, "Gurrrl. . . that suburban drag does nothing for you—bless your little heart."

Betty, in a leopard-skin pantsuit, electric orange blouse, white sandals, and tiger-stripe sunglasses, strode to a nearby waterfront park. He sat down at an empty picnic table as Helena sheepishly followed.

"How did you know it was me?" she asked, once seated across from her old friend.

Betty smirked. "Don't worry. Your secret's safe with me. I've been on the lookout for you, sweet cheeks. I know better than most what it takes—the makeup, shading, and such—to camouflage features, so I stripped those things away in my mind, and, Voilà, there you were.

"Delighted to see you. I worried something was up when you went underground again. Was it because of the gallery shootings?"

"Right in one, Betty, though I shouldn't talk about that."

"C'mon, Helena. This isn't some queen at the next dressing table. This is me, Betty. Do I need to start the 'I knew you when' shit to coax the 'T' out of you?

"Besides, you owe me for that whole Sea Hunt routine; say nothing of voiding the race. We'll need a rematch, by the way, or we'll lose all those lovely donations. I gotta tell you, though, I had a ball messing with Brandt's head. I almost miss the son of a bitch. For a straight man, he was a fabulous straight man."

Helena shrugged. "Well, OK. You *do* have a point."

Betty listened attentively as Helena recounted all that had happened since the race. When she finished, Betty removed her sunglasses and twirled them in her right hand.

"So, you suspect some super-rich guy wants a comprehensive collection of Provincetown Art? That doesn't seem as outrageous as you might expect. When I was at the Miami apartment last winter, a fellow down the beach raided Art Basel for every Robert Motherwell he could get. He dropped four million without even attending the show. Did it all through art brokers."

"Do you know why?" Helena asked, leaning forward.

Betty did the same. To someone watching from the street, they looked like two girlfriends sharing confidences.

"He said he collected Provincetown Art and always got whatever he wanted, whatever way he could. We were at the same table at Faena, but he was far more interested in the waiter than talking to me. It's inevitable. When a girl reaches a certain age, the old charms just don't cut it. I should have been smart like you and married when I was asked."

"Yes, darling, but then Cary Grant would never have had his film career. Take comfort that the entire world benefited from your sacrifice."

"Bitch, I've missed you," Betty said, clutching Helena's hand with a firm grip.

"I've missed you too, dear one. More than I can say," Helena said, turning away to compose herself.

Betty, respectful of his friend's emotions, continued his tale. "I wasn't surprised to see that same waiter onboard *Scamp* around the time of the museum opening. If he knows what's good for him, he'll get a ring on it before there's more onshore dining. His finger, I mean, in case you were thinking otherwise."

"I remember that yacht," Helena said. "She tied up at Fisherman's Wharf, just past *Dame Edna*. I seem to remember watching *Scamp* leave the day we discovered the vandalism in the museum. Was the waiter from Faena working or a guest?"

"Well, I'm not sure we can consider his duties work," Betty said with a knowing glance. "His boss is fifty-five or so, though he's still sort of hot. But if you're asking whether the waiter was serving dinner on board, the answer is no. Whatever he was serving up was definitely between the sheets."

"Who owns the yacht?"

"Oh, didn't I say? His name is Lance Kensington. He made an absolute fortune around twenty years ago, developing web protection for banks and credit card companies. He's also got some history in town. *Scamp* has visited several times, docking at the long wharf facing the breakwater. You know where I mean, the 'size queen's section,' just past our boats. Are you telling me you haven't met him?"

"Come to think of it," Helena mused, "someone by that name visited the museum just before the opening. He offered to assess our security systems for free, but I told him we had things covered."

"Did you give him a tour?"

"Yes, as a courtesy, though we hadn't hung Mavis's work yet. Do you think he was casing the joint?"

Betty lit up as she began to dish. "Honey, from what I've heard of this guy, nothing would surprise me. He's got all sorts of shady deals and underworld connections. Rumor has it he used to turn tricks before hitting it big with his security firm. Apparently, he was among the first to offer his wares over the Internet. You remember, in the old days, before Grindr and Scruff, when guys hooked up in chat rooms?"

"And dinosaurs like us roamed the earth," Helena added with a laugh. "It's a long way from cybersex to cybersecurity, though."

"Not as far as one might think," Betty mused, stopping to watch a handsome young man stroll to the water's edge. "The porn and escort industries led the way in many technological breakthroughs—just like NASA but less boring. From what I've heard, his company developed the remote cam concept as well as by-the-minute billing. And to think, I could have had him for eighty bucks a toss back in the day."

Helena feigned shock. "My dear, what *are* you saying?"

Betty laughed. "Don't bullshit me, honey. I know how many miles are on your odometer. He was a bartender here in P'town one summer, long before you arrived on the scene. Everyone always said he was selling himself on the side, with women sometimes—but mostly men. There was something about a college fund. Of course, that's the oldest story in the book."

Helena watched her friend with intense interest akin to joy. Chatting with Betty was the first moment of relaxation since she'd discovered Mavis's defaced paintings.

Betty paused for effect. "If I recall—and it is from the depths of time I pull this tasty morsel—he was kept by that dreadful Cheswick Wilks for much of the following year. Wilks even brought Lance back to Manhattan at the end of the season. The story was that he was a houseboy, though no doubt there were extra duties. In fact, I'm fairly sure it was Wilks who funded Lance's startup, but I could be wrong about that bit. Much as I hate to admit, it was a long time ago."

"Wilks keeps rattling around in my brain. What more can you tell me about him, darling?" Helena asked, appreciating Betty's vast store of gossip more than ever before.

"A sorry creature, in my estimation. I've often wondered why he didn't fall on his face, given those spindly legs and that big gut. He's always been that way: the pale skin, long, pointy nose—and those creepy eyes with the half-glasses. Years ago, he'd have himself hauled onto Herring Cove Beach in a sedan chair carried by four muscular boys wearing matching speedos that left nothing to the imagination. Another group of boys carried enormous picnic hampers. One week they'd all be blond. The next week, brunette. The boys, not the hampers. Those were the days. Anything and everything used to go on out at Herring Cove. But I digress.

"He'd serve brunch and hold court, smoking pot through a long cigarette holder. If I recall, they used to call him 'The Penguin' after that character on *Batman*. You know, the old TV show, not the movie. Wilks spent money like water and used to dine out on his family lineage—the Astors and that horrid woman, the 'Witch of Wall Street,' until people were downright sick of hearing about them. What was her name?"

"Hetty Green?"

"Yes. That's the one. World's worst woman miser, they call her now, but she had to have been a smart businesswoman to go as far as she did back then. That beautiful old house in the East End, the Stull house, is all Wilks has left. The banks foreclosed on his Manhattan townhouse two years ago. It had been in the family for ages. From what I hear, his place here is crammed to the gills with stuff from the townhouse. A friend who had dinner there recently told me the place made Grey Gardens look like *House Beautiful*."

"And now Wilks' former boy toy, Lance, is the one that's filthy rich," Helena said.

Betty chuckled. "Oh yes, dahlin'. He makes our combined fortunes look like pin money."

"And obsessed with art?"

"I'd say so, given the swath he cut through Art Basel last winter."

"And is here in town?"

"Was here. *Scamp's* been back now and then, but that doesn't mean much. Lots of rich folks park their yachts at a marina and then fly off someplace else.

"I don't recall seeing Lance in the flesh save that one time just before the museum gala. I was overseeing repairs to *Tough Cookie*. He walked up the pier and didn't recognize me—no doubt he was distracted. I'm sure he had his hands full with that waiter. And I mean both hands."

"Darling, as captivating as that image may be, I've got to go," Helena said, rising. "I can't begin to thank you enough for this information. You may have just broken the case wide open."

Lady and the Scamp

Over dinner that night, as Shirley-Mae ladled out her famous firehouse chili, Helena turned to Butch. "I need some of your superb nautical know-how."

"What are you up to now?" Butch asked, taking a spoonful and blowing to cool it.

"How can I find out where a boat has been?"

"When you say 'boat,' do you mean a big boat or a little boat?"

"I need to know where a yacht has been for the last couple of months."

"That's easy. I've got an app on my phone. What's the name of the vessel?"

"*Scamp*. As in *Lady and the Tramp*. And no, before you say it, I'm neither the lady nor the tramp."

Butch opened the app. "You don't fool around. *Scamp* is one of the largest yachts afloat at two-hundred-thirty feet. Why are you so interested? You're not planning on upgrading, are you? *Dame Edna* was at the far end of our price range."

Helena laughed. "No, not at all. It's just that I ran into Betty today."

"You talked with Betty? Can you trust him not to blow your cover?"

"He spotted me in my Kelly drag, but I know he'll never say a word."

"If he spotted you, others could too," Shirley said, helping herself to some shredded cheese.

"I don't think so. Betty knows what it takes to create a believable impersonation, while most people only observe the end result. In any case, he told me about this super-rich cybersecurity mogul who used to be here in P'town years ago. He owns *Scamp*, which was at Fisherman's Wharf around the time Mavis's paintings were defaced. And," Helena paused for maximum effect. "Kensington set a record at Art Basel last winter, purchasing every available work of one Provincetown artist."

"What else did Betty have to say?" Butch set down his spoon and gave his full attention.

"Rumor has it that dreadful Cheswick Wilks kept him when he was younger."

"I got cornered by that sonnuvabitch at the private view," Shirley-Mae said. "He kept rambling on about his weird aunt and his big old house. Even invited me over for drinks. If he was keeping any young kid, it would scar the poor boy for life."

In the Shadows

The next day, Helena, her Kelly drag tempered by a headscarf and sensible shoes, made slow progress over the two-mile walk from the hideout to Fisher Road. She'd had to carry C.J.'s dog, Moppet, for the last mile. The pup had grown tired, sat down in the sand, and refused to budge.

It was dusk by the time they finally arrived at Mavis's house. Approaching with caution, Helena spied a man dressed in black outside the studio. As she drew near, he turned and vanished into the woods. Reaching the spot where he'd stood, she could see Mavis hard at work. When Helena finally captured the artist's attention, Mavis flipped a cloth over her easel, then hastened to let her in.

"There was someone out there just now," Helena said. "Did you see him?"

"Not this time." Mavis sounded blasé, but Helena sensed she was anxious. "But I've had a sense there was another one around lately."

"Another what?"

Mavis directed Helena to a stool by the window. "Wanna-be artist. They stalk me sometimes, trying to get me to teach them what I know. I fend 'em off with this." Mavis brandished her vintage shotgun as Helena flinched. "In your case, I'd hate to be mistaken. You have so many wardrobe changes I can't keep track. We need a secret bird call so I know it's you."

Helena wasn't so sure.

That was no art student—there's something both sinister and familiar about that man in the shadows.

"Keep the safety on that thing, Mavis, if it even has one. I didn't dare call you. I'm sure they're tapping your phone line by now. And you won't take a burner phone, so how does a girl stay in touch?"

"OK," Mavis sighed. "I assume this isn't a social call. Would you care for a cup of tea? I've got mugs out here, though my favorite is still a piece of evidence. And you know, somehow, the tea just doesn't taste the same. Nice dog, by the way."

After filling Mavis in on the latest developments, Helena asked if she ever knew a Lance Kensington.

"Sounds like one of those pornstar names, but it is familiar," the artist said, petting the puppy. "Where do I know it from? Oh, yeah. Now I remember. That asshole!"

Helena, cup in hand, moved closer to monitor Mavis's expression. "Exactly what do you remember?"

"He was an artist model back when I taught at the Art Center. Young, not over twenty-five. Good looking for a fella but taken with himself. He had a hard time as a model—literally."

Helena chuckled. "Do you mean what I think?"

"Yup. One of those exhibitionist types you have to watch out for in my line of work. Standing up there naked in front of an audience got him quite worked up. A few of the Chatham ladies and most of the men found that quite intriguing. I remember wondering if he was advertising his wares."

Helena sensed a change in her friend's mood.

Where normally she'd make a wisecrack, she's subdued. I wonder if there's more to this story than she's willing to say.

"Was that all the trouble you had with him?"

Mavis looked down at Moppet, who stared up at her, tail wagging. Her voice dropped to a whisper. "No, that was the least of it. The Association paid his fee, but on top of that, he demanded a cut on the sale of my work."

"Say more?"

"Until I learned better, I'd paint along with the students. At the end of the week-long figurative class, I had four finished portraits of him in all his glory. If I remember correctly, I worked out a deal where this wealthy woman from Pocasset bought them from me but also donated to the Art Center.

"Turns out Lance was quite the narcissist and obsessed with the portraits from the moment he saw them. He insisted on getting one as a commission, claiming they wouldn't exist without him. I told him if he wasn't careful, I'd give him a commission, all right. I'd commit to sticking his head where the sun don't shine."

Helena's laughter seemed to lift Mavis's spirits. Her eyes brightened, and she appeared more relaxed. "He gave me a lot of lip but backed down in the end. Last I heard, he'd taken up with that Cheswick Wilks fella. I left town for a bit after that. By the time I returned, Lance was with him in New York."

Mavis ended abruptly. Her face was taut, and the corners of her mouth curled in a distinct frown.

Helena studied her for a moment, then asked, "Do you remember the name of the woman from Pocasset?"

Mavis chuckled. "Sounds like the man from Nantucket. No. Can't say I do. Those blonde trophy wives look alike after a while. Present company excepted, of course."

Helena tossed her tresses, which coaxed another smile from the artist.

"They'd know at the Art Center, though. It was the first class I taught there in 'eighty-seven."

"Excellent," Helena said, coaxing the puppy onto her lap. "Actually, there was something else I wanted to discuss."

"What?" Mavis asked, hesitating slightly.

"This is Moppet. He used to belong to C.J. Strongue."

Mavis paled, and her voice grew somber. "I wouldn't let her bring him."

"To the meeting at your studio?"

"Yes. I did everything I could to discourage her."

Helena's voice was soft and encouraging. "It's a good thing he didn't go, Mavis. Can you see that? He would have been there when—"

"I know. I know. I feel guilty for making C.J. climb up to my studio to see a painting I knew she'd hate. If she hadn't pushed me—"

"Let's not dwell, Mavis. C.J. was maladroit and sometimes inappropriate but essentially a well-intentioned person who'd had a tough life. She had no living relatives. Moppet was at a kennel for weeks before Marc and Cole took him home. Frida would be devastated if they kept him, so we thought maybe you'd like to have him."

"All I'd see is C.J. lying there," Mavis said, her voice cracking.

"Or perhaps you might think of it as doing a good turn for the poor soul," Helena said gently. "She loved this dog more than anything else. I'm sure she'd rest easier if he had a good home."

With that, Helena set the pup back on the floor. He let out a little whimper, and Mavis bent down to pick him up. Looking up at Helena with tear-filled eyes, she nodded once.

"Thanks, Mavis. As always, you're a doll," Helena said, rising and kissing the temperamental artist on her cheek. "I'll ask Marc or Cole to drop off his food first thing tomorrow morning. Moppet is set for the night. I fed him already.

"Before I go, may I see what you're working on?"

Mavis shook her head. "Not ready yet. And don't call me a doll. The last guy who did sang soprano for a month."

The Dark Web

Helena walked the short distance to the Fisher Beach lot, where Charlotte and Chief Louie were waiting in his Volvo.

"Did you have any trouble getting away from your shadows?" she asked while sliding into the back seat.

Charlotte grinned, saying, "Afton led them on a wild goose chase."

"So what did you figure out?"

"It's all written here," Charlotte said. "I've covered the details with the chief. I'll just state the high points."

She handed several pages to Helena, who put them in her purse.

"Before we get into that, Louie was just telling me something I think you'll be interested to hear."

The chief turned to look at Helena. "Sergeant Brandt brought in the Bureau of Criminal Investigations to review the wiring in Mavis's studio. One of several things he failed to report was that the crew found wireless transmitters and surveillance cameras inside the studio. Whoever set the trap would have seen C.J.'s death and known they'd killed the wrong person. I suspect Brandt knew C.J. was dead all along.

"This was a sophisticated effort. Mavis was fortunate to have forgotten that meeting. I think whoever was behind the murder attempt knew she would make herself a cup of tea as soon as she arrived."

Helena nodded in agreement.

Everything fits, but there's something Mavis is still not saying

The chief cast a knowing glance as if to say, *I know what you're thinking, but now is not the time to discuss it.*

"That's all I've got, but wait until you hear what Charlotte has dug up."

A car parked behind them. Charlotte looked straight ahead but whispered, "Kensington Security fronts as a cybersecurity operation with several legitimate clients, though most of its profits come from hosting some questionable websites. Not just porn, but also merchant sites on the dark web."

"They've got to be making their money from more than provider fees, don't you think?" Helena asked.

"There are allegations that KS, as the company is known these days, has been skimming off the top of the shadier financial transactions. Lance Kensington has been buying a lot of art while liquidating most of his other physical assets. He sold a penthouse in South Beach, a home in Mexico, and another in Guadalupe, along with a large amount of company stock to pay cash for *Scamp*."

"Is he still running the business?" Helena asked.

Charlotte smiled her appreciation for the question. "Someone allegedly close to Russian oligarchs handles day-to-day operations. Kensington talks of retiring, but tales of extensive drug use, prostitution, and fraud might be forcing him out. My contacts at Treasury say witnesses are intimidated and hesitant to admit doing business with KS. Even so, indictments are expected within the year."

"This sounds simply too James Bond," Helena said. "You can't tell me these sorts of goings-on have come to little old Provincetown."

Chief Louie shook his head. "In my line of work, I've learned never to say never. I'll drop you off on the way back, Helena."

***

Walking up the driveway to the hideout, Helena felt that pieces of the puzzle were finally within her grasp.

So Kensington's on the ropes, and the lady from Pocasset is sitting on paintings worth a quarter of a million each—if she still owns them. But why steal a town's artistic legacy? We need more answers. Perhaps the best way to get them is to come up with better questions.

Putting It Together

The following day, Marc and Cole hosted another hastily arranged meeting at Staunton's Lookout, their contemporary house atop the dune. While Afton checked for listening devices, two security guards distracted the men monitoring HomePort and Telegraph Hill. Then, "The Irregulars," as the deputized friends proudly referred to themselves, parked out of sight behind the house.

Mavis was conspicuously absent from the gathering in Marc's study. The large room, filled with portraits painted by Cole, had panoramic views of the harbor, Cape Cod Bay, and the Atlantic. Varnished wood, brass fittings, and a mounted telescope gave the impression of a ship at sea. A set of the captain's journals had pride of place in a bookcase on the eastern wall, each of the twenty volumes delicately numbered in gold. While the original journals were in the museum, the Historical Society had published an edition including Marc's tale of his arrival at HomePort and the vindication of Captain Staunton.

Marc wrote at the captain's desk from a spot overlooking HomePort's tower, where both men had gone to write in all sorts of weather.

Q and A

Dan Andrade, seated at the head of a long, gate-leg table, kicked off the discussion. "Thanks for coming at such short notice. When

Helena called yesterday with her list of questions, it seemed wise to farm them out in advance. I hope you all did your homework.

"First question on her list: where was *Scamp* during recent events? Butch, what could you find out?"

Hair still blond, Butch was seated to Dan's right. "She was docked in Plymouth when the hijacking attempt occurred on Route 3, which is nearby. *Scamp* was in P'town overnight when the murder and break-in occurred. She cast off the next morning, several hours before C.J.'s body was found."

"Was she here when either of the shootings occurred, Butch?" Amy asked from her seat to Dan's left. She was dressed in a dark suit with a white scarf and held a cup of coffee in her right hand.

"No. She stayed in international waters, which means at least twelve nautical miles offshore. Cruising yachts usually hug the coast for the scenery, but *Scamp* remained beyond territorial limits most of the time—except for one overnight in Buzzards Bay."

Amy consulted notes on a yellow pad. "Where was she on the twenty-first?"

"Interesting you should ask. That's the day she anchored off the coast of Marion in Buzzard's Bay. What about the twenty-first?"

"That's the night that Deidre Hamilton's waterfront home was broken into, and four male nudes by Mavis Chandry were stolen," Amy said, grinning at Dan as if she'd won a wager.

"What?" Helena exclaimed. "The woman from Pocasset?"

As the others listened intently, Helena shared Mavis's story of young Lance and the four portraits.

"Butch, does this suggest the robbers came by boat," Amy said.

"*Scamp* has a so-called 'limousine tender' that can hit thirty-five knots, which would make the trip from Marion to Pocasset easy enough. It could also get someone into Hyannis Harbor. After that, it's less than half a mile's walk to the hospital to kill Brandt."

"Mrs. Hamilton reported the theft to Pocasset police," Dan said. "No one at the station knew to tell me—an oversight that cost us time."

Helena said, "The Art Center gave me some background on those works that Mrs. Hamilton bought. They believe they were the only male nudes Mavis has ever painted."

Cole's eyes widened. "Until now, you mean, when she painted the one she was going to give you."

His conversation with Mavis's art dealer had confirmed there were only five male nudes. The dealer kept a database of all the paintings, including her most recent work. Whenever a work sold, he added the new owner's information to the painting's blockchain record. As a result, few forgeries had been attempted.

"Mavis sent him an image of your painting, Helena," Cole said. "He said it was one of the best things she'd ever done and was devastated to hear it had been stolen."

Charlotte, who had been listening intently, chimed in. "So anyone with access to that database would know the current location of all Mavis Chandry's paintings."

"Exactly," Dan said. "And the next question on our list?"

"Why are Mavis, Melody, and Cole's paintings sequestered from the rest of the stash at Creek Hill Road? Why does Doctor Woodman have them? And what's Henry Boorstin's role in all this?" Helena replied.

"That's the next three questions," Charlotte said, wagging her finger.

Helena hung her head. "I know. But if we can figure those connections out, I think we'll know who's behind all this."

"Perhaps," Amy said, almost to herself.

Dan glanced her way. "Say more?"

"According to Butch, we can place Kensington in town for C.J.'s murder, but not Brandt's. We should keep that in mind. But let's tackle Woodman and Boorstin first."

Marc grinned. "Sounds like the reporters who investigated Watergate."

Provenance

"Let me start this one," Amy said, walking to a whiteboard Marc used to plot his books. She wrote two names and drew a line between them. "What do we know about their connection?"

"That Boorstin was Doctor Woodman's architect," Marc said.

"That the doctor implied he got *Grace* from Boorstin when we know it was stolen," Helena said. "And, of course, we know Woodman has Mavis's original phoenix painting."

"That the transmitters revealed three of our decoy paintings have also found their way from Boorstin to Woodman," Melody said.

"That all those paintings are loosely related in style. Remember, Melody and I patterned our works after Mavis's," Cole said.

Marc hesitated, then added, "The four paintings stolen from Mrs. Hamilton and the phoenix painting the doctor has account for all of Mavis's existing male nudes. But how to explain the sudden interest in Cole and Melody's art?"

"Lineage," Cole replied.

Amy wrote the word on the board. "Say more?"

"Works by those who study with the master. It's an arcane concept. Most artists don't have acolytes who doggedly paint in their style."

"I can think of a couple in town who do," Marc said with an arch grin.

Cole laughed. "Leaving that bit of local color aside, a collection containing not only the artist's work but also those of their school might interest some buyers. And remember, the hijacking was meant to steal all of Mavis's previously unknown works."

"So you're saying we should assume the thefts center on Mavis?" Dan asked.

Helena took a sip of water. "A better way to say it might be that Mavis is at the core of whatever's been happening. That's why I asked you not to invite her, Marc. Remember, Lance Kensington thought he should have made money off those early nudes. And now he's probably gotten them for free."

"But why obsess over a modeling gig that happened three decades ago?" Charlotte asked. "And if Mavis is the key, why are her paintings with Doctor Woodman?"

"I think I'm starting to see how things fit," Helena said with a smile. "If we assume Mrs. Hamilton's paintings went by launch back to *Scamp*, then the only other 'school of Chandry' works outside the museum are with the doctor. Kensington could recover those works in one stop by stealing them from Woodman. Remember, the market won't touch a painting that isn't in Mavis's database, which rules out all the unsigned pieces in her studio.

"Bear with me for a moment. Many of the works stolen over the summer are quite large, aren't they? Like six feet tall, some of them?"

Cole nodded.

"And they'd have to be crated if they were traveling any distance. Correct?"

"Yes."

"But the paintings the doctor has—"

"Are small enough to be moved at short notice," Cole said, catching her drift.

"And if the police find the big ones, these smaller, Mavis-related works are someplace else," Marc said.

"She's old, and there's no doubt her paintings will appreciate in value when she dies," Helena said. "I can see why he's set them apart. If I'm right, those paintings will be removed from Doctor Woodman's house when Kensington decides to clear out for good."

Charlotte's phone pinged. "My contact at Sotheby's just texted me. He reviewed sales of Provincetown Art for the last year and found potential evidence of shill bidding. The thefts may not be just about amassing a collection; they might be part of a scheme to fix prices. After all, if there's less Provincetown art to go around, each piece that comes up for sale will be more valuable."

"This is beginning to sound like an art-funded pension plan or insurance policy," Butch said. "*Scamp* can go almost anywhere in the world. She'd have the telecommunications capacity and could deliver paintings to any continent. If Kensington is running from the Russian mob, this is a damn good way to keep moving yet have his assets with him. If he needs money, he can sell a painting from anywhere."

"If so, those small works the doctor has *must* be the key to when Kensington is going to leave," Dan said. "We have to know immediately when someone comes to get them."

Helena glanced at Melody, who promptly said, "Consider it done."

The Night Watch

Melody organized the buskers to monitor Doctor Woodman's house around the clock. On the third day, when she spied Henry Boorstin's car careening into the driveway, Melody was positioned beneath the kitchen window within two minutes of his arrival.

"You can't keep them," Boorstin shrieked. "I've got to have them now! Here's a check for every cent you gave me."

"No way. They're mine, and there's nothing you can do," the doctor replied. "I've got your bills of sale marked paid in full. And I doubt you'll want to confess to selling stolen property."

Boorstin slammed his fist on a counter. "Stolen property? What the hell are you talking about?"

"I've had this," the doctor replied, pulling a piece of paper from his wallet, "from an acquaintance who was decent enough to warn me. I'll read it to you:

"Dear Dr. Woodman,

I've so enjoyed the tours of your art collection. Because you were so kind to me, I want to return the favor. I told Melody Carpenter you had one of her paintings. When I described the portrait known as Grace, Melody told me it had been sold to a Mrs. van Dusen. When Melody checked, Mrs. van Dusen told her the painting was stolen from Henry Boorstin while he was taking it to be framed.

I feel it my duty to warn you that you are in possession of stolen property.'""

Woodman didn't share that the note was signed by Candace Lagasse.

"And now here you are trying to buy them back. Did you steal *all* of them?"

Boorstin sank into a chair. "No. I got them from some people—don't ask me their names—who threatened to expose questionable business deals if I didn't find a hiding place for the paintings. One painting *was* stolen from me to fake out the owners, this rich blonde ditz and her husband. I got it back the same day. Don't ask me to say more than that."

Woodman was red with rage. "So you used my house as a stash? What were you going to do, take my money and then steal them back from me?"

"I'll pay ten thousand more than you paid me." Boorstin's face was contorted in fear. "They'll kill me if I don't bring them back."

"Not my problem. You got yourself into this mess. Get yourself out of it and get yourself out of my house!"

Boorstin stopped at the front door. "You better watch your step. They don't take prisoners."

"Neither do I," the doctor yelled, hurling a plate at the despondent architect, who ducked just in time.

One Step Back

"So the theft of your painting was a ruse," Helena said to Melody after being summoned to Buskerville Hall. They were seated on the bed in Melody's room, which overlooked the doctor's house.

"Sure looks that way. Boorstin must have bought my harbor scene for himself and sold *Grace* to Doctor Woodman after the fake robbery."

Helena scowled. "Boorstin is more of a louse than even I imagined. I can't believe I'm saying this, but I sort of feel bad for the Flying Asshole. Woodman doesn't have a clue what kind of crowd he's gotten tangled up with."

"I bet Boorstin figured they'd steal them back, and he'd make money on the deal," Melody said, parting the curtain to check on Woodman's house.

"That seems likely," Helena said, "but why not do just that? Why is Boorstin now so eager to buy them back?"

Melody paused. "Because the gang knows we're on to them? Do you think they've spotted the plainclothesmen Chief Silva has monitoring Creek Hill Road?"

"That's probably it. I'll go warn the chief."

***

Helena recounted the conversation to Chief Louie, who called Dan Andrade on a burner phone.

"My guys tell me there's a van at Creek Hill Road that's unloaded a lot of plywood and two-by-fours. We figure they're building crates to pack the paintings. There's a hitch, though, Dan."

Helena described what Melody overheard.

As always, the chief was methodical. "Helena, do you have any additional thoughts why those paintings aren't with the others?"

"We suspect works associated with Mavis and her school are kept separate in case the larger haul was discovered. Those are the paintings Kensington wants most."

"That supports the theory he'd retrieve them right before he skips town."

Helena pursed her lips. "Which is why that snake of an architect tried to get them back. The gang must have made it his problem because they know they're being watched. I can't help but enjoy how Boorstin must be feeling just about now."

"I recommend we pull the detail," the chief said. "We've got the transmitters hidden in the paintings taken from the museum. Two are in the stash at Creek Hill, and the rest are at Doctor Woodman's house. When those paintings are moved, we'll know."

"There's one more piece of the puzzle," Helena said. "Where's *Scamp*?"

The chief looked pleased with himself. "I found that marine app your husband uses and checked on her an hour ago. She's in international waters off Chatham, heading parallel to the shore toward Provincetown. That makes me even more certain Kensington's planning to leave."

"Agreed," Dan said. "Shut down everything but the surveillance camera across the street."

The Road Less Traveled

Later that day, Helena and Butch strolled a narrow path near the hideout. One side of the trail was a steep hill covered with oaks, pines, and beech trees as far as the eye could see. The other side dropped precipitously to the moors below. Grasses undulating in the breeze, water flowing through a stone culvert, and the all-encompassing stillness made Provincetown seem a thousand miles away. The past revealed itself along the worn route: a cemetery with five headstones amid a pine wood, a solitary lilac that once graced the doorway of a long-forgotten homestead, and stone walls that demarcated fields now reclaimed by woodland.

Helena gazed across the hollow. "I agree with Louie. Kensington's gang is ready to leave. But something troubles me. Why would they make such a big show of moving lumber into the house? And why wait until now to pack? What if that's all a ruse? They've deceived us before."

"You're right," Butch said. "It would make much more sense to have the art crated and ready in case they had to cut and run. So you think the van and the plywood are a decoy?"

Helena was pleased Butch understood. "I do. They've always known they'd have to rendezvous with *Scamp*. Why delay packing when the order to leave could come at any moment? What should we do? You didn't ask to be dragged into this, but I'm fresh out of ideas."

Butch responded without hesitation. "I've never been sure Louie and Dan had the entire picture. No more conferences or speculation. It's time for action. You and I should strike out on our own."

"Now that's the guy I married," Helena said as they reached the railroad bed where trains once transported famous artists and writers to and from New York. "Race you back to the house."

Incommunicado

Chief Silva monitored a video feed from the thieves' hideout on Creek Hill Road. It had been four hours since every human observer had left the location. Suddenly, the feed went dead. Perplexed, the chief scrolled through other webcam sites in town. The Monument, Spiritus Pizza, Town Hall; every site was down.

"Goddamn it. I should have expected this," Louie yelled, bringing Officer Chase running. "Get over to Creek Hill Road and see if anyone is still at the house. I'm heading to MacMillan Pier."

En route, Chief Louie tried to use his radio, then his cell phone. Neither worked. Driving to the end of the pier, he was surprised to find Marc and Cole standing there.

"Helena called three hours ago," Marc said, "and told us to monitor any suspicious vessels leaving the harbor. So far, all we've seen is a fishing boat."

"Cell coverage and police frequencies are down," the chief said. "Looks as if Kensington and his crew have jammed the signals so they can make a run for it. I need to check on a couple of things. Keep watching. I'll be back."

Crossing the Line

Chief Louie drove to Creek Hill Road, where Officer Chase informed him the hideout was empty.

"They may be stealing the paintings from Woodman," the chief said. "The trackers showed the art was still there just before the signal stopped. I'll drive over there to see if I can intercept the thieves. Wait here."

The front door of Woodman's house was ajar when the chief arrived. Gun drawn, he entered. There were blank spaces on the wall where the valuable paintings had once hung. The transmitters were lined up on the kitchen counter as if to mock those who had faith in them.

Boorstin and the doctor, tied and gagged, lay on the kitchen floor. Neither man seemed to realize anyone was in the room. Their vital signs were weak, and there were no bruises, but the chief noticed a slight trace of blood on their right arms, indicating a possible injection. He dialed the Rescue Squad from Doctor Woodman's landline.

After tending to the men as best he could, Chief Louie tried to reach Helena, then Butch. When neither answered, he called Charlotte, who picked up on the first ring. She'd not seen them all day and suggested he call Melody.

"Melody," the chief exclaimed. "Shit. I forgot she was watching the house."

The chief found her stretched out in the elaborate flower bed. She, too, had been drugged.

Just then, the Rescue Squad arrived. The paramedics were tending to Melody within seconds. When she stirred a few minutes later, the chief asked about her condition.

"Drugged with a strong sedative," a squad member replied. "Vital signs are suppressed, but she should be out of danger now we've administered a stimulant."

"Same here," a voice said from a nearby window. "These two got enough to kill them. Good thing you found them when you did, Chief. They'll be out for hours but are stabilized. We should get everyone to the hospital for observation just to be on the safe side."

Chief Silva paced the lawn watching the ambulances depart, his brow furrowed.

What's happened to the small town I grew up in? This used to be the safest place in the world. We never locked our doors. Everybody knew and looked out for each other. Now, this?

Forcing himself to focus, the chief went inside and called Charlotte. Informing her of Melody's condition, he asked that Charlotte meet him at MacMillan Pier. Then, without success, he tried Helena and Butch a second time.

Once back in his cruiser, Chief Louie raced along Commercial Street, lights flashing. At the Coast Guard station, he asked to see Commander Raúl Vega at once. The gates opened. A tall man with a crewcut ran out of a long gray building to the right of the drive.

Chief Louie wasted no time. "I need you to run an intercept. We've lost cell and police communications. Are your frequencies still active?"

Vega spoke into his walkie-talkie and got a response. "Appear to be."

"I need you to intercept the yacht, *Scamp*. Last I knew, she was heading toward Race Point from Chatham. We're investigating the owner for art theft and possible murder. I suspect he'll return to international waters after picking up stolen artwork."

Vega told Chief Louie the nearest cutter was the *Ida Lewis*, at least an hour away. He could deploy air search and rescue from Air Base Cape Cod, but if *Scamp* reached international waters, he couldn't pursue and board her unless there was a reciprocal agreement with the vessel's flag state or proof of a crime.

"I'm sure there isn't an agreement," the chief said. "What's more, the yacht can make fourteen knots. I also doubt *Scamp* will enter the harbor, so we should expect a second vessel to deliver the paintings. If we can observe the transfer of stolen property, you'll have what you need to board her. I'll see you at MacMillan Pier."

"I'll do whatever I can, Chief," Vega said before sounding the general alarm.

***

The chief found Marc and Cole in a tense discussion when he returned to the pier.

"A trawler could easily transport crates of paintings to *Scamp*," Marc said. "There must be a crane to haul the limousine tender, which they could use to hoist the crates on board, especially on a calm sea like tonight's."

"We saw a New Bedford trawler head out some time ago," Cole explained to the chief. "We didn't put it together at first. Now, we're convinced they passed within ten feet of us with everything below deck—the paintings *and* the thieves. We feel like idiots."

"If I beat myself up for everything I ever missed, I'd be in a straitjacket," the chief said. "Give yourselves a break. Have you seen Helena and Butch?"

"No," Marc replied. "*Dame Edna's* still docked, but there's no sign of them."

Charlotte strode toward the three men. "What's Melody's condition?"

"What?" Cole and Marc exclaimed.

"She'll be OK," Chief Silva said. "I'll fill you in later."

Charlotte grabbed the chief's arm. "I googled *Scamp*. She has a helicopter deck. The paintings Woodman had are small enough to fit in a helicopter."

"Good thinking," the chief said. "They're not at his house, and the thieves found the tracking devices. I'm sure you're right. We need speed and backup—and here it comes."

Two Fast Response Boats raced toward the pier. Once nearby, Commander Vega yelled, "A Cape Air pilot spotted a yacht off Peaked Hill Bars with a trawler offloading onto it. Shortly after, a small helicopter landed and delivered some parcels before it left again. We've got all we need for boarding so long as we can catch up with *Scamp*. I'm pretty sure I can get these FRBs there in time."

"Take us with you," the Chief yelled.

"A bit irregular, but given Congressman Mullin's prior involvement, I'm down with it."

***

The chief and Charlotte boarded the commander's boat as Marc and Cole jumped onto the second craft. Both FRBs set out at maximum speed, leaving wakes that shimmered in the moonlight as the sound of their powerful engines echoed across the harbor.

"What's the speed on these?" Chief Louie asked Commander Vega, shouting to be heard. The chief wore a life vest and gripped a metal bar beside Vega, who was piloting the FRB. Between the rapid forward movement and the bouncing of the inflatable, both men were hanging on as tight as they could.

"They can hit forty knots on a calm night like this," Commander Vega yelled. "But we're not armed other than our handguns. The *Ida Lewis* has the heavy artillery, and she's still more than an hour away. The best we can do is track *Scamp* until she arrives."

Long Point and Wood End lights passed in a blur as Provincetown receded into a misty haze colored by reflected light.

The commander pointed to the radar, where a shape was moving toward the Cape Cod Canal. "There's your trawler. We've got a fix on their AIS transponder and know who they are. When they reach the canal, a team from Base Cape Cod will intercept them."

"What's AIS?" Charlotte asked, leaning forward to be heard.

"Automatic Identification System. It's how we identify vessels at a distance. Every large boat should be equipped with it by law, like a black box on a plane. *Scamp* has blocked her AIS signal, but since she's the largest vessel in the area, I can track her on radar. She's proceeding toward international waters at fourteen knots. We should be able to intercept her in about twenty minutes."

Commander Vega took a call on his radio. "And we've got visual contact from the two helicopters out of AFB Cape Cod. There's one more vessel showing on the radar, but they've also shut off their AIS. I suspect that's just a passing yacht or maybe a smuggler. We should continue to monitor them, though."

Funny Girl

The two FRBs surged ahead at full speed. Soon, the navigation lights of a large vessel appeared in the distance. When the FRBs drew near, Commander Vega hailed the yacht.

"Motor Vessel *Scamp*, heave to and prepare for boarding."

There was no response.

Vega set his vessel on a course to block the yacht, giving way only when the boat's bow was upon him. Two helicopters focused their spotlights on the deck, where three men defiantly waved their guns.

"They'll cross over into international waters in less than five minutes. What the hell?" Vega pointed to his radar, where a second vessel was on a collision course with *Scamp*. When the helicopters' floodlights illuminated the area, Marc recognized Butch's fishing boat, the *4theHalibut*.

Helena stood in front of the wheelhouse, her hands outstretched in supplication. She was clad in an old-fashioned orange outfit with a long skirt and a fur cap and clutching a bouquet of yellow roses. As the FRBs slowed to a halt, those on board heard the strains of Barbra Streisand's version of "Don't Rain on my Parade."

"I don't believe it," Cole said to Marc.

"Oh, I do. But I fail to see the point."

Scamp's searchlights played over the water, and her horn sounded mighty blasts, but she made no attempt to reduce speed or avoid *4theHalibut*.

"Less than a mile to international waters," a crew member informed Commander Vega, who had been staring at Helena as if he were hallucinating.

4theHalibut slowed to a stop just to the port side of *Scamp*'s bow as Helena continued her lip sync performance. The scene was glamorous, as if she were on an outdoor stage illuminated by spotlights against the night sky, but absurdly dangerous given she was miles out to sea and in the direct path of an oncoming vessel.

As *Scamp* bore down on *4theHalibut*, Butch, grasping the wheel, made no effort to avoid a collision. At the last possible moment, *Scamp* turned to starboard, passing so close her wake washed over the fishing boat's stern. Helena clutched a nearby rail with both hands when the waves hit, then turned back to watch the departing yacht. Suddenly, *Scamp* shuddered. Her engines whined, then stopped altogether. Once the waves subsided, Helena continued to lip-sync as Barbra brought the song to a close.

A minute later, the lights of the *Ida Lewis* came into view. Helena turned toward the FRBs and took several bows.

"*Motor Vessel Scamp. Attention all crew. Drop your weapons and raise your hands where they can be seen. Prepare for boarding,*" Commander Vega ordered as a team of four men rappelled from a helicopter onto the yacht's forward deck.

The second chopper hovered so close that those in the FRBs could see four Coast Guardsmen training their rifles on the men on deck, who dropped their weapons and raised their hands.

In the distance, a small black helicopter approached, then circled back toward shore. One of the Coast Guard pilots radioed for permission to pursue. Commander Vega looked at Chief Louie, who shook his head.

"We may need them to secure *Scamp*. We'll get him when he lands."

"*Negative,*" Vega said. "*Repeat. Negative. Remain with Scamp. Vega out.*"

Butch's voice crackled over the marine radio. "*Urgent. Deploy police to the Fisher Beach parking lot. Repeat. Deploy to Fisher Beach in Truro. Do everything possible to stop that helicopter from landing. It's a matter of life and death.*"

Louie Silva didn't stop to question Butch. He turned to the commander and said, "Have your crew on *Scamp* kill all power ASAP. We've got to shut down the signal jammer and free up the police channels."

Within a minute, even *Scamp's* navigation lights went dark. Silva radioed Truro Police, telling them to send as many cruisers as they could muster to Fisher Beach.

"*Watch out for a small black helicopter coming from the direction of Long Point. Pilot armed and dangerous. Evacuate everyone in the neighborhood. Use force, if necessary, to capture or neutralize the pilot. Silva out.*"

After alerting Provincetown Airport, the chief said, "It figures Kensington would save a potential escape route for himself. I wonder what Butch knows that I don't?"

Commander Vega radioed his team aboard *Scamp* to restore power to lighting only. After five minutes, he received a message. "*Coast Guard boarding team to neighboring vessels. MV Scamp requires assistance due to engine failure. Crew under arrest and secured. No imminent danger. Request tow to Base Cape Cod.*"

Vega replied that a tug would be dispatched and ordered the team to remain on board.

When the RFBs drew alongside *4theHalibut,* Butch remained at the helm, and Helena, still in her Streisand drag, raised a champagne glass. The Coast Guard vessels sounded their horns, and the helicopters played their lights over the scene as she executed a series of deep and protracted bows.

"Don't push it, guys," Marc said to Commander Vega, "or she'll do an encore. And once she gets started, she'll 'sing them all, and we'll stay all night.'"

Apocalypse Now

Mavis Chandry was in her backyard gazing at the stars when a red light appeared low in the sky beyond Long Point. As it drew close, she made out the shape of a small black helicopter. An icy chill passed over her. An elderly, disembodied voice shouted, "*Incoming. Code Red. Battle stations.*"

Mavis scuttled into the house, returning with her shotgun and a shoulder bag full of shells loaded with buckshot. The chopper was now so close she could hear the whir of its blades. Mavis positioned herself behind the ancient oak tree. When the helicopter descended, she fired a warning blast. The copter retreated, then, moments later, a bullet splintered a branch near where she was hiding.

"Lance, you goddamn sonnuvabitch," Mavis yelled, striding out from behind the tree and taking aim. "I've had enough of your bullshit. Do you know how few old oaks are left on Cape Cod?"

She fired a second time just as several police cars swarmed into her driveway and onto her lawn.

A Three Hour Cruise

Leaving *Scamp* under the watchful eye of the *Ida Lewis* and Commander Vega, the friends boarded *4theHalibut* for the long trip back home.

After several minutes, Chief Louie confirmed that telecommunication and web services had been completely restored.

"According to the Coast Guard, they've never seen such a sophisticated operations center on a private vessel, but they were able to deactivate the jamming device."

Truro police radioed the copter had changed course toward Provincetown after an exchange of gunfire. No injuries were reported.

Chief Silva turned to Butch and asked, "OK, what's with the Fisher Beach business?"

Helena's cell phone rang before he could answer. "She is? He did? She did? Thank God! We have a hideout nearby. Take her there so she can rest. I'll text directions. And call me back when you get her settled."

Helena finished her text, took a deep breath, and said, "Kensington was going to kill Mavis."

Cole was incredulous. "What could she have ever done that he'd risk his freedom to kill her?"

Helena's response was somber. "He's been trying to murder Mavis from the start. I saw him outside her Truro studio one evening. He seemed familiar, though it was a while until I remembered him from when he staked out the museum. When we foiled his attempt to escape on *Scamp*, Butch and I were certain he'd fly back to kill her."

"How'd you know that?" the chief asked.

Helena was pale, with no trace of her usual bravado. "I'm afraid I'm not at liberty to say just yet. Kensington tried to land, but Mavis fired her shotgun. When the police showed up, he took off toward Provincetown. Mavis told Elise and Gwen she might have hit the fuel tank. They'd heard the gunfire and went to see if she was safe. They're bringing her to the hideout now."

Silence overtook the group. For several minutes, the only sound was the throbbing of the boat's engines.

"OK, you two, out with it," Charlotte said, pointing at Butch and Helena. "How did you figure out how to be in the right place at the right time?"

Helena explained how they suspected the art had already been crated and that a trawler would deliver it to *Scamp*. They called Marc and Cole once *4theHalibut* was out of the harbor, then followed *Scamp* on radar, adjusting their course to intersect with her before she reached international waters.

"We never thought of *4theHalibut*," Marc said. "We figured you might try something with *Dame Edna*. I applaud your foresight, but it doesn't explain how you stopped that yacht. Her engines ground to a halt."

"And will cost a mint to fix," Butch said, grinning at his spouse.

"Don't look to me for technical explanations," Helena said. "My specialty is making a place look like home. This is Butch's boat, but I've tried my best to bring the amenities onboard, such as the champagne bar, sound system, and jacuzzi."

"Say nothing of the wardrobe from what I can see," Marc said with a grin.

"Well, a girl must be prepared. This was supposed to be my Blessing of the Fleet costume until I had to go into hiding. Everything was already on board, including the CD and the plastic roses."

"And you stopped the boat, how?" Charlotte asked, eager to get Helena back on track.

"Well, darling, I'm not saying anything definite, but Butch may have hit that thingy that lets the whatsis over the back just before I went up on deck for my 11 o'clock number."

"It's the stern, Helena," Butch said, shaking his head. "How many times must I tell you, you crazy queen? It's not the back. It's the stern. And your 'whatsis' is the trawl—the net—which you knew damn well would clog *Scamp's* impellers."

"Champagne, darlings?" Helena said, looking smug while opening another bottle of Dom Perignon. "I think the occasion calls for it."

"Isn't this a fishing boat?" Chief Silva asked, glancing around as if to confirm his point.

"Well, yes. But no one said fishing needs to be uncomfortable—like camping. The kind in the woods, I mean," Helena said, smirking at Marc, who was still shaking his head.

The radio crackled to life just as Race Point Light came into view. "*Fishing Vessel 4theHalibut. Mass. State Police for Chief Silva. Over.*"

"*4theHalibut, here. Silva speaking.*"

"*We've found an abandoned helicopter at the Provincetown Monument. Suspect still at large.*"

"*Thanks. Keep us posted. Over and out.*"

"Damn," Chief Silva said, slamming his hand on the rail.

"Be of good cheer, darling," Helena said, wrapping an arm around his shoulder. "Why not use those powers of yours to have the State Police block off the airport and all roads out of town? Then radio Commander Vega to seal off the harbor. If you remove Kensington's escape routes, you'll find him soon enough. For now, there's not much else you can do until we get to shore.

"Dolores insisted on packing an enormous picnic basket. There's no stopping that woman, and there's more than enough to go around. Have another glass of champagne while I set out the food. I've got some delicious pâté and a lovely Stilton. May I offer you some?"

Intensive Caring

By the time *4theHalibut* docked, it was six in the morning. Helena and Butch left for Cape Cod Hospital at once, using a special pass from Chief Louie to drive through numerous roadblocks.

At the hospital, the staff gaped as Helena, still in her Streisand drag, strode through the main door. She paid no mind, declared she was Melody's great-aunt Barbra and demanded to see her niece at once.

Arriving on the fourth floor, Helena and Butch passed the heavily guarded rooms where Boorstin and Doctor Woodman were being treated. Passing a solarium, Helena waved to an elderly woman, who cackled at the sight of Helena's orange outfit and fur hat.

"Streisand was at her best in that one," she yelled as Helena strode past.

An elderly man in a wheelchair turned to face the window, seeming to disapprove of such frivolity.

When they reached Melody's room, Helena flung the door open, startling a nurse and the young artist, who was seated upright in bed drinking water through a paper straw.

"Helena!" Melody squeaked, throwing open her arms. "You didn't have to dress up to visit little old me!"

The nurse started to reprimand them, then shook her head and left the room muttering, "Provincetown. . . I just don't get that place. . ."

"How are you, darling?" Helena asked, seating herself on the side of the bed.

"A little weak and groggy, but fine. The doctors say I can go home today."

"You're not going home," Butch said, brooking no argument. "You're coming with us."

Melody's eyes brightened. Whatever effect the drugs might have had, she'd recovered quickly.

"We've got so much to tell you," Helena said. "But we'll wait until you're up for it. Excuse me for a moment. Everyone is worried sick about you. I'll call Dolores and ask her to get the word out that you're OK."

"Which means the entire town will know in ten minutes," Butch said, taking Melody's hand. "I'm so relieved you're safe. And I'm sorry we put you in the position we did."

"What position?" Melody bristled. "So I passed out and found myself in Hyannis. Big deal. I bet it's not the first time that's happened to any of us."

Helena called Chief Louie, who reported a fuel leak had forced the helicopter to land at the Pilgrim Monument. Kensington had escaped into the woods near Route Six. Then, she spent time at Wally Trieste's bedside. His color seemed promising, but he was still comatose.

***

On the ride home, Butch and Helena shared the details of *Scamp's* capture with Melody.

When they described Helena's Streisand performance, Melody stared in disbelief. "But the guys on *Scamp* had guns. They could have picked you off in an instant."

Helena laughed. "In front of the Coast Guard and their helicopters, darling? With machine guns trained on them from all angles? Not likely."

Helena explained how it wasn't in the crew's best interest to fight if Kensington wasn't there to force them. Firing on the Coast Guard would have given them instant authority to pursue *Scamp* anywhere in the world. Knowing that, they surrendered instead.

Helena was enjoying herself. "And besides, with Ida what's her name on the horizon, they'd have been outnumbered within minutes. The captain couldn't be that stupid. I wasn't all that worried."

"I don't know if I'd ever be so brave," Melody said.

"No, darling, you merely eavesdropped on two desperados and got yourself drugged by the same goons who nearly killed them," Helena said. "I'll take my chances on top of a wheelhouse with the Coast Guard as my backup group any day. 'Thanks ever so.'"

Not on my Watch

Helena, Butch, and Melody returned to HomePort. To their surprise, Mavis and Shirley-Mae were seated in the kitchen with Dolores.

"Well, there you are at last!" Shirley exclaimed. "What the hell is going on? After Gwen and Elise dropped Mavis off, I got worried. We thumbed a ride back to Mavis's, then drove here to see if Dolores knew anything."

Helena bent to kiss Shirley, then clasped both her hands. "Darling, I'm sorry. I've been so busy I didn't have time to get back to you."

Her grandmother wasn't mollified. "We had to pass through a roadblock. I get anxious at roadblocks. Always have."

"Well, at least this time, the APB wasn't for you," Helena said. "That must have made for a pleasant change."

"Don't start with that ancient history," Shirley-Mae said. "I told you a thousand times that last manhunt was a misunderstanding."

Mavis raised her eyebrows as Helena said, "Must have been strange for the shoe to be on the other foot."

As everyone laughed, Butch took a call from Chief Silva.

"Any news on Kensington?" Mavis asked when Butch hung up.

"Nothing new," Butch said. "He's got to be holed up somewhere in town. They're looking everywhere, even patrolling the dunes, but no sign of him yet."

Helena reached for her phone. "I should get in touch with Quincy and let him know we're OK. He gets cranky when he's left out. Besides, I need to make an appointment with him."

Unwelcome Company

The following morning, Quincy was not in his office at the agreed-upon time. When Helena called, there was no answer.

"That's odd," she said, "He always picks up this number."

"Leave him a message," Butch suggested. "He may have forgotten and still be out on the golf course."

"He doesn't have voicemail on this line. If he's tied up, he texts. And he hasn't."

Butch had the car started by the time Helena hung up.

***

Arriving at Quincy's stately captain's house, Helena saw his vintage Avanti parked in the driveway. Then, she noticed his living room curtains were closed.

This isn't good. Quincy's up at five and always opens them before leaving to play golf. We have a standing joke not to knock if they're drawn. This isn't like him.

Butch said, "The curtains aren't evenly closed. That's not Quincy. Let's get the chief out here. Just in case."

Helena was about to call when a bullet whizzed past and hit the curb.

"Duck!" Butch yelled. "Get behind the car."

Helena and Butch crawled behind the Land Rover. Once there, she texted the chief.

(Helena) *At Quincy's. Someone's shooting at us. Kensington may have taken him hostage.*

(Silva) *Don't engage. Stay put. On my way.*

A swarthy man with a crazed stare stepped out the front door of Quincy's house, pushing the attorney ahead of him, a pistol to his head.

"Put your keys on the dashboard. Then step away from the Rover," the man yelled, his voice raspy and tense.

Butch immediately did as he was told.

"Now, both of you. Hands up!"

Two shots echoed across the neighborhood, leaving Helena and Butch's ears ringing as the Avanti's front tires deflated.

Kensington gestured with the pistol. "You. Lady. Over there. You, boyfriend, or whatever you are, get back across the street. Old man, come with me."

Helena glanced at Butch, whose eyes pleaded she not disobey.

"Take me instead," she called out.

Butch grabbed her arm. "No, don't do it!"

Quincy yelled, "I forbid it, Helena. You've got your whole life ahead of you."

Helena adopted a casual tone. "Darling, you're not that old. Besides, if you go, you'll bill me for your time. Who knows how many hours you'd rack up."

Quincy's eyes were rich with emotion as Helena slowly walked toward him, still holding her hands in the air. "Lance, I can get you into the museum. I'll give you *all* the paintings—even the masterpieces—if you take me instead of him."

Butch moved to join her until Kensington pointed his gun at him. "You. Loverboy. Stay where you are."

Kensington looked as if he'd had no sleep for days. His scruffy white beard, incongruous in contrast to his slick, dark hair, made him look even more wasted. It took time for him to come to a decision.

At last, he spoke, "You, old man. Get over there with Romeo. And you, museum lady, come with me. Anyone who doesn't do what I say gets it between the eyes."

Quincy refused to move.

"Look, Grandpa," Kensington snarled, growing more agitated. "I said move it."

"Not on your life," Quincy replied softly, looking right at Helena, whose hands dropped to cover her mouth.

In one swift movement, Kensington cracked Quincy on the head with the butt end of the revolver, then pointed it back at Helena.

The lawyer slumped to the ground without a sound as Helena walked deliberately to where he had fallen. As she bent to tend to her friend, Kensington remained silent.

"This is too much, Helena. Too much," Quincy whispered as she checked to see if he was bleeding.

"I love you, Quincy," Helena whispered back. "Take care of the family if I don't make it."

"I love you too. Like the daughter I always wanted," Quincy said, his eyes filling with tears.

"Enough," Lance yelled. "Museum lady. Get in the car. Eyes front. You're driving."

Helena got behind the wheel as Kensington opened the passenger door. Then he fired at Butch, who slumped to the ground.

Sliding onto the passenger seat and placing the gun to Helena's head, Kensington said, "Don't look back. Drive to the museum. Step on it."

Follow that Car

Clutching his chest, Quincy stumbled to where Butch was getting up from the pavement.

"Are you all right?" the lawyer asked, his voice trembling.

"Fine. The bullet just missed me. I didn't want him to take another shot, so I pretended to be hit. What about you?"

"Just a few palpitations. It was a glancing blow and didn't break the skin. I was leaving for golf this morning when he pulled a gun and forced me back into the house. That *is* Kensington, right?"

Butch studied Quincy closely as he spoke. "Yes. He must have thought he could hijack your car until he realized it was too recognizable. I've got to follow him."

"Butch, wait," Quincy said in a surprisingly assertive tone. "That man is psychotic, strung out on drugs, or both. This is a job for the police. They're trained for these sorts of things.

"I've got to get my heart medicine. I'll be fine once I take it. Nothing can happen to Helena. I'd never forgive myself, but this is no time for heroics."

"I'll be careful. I promise," Butch said. "Here's Louie. We'll get her back. You take it easy and rest. We'll be sure to keep you in the loop."

Butch flagged down the chief's cruiser, and they set out in pursuit. Convinced Helena would not risk driving Commercial Street at high speed, the chief took Bradford Street and then radioed his officers, deploying them to various locations in the West End of town, the airport, and the National Seashore. When the Range Rover came into view, Kensington held his gun out the window, then pointed it at Helena. Chief Louie slowed down and followed from a distance.

An enormous camper festooned with bumper stickers lumbered down the road, reducing the Rover's speed to a crawl. The chief inched closer until a shot shattered the windshield near Butch's head. Then the Rover sped up and passed the camper, leaving the cruiser trapped behind it until the chief finally passed the ponderous vehicle.

When Helena reached HomePort, she made a sharp right turn into the National Seashore and accelerated.

The chief reached for his radio. "*Silva to all officers. Suspect entering Seashore via Provincelands Road. Coordinate with park service and seal all exits. This is a hostage situation. Approach with caution. Suspect has fired on civilians and an officer. Silva out.*"

Butch and the chief followed the Land Rover at a safe distance. Driving down a steep hill past Herring Cove, another cruiser approached at high speed. With police now ahead and behind, Helena signaled a left turn, swerved into a parking area, crashed through a wire barrier, and skidded onto the fire road leading to Race Point Light. As she accelerated, Helena leaned on the horn. Two men walking their dog jumped out of the way just in time as the Rover navigated the narrow path at an alarming rate of speed.

"He's making her take the dune road to the airport," Butch said. "How the hell does he think he can fly out of there?"

The chief was about to respond when the cruiser hit a pothole, skidded off the path, and slid into a marsh with a sickening thud. Butch clambered from the stranded vehicle and sprinted down the trail. Chief Silva followed, shouting orders into his walkie-talkie.

Crossing the dike near the end of the fire road, they found the Range Rover hung up on a dune, its rear wheels spinning in the air. The passenger door was open, and Kensington was nowhere in sight.

Approaching the vehicle, they heard a familiar voice say, "Next time, I'm taking the Dune Tour—or getting a camel."

Helena leaned over to embrace her husband, who stared at her, speechless, before reaching in, turning off the ignition, and assisting her from the vehicle.

"Oh, Butch. I was never so relieved in my life when I saw you and Louie in the rearview mirror. I heard the shot but couldn't see what happened. I prayed the whole time you were OK."

Butch held her tight, feeling her rapid heartbeat against his chest. "Why didn't you go to the museum? I thought you were going to lock him in. And not for nothing; you scared me to death with that switch you pulled."

Helena grabbed his hand. "I was so afraid you were dead."

"C'mon now, Helena," Butch said. "Focus and describe everything that happened. Where's Kensington headed?"

"He figured out the museum ploy and forced me to go to the airport instead. When the police boxed us in, I told him I had off-road driving skills. Taking the dune road was the only way I could think of to avoid a shootout.

"I better call Quincy and let him know I'm OK."

The Mechanics of Escape

Quincy answered his phone on the first ring. "Helena, that was an incredibly fool-hardy thing you just did. I'm old and expendable. You've got your whole life ahead of you. Not everything is make-believe, you know. When the hell are you—"

"Darling," Helena said, "You're a national treasure. Your public would never forgive me if I let something happen to you."

"Nevertheless," Quincy sputtered, his dudgeon somewhat diminished, "I was perfectly capable of driving that car."

"I never doubted it for a minute, you dear man. But it's all, as you lawyers say, a moot point. Sorry to cut things short, but we've got a fugitive to catch."

Butch called Charlotte, who offered to pick them up. Before walking back to Provincelands Road, Chief Silva surveyed the stranded Rover.

"You sure dug it in. I assume it was on purpose?"

Helena shared how Kensington promised he wouldn't kill her if she got him to the airport. "He was so busy looking behind that he didn't see the dune until the car was already on top of it. I disengaged the four-wheel drive and let us dig in. He got out, took one look, and ran off like a scared rabbit."

Butch put his arm around her. "You took one hell of a risk. If I weren't so mad at you, I'd be damned proud of you."

"Butch, darling, Quincy has a weak heart. There's no way I'd let him be taken hostage. I'd never forgive myself if something happened to him. From the moment we met, he's treated me with dignity and respect. I just couldn't bear it if—"

"I get it, Helena. You're always looking out for the family. Next time, maybe give some thought to what it would do to me if I lost you?"

Helena turned away to hide her tears.

***

When they reached Provincelands Road, the chief asked Helena, "Do you have any idea how Kensington planned to escape?"

"As a matter of fact, I do. We need to get to the airport. Oh, and here's Charlotte. I'll ride with her and meet you guys there."

The chief laughed. "OK. After all this, I guess you've earned the right to keep me in suspense."

Chief Silva hailed Officer Chase, who had been driving the other cruiser. "Chase, are all roadblocks in place?"

"Yes, sir."

"Good man. Radio to let Charlotte and Helena through, then get some men out in the dunes along Route Six. Block the back beach and path at High Head. Leave the dune road to the airport open. Sorry, but I've got to commandeer your wheels. It's going to be quite a job getting those two vehicles unstuck. Stay to oversee that, then get a ride to the station with one of the tow trucks."

Reaching the airport, Charlotte passed several parked cars and pulled up in front of the squat gray building. To her right, she saw the short runway with three private aircraft moored near an old wooden shed.

The Cape Air flight from Boston was landing. Rushing into the terminal, Helena surveyed the line of six passengers awaiting the return trip. Kensington was not among them.

When Butch and Chief Silva pulled up next to Charlotte, Helena ran out to them. "He's not here."

"Damn," said Butch.

"Not to worry. I need to speak with the airport mechanic. We can do that any time before he gets off work. First, I need a drink of water and something to put on my stomach. It's doing back flips."

"Any time?" Charlotte asked, "Whatever do you mean?"

"Stay tuned and find out, darling."

After downing a small bottle of water and a package of crackers from a vending machine, Helena said, "Chief, I need your permission to test a theory."

"What is it?" he asked, his respect and trust obvious.

"I'm certain Kensington will try to fly out of here."

"But we've impounded his helicopter."

"I know. But think back to last night."

The chief played along. "Well, the helicopter landed at the airport yesterday, around eight. Woodman has confirmed that three men burst into his house around nine-thirty, holding Boorstin at gunpoint."

"Did he say what they took other than the paintings?"

"No. It was obvious the art was gone. Beyond that, we can't tell much. Woodman's doctor refuses to allow any more questions."

Helena's tone was forceful. "We need to find out which plane is his."

Chief Silva seemed confused. "Plane?"

"Yes. Doctor Woodman flies up from New Jersey on weekends. I'm certain Kensington knows that. Boorstin would have told him."

"So you think Kensington took the keys to the plane when he was at Woodman's house?" Charlotte asked.

"Or went back for them. Kensington kept his hand in his left pocket as if making sure something didn't fall out when the car bounced."

"But he'd have to file a flight plan, right?" asked Charlotte, her voice trailing off. "No. Of course not. Not if he snuck in after the airport shut down."

"It operates during daylight hours and until eighteen-thirty hours offseason," the chief said. "You're on to something, Helena. Let's get to work."

Within minutes, they were huddled in a workshop beside the terminal. The chief mechanic was a short, rotund man with hairy arms and a dark beard. His hands were covered with grease, his jet-black hair tied up in a "man bun."

"Charles, darling," Helena said, embracing him. "So good to see you. It's been a while since we did a show together. That simply has to change. And soon!"

Chief Silva looked over at Charlotte, the question in his eyes unmistakable.

Charles saw the exchange, grinned, and asked, "How are the flying lessons? You must be about ready to get your wings, right? What can I do for you, sweetheart?"

Come Fly with Me

At ten that night, a shadowy figure crossed the tarmac. Reaching the three planes moored beside the runway, Lance Kensington inserted a key into the door of the first, then the second. Finding success with the third, he released the mooring lines, climbed into the cockpit of the single-engine Cessna 172, and started the engine, which turned over but didn't catch. He was still fiddling with controls when halogen floodlights illuminated the area, and federal agents approached, their weapons drawn.

"Lance Kensington. Step out of the plane with your hands up."

Blinded by the glare, Kensington was taken into custody without a fight. As the agents escorted him across the tarmac, he looked around wildly but remained silent before being pushed into a waiting helicopter.

As soon as the chopper was en route to Boston, the small airport went dark.

Dorian Gray

Back at HomePort, Helena pounced when her phone rang. "Louie? Yes. . . Yes. . . Excellent. Please tell Charles I'll be in touch and thank him again for me?"

"Well?"

Shirley's question reverberated across the dining room where the friends, including Quincy, had gathered around a lavish buffet. Taking one look at Helena's face, Dolores bustled to the wine cellar to fetch champagne.

"The trap worked," Helena said. "As we thought he would, Kensington tried to steal the doctor's plane, but Charles had blocked the fuel line. Kensington is showing classic signs of heroin withdrawal. He hid in the dunes all day and got a hellish sunburn. I suspect he'll also have quite the case of poison ivy.

"The Feds have taken him to a hospital in Boston under some Homeland Security regulation or another. Don't tell anyone. Chief Silva wants it to look like Kensington's still on the loose in case there are more gang members than those caught on *Scamp*."

"The poison ivy couldn't happen to a better person," Shirley sputtered. "I hope he was crawling through it and got it all over his—"

Marc and Cole winced, then quickly tried to change the subject.

Quincy served himself more lobster salad. "He didn't make a hell of a lot of sense holding me hostage this morning. My biggest fear was that he'd hallucinate and shoot me by mistake. I had some idea who he was even though—once again—certain people couldn't manage to keep their lawyer informed."

"Now, now," Helena said, patting his arm, "when you didn't answer, we came right over to see what was wrong."

"And then you took a damn fool risk trading places with me. I'm not some worn-out shell of a man, and I wish you wouldn't treat me as such."

"Quincy, darling, I planned to trigger a security lockdown at the museum. You didn't have the codes to get in. That's all it was. You know how much I rely on your strength."

Quincy appeared to accept Helena's explanation. "In any case, Kensington kept raving he'd been cheated and that he'd get his own back. Mavis, he seemed especially angry at you."

"Did he say why?" Mavis asked, looking ill at ease.

"Yes. Something about your stealing his posterity. He said it had taken him decades, but he'd finally gotten something of his own back."

"Always was a strange duck, that one," Mavis said, draining her glass and holding it out for more champagne. "So I painted his portrait a few times. Who did he think I was, Basil Hallward?"

Shirley looked questioningly at Helena, who explained, "Basil Hallward painted the portrait of Dorian Gray, who never aged, while the painting he kept in the attic reflected all the terrible things he'd done."

"You've got to be more specific than that," Shirley said. "I've known a truckload of old queens who kept themselves young by all sorts of crazy methods. And you'd never believe the pictures they had in their attics."

Until The Fat Lady Sings

Three days later, Quincy and Chief Silva appeared at Helena's office looking uncharacteristically tense.

"Chief! Quincy! To what do I owe this honor?" Helena asked, beaming up at them from her desk.

She wore a black wig in a bun, a red business suit with matching red jewelry, and red "cat glasses." A single strand of hair kept flopping onto her forehead.

The chief refused a seat. "Helena, I don't know how to say this."

"You don't have to. That strand simply won't stay in place. I was just reaching for the Super Glue when you came in."

"It's not that, Helena," he said, struggling for the right words.

"Just come out and say it, Louie. That's always best."

"Well, OK. The thing is, Kensington has a rock-solid alibi for when Wally Trieste and Brandt were shot."

"I've double-checked the interviews and travel documents," Quincy said, his tone tender and protective. "Kensington was in Paris when Wally was shot and didn't return until two days after Brandt died. There's confirmation from Customs, the airline, and security footage. We can't seem to trace a phone, though."

"I saw him throw something out onto the mud flats," Helena said. "If it was his phone, it's useless by now."

The chief's eyes were brimming with affection and concern. "Dan Andrade agrees Kensington can no longer be considered a suspect for those shootings. He *was* in town when C.J. was killed, and we hope to tie him to that murder. And we can prove he shot at Mavis from the helicopter. We have a bullet that matches his gun. But those incidents, the carjacking, and the thefts are all Dan can pin on him so far."

Helena looked over the top of her glasses as the strand flopped down again. "So that means—"

"Whoever shot Wally and killed Brandt is still out there somewhere," the chief said. "We don't think it's any of Kensington's accomplices. All seven have been cooperating, especially *Scamp's* captain, who confirmed the Pocasset robbery. Sadly, our investigators can't identify a suspect for Wally and Brandt's shootings."

Helena murmured, "In a way, that makes sense."

Chief Louie studied her closely, speaking only when he realized she had nothing more to say. "The gang members did tell us they found the transmitters on the paintings at Creek Hill Road. They used Boorstin's kidnapping as an opportunity to steal Grace and move the crated works to another location. I've not told Boorstin we know that.

"We also tracked down the fishermen who delivered the accomplices and paintings to *Scamp*. They were paid enough not to ask questions and instructed to drop off some boxes to a customer wanting to avoid dockage fees. Dan has decided not to charge them.

"Helena, all I can say is that we're revisiting every detail to find those responsible for the two shootings."

"I assume I'm not on the list this time?" she asked with an arch look.

"You never were with anyone but that damn fool, Brandt. But we are back to square one on his murder," Louie said, his frustration apparent.

"What's going on with Boorstin and Woodman?" Helena asked.

"We still don't have sufficient evidence to hold Boorstin. We have him under surveillance, though it will break my budget if it goes on for too long. Doctor Woodman is another matter. He has paid bills of sale for all the paintings stolen from him—including the one taken from C.J.'s studio. So far, he's been cooperating with our investigation to avoid charges of receiving stolen property. Or should I say, he appears to be cooperating."

"And what's Kensington saying at this point?" Helena asked after making a note on the back of an envelope.

"Nothing of much use. He's being treated for addiction, but his anxiety appears to be more than just the symptoms of heroin withdrawal. He seems more afraid of the Russian mafia than a possible murder charge. I saw a video of one interview with him, and I've never seen anyone so unstable.

"We found traces of fingerprints on the inside of that dummy circuit breaker in Mavis's studio. Because of the melted plastic, we had to send them to the FBI lab, but we should know something soon. I hope it will tie him to C.J.'s murder, but it's a long shot."

"What does Boorstin say now that Kensington is in custody?" Helena asked, gazing down at the museum atrium, where a group of students stood in front of the Mansion Suite.

"Not much. He's upset we didn't post a security detail outside his house. Of course, he doesn't know he's under surveillance. It's not Kensington he's afraid of. Someone else has him petrified."

Helena tapped a pencil on the desktop in short, staccato bursts. "So he's frightened by a person or persons unknown. I find that most satisfying. What's your plan?"

"We're going to play on Boorstin's fear and see if we can get him to talk. I'm not too optimistic about that, though," Chief Louie said, his voice somber. "My major concern is that you may still be in danger. After all, you're a witness to both shootings. Speaking of that, is there anything you might have overlooked when we talked two days ago?"

"Nothing more than a nagging feeling I'm missing something. I'm going to ask Charlotte to double-check a few things. I assure you, if anything comes out of that, I'll let you know."

"I've heard that one before," Quincy said, rolling his eyes.

The Devil in the Details

Charlotte and Helena met a day later at the house on Telegraph Hill to discuss what might have been overlooked in their investigation. The day was bright and unseasonably warm. The tide was out, and crews were working oyster grants in the bright, reflected light.

Seated at her desk, Charlotte consulted her notes. "For a small operation, Dan Andrade's office sure knows how to gather information."

She explained how the Russians had loaned Kensington money at low interest rates in exchange for a percentage of his company. Then, KS had sold transaction data, angering some dangerous people. As a result, Kensington had been liquidating assets and distancing himself from his previous life. The boyfriend he traded in for the waiter had described Kensington's behavior as abusive and irrational in a palimony suit.

"According to the boyfriend," Charlotte said, looking up from her report, "We're talking drug-fueled drama. Raw, unadulterated addiction and greed."

"That fits," Helena said. "I've been thinking how Kensington came to town just like a modern-day Black Sam Bellamy, plundering the local art market."

"While jacking up the prices of Provincetown art at major auction houses," Charlotte added. "He also traveled to European sales, which makes little sense since he could have phoned in a bid."

"No doubt, he made sure to be out of town for the hits on Wally and Sergeant Brandt," Helena said. "Any connection to Boorstin?"

Charlotte explained she'd met with Dan Andrade's forensic accountant and dug a bit more into the architect's personal life.

"He's been paying some sort of silent partner while also making significant wire transfers to an offshore account that isn't his."

"So you're thinking blackmail?" Helena asked.

"For what, we haven't been able to figure out yet."

"How much has he shelled out?"

"Just under four hundred thousand. More than enough to pay off his current obligations."

"Fascinating," Helena said, staring out at a departing yacht. "What did you learn about Woodman, and what's his relationship to Boorstin?"

Charlotte described the doctor as affiliated with a small hospital near Newark. "About three years ago, he inherited money from an aunt, which enabled him to buy the plane and his Provincetown home. Doctor Woodman *has* had run-ins with Boorstin. In the most recent case, it seems the doctor's roof leaks. Boorstin said the problem was corrected. Woodman said it wasn't and filed a lien, subsequently withdrawn. Other than converting his mother's home to a duplex and selling it, there's no history of Woodman developing any real estate."

Helena pondered this for a moment, then said, "Could he be someone other than he seems to be?"

Charlotte took time to answer. "If that's the case, he's chosen an intriguing persona. From what we learned, the doctor is more of a blowhard, plumping up his self-image, often making a fool of himself. Dan's team couldn't find anyone who spoke well of him. Instead, they heard words like maladroit, compulsive, and status-conscious."

"That jibes with what my gut tells me. Not a crook, just frantic to gain entry to what he considers 'P'town Society.'"

Charlotte chuckled. "Heaven help him. Perhaps we should warn him he's signing up for endless dinners, a torrent of emails, and frequent assaults on his bank account."

Helena held up her right hand. "Now be fair, Charlotte. There are a lot of deserving charities in town. And many fine people who support them. You know we've been dealing with a smaller group of arrivals who haven't figured out what it means to live here. The real risk lies in making sure they don't turn us into the Hamptons—an overabundance of money and pretense with no place for regular folks to live. That said, we'll leave Doctor Woodman to discover the social nuances for himself—along with a few other surprises."

Too Quaint for Words

The following morning, Helena, back in her Kelly van Dusen drag, studied the knocker on Henry Boorstin's front door.

Helena lifted the bronze casting of Medusa's head and dropped it with a thud.

Nothing says welcome like a head covered with snakes.

The architect, looking uneasy, peered out a nearby window.

"Oh, it's you, Kelly," he said, opening the door a crack.

"Yes, Mr. Boorstin. It *is* me. I thought I'd stop by and say hello."

The architect hesitated, then opened the door. He was wearing a faded blue shirt and brown cargo pants, both of which needed ironing. "I don't mean to sound rude. But may I ask what brings you to my home that couldn't wait until Monday?"

"I apologize for the intrusion," Helena said, looking far from contrite, "but I'm leaving for St. Barts tonight. We didn't have time to visit that Wellfleet property together, but I wanted to be sure you knew I'm moving forward with the purchase."

Boorstin's features brightened. "No problem. I was just watching one of the Sunday news shows. Do come in."

As Helena had expected, the main floor of Boorstin's home was one large room. The old pine floors were pickled the color of weak coffee. Oversized leather sofas took up much of the living area, serviced by a series of glass-topped coffee tables. What little art hung on the walls was primarily portraits of sea captains or fishermen in rain slickers, save for one sad clown holding a bent sunflower. A colossal air handler overshadowed the fireplace, whose bricks had been painted black. Beneath the unit was an enormous flat-screen TV. Helena glimpsed entwined, bare flesh before Boorstin quickly shut it off.

"May I offer you coffee?" he asked, glancing longingly at an elaborate bar crammed with partially empty gin, brandy, and Scotch bottles. "Or something a little stronger?"

"I'd love a Mimosa if you have one," Helena cooed.

"Coming right up."

Boorstin hurried to the bar, opened a wine chiller, and produced a bottle of cheap Asti Spumante. Though he tried to block the bottle from Helena's view, she saw its label and stifled a shudder.

Sashaying to the refrigerator in the galley kitchen at the far end of the vast room, the architect filled a flute with orange juice and added the questionable wine.

"There you are," he said, traversing the length of the house to deliver her drink, his footsteps echoing across the expanse. "There's plenty more where that came from, dear lady. I hope it's to your liking."

"I'm sure it will be," Helena said between clenched teeth.

Boorstin returned to the bar and opted for an enormous glass of Scotch with no ice. "Now then, it sounds like all systems are go on Wellfleet."

He gestured for Helena to sit.

"Oh, yes. Indeed they are. More than ready. It's amazing how cash can move things along."

"You paid cash for fifteen acres in Wellfleet?"

"Yes, of course. Mortgages can be so tiresome. Especially when your accountant is in France."

Boorstin stared at Helena as if she were a large dish of ice cream. "So what can I do for you, dear lady?"

Helena announced that, in addition to the main house, she wanted a stable as well as guest quarters. She'd also need a series of walking paths throughout the site and a separate drive extending to the guest house.

"I want you to design the drive and paths just like those Jackie had on Martha's Vineyard. I used to love that place when I visited as a girl."

Boorstin took a large sip of Scotch and stared out the front window as if he were dreaming. "Separate guest quarters is an excellent idea. Company can be so underfoot at times."

"Thanks for reminding me. I forgot two of the other buildings. Silly me." Helena sipped her drink and struggled not to grimace. "We need staff housing. Five separate suites, kitchenette, living room, bedroom, and bath. Out of sight of the main house, halfway to the guest house. And then, of course, the garage: eight bays with an artist's studio above. Also, a cottage by the entrance for security staff."

Boorstin scribbled on his pad. In no time, his drink was reduced to a brown residue at the bottom of his glass.

"I'll give you a retainer," Helena said, "so you can get the preliminary drawings underway ASAP. Will fifty suffice?"

Helena laughed when Boorstin looked puzzled. "Fifty thousand, of course. My husband always says I'm hopeless with numbers. I've got the cash in my purse."

What Matters Most

After extricating herself from Boorstin, Helena drove the short distance to Chief Silva's home.

"Louie, I hate to barge in like this, but do you have an antacid? I just drank the worst Mimosa since I did the brunch show at the Moby Dick Lounge in McKeesport, Pennsylvania. I saw Boorstin, and I'm paying for it in more ways than one. He took the money like a hungry dog, though. It should be easy enough to track what he does with it."

"I'll let Dan Andrade know," Chief Silva said as his wife entered the room. "Honey, do we have any antacid?"

Mrs. Silva, a tall, svelte woman with dark hair and prominent features, retrieved a small bottle from the kitchen.

"You're a goddess, Eileen," Helena said, quickly chewing the tablets. "Haven't I always said how fortunate you are, Louie?"

Eileen smiled warmly. "I suspect you two are hatching another of your schemes, so I'll leave you to it. Sing out, Helena, if things don't improve."

"You're one lucky man, Louie," Helena said as Eileen closed the door silently behind her. "I hope you know that."

"I sure do. I've felt that way ever since she agreed to be my dance partner in the third grade."

The chief pointed to a photograph of two small children doing what appeared to be a waltz. The young Eileen was beaming at the camera. The young Louie was staring intently at his feet.

"Even back then, you were methodical," said Helena. "And Eileen was ready to tackle the world. Tell me something?"

"Sure, what?"

"With all the demands of your job, how do the two of you keep the spark going between you? It's obvious you guys are still crazy about each other—even after all the years."

Chief Louie grinned. "It took time to establish the ease with each other we have these days. When the kids came along, they stayed with alternating sets of grandparents every Friday night, so Eileen and I got what they call a date night these days. And most importantly, I learned how to say no to all the distractions in this town."

Helena was enthralled. "How could you do that? You're a local institution."

"A friend once told me this secret: 'Whenever you're asked to have people come to visit, join a committee, whatever it is, if you have the slightest hesitation, say no first. Change your mind if that answer doesn't feel good later, but start with no. It does two important things: One, it makes people less likely to ask if they don't really need you. And two, it buys you time to figure out what your hesitation was about.' Since I learned that lesson, I've been OK. You can get swept off your feet in this town without even knowing it."

"I'll have to remember that," Helena said, more to herself than the chief. "I'm starting to think Lola became a recluse to avoid everything I've been dealing with at the museum."

Chief Louie seemed to understand. "I suspect there's some truth in that. I'll never forget what she said when I wanted to honor her for her donations to the police association. 'Louis,' she said—she never called me Louie; said it wasn't proper—'I give because I can, and I want nothing in return but the pleasure of your company now and then. Late in my time on earth, I found the secret of life: do your bit to help others, ground yourself, find the joy within, and don't let anyone intrude on it. Some people say that's selfish, and perhaps it is—in the sense that one looks out for oneself. But I'll tell you something, Louis, when you get to be my age, you don't remember the moments of adulation or recognition. You remember exquisite moments like this. Quiet times with a dear friend.'"

Helena and the chief paused, savoring their fond memories of Lola. Then Helena said, "Thanks, Louie. I'm glad you're that kind of friend."

"Don't thank me. Thank Lola," was his humble reply. "She taught me what little I might know on the subject."

An Inevitable Conversation

Helena's next stop was the old house near Fisher Beach.

Mavis, seated at the kitchen table with Moppet on her lap, waved Helena inside, her voice a monotone. "I suppose I should thank you for having Elise and Gwen watch out for me after that helicopter business. I figured you'd be along eventually, so I waited to say so."

"I knew you'd be expecting me," Helena replied. "What did Kensington mean when he said you stole his posterity? It doesn't sound like he was talking about nude portraits."

Mavis seemed to come to a decision. "Damn it to hell. I'm tired of keeping everything bottled up inside. I'll tell you if you promise to be discreet and not think too ill of me."

Helena sat down beside her. "Of course, I'll be discreet. Nothing you could ever say would make me think ill of you. Where's the child? They must be at least thirty by now."

Mavis sat bolt upright. "You knew?"

"When someone speaks of their posterity, it's usually ego-driven. Kensington had enough money to build monuments to himself. I figured he was obsessed with something money couldn't buy."

"Right in one," Mavis said with a nervous laugh.

She told how she met Kensington when she was just coming off a breakup with her first girlfriend, a baker named Lois. They'd been together for more than ten years until Lois cheated on Mavis with a waiter from the Lobster Pot.

Mavis was angry but found she was also curious. "Lance was horny as hell, waving his wand around in my art class, so I figured, why not? I wasn't as chunky back then. Turned out he was easy enough to be had—for a price. One night when I'd gotten good and drunk, I gave Lance a hundred bucks and took him to bed."

"And?"

"It was a disaster, but it sure cleared up what I wanted and, more so, what I didn't. Two months later, I realized I'd messed up big time. The money from those four portraits came in real handy. It allowed me to leave town just when I needed to. The baby boy hadn't developed the way he should, and the doctors told me he'd need special care for his entire life."

"Was his foot deformed? Like in your painting?"

"Yes. Still is. You figured everything out from that?"

Helena clasped Mavis's hand in hers. "The love displayed in that painting had to be a mother's love. And, of course, Kensington's ravings about his posterity solidified my thinking. How did he find out about his son?"

It took time for Mavis to find the right words. "I took one look when Kevin was born and knew I could never say a word to Lance. That misshapen foot was sure to turn his vain father against him. The poor child never came home from the hospital. Instead, I got him into a long-term care facility in Northampton.

"Along with his cognitive disabilities, Kevin developed cerebral palsy. He's a sweet boy. As gentle as a lamb. I go to see him as often as I can. Even though he has no idea who I am, I gotta tell you, there's no better feeling for me than seeing that look on his face when I walk into his room. Of course, leaving him is hell. He cries, and I hear his voice for days afterward. I wish I could be there every day, but I've got to work to keep the money coming in but also to stop from losing my mind. It's a hellish situation. All because of one stupid mistake."

Mavis spoke of running into her ex-girlfriend, Lois. "She was gay again, a real stone butch. But still angry over what she claimed I did to drive her away. It was a fine mess. There I am with a son I hadn't acknowledged. And there's Lois, the new head of security for the place that was caring for him."

Mavis took Lois to dinner that night. After several drinks, Lois admitted the breakup was her fault and explained it took twenty years to get herself straightened out.

Mavis was touched by this. "We drank more. Eventually, I told Lois about my fling with Kensington. When I did, it was as if a switch flipped. Suddenly, she needed money. The threat was implicit, but I wrote her a fat check on the spot out of a sense of responsibility—and for old times' sake."

Helena studied Mavis closely. "So what happened after that?"

"The next morning, I woke up with a tremendous hangover and an even bigger dose of fear, so I moved Kevin to another home within the week. When Lois showed up in Truro a year later wanting more money, I told her to go pound sand. That's when she threatened she'd knock me off my high horse if it was the last thing she ever did.

"Lois said she'd paint me as a total hypocrite and uncaring mother. This would have created a furor in the feminist groups I worked with. Even so, I said no to her, and that's when she went looking for Lance."

"And found him," Helena sighed.

Mavis explained that Kensington showed up a few days before the museum opening. "Thanks to Lois, he knew about Kevin and wanted to see him. I tried to explain the child was incapable of understanding and well cared for, but it wasn't enough. Lance said he'd take me to court to claim paternity and even boasted his nude portraits would show the judge how obsessed with him I'd been.

"Lance couldn't concentrate, wouldn't listen, and scared me to death. He even said something about Kevin being better off dead—that maybe it was the best solution. There was no way I'd let him near my son, and I told him so."

"Mavis," Helena said, "I don't mean to pry, but who inherits when you die? Is it Kevin?"

"Everything goes to a trust I've set up for him. Once he dies, the remaining funds revert to a charity for brain-damaged children, but my entire estate will be set aside for him during his lifetime. Kevin's future is secure should he live to be a hundred and ten, which I hope to God he doesn't."

Mavis stared at the table. "I better admit the rest, Helena; it's been tearing me apart. I knew the moment I saw my damaged paintings that Lance was responsible. When we found C.J.'s body, I was certain it was me he was trying to kill. I accused you in order to protect my secret and keep Kevin out of the limelight. I'm so sorry. Please forgive me."

"It's OK, Mavis," Helena said, her voice calm and soothing. "I figured that out some time ago. When Lance couldn't steal your paintings before they got to the museum, his Plan B was easy enough to imagine."

She then explained how, with Mavis dead, Lance could lay claim to, or at least manage, her estate. With DNA proof of paternity, he'd be likely to gain control as Kevin's court-appointed trustee or conservator.

"He's an expert at hacking. I suspect he's seen your will, the database with the locations of your paintings, and all your financial records. It's reasonable to suspect he'd find a way to sell the collection or embezzle money from your estate. Things like this have happened before, despite the best safeguards. Your money and art are why he's been so obsessed. It's not out of any love for his son."

Mavis looked down at the table and rubbed her right thumb against her index finger. Moppet, seeming to sense she was upset, licked her face.

Helena waited until Mavis looked up. "You were in real danger, darling. Lance had you under surveillance in your studio and saw you always made a cup of tea before getting down to work. We don't have definitive proof yet, but we're confident he replaced the working circuit breaker with a dummy, shaved the insulation on the teapot's cord, and repainted it to mask the copper underneath."

"So rather than just killing me with a gun, he went to all that trouble? Why?" Mavis asked, cradling Moppet against her chest.

"To have an alibi. Lance monitored everything from his yacht so the crew could confirm he was onboard when something happened to you. Lance knew C.J. was killed by mistake, so that same night, he tampered with the museum's security network—again remotely—and had his crew deface your paintings. If you had removed your work from the museum, I'm sure he was prepared to hijack the truck on the return trip. This time, with whatever it took to get your work."

"And I encouraged Sergeant Brandt to think it was all your doing," Mavis said.

Helena grasped her hand. "Stop persecuting yourself. Brandt was working for Lance, who no doubt had him place suspicion on me. It was important to draw attention away from the actual issue—getting control of Kevin's inheritance. Lance would have set me up even if you hadn't said a word. Once you decided to keep the paintings in the museum, his only alternative was to kill you before you signed the bequest. I saw Lance outside your studio when I visited you a while back, and we both know he was coming for you the other night in his helicopter."

"Do you think I killed Brandt to protect Kevin?" Mavis asked, her voice a whisper.

"Not for a moment, darling. Someone else is behind the shootings of Brandt and Wally. Lance was the mastermind, but I believe them to be a powerful force in their own right. I'm pretty sure I know who they are. I can't prove anything yet, but I can say for sure you're not a suspect."

Helena saw Mavis's bottom lip quiver and rose from the kitchen table to wrap her arms around the old woman, who burst into tears.

***

After returning to HomePort to change her outfit, Helena felt her phone vibrate. A group text from Chief Silva read:

(Silva) *Boorstin is on the move. Currently on Commercial St.*

I have an officer ready to follow him at the bottom of Pleasant.

(Helena) *And a deputy on her way.*

(Silva) *Report any developments and STAY SAFE.*

Covert Ops

Helena parked in the Johnson Street lot. Because she was wearing her usual attire, several friends crowded around to welcome her back. After chatting with them, she sat on the wall in front of the library. Looking west on Commercial Street, she saw Boorstin strolling toward her carrying the manila envelope filled with cash she'd given him just hours before. Then she heard footsteps approaching from the east.

"You're a natural, Helena," Amy Morgan said, sitting beside her.

Helena leaned over to kiss her cheek. "No one has ever said that about me before, darling."

"A natural detective, I mean. Dan has kept me up to speed on what you've uncovered."

"I've been wondering what happened to you, Amy. I haven't seen you for days."

The detective leaned close. "KS is incorporated in Miami-Dade County, so I went there to research the company's origins. Charlotte's findings were an immense help."

"Why are the company's origins so important?" Helena asked.

"I figured Lance Kensington's rise from rentboy to software mogul might hold some clues as to his associates. Thirty years ago, he was a bartender and artist's model. Now, he's worth over a hundred million. And that's only the assets we could uncover. He was in the right place at the right time, but there had to be seed money to give his firm a decent start. At least enough to fund the original porn operation. The equipment alone would cost a pretty penny, say nothing of technicians, actors, room rentals, and the like."

Helena's eyes lit up. "So you think he had a fairy godmother—"

"Godfather. I keep coming up with one name: Edward Mott Robinson."

"Who's he?" Helena asked, sneaking a discreet glance only to discover a crowd of tourists blocked her view of Boorstin.

Amy smiled. "That's the point. Who *is* Robinson? I know he lent fifty thousand to Kensington to get the porn operation up and running. He's even listed as one of the principal shareholders of KS. But I can't find a trace of him."

Helena spotted Boorstin once the crowd passed. He stood alone on the sidewalk as if waiting for someone.

"Maybe Robinson died?"

Amy shook her head. "When I say I can't find him, I mean I can't find a birth or death certificate. No tax records. No medical records. Edward Mott Robinson is a total cipher."

"I assume you Googled him?"

"Of course. And the only thing that comes up is some guy who owned a whaling fleet in New Bedford in the mid-eighteen-hundreds."

Amy grew silent when a prissy voice called out from across the street. "Helena, dear lady! What a delight to see you in the flesh! You were sorely missed. I'm overjoyed you've come home to us at last. And do I ever have a bone to pick with you. I've invited you more than once to see my library, and you've not come. Where *are* your manners?"

"Oh, hello, Cheswick," Helena said, masking her annoyance as she watched Boorstin hasten down a side street. "I've just gotten back. I haven't forgotten. In fact, how about tomorrow?"

"Oh, that would be delightful. Shall we say four p.m.? That will give us time for a cocktail or two. Ta-ta for now."

As Cheswick Wilks sashayed toward the east end of town, Helena eagerly scanned Commercial Street.

"Boorstin took off, Amy. Did you see if he met someone?"

"While you were talking to Wilks, I didn't see him speak to a soul."

"Did he still have the envelope?" Helena asked, unable to mask her disappointment.

"Yes."

"Damn it. Boorstin was waiting to deliver that money to someone. I know he was. He must have heard Big Bird call out my name and bolted."

"Big Bird?" Amy asked, raising her eyebrows.

"Long story, darling. I'll tell you some other time."

A Stove Boat

Helena woke with a start at three the following morning. She'd dreamed of a harpooned whale ramming a whaling ship, which sank in minutes. Then she'd heard a voice say, "*It was one of the few losses for 'Black Hawk' Robinson. Other owners were far less fortunate, so I constantly reminded myself.*"

Racing downstairs to the library, Helena pulled the index to Captain Staunton's journals off the shelf.

Journal number twelve contained the exact words she heard in her dream and an additional notation: "*I'd always make it a point to have a gam with the captain of a Howland ship. Many knew Robinson. I listened and learned all I could.*"

In a later volume, Helena read a telling entry from 1916: "*So Black Hawk's daughter, Hetty Green, is dead. 'The Witch of Wall Street,' they called her. I remember meeting her at a cotillion in New Bedford just before I met my despicable wife. Hetty was a homely, coarse, and inconsiderate woman, though they said she once danced with the Prince of Wales. Her son, Ned, was a flawed being if ever there was one.*"

And in June of 1936: "*So Ned Green is dead. Imagine him marrying a prostitute. What would his stern Quaker ancestors have had to say about that? Rumor has it she doesn't stand to inherit a cent. It all goes to his sister, Sylvia Ann. Her husband, Matthew Astor Wilks, is dead these ten years, which means the enormous Howland fortune descends to a sixty-five-year-old widow who seldom leaves her New*

York apartment. What an ignoble result for all Black Hawk's hard work. Will my line suffer the same fate, or will my dearest Lola see to it the Staunton legacy endures?"

Then finally, in August of 1951, the year the captain died: *"Sylvia Ann is dead, and the entire Howland fortune has been spread far and wide, like chaff to the wind. Millions in anonymous bequests! Black Hawk must be rolling over in his grave. And so his name recedes into history.*

"As death summons me, I see my daughter, estranged from her sister, growing more eccentric and reclusive with each passing year. Is there nothing I can do to ensure the Staunton name escapes Black Hawk's fate? To have worked so hard and not be remembered seems the cruelest cut of all."

Helena made several Internet searches on her laptop, closed the cover with a satisfying snap, and returned to her bedroom.

Now, how did I think of that? Helena asked herself as she slid under the covers. *Or did I? Perhaps Marc is right, and Captain Staunton still has an oar in around the place. Either way, I know all I need to know.*

Then she fell into a deep, restful sleep.

The Stone Fleet

The next afternoon, Helena dressed in a gray tailored suit and a black wig pulled back in a severe-looking bun. Choosing black glasses and a black leather bag, she pinned a sunburst brooch to her jacket, added a silver bracelet and pearl choker, then surveyed herself in the mirror.

It's the right look, studious and non-threatening, but for the life of me, I look like Lois Lane. Will Superman come to my rescue if I need him? Who knows? I just might.

Then she took off the pearls.

A Social Call

Cheswick Wilks greeted Helena with a kiss on both cheeks, which, for once, she did not fend off. His thin mustache was like sandpaper, and his clammy lips felt reptilian against her skin.

"So punctual. A forgotten courtesy," Wilks said, pushing up his half-glasses and escorting her into a dimly lit hallway.

Helena, a former housekeeper, surveyed the space with a practiced eye. There was a handsomely carved staircase on one side of the entrance hall. On the other was a row of bookcases, an antique gilded mirror, and a series of old portraits. The Victorian furnishings were dingy, bordering on grimy.

No wonder the place is so dimly lit. It's not just vanity on Big Bird's part. Anyone who saw all this dust and dirt in the light of day would run screaming onto Commercial Street.

"Are these family members?" she asked, pointing to the portraits. "I see a resemblance. Especially around the eyes."

Wilks nodded. "Why, yes. This is Uncle Matthew. And this is my famous Great-Aunt Hetty, of whom I'm sure you've heard."

"It seems to me she got a bad rap," Helena said. "If a man had accomplished all she did, they'd say he was a titan of industry. What was it they called her because she was a woman?"

"The Witch of Wall Street," Wilks replied, "but not without some justification. She used to buy the newspaper, read it, iron it so it looked new, and send Cousin Ned out to sell it again."

"I'm sure that was nothing more than Yankee frugality," Helena said as Wilks escorted her through another parlor filled with overstuffed furniture. "You had some information about Captain Staunton, I believe?"

Her host seemed pleased she'd remembered. "Oh, yes. Hetty's father ran the Howland Fleet, one of New Bedford's largest whaling operations. He and the captain knew each other."

"Captain Staunton had some work done on the *Andoria* in New Bedford before his last voyage," Helena said, appearing to warm to the topic.

Wilks smiled, his thin mustache stretching to reveal yellowed teeth. "You *do* know your history. That's so refreshing. Most people don't care about such things. My family was once the most powerful in the country, and now no one even listens to us.

"I've got White Russians chilling—the drinks, not the aristocrats. Shall we head to the library and introduce ourselves?"

Helena giggled. "How delightful! Lead on, kind sir."

Wilks ushered her to a room at the rear of the house. The octagonal space was crammed with several glass-fronted bookcases, a faded Chesterfield sofa, and two wingback chairs with a marble-topped table between them. The so-called library looked more like a used-book emporium. Moldering volumes were piled up on the floor in untidy stacks that appeared as if they might topple at any moment. The room smelled musty and felt close.

Wilks escorted Helena to a chair. "It took a devil of a time to find this, but I did," he said, pointing to a leather-bound volume. "It's the log of the *Leonidas*, piloted by Master John Howland. She was part of the Stone Fleet."

Settling onto the sofa, Wilks explained how the North sank old whaling ships filled with stone to blockade Southern Harbors during the Civil War. The *Leonidas* was scuttled off Fort Sumter.

Helena feigned rapt attention. "I've heard of the fleet but not the *Leonidas*. Did any Staunton ships participate?"

Wilks' tone grew glacial. "Master Howland wrote in this very journal that the Stauntons refused."

Helena felt her pulse race.

Is he ticked off about something that happened during the Civil War or at me? Perhaps it wasn't such a great idea to come here alone.

"How interesting. The Museum has no record of that."

Wilks glanced out the window as if looking for someone. "It raises the question whether the Stauntons avoided their patriotic duty."

"That seems hard to believe," Helena said, following his gaze, "but we'll research the issue thoroughly and make the results public, whatever they may be."

"I admire your honesty. In fact, I propose a toast," Wilks said, taking a pitcher from an ice well on a side table. He poured the mixture of vodka, Kahlua, and heavy cream into two glasses. Handing one to Helena and raising his, he said, "Here's to integrity!"

Helena smiled and raised her glass. "And in the same spirit, here's to you, Mr. Robinson."

Rear Window

Wilks swallowed half his drink and choked. "How much do you know?"

"I know of your dalliances with and financial support for Lance Kensington, who hid out here the night the Coast Guard seized his yacht."

"How could you possibly be aware of that?"

Helena maintained a calm demeanor. "There's an aviation headset on the settle beneath Aunt Hetty's portrait."

"I use it for video conferencing."

Helena tried to sound apologetic. "Sorry, Cheswick, I'm three flights from my pilot's license. I know it's aircraft issue, the KS company logo notwithstanding."

Wilks glared. "How is it you're *always* so certain?"

Helena spoke slowly. "My certainty is not at issue, Cheswick, and you know it. Come clean about Lance before things get worse."

"He was a gorgeous boy once," Wilks said, staring out the window. "Impossible to resist. But, as they always do, he moved on. He *was* better than most at keeping in touch, though."

Helena set her untasted drink on the table. "Even when he wasn't asking for money?"

Wilks seemed offended. "Lance didn't contact me *just* to ask for money. Though he knew I'd do anything for him, I believe he genuinely liked me. At least he was kind enough to offer investment opportunities."

"Like funding his startup under the name of Edward Mott Robinson?"

"Robinson was my great-great-uncle," Wilks said as if reciting family history.

"I know," Helena said. "You couldn't risk attaching the illustrious Wilks name to a porn operation. Did Lance ever pay you back?"

"He's going to," Wilks said in the same dreamy tone.

Helena lifted her glass, hesitated, and set it down again. "Say more, please?"

"Lance is liquidating his company. I'll get the current market value of my investment once he's fully cashed out. That money will solve a lot of my problems."

"I imagine even an Astor fortune runs low over generations," Helena said, sounding sympathetic.

"Oh, yes. And, of course, Cousin Sylvia, Hetty's daughter, wasted her inheritance on *all* sorts of lost causes. The Howland fortune would be worth one point five *billion* today—and she didn't leave one red cent to my side of the family."

"How inconsiderate!"

"I heartily agree." Wilks reached for his drink. "I've been living hand-to-mouth as a result. A place like this requires a lot of maintenance. Say nothing of the social reciprocity my position demands. It all adds up."

"Is that where Henry Boorstin comes in? He seems to have taken on your upkeep."

Wilks gaped at Helena. "You can't possibly know about that. The checks go to an—"

"Offshore account in the Cayman Islands," Helena said softly. "Except for the cash he was bringing you yesterday."

Wilks leaned back in his chair, his face bright red. "Are you some sort of witch?"

Helena laughed. "Not of Wall Street, I'm afraid. I rely on Charlotte Grubb for my financial advice. It's all rather simple. I gave Boorstin the money, darling."

Wilks seemed incredulous. "*You're* the ditzy blonde client he told me about?"

"As I live and dye," Helena said with a forced smile. "What did you have on him?"

Wilks glanced out the window again, then down at the table where Helena's drink remained untouched. He closed his eyes and took a deep breath. "These old floors were sagging with the weight of my New York furniture, but I couldn't bring myself to dispose of it. Boorstin drew up a plan to strengthen the sills and joists, but he didn't specify the steel-core beams needed to support the weight. I hired an investigator who found enough shoddy work to put Boorstin out of business. He had no choice but to pay."

Helena tried to sound sympathetic. "But you had more on him than that, Cheswick. Otherwise, he wouldn't have involved himself with stolen paintings."

Wilks seemed eager to correct her. "I didn't. Lance did. He's marvelous with computers—so talented. He traced my Cayman Islands deposits to Henry Boorstin and discovered he'd failed the architectural licensing exam countless times. The real Henry Boorstin, who has a degree from Yale, holds the license and runs a scam with dozens of would-be architects. As for the fake Boorstin, he saw a hot market and took advantage of it despite having no talent whatsoever."

"That explains his architectural choices—or, better said, the lack thereof."

Wilks chuckled. "I see we agree about that much, at least. He copies buildings from Chatham and Nantucket, then plunks them down in Provincetown with no sense of the impact on their surroundings."

"With no sense at all," said Helena. "And Lance found all this out?"

"Yes. And made Boorstin store the most desirable paintings until it was time for *Scamp* to leave."

Helena tried to stifle her satisfaction. "And Boorstin sold them to Doctor Woodman."

"He didn't want to get caught with them and figured Lance could always steal them back," Wilks said, his voice tentative. "Lance was furious when he found out. He did get the paintings back, though I've learned the hard way not to ask too many questions when he's riled up."

Helena made sure to sound worried. "Are you that afraid of him?"

Wilks seemed distraught yet still besotted. "Recently, yes, I must admit, I have become alarmed. He frightened me, barging in as he did last week. He wasn't himself."

Helena leaned forward and asked, "Did he need your help to escape?"

"He did, but my car had just broken down."

Helena noticed a beautifully patterned cobweb in a far corner of the library. A spider was rushing to capture an entangled fly.

"When you say Lance knew you'd do anything for him, don't you mean you *did* do things for him? Questionable things?"

Wilks stared, his eyes cold and threatening. "Whatever could you mean?"

Helena took a deep breath. "Why did you shoot Wally? He's such a fine young man."

"You're not drinking your cocktail, my dear," Wilks said, his voice eerily calm. "I'm afraid I'm out of cream and can't make another round. If you won't be drinking it, may I? It seems a shame to waste good liquor."

"I haven't decided yet," Helena said pointedly. "Why don't you tell me about Wally while I make up my mind?"

Wilks smiled as if to say, *touché*. "Lance was certain Wally would tell you his security list had been hacked."

"He started to at the party in Truro. Just before you shot him."

Wilks' tone was defiant. "Lance said there'd be trouble if they traced the break-ins back to *Scamp*."

Helena struggled to contain her anger, staring out the window as she spoke. "And you shot that charming young man to protect an old boyfriend?"

Wilks followed her gaze. "You don't know Lance. He could be so kind, but he could also be horrible. The things I've seen him do over the years. . . He'd have killed me if I didn't shoot Wally. You must believe me."

Helena continued to stare. "So, at the party, when you heard a young man wanted to see me, you figured it might be Wally, pretended to leave, and waited outside for the right moment."

"Yes. That's just how it happened. Wally was so handsome. I didn't want to kill him. I was glad to hear he's still alive."

Helena noticed the spider had reached her victim. "I believe you, Cheswick, but I doubt you felt the same way about Sergeant Brandt. Lance dug him up somewhere on the dark web, didn't he? And created his fake resumé?"

Wilks confirmed this, then described how Brandt drugged Afton's brother to get Afton out of the way before the museum break-in.

"Brandt knew the trap in the studio was meant to kill Mavis Chandry, not C.J. Strongue. When blaming you didn't work, and threatening you didn't make any difference—"

"Brandt sent that anonymous letter," Helena said. "It always seemed overkill to me."

Wilks' words poured out in a breathless torrent. "Brandt knew Lance had set the trap himself but wanted the glory of catching a murderer. He didn't care who it was so long as he got to play cop. That's all that mattered to him in the end—being the macho man with the badge."

"So Lance killed C.J.?" Helena asked, leaning forward to mop up a drop of White Russian she'd spilled on the table.

"Oh, yes. He did that on his own," Cheswick said with pride. "When C.J. died instead of Mavis, Brandt wanted to arrest one of Lance's crew. That got Lance even more worked up. The last thing he needed was any more screwups."

"Are you saying Brandt went rogue?"

Wilks nodded several times. "Yes. Exactly. He'd become a liability. Lance said he'd pay me a million dollars on top of my investment to eliminate him. He knew I had a gun and silencer."

Helena tried to seem supportive. "It might have been a smart move to throw them away after shooting Wally."

"Lance told me the dates he'd be in Europe and said to kill Wally and Brandt while he was away, so I couldn't."

As Helena watched the spider wrap its prey, Wilks spoke slowly as if he'd run out of steam. "It proved easier than I'd thought to shoot Brandt and slip away."

Helena cradled her drink, then set it back on the table again. "But you didn't kill him. Not then."

Wilks, taken by surprise, paused, then shrugged. "No. Unfortunately, I couldn't risk two shots—too many people around. Lance was furious when he found out Wally and Brandt were still alive."

"And insisted you finish the job?"

Wilks spoke as if recounting a distasteful memory. "Well, yes. I suppose you could say it that way."

Helena stared out the window assessing her options.

It's crucial he feels empathy for being put in what I'm sure he thinks of as an unseemly situation. His life is ruled by manners and other peoples' opinions. How tragic.

"So you checked yourself into Cape Cod Hospital. . ."

Wilks explained his heart often went into arrhythmia before an epileptic attack. "They know me there. Unless a seizure hits, I have free rein of the place, so I moved my wheelchair to the hall, as I usually do, and waited for my chance."

It wasn't long before the guard took a break while Sergeant Brandt was asleep. Wilks injected the solution Lance had provided into Brandt's IV and returned to the wheelchair just as an alarm sounded. The staff rushing to assist the sergeant made it impossible for Wilks to get into Wally's room.

"After I checked myself out, I had a genuine attack and had to return. In fact, I saw you come to visit that girl who sings in front of the town hall. They discharged me that afternoon, and I came home to find Lance waiting for me."

Helena smiled. "You turned away so fast I wasn't sure it was you. But it got me thinking."

"That's what I was afraid of," Wilks said with a sardonic laugh that sent chills down her spine. "I kept telling Lance that anyone who underestimates you does so at their own peril."

"I assume you'd be far away if he'd already paid you," Helena said, trying to keep her tone both calm and interested.

He's heading over the edge. One false move could set him off.

All at once, Wilks seemed heartbroken. "Lance said he had funds in Switzerland and that he'd wire the money to my offshore account once we were safe. I always believed he'd do right by me in the end. You know what they say, 'Hope springs eternal.'"

"That hope, my dear Cheswick, has been your downfall all along," Helena said as he peered out the window, looking desperate. "I feel sorry for you. Honestly, I do."

Wilks choked back tears. "Thank you for that, my dear. No one seems to care about me anymore. Not the way they used to. Back in the city, I filled my townhouse with love, but when I had to give it all up..."

Wilks stared into his empty glass. "I wish things had been different, and we had become friends. You must believe me."

"I do," Helena said with genuine sadness. "As a friend, I should tell you they arrested Lance at the airport the night after he left you."

Wilks heaved a deep sigh. "I figured something happened when I couldn't reach his burner phone. I just didn't want to admit it to myself."

"I saw him toss it in the dunes so no one could track him," Helena said.

Tears streaked Wilks' face. "I've left several voicemails since I got the money, but he hasn't called me back."

"The money you just got from Henry Boorstin?" Helena asked, her voice a gentle whisper.

"Yes. When I threatened Lance would pay him a visit, Boorstin came up with the money in a heartbeat. Lance and I planned to fly a private plane to Canada and then get a commercial flight to Moldova.

No extradition from there, you know. He promised I could go with him. That's why I still had his headset. Lance knew the Feds would freeze his U.S. assets, so I was his only hope. My bags are packed and everything."

Helena stared at Wilks as resignation clouded his features. "And you kept hoping he'd appear. Even just now. You must love him very much."

Wilks wiped his eyes, then spoke in a petulant tone. "If you're not going to drink that cocktail, Helena, I could certainly use it. This conversation has taken a lot out of me."

"I'm afraid I'm not in the mood anymore," Helena said, handing him the glass, "though it looks delicious."

"Here's to you, my dear. You've been most understanding," Wilks said, draining her glass. "The least I can do is spare you the agony of Lance's revenge. He was furious with you for stopping his yacht with all those paintings on board. There's nothing he can do about that now, though.

"My weak heart should make things easy enough, so don't blame yourself—"

Wilks' head lolled onto his right shoulder as the glass dropped to the floor. Helena reached over to check his pulse. There was none.

"Did you get all of that?" she whispered into the microphone tucked into her bra.

"Every single word. I've got the video, audio, and a real-time backup," Amy Morgan replied in hushed tones.

Not waiting to answer, Helena dropped an earpiece into her purse and ran outside to await the police.

Postmortem

When the medical examiner had completed her work, Amy and Helena retired to Bubala's. They chose a table away from Commercial Street where they could talk without being overheard.

"Now I really *do* need a drink," Helena said as a server placed a large, ice-cold Martini in front of her.

Are you sure you're OK? Amy asked. "That scene at the end was intense. My heart was in my mouth, especially when Wilks kept looking out the window. I was worried one of Kensington's men was waiting for a signal."

Helena took a moment. "I'm all right. Not fabulous, given I just witnessed a pathetically messed-up guy commit suicide with a poisoned drink meant to kill me—but all right. I think Wilks was still waiting for Kensington to rescue him. Imagine falling in love with someone you paid for sex. Especially someone so manipulative. Poor man. All those years. All that abuse. And he was still crazy about the guy. Crazy enough to kill for him."

Amy lowered her voice. "The poison must have already been in your glass, but how did he think he could move your body or even dispose of it? He was an old man with a bad heart, a broken-down car, and not a friend in the world. And we just learned the bank foreclosed on his house last month. He had to vacate in six weeks. There's no way he could have hidden a body for long."

Helena wasn't surprised. "Until I told him Kensington was in custody, I suspect Wilks believed he'd be carried off to foreign lands by a knight in shining armor. If he'd lost his precious house *and* Lance, I'm certain he had no reason left to live."

Helena took another long, satisfying sip. "Seeing Wilks in that filthy place, surrounded by all the fancy art, statues, and furniture, made it clear to me that his possessions controlled him. I've never seen that side of hereditary wealth before. Paying for Kensington's services allowed Wilks to love him as if he were another acquisition—the only way he knew how to love. Kensington was savvy enough to use that to manipulate him into paying for his startup. No doubt he kept dangling the notion of their escape together over Wilks to be sure he did whatever he wanted—including killing me."

Amy stared at Helena as if seeing her for the first time. "Wow. That's profound. Did you study psychology?"

Helena shrugged. "Psychology, no. People, yes. Most folks let their guard down when they don't know who you are. That's why drag works so well to disarm an audience—and why I try to maintain a consistent look when I'm not performing. Otherwise, folks might tell me things they'd regret later.

"Oh, and here's the camera," Helena said, unfastening the sunburst brooch and handing it to Amy. "That was a stroke of genius, building it into a piece of antique jewelry. Wilks never noticed."

Amy put the brooch in her purse. "Quite the gimmick. We're not as unsophisticated as people might think in the DA's office. Dan Andrade has a lot of tricks up his sleeve, but even I was surprised he had something drag-compatible. I wonder if I should start using it?"

Helena chuckled. "Don't get too used to it. I may need to borrow it back to keep my donors honest."

Amy took a sip of her Cosmopolitan. "Wilks seemed to confirm that Boorstin peddled the paintings to Doctor Woodman to dodge the rap and pick up some much-needed cash."

"I know you and Dan will nail all that down," Helena said, holding up her empty glass to attract the server's attention. "No doubt Boorstin has numerous fraud charges looming, say nothing of architectural crimes against humanity. Fraud may be one thing, but some crimes are simply unforgivable."

Amy paused as if rehearsing what to say next. "And while we're still on the topic of honesty, Helena, there's something I have to tell you."

"Shoot," Helena said, looking puzzled.

"Before I met you, I hated drag and insisted it demeaned women. After going through all this together, I see the courage and truth drag enables. I wanted to tell you that and say I hope you'll still be my friend."

Helena held Amy's hand and gazed into her eyes. "Many women feel that way, and I *never* blame them. Some female impersonators *do* mock women. I've always tried to poke fun at men's definition of femininity while turning their notions of masculinity on its ear. Have no fear, Amy. We'd be friends no matter what. As my husband Butch taught me, some relationships are just meant to be. There's no point in over-analyzing why they happen. They're a life blessing that only a fool would forgo."

Amy blushed slightly, then glanced at her phone. "Dan just texted. Wally is out of the coma. The doctors say his recovery will be gradual, but he made it clear it was Wilks who intimidated him into admitting there was a password list."

Helena raised her glass. "Here's to Wally. He's a good kid. Naïve, but I never doubted him for a minute. I'm going to hire him to beef up security on the estate when he's up to the job. I'm sure he's learned his lesson."

"You don't think you're moving a bit fast on those Martinis, do you?" Amy asked, her eyes growing wider when Helena ordered a third as soon as her second arrived.

"If you'd ever had tea with Lola Staunton, you wouldn't be so concerned. One of the hidden benefits of my years at HomePort is that I can drink almost anyone under the table."

"How do you do it?"

"Practice, practice, practice."

Amy lowered her voice. "Speaking of drinks, did you know beforehand Wilks had poisoned yours? I'm not asking professionally; this entire conversation is off the record."

Helena grew pensive. "Not at first. I thought it odd he'd chosen White Russians rather than asking my preference. I didn't dwell on that until something about Miss Marple popped into my head. Remember *Nemesis?*"

"Yes," Amy said. "I love that story. Miss Marple figured out the murderer was the wacky sister and didn't drink the milky drink that was supposed to help her sleep."

Helena surveyed Commercial Street. Miss Ridgefield was posing for pictures with a group of Japanese tourists as Melody was preparing for a performance. The scene seemed more vibrant, the people more animated than Helena had ever noticed.

This is life. And I appreciate it so much more after a near-death experience tempered by a couple of Martinis. Yes, Norman Mailer, this is a town genuinely worth fighting for.

Helena set down her glass. "As I was about to take a sip, I distinctly heard Lola's voice say, '*Nemesis*.' Just that one word. Between us, I've always sensed Lola and her sister watching over me. And I'm not the only one: Mavis told me she thought a spirit warned her as Kensington's helicopter approached. That's why she ran to get her shotgun. Who knows? For the record, though—"

Amy held up her hand. "For the record, no one could have imagined there was a massive dose of poison in an innocuous White Russian. Given the condition of the rest of the house, no doubt you were worried the cream had gone bad, which is why you didn't drink yours. I know the Medical Examiner hasn't weighed in yet, but the discovery of a bottle of Aconite in Wilks' kitchen is evidence enough for me.

"What *is* Aconite?" Helena asked. "I'm curious how it works."

Amy hesitated until Helena insisted she continue. "If you must know, it's from a genus of flowering plants containing a potent alkaloid. They have different names, such as monkshood and wolf-bane. A large dose will cause nearly instantaneous death, paralyzing the heart and/or lungs. Its symptoms can be horrific, but fortunately for Wilks, his weak heart gave out just as he said it would."

Amy picked up the menu. "I love the oysters here. Would you care to share a couple dozen? On me?"

Helena hesitated for a moment, a distant look in her eyes. "Only if they're on the half shell, darling. Only if on the half shell. . ."

And Nothing but the Truth

The next morning, Butch and Helena woke early in HomePort's master suite, tiptoed downstairs, and crossed Pilgrims' Park to the breakwater. At its end, they strolled Long Point hand in hand. The couple was blissfully alone, with no sound but lapping waves and the cry of an occasional seabird.

Helena rested her head on Butch's shoulder, far more nervous than she'd anticipated. Her husband wrapped his arms around her waist as they stared across the tiny strip of sand to the bay beyond. Butch nuzzled her neck and spoke so lovingly, at first, she wondered if she was still dreaming.

"I want to apologize," Butch said. "I've got to deal better with the ambiguity and demands of our new circumstances."

Helena stepped out of his embrace and searched her husband's face. "Are you talking about me? I thrive on ambiguity—I'm seldom the same person for more than a few hours."

Butch picked up a flat stone and skimmed it across the water. "That's not true. Whoever you impersonate, underneath, you're always Helena, fiercely protecting your friends and fighting for what's right. Folks in the drag community get what's at stake for others more than most, but you take it to an entirely different level. I wish I had your integrity—and commitment."

Helena stopped walking. "What do you mean? You're always trustworthy and doing your best."

"Thank you for that. But I'm not sure I've done my best lately." Butch guided them toward a small cove lined with reeds. A seal popped up not ten feet from shore and studied them with interest. "When the money came, I started deceiving myself our life would stay the same."

Helena turned to face her husband. "What are you saying? I'm the one who deceives myself and everybody else."

Butch dropped his gaze. "Perhaps. But I wonder if you ever ask yourself the question that literally keeps me up at night."

"What's that?"

Butch hesitated. "How are you and I any different from the onion rings?" His sad eyes probed hers as his voice grew louder. "Of course, there's Lola and Dorrie's money, but that's not what I mean."

Helena tensed.

Get over yourself. He's upset and expressing his feelings. That shouldn't threaten you. Stay present. Trust him. Don't joke or hide out in another persona.

"Say more, Butch."

"Are you sure you want to hear it?"

"Absolutely."

One if By Land

Butch stopped walking but avoided Helena's gaze. "OK. So consider this: we have our laughs at the onion rings' expense, right? It's all so easy. We live here and understand how things really work. They arrived en masse, clueless and ill-suited to our way of life, desperately trying to sustain their urban existence. Making fun of them is a way of diminishing their impact, but there's a false dichotomy. The truth is, Helena, we mock and demonize them because we hate having to pander to them. It's a devil's bargain. They want in, and we need their money to help with jobs and housing—and to undo some of the damage. But have we ever once considered the cost to us as a couple? I'd like to think we've got more to do in this life than social posturing and vapid conversation—no matter how noble the cause. Why are we spending *all* our time and energy on those things and not living our own best lives? There's no balance. No way to recharge. No time for us."

Butch traced a circle with his foot. Helena mussed it up and coaxed him to sit on the sand beside her.

"I see your point. C.J.'s wasted life hit me hard. I don't want to end up like her, alone, frightened, and misguided."

Butch said softly, "I believe you, but I still see one fundamental problem."

Helena stared at her husband, who wasn't showing anger, but rather the same resignation she was feeling. "What's that, Butch? Whatever you have to say, I want to hear it."

He spoke as if the words couldn't get out fast enough. "Before I left, I was angry, and what I wanted to say didn't come out right. Let me try again. You've become a brand—a fundraising juggernaut that everyone counts on. You get people laughing, just like Shirley-Mae does, and they love you both for it. There's nothing wrong with that, but then everyone lets you do the heavy lifting because you do it so well. Now that the museum's up and running, do you really think they won't expect you to lead the next battle? We've got a few good people outside our family, like Elise and Gwen, but nowhere near enough to make the Staunton Trust stand on its own.

"Everything still depends on you—the queen bee. After all, you made the HomePort Colony a success, then jumped right into the museum project, and now it's the Artisans' Fund. All worthy causes, but why the hell would anyone step up when you're doing all the work?"

Helena stared out over the breakwater's long span. The ocean on the harbor side rippled with waves, while, on the opposite side, the flooded moors were a mirror, calm and inviting.

He's right. Fundraising Barbie, that's me. Goddamn it. How did things get so out of control?

Helena took a deep breath. "I have to own some of this, Butch. I worried if other people got too close, they'd see I was a fraud. That's why I insisted on doing so much myself. I wanted to be able to hide any mistakes I made. It was childish and insecure—and it hurt our marriage. Can you ever forgive me?"

"Nothing to forgive," Butch said, kissing the top of her head. "I wasn't a full day on that yacht before I realized I resented those people taking you away from me even more than I resented all the bullshit they brought with them. We both want to help others. The question is on whose terms. And we need backup if you and I step aside every once in a while."

Helena felt herself growing lighter. "Exactly. Though I can't imagine how to dig myself out of the mess I've made."

Butch's gaze was so intense the sunlight glimmering on the water seemed dull by comparison. "It's simple. We've got to change the way the game is played. Figure out how to manage and focus the momentum rather than you doing it all yourself. You've been going full tilt for years without a vacation or chance for us to reconnect. It can't be that way anymore. Right?"

The couple reached the breakwater. Across the harbor, the town glistened in the early morning sun. HomePort, high atop its dune, shone in the distance like a castle in a fairytale.

After meeting her husband's gaze for as long as she could, Helena began to cry.

Butch pulled her close. "C'mon now. Together, I know we can fix this. And I even think I know how."

Helena took a step back. "In the name of God, tell me!"

Butch looked serene and confident. "I've thought about nothing else the whole time I was away. What's called for is a major change of course. I'm calling my plan 'One if by land, and two, if by sea.'"

"What's one?" Helena asked, feeling relief at the sound of his confident voice.

Butch grinned. "We head back and give that big four-poster a long-overdue workout."

"I thought you'd never ask," Helena said in her best Mae West voice, savoring the return of playfulness and ease between them. "And two, big boy?"

Butch laughed before reciting what seemed a pre-rehearsed speech. "The night before Shirley called, I stared for hours at more stars than I'd ever seen. I told myself I'd take you across the oceans—just the two of us—and teach you the name of every single constellation. Then, I grew discouraged. I couldn't imagine how you'd ever get away.

"If you're willing to do things differently, we'll figure out the details together and set sail. We'll get a new executive director, create more positions—whatever it takes—but we've got to get you out of here for a while. It's the only way. If you're gone, others will have to step up. I bet Marc, Cole, and Charlotte would help manage the transition. But first things, first."

Butch took her in his arms and kissed her with such passion that Helena lost her balance. Then he ran toward the breakwater. Helena chased after him. She'd never felt so free.

***

Up in HomePort's tower, Shirley-Mae handed the captain's telescope to Dolores, smiled contentedly, and took a swig from her flask. "What do you say, hon?" she said to the housekeeper, who, after glancing through the lens, wiped her eyes with a handkerchief fringed with violet tatting. "How 'bout we saddle up the Edsel, head up to Hyannis for a day's shopping, and then maybe hit a couple of bars? Looks like the kids are gonna want the place to themselves for a spell."

The Tide Turns

Two weeks later, Freddie Chalmers, whose article on the art thefts in the *Provincetown Free Press* had garnered national interest, returned to HomePort.

Dolores and Shirley were handing around trays of canapés in the front parlor while the Bradford Street Irregulars and a small group of friends waited for Helena and Butch's arrival. The space was hung with its first student show. Lola and Dorrie's portraits seemed at home amid the vibrant colors and vivid subjects. Melody was studying the artwork, trying to keep as far away from Mavis as possible.

"I was beginning to worry it was a mistake to move all the original items to the museum," Cole said. "Now there's enough art on the walls, though, I think the space works well."

"It does, Cole," Helena said, pausing at the doorway with Butch at her side. "After all, it wasn't the things in the room that made it special. It was the people. Speaking of people, I think that must be our guest of honor at the front door. No, Dolores, you stay put. I'll let him in."

Just Deserts

Helena guided Doctor Woodman into the room, followed by Chief Silva.

The doctor was confused and nervous as Helena made introductions, saving Melody for last. "I believe you know Melody Carpenter, the artist. You had her paintings for a while, if I recall."

"We may have met," Woodman said, avoiding Melody's glare.

Helena strode to the ornate fireplace and faced the assembled company. "Doctor, you once told me you came to Provincetown to know the 'movers and shakers,' as you so quaintly put it."

"I believe I said that at one time," he replied sullenly.

"At one time?" Helena asked, her eyebrows raised. "Have you come to think differently?"

The doctor was slow to respond. "Not really. You need the right connections to get ahead in the world."

Marc and Cole exchanged a glance that signaled *Oops! Wrong answer.*

"So you still don't see the importance of doing one's best and making others happy?" Helena asked with a slight edge to her voice.

"We never discussed such drivel," the doctor said. "Why am I here? What do you want from me?"

Melody tried to hide a smile.

"Allow me to jog your memory." Helena subtly shifted her facial expression. Using a different tone, she said, "You don't remember me telling you that when I came to look at your paintings, better said, the stolen property hidden in your house?

Woodman steadied himself against the back of a chair. "That was you?"

"Candi Lagasse, at your service," Helena said, making a curtsey.

Woodman scowled and shouted, "You had no right to—"

Helena hoisted herself to her full height, towering above the doctor. "No right to do what? To come into your home at your invitation? To see the worst collection of tourist art on the Eastern Seaboard? To listen to you hold forth ad nauseam with outdated notions that went out with *The Bonfire of the Vanities?* Just what is your objection, Mr. Tin, ehr, *Doctor* Woodman."

As Shirley-Mae looked around the group as if to say, *I raised that one*, the doctor stammered and made several false starts.

When it became clear he had no response, Helena continued. "Many of your so-called 'movers and shakers' spend short amounts of time here, overpay for property, and think they own the town. They soon discover they're in the distinct minority and move on—but not before doing plenty of damage. If you are remembered for anything at all, which I sincerely doubt, it will be for your attempt to force the buskers from the one place in town where they can still afford to live."

"Now, wait a minute," Doctor Woodman bellowed, his face growing red. "A man has every right to purchase property and make improvements."

Helena clapped her hands. "I'm so glad you said that. We'll get back to your point after I spell a few more things out for you, darling: First, you have no future here. As of tomorrow's edition of the *Free Press,* the entire town will know Henry Boorstin set you up to receive stolen property. *And* that you were too blinded by greed to notice."

The doctor looked around the room for support. Seeing none, he seemed to shrink into a large, round ball.

"Speaking of new developments, *Doctor* Woodman," Helena went on, "My advice is for you to get out of Dodge. The sooner, the better. To that end, I'm prepared to offer you one hundred thousand dollars over market price for your home—*in cash*—so *I* can do with it whatever *I* want. If you accept, I'll expect you to vacate in a week. You have three minutes to decide, then my offer drops by ten thousand each additional minute you delay."

Helena returned to the replica of Lola's swan chair, sat down, picked up her teacup, and took a large swig of the gin it contained.

When, at last, the doctor nodded, she raised her cup in a salute. "A wise decision. You were almost out of time."

Woodman started to leave, only to be thwarted by Afton, who blocked the doorway, saying, "I don't think the lady is quite done with you yet." Then he pushed him into a nearby chair.

"Afton is right as always," Helena said. "I do have one last question for you." She winked at Melody. "What's your favorite movie, Doctor?"

"Huh?"

"Tell me the name of your favorite movie."

Woodman's features grew dark. "Go to hell."

Helena laughed. "Where *are* your manners? At the risk of sounding like an Edward Albee character, I'm the hostess, and you're the guest, so you've got to play my little game."

The doctor looked incredulously at Chief Louie, who said, "Answer the question."

"I dunno, maybe *Wall Street*?"

Marc whispered to Cole, "That was a no-brainer. Where's Helena going with this?"

Cole shrugged.

"An interesting choice. Explains a lot," Helena said, looking toward her audience as if to say, *Wait for it.* "Would you care to know mine?"

"Not really," the doctor muttered, "though I have a strong hunch you're gonna tell me."

Helena smirked. "Another example of those impressive social skills that have gotten you so far. But you're right, I am going to name my favorite movie. It's *Auntie Mame*."

"So what?" the doctor snarled, his hands clutching the arms of his chair. "What the hell does that have to do with anything?"

"And do you know my favorite scene?" Helena continued, unfazed. "It's the one where Mame Dennis announces she's bought the property in Mountebank for a home for Jewish war refugees. I've always loved it when the Upsons, those pathetic, racist social climbers, got beaten at their own game."

When the corners of Charlotte's mouth twitched, Helena pretended not to notice. "Charlotte, darling, would you care to explain to Doctor Woodman what the hell this has to do with anything, as he so eloquently put it?"

Charlotte opened a notepad and read, "The building affectionately known as Buskerville Hall will be combined with your property, Doctor Woodman, to form the Annie Machado Musician's Retreat. Named in honor of the late Dorrie Machado Staunton's mother, the Retreat will offer low-rent residences for eligible street musicians."

Doctor Woodman leaped from his seat, apoplectic. "Now, wait a damn minute. Henry Boorstin told me some rich woman from Europe—van Dusenberg or something—bought that old guest house out from under me. She won't sell. She's going to develop the place just like I was."

"Adopting her Kelly van Dusen voice, Helena smiled Kelly's insincere smile and said, 'I simply *adore* street musicians. There's something just so *down-to-earth and reassuring* about *the little people* playing for spare change on the sidewalk, don't you agree?'

"The hell with it!" the doctor bellowed. "I never should have come to this goddamn town. That's what I get for—"

"Having your head up your ass," Shirley-Mae said with a guffaw. "At least you've got the skills to pull it out if you ever learn to behave like a decent human being."

The friends applauded as Helena took one sweeping bow after the other, as grand as any diva at the Met. Taking advantage of the distraction, Doctor Woodman snuck toward the door. At the last possible moment, Afton stepped aside to let him pass.

"My lawyer will be in touch with the paperwork and the check!" Helena called out just before the front door slammed shut. Then she turned to Freddie. "Darling, did you get all that?"

"Every word," the reporter said. "Enough for a full article in my upcoming series on the housing crisis. When you make a deal with a reporter, Helena, you sure keep up your end of the bargain."

Phoenix Rising

The group shared observations and appetizers until Mavis stood to speak, her deep voice unusually subdued. "I got my painting back—the one meant for Helena. Chief, would you be good enough to fetch it?"

Chief Louie returned with the painting of the young man and the phoenix, which Mavis placed atop the mantel.

"C'mon over here, you," Mavis said, pointing to Helena.

As Helena drew close, she stammered, "That's me in that picture. However did you know, Mavis?"

"Trust me. Somehow, I just did," Mavis said. "Now, Dolores, honey."

Dolores entered, holding another canvas covered in thick, white cloth.

Mavis pointed to it. "The painting under wraps is the proper companion to this phoenix painting—not the one I dashed off to trap Lance Kensington. No one has seen it but my agent and me. And now it's ready for you, Helena. Before we unveil it, though, I want to say a few words."

Mavis displayed a tender smile, which made her look much younger than her years. "I've come to think of life as existing in two segments: the part where we're young, making mistakes, and the part where we're older and have figured out who we are. Or at least we know more about ourselves," she said, turning to look at Helena. "I always envisioned this series as a diptych. The first is the beauty and potential of youth hobbled by the tensions of self-doubt. The second is the wisdom and power that comes from knowing one's truth. I wanted to show that progression in these two paintings.

"Butch, would you be good enough to do the honors?"

He removed the covering in one rapid movement. The second painting, in shades of gold, emerald, and red so vivid it seemed aflame, was a portrait of Helena as a mature woman. She seemed regal and confident, wearing the Staunton jewels, and dressed in a gown embroidered with the phoenix from the companion piece. A man in a simple white toga tied at the waist knelt at her side, looking up at her. There could be no doubt this priest-like character was Butch. His adoration lit up the entire canvas.

Marc took Cole's hand and whispered, "The love. I can feel it. She painted the love Butch has for Helena. How the hell did Mavis do that?"

"Damned if I know. I feel it, too," Cole said as he squeezed Marc's hand. "I never thought a painting could convey something so powerful, yet so intangible."

Helena stood in silence for some time, then said. "Mavis, this is the most beautiful thing I've ever seen. I've dreamed all my life someone would look at me like that. How in the name of Rembrandt were you able to capture the emotion?"

Before Mavis could answer, Shirley-Mae marched up to Helena and brandished an index finger in her face. "Jumpin' Jehoshaphat, child. I've never seen such a crock of horse shit since I worked the stables at Preakness. Butch looks at you that way *forty-seven* times a day. From what the fellers tell me, he looked at you that way the night you met—and every day since. You goddamn fool. Are you so blinded by your pain you *still* can't see that?"

Helena turned to look at her husband, who sported such a smug grin she began to blush.

Taking Mavis's hand, Shirley said, "You saw what she was doing all along. Didn't you? Using sarcasm and personality changes to hide from herself. Now, maybe between us and those two broads that haunt the place, we can force some sense into her brain. If there is still one beneath all that foundation and blusher."

As her grandmother was overtaken by emotion, Helena squeezed Butch's hand so hard his fingers turned white.

Shirley regained her poise and took a deep breath. "Mavis painted these so you'd see the same damn thing I've been trying to show you most of your life. Yes, Helena, you were a young, frightened boy once. And yes, you dealt with a lot more hurt than any child should ever have to bear. But you burst through that pain, like this here bird. What's it called?"

"A phoenix. It comes from Greek mythology," Cole said, looking at Marc, his voice cracking. "It rises from the ashes. Again and again."

Shirley held Helena in her defiant gaze. "No better way to say it; you rose from the goddamn ashes. And you became a rock for your friends and a lifesaver for your worn-out old Gandma. Nobody gives a tinker's damn what you wear, who you love, or where and how you find your joy. They *admire* you, Helena. You're *the only one* who doesn't see yourself as you really are. Instead, you hide behind your fancy getups and goofy characters.

"What this amazing artist has done," Shirley said, pointing to the second portrait, "is to paint you not as you pretend to be but *as you are.* The person worthy enough to take Lola Staunton's place at the center of this here family—a family I've hoped for all my life and finally found."

Seeing something in Helena's eyes, Shirley paused. When she spoke again, her voice was a whisper. "You know, Helena, your mother—my daughter, just in case you forgot—left me, too. The difference between you and me is I forgave her. You never could. And that's what you need to do now, honey child. Forgive her, make peace with what happened, and set yourself free. It's all over, baby. You made it. You're just as safe and loved as that young boy ever dreamed you'd be.

"Come here, girl. You need a hug, and so do I. You too, son," Shirley said, pointing at Butch. "And I mean that just as it sounds."

As Butch and Shirley pulled Helena into a deep embrace, their chosen family began to tiptoe away. Then, Helena said, "No, everybody, wait. Mavis, I have a question. How did you see through to the real me?"

The artist seemed unsure how to answer. "To be honest, there were times the brush took me places and did things I didn't think were possible. And I swear, sometimes it felt as though someone was looking over my shoulder whispering what to do next."

Helena gazed at the portraits of Lola and Dorrie, then, seeing Mavis focused in the same direction, pulled the artist close.

Two if by Sea

The thick planks of Fisherman's Wharf were tinged with frost. The Bradford Street Irregulars stood in a single line along the pier, shuffling to keep warm.

As the sun rose, the fully provisioned *Dame Edna* was preparing to cast off. Helena was at the helm, and Butch was doing last-minute systems checks. *Tough Cookie* was at the next slip in a similar state of readiness. Betty, dressed in a fur-lined parka trimmed with rhinestones, was checking his chart plotter.

"Don't cry, Gandma," Helena said to Shirley-Mae, who was reaching for her flask, eyes red, her nose running. "Remember, we've got the villas at Las Hadas lined up for three weeks at Christmas. Did you know they have a brass trio that plays when a boat arrives? And they fire a cannon so you'll know to meet us at the dock. I'll expect to see all of you waiting there when we arrive.

"Easy now, Gandma. Please don't worry. We'll be together again before you even know it. Then we'll have Easter in Bora Bora. I'd thought Easter Island might be more appropriate, but Butch convinced me that's living a bit too rough."

"I suppose conservationists everywhere are relieved," Marc said, sniffling and squeezing Cole's hand. "You'd never have resisted giving at least one of those statues a head-to-toe makeover. But, oh, wait a minute, do they even have toes?"

Helena welcomed the distraction. "You're probably right," she said, taking Butch's hand in hers. "Thank you all for supporting us. It was a tough haul getting the museum up and running. It did us both in."

"Say nothing of going into hiding to dodge a murder rap without informing your attorney," Quincy added.

Helena heaved a dramatic sigh. "That, too. If you folks weren't willing to pick up the slack, there'd be no way we could ever leave. I know you understand how important it is for Butch and me to get away by ourselves. We're so grateful."

Betty finished his adjustments. "Afton, we'll check in with you and Aaron when we're a day out of Montego Bay, so you can set up the finish line."

"Just so you know, we won't be hanging any scuba gear from the mark," Afton said with a laugh. "This time, you've both got to finish the race. I'm damn tired of the drama."

"Oh, Betty, are you going somewhere, too?" Helena teased.

"Is your brain so bleached you've already forgotten? I'm with you as far as Jamaica," Betty replied in mock indignation, making it all too apparent the rivalry between the two captains would continue unabated until a winner was declared.

Helena blew Betty a kiss. "But not on board, darling, thank God. And remember, 'If the boat is rockin', don't come knockin'."

The friends' laughter echoed across the water, startling a flock of pigeons that soared upward from the marina roof, bobbing and weaving in the dawn's light

Helena turned to face the folks on the pier. "As I was saying before being so rudely interrupted, with all your help, I've fulfilled Lola and Dorrie's wishes. Now it's time to clear my head and make peace with my past."

Helena looked at Mavis, who was grappling with potent emotion. "What can I say, darling? I'm so grateful to you for all you've done."

Mavis's deep voice lacked its usual authority. "Look, Helena. Just let it all go. You've done your bit. It's time for others to step up. Things will work out just fine. People need to get outside their social media bubbles and see what's happening to the place they love. And we'll make damn sure they do."

Butch put his arm around Helena. "Thanks for sharing her with me. I promise to do everything in my power to make her the happiest female impersonator on the Atlantic *and* the Pacific—and to return her to you safely."

"We'll hold you to that," Dolores said in mock severity as the group cheered and the birds took flight again.

"Well, I guess the time's come to shove off," Helena said, sounding hesitant. "It's been a tough stretch for me, and now I want to—"

"Get back to nature," Marc chided, "on a million-dollar yacht."

"OK, Marc," Helena said, laughing. "Perhaps I'm not exactly roughing it, but trust me when I say I've got some rough work ahead of me to change the habits of a lifetime. I'm humbled to have what I have and the opportunities it offers, but I'm telling you, for the record, if I had to get on a mule and ride across the desert to be alone with Butch, I'd do it in a heartbeat."

"Honey, I've done that, been there, and got the T-shirt," Shirley-Mae said, wiping her lips. "Trust me. It ain't all it's cracked up to be. Nothing worse than finding you've ridden an ass a thousand miles on your own ass only to end up stuck in some flea-bitten motel with yet another one."

Butch shook his head and turned the ignition key. The engine sprang to life. Marc and Cole tossed the dock lines to Helena, and *Dame Edna* backed out of her slip. Then the two men ran to *Tough Cookie* and assisted Betty with his departure.

Both yachts cruised to the middle of the harbor, then headed into the breeze to raise their sails. With the rising sun as a backdrop, they looked majestic, filled with hope and the promise of a new chapter in Provincetown's ongoing love affair with the sea.

The friends stood in silence, watching the magnificent vessels round Long Point and Wood End until their sails faded from view. Then, the group strolled down the wharf to the parking lot, where they congregated at Quincy's Avanti, unwilling to let the moment end.

Shirley-Mae wiped away yet another tear and said, "Anyone for cocktails at the house tonight? Dolores and I don't want to mope around that big place, especially right after sending our kids off on the high seas. C'mon over around six and keep us company."

Even Quincy eagerly agreed.

The Rough Cut

The following afternoon, the Bradford Street Irregulars gathered in the museum theater to view the rough cut of Paul Schroeder's documentary. Helena and Freddie's conversation with Paul, followed by the montage of the town, were high points, though it was clear to everyone the film lacked a satisfying ending.

As the applause died out, Freddie stood to speak. "You know how the *New York Times* always does a piece on Provincetown each year? For once, this one will have some substance instead of droning on about how eccentric we all are. They're sending reporters to interview us about our housing and climate work, and I've been asked to be a major contributor. If you and Helena hadn't included me in this documentary, Paul, I'd never have had this chance."

Jaunty, as usual, the filmmaker gave two thumbs up. "After all those great articles you've written, Freddie, I'm not surprised in the least. Speaking of surprises, I've got one, too. The last segment still needs a few minor edits, but I want you all to view it while the rest of the film is fresh in your minds. I think you're going to like what you see."

***

The final scene was shot at Mavis's HomePort studio, as she and Paul sat on wooden stools in the light-filled space. Behind her were four large canvases covered by white cloths. The ancient skull she'd once used as a mug was nowhere to be seen.

"I understand you have something special for our viewers," Paul said, as the camera focused first on him, then on Mavis.

"Yes," Mavis said, smiling broadly, "I thought they might enjoy an unveiling. I finished glazing the last piece this morning after working night and day for weeks."

Mavis removed the first cloth to reveal a host of Pilgrims watching a group of Native Americans walk single file into the woods. The Pilgrims' features were hostile and judgmental, the displaced natives' sad and resigned as they looked back at land they'd called home for millennia.

A work portraying the banishment of Goody Hallett was under the second cloth. Again, those casting her out were accusatory and hateful. She, too, stood by a path at the forest edge, looking past her tormentors to the ocean, her face contorted in grief.

The third painting was of Mavis cradling a child with a malformed foot as a crowd pointed and jeered.

The fourth was of Mavis chasing C.J. Strongue from Fisher Beach as people laughed and held up their phones to videotape the scene.

The beauty of the paintings' backgrounds amplified the ugliness of the crowd, whose wardrobe changed according to the period but whose faces remained the same. Their malevolence was frightening, the embodiment of mob mentality, prompting the question how such hatred endured over centuries without burning itself out.

Mavis pointed to the fourth painting. "The murder of C.J. Strongue—the woman running away from me—deeply affected me. I thought she was an old biddy with some crazy idea for another monument we didn't need or want. And I chased her off, as you can see. Weeks later, ashamed of myself, I agreed to meet with her, though I didn't remember to show up when the time came. She died as a result.

"C.J. Strongue was new to the Outer Cape and naïve about our ways. She thought she'd be accepted if she built a monument to honor

Goody Hallett—this girl here—who was exiled for having a child out of wedlock."

The camera focused on the intense longing on Goody's face as she stared out to sea.

Mavis continued, "The monument may have been a misguided notion, but the thoughts behind it were not entirely without merit. Ms. Strongue knew, more than most, that to truly belong to a community, it's essential to give whatever you can in whatever way you can. Small town living is a commitment—not an entitlement."

Mavis surveyed the painting again before turning back to the camera. "Ms. Strongue's monument project brought to light a dark truth passed down through the centuries. A truth I've tried to represent in these four paintings. Isolating and driving people away—what they called shunning in the old days—has been a part of this place since the Pilgrims landed. The labels have varied over the centuries from Saints and Strangers to North and South, Black and White, Gay and Straight, Conservative and Progressive, to name but a few. Even something as nebulous as 'townies and washashores' sustains the notion of an insider and outsider—an 'us' and 'them.'

"Four hundred years of keeping ourselves separate—focusing on our differences—fostering the distance between us despite our being so very much alike. It's a disease that, with my near escape from death, I recognized in myself."

The camera zoomed in on Mavis's features, craggy and careworn.

"I judged Ms. Strongue a nag and a colossal nuisance. I, too, shunned her, just as I once feared I might be shunned—the same way Goody Hallett had been nearly three hundred years ago for having had a child out of wedlock. That's my illegitimate son in the third painting. His name is Kevin, and he's the love of my life despite being so developmentally challenged he'll never know I'm his mother."

Mavis looked away from the camera before taking a deep breath and regrouping. "If Ms. Strongue had not come to my studio that day,

I'd have been killed, not her. Instead, I lived to care for my son, make more art, and have a chance to make things right.

"What do I mean by making things right? Questioning my assumptions, trying to bridge the distance whenever I can, and checking in with myself each day to be sure the aches, pains, and general disillusionment of old age aren't preventing me from living my truth and fulfilling my obligations to others."

The camera switched to an exterior view of the Stull House, prompting whispered speculation in the darkened theater. Mavis's voiceover described the home's history during a visual tour of the interior that revealed the books, portraits, and antique furniture cluttering every room.

The artist let the images resonate before resuming her narrative. "There were two attempts on my life. A recent suicide in this house is related to the second attempt. Had the man who tried to kill me not been apprehended, I suspect the house's former owner would still be alive.

"Confronting death—not once but twice—has forced me to accept my mortality. I've spent weeks thinking about how I should use what remaining time I may have. Time, I must admit, that has become even more precious."

Mavis hesitated for a moment, then a slight smile transformed her face as if she were anticipating the impact of what she was about to say. "I've purchased the Stull House and all its contents. My hope is that it will become the home of the C.J. Strongue Memorial, a training facility where interested young people can conserve the property and furnishings while earning a wage that allows them to remain in town. It also is my intention, as laid out in the document I'm about to sign, to donate this polyptych, the sixty-three works in my current show, and any items of historical merit in the Stull House—as well as the house itself—to the Staunton Trust."

Mavis picked up a fountain pen and signed the bequest. When she finished, the documentary switched to an offshore view of

Provincetown at sunset, looking majestic, welcoming, and, somehow, far more secure.

When the film ended, Paul turned on the lights as the small audience of friends sat in stunned silence. Then, slowly, they stood and clapped. Mavis remained seated, hands crossed in her lap, her eyes downcast until the last person left the room.

A Benevolent Muse

A few minutes later, Melody returned to the theater, entering the room with dread in her downcast eyes.

"I got your note. Is something wrong?"

"Thanks for hanging around," Mavis said, placing her hand on the young woman's shoulder. "Nothing's wrong. I have a few things to say to you, and I don't know any other way than to come right out and say them.

Melody blanched and sat down. Mavis followed suit, chuckling softly. "Fear not, kid. It's all good news. I talked things through with Helena before she left. We're thrilled and honored to invite you to be my apprentice in a new mentoring program. If you're willing to accept, Melody, you and I will spend the next year studying, painting, and exploring the art world. Then, the following year, we'll tour museums and private collections in Europe and Asia."

Melody opened her mouth, but no words came out.

"Hard as it may be to believe, I was once like you, kid," Mavis said, her voice rich with emotion. "Full of piss and vinegar, yet so lacking in artistic confidence, I'd paint over everything I did before anyone could see it. When Helena and Cole used your work as bait, I sent my housecleaner to buy one of your paintings. The self-portrait. I've studied it inside out and sideways. You've got what it takes, and I'm going to spend the next two years making sure you believe it. I've got all the money I need for my son and more than I can ever use for myself, so, to my way of thinking, it's about time to invest in the future. And, when it comes to my artistic legacy, I see you as that future."

Melody took several deep breaths, then studied the old woman, whose eyes were filled with tears.

Mavis met her gaze, let silence prevail for a few seconds, then said, "There's one more thing, kid. We'd like you to head the selection committee for housing at the Machado Home. We need someone who understands the challenges the buskers face. You'll have a stipend, a free place to live, and a studio at the HomePort Colony. And I guarantee the committee work won't intrude on your painting time or apprenticeship."

"Yes. Yes. Of course, I'll do all of it," Melody said. "Do you know what a secure place to live and work will mean to us?"

Mavis clasped her right hand and held it, her gaze maternal. "Only good things, kid. Even great ones. All things are possible when you're young."

A Love that Endures

That same evening, the board of the Staunton Trust met in Captain Staunton's former study. The brief discussion preceded a festive gathering, which lasted until two in the morning.

"Not a bad meeting," Quincy said to Mavis as Shirley escorted them to the door.

"A decent start," Mavis said. "I'll feel more comfortable when we have more staff in place. I'm glad Chief Louie is considering our offer to join the board. He didn't say no outright, which is an excellent sign. And there couldn't be a better choice than Freddie for that last empty seat. My biggest worry is the new executive director. If they see sweet reason and keep the hell out of the way, we'll be fine."

"And if they don't?" Shirley-Mae asked.

"Easy enough to solve that problem," Mavis chuckled. "I'm always looking for bait for my lobster traps."

Dolores left soon after, and Shirley found herself alone in the parlor, where she studied the portraits of the Staunton sisters, occasionally turning to admire Mavis's diptych on the opposite wall. The paintings' brilliant colors and masterful execution glowed in the dim light, the effect that of a moonlit cathedral.

Turning back to the Staunton portraits, Shirley raised her glass in a toast. "Don't get me wrong, ladies, I'm in favor of the kids having all the time together they need and thrilled Helena is ready to make peace with her past. I'm still worried, though. Not about them being at sea. About what happens when they come home. I don't want them to fall back into the same rut. Folks in this town can wear a body down to cinders in no time."

Shirley-Mae started when a crotchety voice said, "If you let 'em, dahlin'. Only if you let 'em. Don't borrow trouble. You and the artist woman can get the right people involved. You know you've got what it takes to do that. And if you do, the kids will come home to a better life, sure as my name is Dorrie Machado Staunton."

"But Dorrie, that's the thing," Shirley said. "Even if it meant cutting my life short, I'd do whatever I could to ensure Helena gets all the time and space she needs. Butch, too, for that matter. What bothers me is whether I'll even be here to see the results. I want to know Helena is settled and at peace before I cash in my chips. It's all I've ever wanted."

Shirley walked closer to Dorrie's portrait, staring into its eyes. "The problem is—and I don't really have to tell *you* this—at my age, I feel lucky to wake up in the morning. And after all the booze and food tonight, tomorrow looks especially challenging. What if I never know whether Helena gets her act together? What if I never see her and Butch again?"

Tears streaming down her face, Shirley was suddenly a bone-weary old woman who looked every year of her nine decades, if not more.

"My dear," Lola's patrician voice intoned, "steady on, now. Steady on. Of course, you'll see them. You'll always be here—one way or the other. What's more, we promised Helena we'd look after you, and so we shall. You have my word on it as a Staunton.

"Come talk to us if you ever get lonely. This room is where the family has gathered for centuries—especially the women when their menfolk were at sea. I see no reason it can't continue to function as it always has.

"We worried about Helena, too, you know. In the end, it was the love you and Butch have for her that made things right. Love is all-powerful, my dear. It drives the universe, and ours for our family—

which includes you—enables us to stay on at HomePort. Have no fear, Shirley-Mae. We're here to help in any way we can. And believe you me, we know a thing or two about endurance."

Shirley gazed at Mavis's portraits of Helena until Dorrie's voice, far less lofty but just as forceful, chimed in. "You need a good night's rest, girl. That's all. Nothing wrong with you that a good forty winks won't solve. You know what you gotta do, and there's no one better suited than you to do it. You'll have them laughing all the way to the bank. You're a broad after my own heart, but you gotta pace yourself. So get to bed and recharge those batteries before your tits sag another inch!"

And with that, Shirley-Mae Moutree, Executive Director of the Staunton Trust and toast of Provincetown, raised her middle finger to Dorrie's portrait and tottered from the room. Taking hold of the ornate banister, she began the steep, slow climb up the grand staircase to the second floor of the empty mansion.

When Shirley reached her bedroom door, Dorrie's voice rang out one last time. "See ya in the mornin', dahlin'. Our executive board meeting starts right here at eleven a.m. on the dot. Be there or be square."

Now, Voyager, Sail Thou Forth

Tough Cookie's navigation lights were barely visible in the darkness when Butch called out to Helena, who sat on *Dame Edna's* aft deck, gazing up at a night sky ablaze with constellations. Bundled in a fleece-lined parka, she peered over the gangway at her husband, who looked heroic in nothing but a pair of boxer shorts.

"I've found Virgo, Butch. At least, I think I did. Will you check if I'm right this time? Just once more, darling?"

Butch raised both hands. "It's too cold. Right now, Helena, there's only one star I care about and only one place I want her. There'll be plenty of time for stargazing when we're further south. And just wait until you see the moon taking center stage up there in the night sky."

As she stepped down into her husband's outstretched arms, Helena blew on her hands to warm them, stroked his muscled chest, and, choosing a sultry tone, whispered, "To hell with the moon."

-THE END-

Author's Note

As I worked on this book, Covid-related issues and increased hatred toward the drag and transgender communities made me wonder if another HomePort novel had a place in such a dysfunctional world.

Pandemic flight, retiring baby boomers, the Great Resignation, and remote work had brought momentous change to rural towns across America and Europe. Despite our relative isolation, Provincetown was not immune. Significant numbers of people relocated here to escape the urban horrors of the pandemic or because they wanted to change their lives.

Some who already lived here felt threatened, not only by the virus but also by the societal changes it had unleashed. A handful insisted bridges over the Cape Cod Canal be closed and the town sealed off to all but full-time residents. As demand for real estate increased, off-Cape developers swooped in, displacing workers and retirees by converting rental properties to private homes or condominiums. Real estate prices soared. Luxury vehicles—many with out-of-state license plates—glistened in driveways that once hosted pickup trucks, bicycles, and lobster traps.

The winter sounds of carpentry, heavy machinery, and stonecutting disrupted the summer months. Yachts in the harbor grew longer. Film crews blocked off streets as rumors spread about which stars might be in town. Money and celebrity had discovered funky old Provincetown.

A few long-time residents spoke of being driven out by a "tsunami of wealth," while newcomers and recent retirees felt unwelcome and guilty for living in the home of their dreams. I repeatedly asked myself if the unique qualities that had attracted so many to Provincetown—strong community ties, tolerance, freedom of expression, natural beauty, and room to breathe—would survive the inequities the pandemic had exacerbated.

I found signs of hope in the generous donations to stave off food insecurity and the outpouring of support for essential workers and LGBTQ-owned businesses. Nearly two hundred thousand dollars was raised for those impacted by flooding in December 2020, highlighting the town's continued willingness to care for its own—and the increasing threat of climate change.

Even so, P'town seemed to be splintering into disparate factions. I resonated with the frustrations on both sides but couldn't shake the notion that the underlying causes were not being addressed. A head-in-the-sand approach to the long-term impacts of the housing crunch was but one piece of what I considered a complex and disheartening puzzle.

One gray afternoon, as I revisited Mary Heaton Vorse's 1942 opus, *Time and the Town*, a quote leaped off the page: "*Truro sitting discreetly in the folds of her moors looked down her nose at Provincetown and still does.*" This got me thinking that if anything remained a constant these days, it was the Cape's opinion of "the folk on Land's End." What other constants might there be?

A chapter on the aftermath of the first World War also struck home. An influx of urbanites, abetted by mass production of the automobile, challenged the town's way of life. Sail-based industries, such as whaling and fishing, gave way to technologies requiring fewer workers. Yet, Provincetown's best attributes survived the transition: tolerance, caring for its own, and a contrarian viewpoint exquisitely enhanced by unbridled joie de vivre. I was struck by the parallels between then and now, which prompted me to consider how one might counter the inexorable forces of "progress" in today's polarized environment. That's when this novel found its groove.

P'town's ongoing struggle to maintain its unique identity could be the perfect outlet for Helena's passion, loyalty, and sense of justice. The drag community has always been in the vanguard of the battle for change and equity, which is one of many reasons performers are often targeted. The most appealing aspect of drag, to me, is the creativity and self-expression it enables. It also has a long and complex history with roots in various cultures. Those who practice it have the freedom to push the boundaries of gender and fashion—and to create their own unique looks *and* personas. At its core, drag is about self-expression and creativity; a way for performers to play with gender, identity, and performance, much as I have tried to do in this book. There are no limits to what a drag performer can do, which makes Helena such an appealing character to me.

HomePort's chatelaine would fight hard for the town she loved. And I instinctively knew what she would do. Restoring and repurposing old buildings would provide year-round jobs and allow people to remain in their neighborhoods rather than be relocated to the edge of town or driven out altogether. Perhaps, in time, divisions and misconceptions might be laid to rest as neighbors bonded in their shared love of this remarkable place. The concept was admittedly naïve, but I yearned to see it play out, if only on the page.

My remaining concern was whether this sort of struggle was still relevant, given all the tensions in the world. Then, one day, while discussing the plight of the drag and transgender communities, I heard someone say, "Provincetown is America's lifeboat."

Hearing this, I felt even more grateful for my hometown and recognized its place in the American psyche. And in these words, I also found my answer: Even in times of great upheaval, some things remain constant. Despite incredible odds, kindness and decency *can* prevail. A chosen family and a community of like-minded people can make all the difference.

***

Unlike Butch and Helena, I have neither inherited millions nor a yacht I can sail to Bora Bora. I'm still anchored here in Provincetown, confident that, as Mavis Chandry said, "Small-town living is a commitment—not an entitlement," and that somehow, those who currently call this bit of sand home will find a way to perpetuate that ideal.

I hope to be around long enough to see how this new chapter in the town's history unfolds—and perhaps even write about it.

I hope you enjoyed *The Distance Between Us.*

ACB–December 2022

About the Author

A. C. Burch's debut novel was the award-winning *The HomePort Journals*. He is also the author of a short story collection entitled *A Book of Revelations*.

His first decade as a Provincetown resident was spent living in a condominium where drama reigned supreme (see the short story, *Even in Death* in *A Book of Revelations)*. In 1997, he bought an 1881 Cape in dire need of renovation and has been working on it ever since. The prior owner, whose family owned the property for 92 years, described it as haunted by the ghost of her grandmother, who was born, lived, and died in the house. Any odd occurrence is always attributed to "Bridey," who was said to have regularly chased painter Charles Hawthorne and his students off her dune-top property. No doubt, the spectral denizens of HomePort owe their presence to her example.

An avid sailor, photographer, and gardener, A.C. seldom goes anywhere without his adorable—if demanding—Golden Retriever, Dori, known to her devoted fanbase as #DoritheWonderDog.

Visit ACBurch.com and follow ACBurchAuthor on Facebook and Instagram to learn more.

Acknowledgments

This book would never have come to fruition without the wisdom and generosity of my fabulous editor, Elizabeth Sims. Her talent for offering gentle encouragement and honest feedback with warmth and humor is unparalleled.

Cover designer James Iaocobelli, thank you for sharing your extraordinary abilities. It's been a pleasure to work with you.

I'm honored Pamela Parsons allowed her artwork to be licensed for the cover, fulfilling my vision of a Mavis Chandry painting.

To Madeline Sorel, illustrator and resident goddess: once again, you've captured the whimsy of HomePort in your drawings. Thanks for the creative opportunities and joy you bring to my writing and my life.

To Ric Ide, photographer extraordinaire: what can I say? You turned a terrifying task into a joyous experience.

To Colin, whose astounding intellect and inquisitive nature spawn so many enjoyable conversations: I couldn't have done this without your support and insight.

To Vee, whose graphic wizardry and artistic eye contributed so much: you represent the best of your namesakes. There is nothing you cannot do.

To Victoria: Thanks for your support when I was overwhelmed by doubt.

To Bob, who read more versions of this book than friendship can rightfully expect: thanks for your candor and support. Couldn't have done it without you.

To Jeff, whose input is so valuable: thank you for the oh-so-constructive feedback in the final round. By the way, Dolores sends her love.

To Jeannette: our collaborative friendship is the source of so many good things. Thanks for your expertise and encouragement.

To Arthur, whose words and deeds exemplify the importance of everyday kindness: I'm honored and humbled to have known you for most of my adult life.

To Dr. Ben Andrulot, who not only keeps my spine adjusted but also my brain: from now on, "No" is the new "Yes."

Finally, I want to offer my heartfelt appreciation to those whose efforts made living in Provincetown during the pandemic safe and bearable—as well as an opportunity for personal reflection and growth. There are too many people to list individually, but I will always treasure your generosity and commitment to this tiny place we call home.

Thank you all.